"I fear my heroine is going to prove an utter fool," said Vitra.

"Your heroine? You've decided on a female protagonist?"

"You didn't catch a glimpse of her then? Her name is Vel Thaidis. Behold my invention!"

With the smallest of the strong and versatile fingers of her right hand, Vitra depressed a key in the tray. In midair, just above the blanked viewing screen, an image evolved. It was that of a young woman of a different, voluptuous, full-breasted slimness, golden-skinned, green-haired, clad in elegant curious draperies, and with an odd darkening over the eyes.

"I have been meticulous, you see," said Vitra. "Notice the polarizing inner lids to protect vision from the ghastly ever-present sun. All my characters possess them."

"The polarizing lids are very interesting," said Vyen, examining the image. "Not so interesting to set the drama on the hot side of the planet, which in reality is an uncharted airless desert, uninhabitable by beast or man. . . ."

# DAY
# BY
# NIGHT

**Tanith Lee**

**DAW BOOKS, INC.**
DONALD A. WOLLHEIM, PUBLISHER

1633 Broadway, New York, N.Y. 10019

FIRST PRINTING, NOVEMBER 1980

1 2 3 4 5 6 7 8 9

**DAW**ᴇꜱᴔ
**BOOKS**

DAW TRADEMARK REGISTERED
U.S. PAT. OFF. MARCA
REGISTRADA. HECHO EN U.S.A.

PRINTED IN U.S.A.

# Table of Contents

# DEDICATION

To Bernard Lee, my Father,
who generously gave me a planet, and all
its problems.

# CHAPTER ONE

## Part One

Half a staed below the palace of Hirz, the formal gardens gradually smoothed themselves into the curve of the lake shore. Here, where jade-green undulations of liquid broke on the pale gold sand, stood a golden young woman and her three attendant robots.

Apart from the Hirz Palace, no other building was visible above or along the arms of the shore. This portion of the Yunea, for twenty staeds along the Ring in either direction, was the property of Hirz. Hest, lay the holding of the Domms, to hespa, the decadent estate of the Thars.

It was the fifth hour, as two or three singing clocks within the palace had just announced. It was also Jate, the waking time. Nevertheless, customs had changed. Only the girl and her three robots occupied the scene, and before them the lake spread its empty, sun-flecked sheet under the wide green sky. Then the Voice Robot spoke.

"Vel Thaidis, your brother is coming."

Vel Thaidis did not bother to glance either way, since her sight could not match the optics of the robot. Instead, she looked at the robot itself in the form of Courteous Address.

"You are certain that it's Velday?"

"I will check the patterns. Yes, they are his. There are also companions."

"Who?" Vel Thaidis said, and the inner polarizing lids of her eyes flickered as if with tension.

7

"There are altogether five extra persons of both genders. Shall I name all of them?"

"No. Is Ceedres Yune Thar among them?"

"Yes, Vel Thaidis. He is riding with your brother."

Vel Thaidis turned and looked at the lake, adopting the Distant Address.

"Advise me. I wish to avoid Ceedres Yune Thar."

"You should return to the palace and shut yourself into your own apartments immediately."

"Bad counsel, Voice," Vel Thaidis said sharply. "Velday will give Ceedres free rein in the palace. Ceedres will batten on our hospitality, as always. If I'm there, perhaps I can keep some control of the situation. I can't avoid him after all."

"Hespa, the sand cloud your brother's vehicle is creating is now apparent to the human eye," said the Voice Robot.

Vel Thaidis, angrily, turned once more and gazed to her left, hespaward, through the dark lenses of her polarized inner lids. The three robots also turned. They were of a blond matte plastum, creamily shining in the unchanging sunlight. In shape they resembled women, with delicate doll-like features, blond spun hair and colored mineral eyes, to enhance their aesthetic value. The voice of the Voice Robot was rather high, but pleasant and not unnatural. Yunea science had long perfected such matters.

The young woman herself, Vel Thaidis Yune Hirz, had been formed in one of the Yunea Matrixes, a formation both genetic and human. Burnt gold of skin like all her race, she had the curvaceous graceful figure which the women of her line inherited, and the beautiful face that reappeared, in either sex of the Hirz, at regular intervals. Her hair had been bleached and tinted a faint milky green, then arranged in folds and coils over her head and down her back. Her long draped garment was smoke-white, and bracelets of apricot metal ringed her slim metallic wrists.

The sand-cloud neared like a running plume along the fifth-hour hespan shore. Now she saw the open car, the green parasol wobbling above like a long-stalked flower growing out of it, and the two madly racing lion-dogs of plated bronze thundering before. And now she saw Velday, her brother, a figment of the same Hirz beauty, grinning as he twitched the reins, and the wind of the race parted his gilt-color hair. And finally she saw Ceedres Yune Thar standing beside Velday, also handsome, also gilt-haired, the driver-box held casually in his hand. He grinned too, a grin exactly like Velday's grin,

8

for much of Ceedres' fascination for others lay in masterful tricks of imitation. And as he grinned, he skimmed the speedometer of the box up and up the scale. Now the lion-dogs leapt in an ecstasy of propulsion, and sparks showered from their open mouths. One instant the chariot was a staed away, next instant the fore-whip of flying sand stung across Vel Thaidis' bare arms and her throat. Then the chariot was stationary, the bronze beasts petrified in a crouching posture, the reins slack in Velday's hands, and the driver-box idle in the hands of Ceedres.

"How lovely you are," Ceedres said directly to Vel Thaidis, without preliminary, the compliment-as-insult method he was so good at.

She stared at him, and immediately he copied her stare, staring back with all her own intensity reproduced.

"Oh, come now," said Velday. "You're not going to fight already. My sister and my friend should like each other."

"She mistrusts me, I fear," said Ceedres softly. His polarized eyes went on and on, staring at her. "How can you be so cruel to me, Vaidi, when I—"

"Don't call me that," she said to him. It was a trap he had set her, of course, to force her into speech with him. Even so, she would not allow him to use the diminutive of her name: Vaidi, the abbreviation due to family, intimate or husband.

"I'm sorry, Vel Thaidis," Ceedres said. The sun glinted on his fair hair like a mesh, more polished than the hair of her brother. Polished as Ceedres' manner, now. "Truly sorry. I beg your pardon. And yours, Vay," he added, deliberately showing her that Velday permitted him the diminutive.

"Oh, don't *trouble* yourself, Cee," said Velday, entering wholeheartedly into the game.

She forgave her brother. Ceedres had enchanted him since childhood: Ceedres could enchant almost anyone. Only she, it seemed to her, could fathom the roots of what Ceedres was. But she was accustomed to this triangular situation, which had also existed between the three of them since childhood. And though, at some deep level, it profoundly disturbed her, the disturbance was familiar as a garment. Sometimes, too, she admitted to herself that she enjoyed it, the quarreling, the flare of her instinct, warning her. As a child she had been jealous at losing her brother to Ceedres, and Velday had striven to soothe her jealousy, and still did, and these blandishments she relished. She guiltily relished the egotistic awareness that she alone was proof against Ceedres, had analyzed and duly despised him as a parasite. She was not self-blind, but she was young.

"Well," Velday said, leaning on the side of the vehicle, "we kept J'ara in the Slumopolis. The food is always so filthy—great wads of papery stuff and synthetic meats. But the drink, of course, is rare. Only Hirz vintage will do after that marvelous glue they serve at the J'ara Mansions. Cee will be joining us for breakfast, my sister, and about three more—when they catch up. Do you allow it?"

A second, broader plume of sand was just blooming on the hespan horizon.

Vel Thaidis had not kept J'ara, (Jate-in-Maram or stay-awake) but Maram itself, the time of sleep. Now the palace would be filled by whatever sleep-starved aristocrats Velday had collected during his J'ara, half-intoxicated, furiously hungry, argumentative and flippant.

Vel Thaidis felt a little involuntary shrinking, a little surge of mournful excitement. Crowds drew her and repelled. As Ceedres did. As an adolescent, she had hidden herself from gatherings of all types. But her father and mother were dead. Velday and she remained the solitary figureheads of Hirz.

She smiled at Velday, to disarm her words: "When have you ever *asked* me?" she said. "You do as you want."

She was a year his senior. Theoretically, the palace was beneath her jurisdiction.

She stepped aside on to the sand-excluding stone path that led from the shore to the palace. The three robots moved after her.

"We'll follow at our own pace," Velday called.

Ceedres said to him, loud enough for her to hear, "Just give her the space to poison a cup or two for me."

With a flash of exhilarated rage, she looked over her shoulder at him and said, "The only way to poison you, Ceedres, would be to make you swallow your tongue."

An avenue of apple bushes soon flanked the path and drew it into the gardens of the palace. Ten feet in height, the bushes leaned together overhead, their thousands of dark-green fruits, the size of large buttons, hanging from boughs and stems. Beyond the avenue of apple bushes, the garden rose on banks of lawns, set with trees of fleshy, moisture-storing leaves, tiers of foliage that were hardly trees at all, satin cacti of powdery pastel grays and pinks, thin fountains of jade liquid, enormous flowers with plump, wax-white petals,

10

each broader than a man's skull. Bronze and plastum marble, the portico of the house appeared, and its transparent doors slid open in answer to Vel Thaidis' command.

Throughout, the palace was cool and tinged with many soft colors. Its zenith-oriented windows were painted and, blazingly sunlit behind, cast vivid traceries on the floor. Since the sun never altered its position, neither did these traceries. Sometimes an infrequent imbalance in the sky-ceiling thickened the light for an hour or so, and muddied the jewel brightness of the windows. In Vel Thaidis' tenth year, there had been such a happening. An esoteric globe had been produced immediately in the main salon of the palace, and kindled into yellow radiance, while mild prayers were offered to the gods of Yunea science. The globe had to do with occasional religious observance, and communicated with one of the outer temples beyond the great estates. At the second prayer, a button was depressed. An image evolved inside the globe, the transmission of an auto-priest. This mechanical being, regaled, obviously, in the Courteous Address, replied with reassurance. Yet, itself a symbol of the law, morality and religious ethic of the Yunea, its reassurance was conceivably as symbolic.

If the gods were vague, so too was the unease caused by the thickening of the light. The aristocrats of the Yunea did not believe any true harm could come to them. In the Slumopolis, she had been told later, robot lawguards had mobilized to contain an upsurge of panic. But what else could you expect of the Slumopolis? Naturally, its people were educationally ignorant of the function of the sky-ceiling of the planet, which provided an enclosed atmosphere for the species below. Vel Thaidis, however, had realized, even by her tenth year, that though the Yunean aristocracy was educated in all the facts and mechanics of its world, it no longer comprehended them. Science cared for her favored children. They had no need to comprehend. Their assurance and bravery at the time of half-darkness was due, therefore, not to knowledge, but to complacency, for they were spoiled and supposed the gods of science loved them and would protect them always. They were even conscious of their own attitude, but it was impossible for them not to succumb to it, and Vel Thaidis had succumbed with the rest.

Now, she placed her hand on a wall panel.

"Prepare breakfast for my brother and five companions, with caffea and the last-chosen wine from the cellars."

11

The panel sang, and she sensed activity pour through the house, unseen; circuits, synapses, passing the message, and the kitchens buried beneath brimming into life.

She wondered if her brother would sleep after the breakfast and the J'ara, and doubted he would. Infants were taught to compose themselves for sleep somewhere during the eight hours of Maram, but the training did not always hold. Velday was now one of those who inclined to sleep only one Maram in six, with an hour every second or third day under the dream-wash technique, the machinery every Maram chamber provided.

Vel Thaidis herself chose seven hours of sleep at most Marams. Suddenly, standing in the pale shade of the palace, she beheld her unlikeness to her brother, not only regarding J'ara, but in all things, with a bewildered surprise. She had never properly thought about it before. Like the running battle with Ceedres, the dissimilarity had always been there. Yet she and Velday were near in affection. Or were they?

At their inception, their parents had been old, a father in his three-hundredth genetic year, a mother barely younger. The pair's rapture with each other had kept them from procreation a long while. Finally, reluctantly, they had obeyed the law. They had permitted the reproduction elements to be taken in order that two children might be matrixed.

No disease existed in the Yunea. Even in the Slumopolis, specific illness, when detected, was swiftly erased. But among the aristocrats whose existence could be lengthily prolonged into three or four hundred spans, boredom came to be the killer, a bizarre running down, a sort of decline and decay, nonphysical but fatal. To this malaise, the father of Velday and Vel Thaidis had submitted in his three hundred and twentieth year. Their mother lived a year longer. Now only their dust remained in golden urns. During their lives, in any case, they were reclusive, and hardly more affectionate than the two urns they had ultimately become. They had ignored the compulsory offspring scientific tradition demanded of the princely houses. Beyond strictures of behavior and religious vagaries, no communion linked parent with child. Was it merely this, then, which had formed an alternate bond between brother and sister?

Velday was really the only person who had proper significance for Vel Thaidis. Nobody else had ever seemed—what word was she seeking?—*accessible*. By which she meant, surely, sympathetic—*safe*. Vel Thaidis frowned, peering into

12

her own mind in this way, and unnerved by it. If her link with her brother were spurious, probably he had already spiritually broken free. And she, what was left for her?

Within doors, the inner polarized lids had lifted from her eyes, which showed clear and dark and now quite blank with insecurity.

She heard a dim whirring as the main salon prepared itself, and outside the distant clatter of chariots and the robot liondogs bounding into their mechanical stalls. Strains of laughter were floating on one of the terraces, then a great shout lifted and more laughter—some joke or antic, probably of Ceedres' devising.

As so often in the past, Vel Thaidis felt herself shut from the feast, an eavesdropper and misfit.

The salon was reached by an escalator, and was located near the roof on the zenith side of the palace. The salon's zenith wall was all one great painted window, and so a reflected tracery of crimson, lavender and topaz flowers lay draped like ghosts across the whole chamber. Scattered about, Velday's guests lolled at their individual tables, while the service robots helped them to hot and cold dishes, wine, steaming caffea, sweets, from the opened food hatches to the rear.

A voice-service robot came to Vel Thaidis as she entered. It too, like her attendants, was attractively styled and had a pleasant tone.

"Shall I set a place for you, Vel Thaidis?"

She had already eaten, but refused the robot in the Courteous Address, and asked for a goblet of fruit juice mixed with the amber Hirz wine. Velday's guests were now calling to her, in their own mechanically courteous way, trying to propitiate her. *How strange*, she thought, taking the cut-crystal glass in one hand, the paw of Kewel Yune Chure in the other, *I am wary of these people, and they are equally wary of me. How stupid it is.*

Aside from Kewel, Darvu Yune Chure was also present. Chure was an extensive family, Kewel and Darvu cousins, attached as brothers, and both idiots—so Vel Thaidis classified them. Another idiot, this time a feminine example, Omevia Yune Ond, reclined against Ceedres' shoulder. An attendant Ond robot waited beside her chair and a live feline sprawled in her lap, its spine under her elegant brassy hand with its black lacquer nails. Ceedres similarly affected the "danger"

13

color of the Yunes—the black of his draped tunic, which had been masked on the shore beneath a white suncloak.

Velday lounged at the other side of Ceedres. Sometimes he pushed morsels to Omevia's feline, which eagerly bit at them, nearly taking his fingers with the food. Velday and Ceedres were telling each other a long and complicated joke, and seemed drunk. Everyone did.

"What then?" Velday said to Ceedres.

"Then," said Ceedres. He paused to make a dramatic, eloquent gesture. "The god forced her to bypass the five hundred and five gates of paradise, and drew her under the ground, and she found herself in a black and unbearable place of nothing. White fires blazed overhead and white venoms underfoot. She could neither breathe, nor speak, nor plead with him. At which the god whispered in her ear: "You requested it. Now you have it. Savor.""

Velday and Omevia were both vociferous with amusement.

"You fool," said Velday, delightedly.

Vel Thaidis, victim of paranoia, concluded that the story, whatever it was, had in some fashion been intended to mock her with its female protagonist. The background details appeared to have to do with ancient Yunean mythology, long-outgrown, concerning a floral heaven and a black hell beneath the planet, into which the gods of science plunged malefactors. Probably Ceedres' black garment had given rise to the tale.

Ceedres now got to his feet. He raised his cup to her.

"I drink to Velday's beautiful sister, who hates me."

He drank, dropped the cup, and cried in a strangled voice: "I'll die young after all."

"Why, whatever is the matter?" demanded Omevia.

Ceedres sank down again beside her, murmured in her ear and "died" gently on her breast. Omevia laughed.

"He says I must inform Vel Thaidis that he has swallowed his tongue."

Dark-skinned as they were, blushes went generally unnoticed in the Yunea. Yet Vel Thaidis felt her cheeks scald.

"I suppose," she said, measuring out the words, "that the house of Thar, having reduced itself to one madman in the past seven hundred years, could be extinguished so easily."

No laughter answered Vel Thaidis' jest. It was vitriol, and in very bad taste. The slow and apparently hopeless fall of the Thar estate, brought about by an ill fortune that struck

14

rarely, yet could strike nevertheless anyone of the princely families, was not usually referred to.

Vel Thaidis noted Velday's remorse and was almost contrite. Then Ceedres sat up and looked at her. She was prepared to be alarmed and defiant before his anger, or abashed before his pride and anguish. Instead, he again simply copied her expression—which she saw was stony, with wide, hard eyes.

"Your scorn acted like a blow between the shoulders," he said, "and, as you see, I've revived. For my house, as you know, a good marriage would save it. What do you say?"

The breath went out of her as it had gone out of the girl in the story. Abruptly, the accustomed triangular garment, which would never be altered, had evaporated. And, as abruptly, she knew what she had had to fear all along.

There was a still, still silence.

Velday broke it, saying, very lightly while smiling, "Can this be a marriage proposal to my sister, Ceedres? Or are you and she in combat to determine who has the least tact?"

"Oh, a genuine marriage proposal," Ceedres replied, now adopting Velday's smiling, cautious face, "uttered from unrequited love (was there ever anything so sad?) and in complete fore-acceptance of her refusal."

Kewel Yune Chure giggled, and threw a candy to Omevia's feline, which sprang to catch it.

Vel Thaidis watched the painted, motionless sun and window pattern reflected on all of them and on herself. The sun did not change, but everything else—

She was in her twenty-first year, her eyes were full of tears and she did not know where to hide herself. She had realized at least how much she distrusted Ceedres Yune Thar, and how much she was allergic to his ambitions and his whims. And that she loved him.


"Let me in," Velday said outside her door.

"Let him in," she told the door. It drew silkenly aside, and her brother walked into the spacious apartment, delicately, as if she had carpeted the floor with crystal eggs.

"They've gone," said Velday. "All of them." He looked at the tall golden chame she had been playing, the six-foot strings and the carved panel of buttons and stops below, where her hands rested. "What he said," said Velday, "was reprehensible, and what you said to him concerning Thar

15

equally so. Couldn't you, for once, reckon your accounts level, and let him alone?"

"Did he mention it to you in private?" she asked, before she could prevent herself.

"He suggested I should apologize for him to you, and he would send you anything of Thar you might care for, in recompense. Though probably there was nothing worth having at Thar now, he said, and naturally, you knew as much, the way you spoke of it."

She shivered.

"I must have scored a hit against his vanity after all, then," she said, and let her finger lick at the strings. They had been playing the rhythm of her heart for three hours, ever since she left the uneasy party above, in the salon. They would have considered it no more than her right to flounce from the room, she supposed, as they would have considered it Ceedres' right to leave following her own remark. Ceedres, however, did not have the pride to do that. Could not *afford* the pride. "I behaved badly," she now said. It was easy, after all, to hide behind the old folly. "You know that he angers me."

"Can't you ever remember our childhood together?"

"Yes," she flared. "How he took you away from me—to ride and hunt, to activities I didn't wish to join, and later to keep J'ara in the Slumopolis, where I was forbidden to venture."

"Oh," Velday said. He went to the open window and stared across the lake, fixedly spangled under the immovable disc of the sun. Little streaks of temporary atmospheric cirrus feathered the sky. There might be a brief dry rain in the thirteenth or fourteenth hour. "There's to be a hunt on the Thar lands at the eighteenth hour in Maram—that is, a J'ara hunt."

"A hunt, using the hunting robots of the Hirz, no doubt."

"No doubt," Velday said reasonably, "when we recall Ceedres has no such working robots of his own."

"He is a parasite," Vel Thaidis said.

Velday flung around on her and shouted: "How else is he to live!"

"In the Slumopolis!" she shouted back. "Where others of his kind have been forced to go."

"Perhaps they had no friends."

"Perhaps their friends were not fools, as the friends of Ceedres are."

16

"I was going to say," Velday said rigidly, "or perhaps they had friends like Vel Thaidis, who cares for nothing and no one except to be mistress of her palace. Suppose our own Hirz technology were to fail—a mere accident of bad luck, as it was for the Thars in the time of Ceedres' father, old Yune Thar. We would have no more means of repairing it than he had or Ceedres has. We too should have to see our home and estate decline into ruin, powerless to prevent it, with exile to the Slumopolis as the end. How can you blame Ceedres for clinging on to what he has, for letting us help him with our own technologies, robots and equipment."

"I blame him for his manner, for his smiling schemes to *use* us—"

"He makes himself amusing, likable, so that we will want to assist him and not regret it. You forget. You don't think, my sister. When he cracked a rib last year on the Domm hunt, he joked all the way to the house, he had us in fits of laughter—and he was in great pain. I asked him how he managed it, after. 'I didn't dare omit clowning,' Ceedres said. He'd been paying for Domm medical treatment, because he could get none at home."

"You love him, he's your friend, your brother," she said bitterly.

"I admit that. But I also love you. You've always squabbled, the two of you. Yet suddenly it has become vehement, murderous. And what he said to you—"

"Concerning what?"

"Concerning marriage, Hirz with Thar. It was clumsy and unfortunate, but there was a reality under it."

Her rings bit into her fingers as she clenched her hands on the carved panel of the chame.

"Well?"

"Well, if you should soften to him—"

Quickly she said, "You'd persuade me to marry him, thereby taking my half-share of the Hirz technology into the Thar palace. True, they would be my machineries, not his, but as his wife, I'd be bound to employ them to renovate the Thar estate. Meanwhile, he would be at liberty to live inside these walls. Which would be the only reason he'd want me."

"Oh Vaidi—"

"No. You're too innocent, Velday, and your *friend* plays on it, as I play this chame." She struck several buttons, producing a discord of many notes.

17

"All right," Velday said, "I see you're adamant. But you'll come to see the J'ara hunt."

"You know I seldom keep J'ara. You know I shrink from hunting things."

"For my sake, then, Vaidi? Omevia Yune Ond will gossip, and the Chures are worse. I'd rather the rest of the princely houses didn't conclude there was bad blood between Hirz and Thar. Particularly not public rage between Ceedres and you."

"You want a garden where no leaves ever fall," she said.

"Maybe. But will you come?"

One of her rings had now cut so deep that blood speckled the rim of it, amber blood, the color of the Hirz last-chosen wine. Vel Thaidis felt the loss of her self-ignorance with raw emotion.

She would join the Thar hunt.

How could she keep away?


# Part Two


A black place, white fires. . . .

This black, these fires, rested upon the transparent vanes of the great dome, as they rested on the whole of the planet's contra-solar surface. They were, in fact, a skylessness of pure black space, seared with bright cold droplets of stars.

Within the dome, in a circular chamber, seated amid the tall banks of the machinery and apparently unmindful of space, a girl in a silver garment was flickering her white hands daintily over a tray of keys. However, perhaps ironically, the hair of the girl (framing a beautiful face, naturally pale as powder,) was a strange abbreviated complement to the eternal void outside and above; black hair, flecked with silver beads, cut straight as a rule two inches from her shoulders.

A vague murmur filled the chamber from the ranks of the machines. In a little round screen a couple of spans before the girl's eyes a bizarre picture exerted itself. Many hundred persons stretched on a cushioned platform, gaping. All looked

18

partly asleep, or rather, mesmerized. All looked wasted, grimy and forlorn. Like hers, their flesh was white; unlike hers, unluminous. Their clothing was piecemeal, murkily dyed and bundled onto them as if to conceal as much of their gray-white human tissue as possible. They were not an attractive or a wholesome sight, and this the girl seemed entirely aware of. Suddenly her hands left her tray of keys and swam to her mouth to cradle a melancholy yawn.

The round screen faded and darkened. The murmur of the machinery retreated a tone or two. At the periphery of the room, a door hissed wide.

"Here you are at last," said the girl clearly. "Come to spy upon the people's storyteller, Vyen?"

"Of course," said Vyen, emerging into the colorless chimes of the light intensifiers, pale as the girl, dark as she, and as slim. In both, it was a hard, a spare, almost a harsh slenderness, yet with something fragile in it, pointed by the delicate metallic ornaments and ornamental clothes both, as aristocrats, adopted. "My sister, Vitra Klovez, Fabulast to the People," said her brother Vyen mockingly, and rotated a silver fiddle-toy between his long thin fingers.

They gazed at each other cruelly. There was always this appearance to them of a pair of affectionate predatory animals staring across a morsel of prey.

Klovez, one of the foremost of the princely houses, had genetically bred Vitra and Vyen as its last two heirs. They were aware of the onus on them and displayed the awareness in many ways. Their method of walking was a graceful stalk; their heads were permanently thrown back, gazing ever down upon the mainly subsurface landscape of their world—a world extremely unlike the burning golden-green outdoor environment Vitra had just been creating in her Fabulism, to entertain the people—or rather the slaves—of the lower echelons of Klave.

"I fear my heroine is going to prove an utter fool," said Vitra now, neatly licking a frozen glass-like alcohol stick.

"Your heroine? You've decided on a female protagonist?"

"You didn't catch a glimpse of her, then? Her name is Vel Thaidis. Behold my invention!"

With the smallest of the strong and versatile fingers of her right hand, Vitra depressed a key in the tray. In midair, just above the blanked viewing screen, an image evolved. It was that of a young woman only about fourteen inches high for purposes of reproduction, but of a different, voluptuous, full-

19

breasted slimness, golden-skinned, green-haired, clad in elegant curious draperies, and with an odd darkening over the eyes.

"I have been meticulous, you see," said Vitra. "Notice the polarizing inner lids to protect vision from the ghastly ever-present sun. All my characters possess them. And the glamorous metallic tan. She's lovely, Vyen, isn't she? But such a simpleton. I fear I'll lose patience with her all too quickly."

"The polarizing lids are very interesting," said Vyen, examining the image with his own cold gray eyes—the same shape and tint as Vitra's. "Not so interesting, to set the drama on the hot side of the planet, which, in reality, is an uncharted airless desert, uninhabitable by beast or man."

"To use the desert is a challenge. Other Fabulasts make up worlds with no sense to them at all. But this has subtle sarcasm. And my ingenuity is perfectly equal to all impossibilities. An airless, scorched desert—in my Fabulism, machinery provides an atmosphere, just as it does for us, and even water." Vitra pressed another key. A view emerged of exotic gardens leading to a jade-green spill of lake.

"*How* imaginative," said Vyen. The fiddle-toy, so necessary to nervous fingers, trembled and twisted. His voice had remained mocking. That his sister had been computer-selected for the role of Fabulast, an essential figment of the tradition of their world, tickled and irritated him. That Vitra was twenty-one, a year his senior, and that this was her first Fabulism, had also influenced his attitude.

"But why do you say the girl is a fool?" he remonstrated now. "She hasn't a foolish face."

"Oh, she's intelligent enough. But emotionally an idiot. I suppose she has to be to fulfill any sort of story. The story, you understand, little brother, which pours irrepressibly into me and through me, such is my huge talent."

"There have been theories that the machinery of a Fabulism chamber makes the story itself. That the Fabulast merely receives, transmits and translates."

"Nonsense!" said Vitra acidly. "If that were the case, why was I chosen Fabulast for my imaginative powers? House Klovez has often produced Fabulasts, which you'll agree is useful. Ours is one of the best technologically equipped residences in the Klave, the reward for genius. No, the machines merely stimulate and assist in visualizing. Their main activity is to project the story to the watching rabble,

20

who lie on their cushions and feed from it like the worms they are."

"Who could anyway expect a machine to outthink my wise and clever sister?"

"Be quiet, Vyen. My tongue's as sharp as yours, and my brain. Sharper. And, to instruct your puerile ignorance, if you suppose machines invent the story I tell, how do you account for this?"

Another key was depressed.

On the air, replacing the Vel Thaidis image and the view of the green lake, two male figures leapt into relief. One was quite clearly Vyen, (though given the name of Velday), but a Vyen much altered, bronzed, athletically muscular, gold-haired, polarized of eye, the sneer replaced by a smiling openness of countenance.

"Now you do shock me," said Vyen, with mild disap-proval. "I'm to be woven into this undisciplined dream, am I?"

"And look who else."

"I perceive Casrus very well. Indeed, that figure is virtually libelous. What if he found out? He's as much a prince as you or I. He might be insulted."

"True, House Klarn is even richer in technology than our own, but not so noble in status. It's produced no Fabulasts, no technologist of any type."

"If Casrus Klarn entered this chamber and saw you'd made him part of your drama for the rabble, next became angry and demanded I fight a duel with him for his honor's sake, I presume you'd be sorry."

"I would laugh very much," said Vitra. "So would you. He'd only seem a dolt if he did such a thing."

"The image is, however, uncomfortably like him."

This was true. Casrus, who practiced daily with fire-sword and knife, who exercised in chariots along the subplanetary concrete tracks of the Klave, was built much on the dynamic lines of the second male image: Ceedres Yune Thar. The structure of the face was as similar as the physique. Libel, and to spare.

"He'll never know," said Vitra. "Only the Fabulast is privy to her own fantasy. That I admit you to the room is a concession. And how pretty you are!"

"Yes, I am pretty," Vyen admitted. "Casrus' fist, sword or gun might make me less so."

"I repeat, only the Fabulast has access to her fantasy as of

21

right, except for the worms who watch the drama played out on the screen in their recreation area, and know nothing about aristocrats, either what they do or what they look like."

"Casrus, however, is the one aristocrat they might recognize, considering his constant forays into the Subterior."

"Never. See how different I've made him, all gold, and so arrogant. Besides, when the worms watch the Fabulism screens they're hypnotized by the machines and forget afterward almost all they saw. Pathetic worms."

"Such contempt for your audience."

"What else? The rabble crawl about on the surface in their airsuits, or through the mines, gathering fuel and minerals to supply the Klave. It's their destiny. My destiny is to mitigate their vile lives with visual stories. I don't have to love them. I'm content to serve them."

"To serve yourself."

"Moralizing precociousness doesn't become you, younger brother."

"Oh, excuse me."

Vitra consumed the last of her alcohol stick, and threw the holder on the ground, from which the machine would shortly clear it.

"Well," she sighed, languidly stretching herself, "the poor worms must wait for the next installment of the fantasy. My service is over for this Jate. I have," she added, "included the ideas of Jate and Maram in the hot desert world of my Fabulism. It seemed reasonable that a place where the sun never sets should have similar sleeping customs to this place where the sun never rises. I've put in jokes about science, too. The hot-sider imbeciles of the story believe gods gave them their science, and pray to them through round golden globes. They think our side of the planet is *hell*, and have a myth about a garden paradise. We abandoned such indulgences long ago."

"Vitra," interrupted Vyen, "we're to dine at house Klastu. Are we going to insult the stupid Olvia by being late again?"

Vitra linked her arm with his. They were almost of a height, very nearly twins.

"Why not? Stupid Olvia is also in my story."

"In other words, you've been singularly uninventive. The least inventive Fabulast the Klave has ever known."

"In other words, I've been economical. Besides secretly displaying my contempt for all houses of the Klave."

Brother and sister laughed and snaked out of the chamber through the opening door.

The Klave, unlike the Yunea of Vitra's invention, was not constructed in a planet-conforming circle. (She compared Klave and Yunea now with slight irascibility. If she had deliberately caricatured certain of her acquaintances, yet she had been original in such items as the Yunea and its tenets, manners and customs. The abbreviated names, for example, were solely her idea, the style of clothing, the furniture and fittings of the fantasy. All these she had been inspired to conjure out of nothing.)

Beyond the chamber of the clear dome, a lift dropped down to a terrace that gave on the subsurface Residencia, the cold-side aristocrats' city. This was as different as might be from the rolling parched splendor of Vitra's Yunean estates. Seen from the terrace, the Residencia was a mathematically cultured lowland of concrete, white metal and crystal. Here and there hills arose, but constructed or hewn, each crowned by its mechanized complex, a diadem of bowls, pylons, bridgework. Indeed, the chamber of the dome was part of just such a complex, situated on just such a man-made cliff, Rise Iu, or forty-six. But Iu, as was occasionally obvious in other of the crowning complexes, possessed a shaft that passed straight up and through the overhead ceiling which contained the underground city. The chamber of the dome gave a direct view of the chill discouraging un-sky of space. Here, in the Residencia, everything was laved by the intensifying lamps, a glow hardly less uncompromising than that of the stars, and definitely no warmer.

Frosty and glittering, the Residencia appeared, and the roadway which spiraled down from Rise Iu to enter it had the gleam of polished ice itself. It was fashionable among the aristocrats to dress themselves to match the state of their inner and outer country, in grays, whites, blacks and silvers. Yet the wretched workers of the Subterior, the cold-side's lower-class multitude, were fed gaudy colors and gaudy deeds by the Fabulasts. And the workers' horrid functional hovels, cold and generally comfortless, were often startlingly splashed with gouts of carmine and russet plastic dye, bought in place of spirits or even food.

Unlike the chariots Vitra had willfully designed for the invented hot-siders, the Klovez vehicle which stood awaiting brother and sister had no mechanical animals. It was raised

23

on enormous air-runners, and thrust forward with a smooth-nosed prow and a curved windshield, from which decorative white streamers floated. Very definitely it was not the sort of chariot employed by those taking exercise. Such a transport would be a mere primitive sling and rail of steel set between big wheels, and drawn by teams of large savage dogga. Probably Vitra Klovez would introduce such dogga eventually into her Fabulast drama. At the moment she was bursting with inventiveness; notions of beasts, situations and geography whirled across her mind whenever she considered her task. But probably inventiveness would flag at some point.

There were ten other Fabulasts among the aristocrats. Their function was traditional and altruistic, their feelings on the matter no longer either. The "worms" of the Subterior who ceaselessly toiled to maintain the princes of the Klave were despised by all, possibly even by themselves, and scarcely considered human.

The chariot car skimmed down the polished road with a panting of its runners, streamers flailing and tiny bells jingling. Its speed was the same as that which Vitra meant to give the hunting chariots of Hirz.

Buildings flew by, silvery wedges, mechanized and humming globules a hundred feet high, and the intermittent palaces, perched in strange rock gardens. The car passed near a flash of gem-studded pedestrians about a radiant blue façade—some theater or arena of exercise. (And Vitra wondered briefly if she should have given her created solar culture more entertainments—somehow she had not envisaged many, save in the decadent area of their Slum.) The car swerved by a grotto of scintillant ice, dashed by other conveyances, stationary or in flight, and over a bridge of wildly scrolled black iron, under which swarmed a multitude of robot and human traffic.

A moment more, and they had reached the gates of Klastu.

It was now Maram, or J'ara for those keeping it, but no clocks had sung in the Residencia. Each aristocrat who cared to carried his own chronometer, along with fiddle-toys, mind games in miniature plastivory boxes, crystal-cinched alcoholic lollipops and other functional jewelry.

Klastu's gates folded aside, and the car ran on.

An avenue of carved trees, hung with fruits of palest yellow luminex, ceased at a portico. The oval entrance was quite unlike the pillared porch of Vel Thaidis' palace, save in the matter of its sliding doors.

The Residencia was artificially heated and filled with breathable atmosphere throughout, yet within its living sectors and their immediate surroundings, this warmth and freshness were concentrated. A tepid scented breeze blew out of the house, followed by a shiny black robotic beetle of enormous size. Klastu had caught the mode of insectile servants. This weird beast now conducted Klastu's latest arrivals into the lift and hence into the salon.

Fountains of gauzily colored oxygen were playing, making several of the party lightheaded and frivolous. The ceiling of the salon was a fake of the space-sky, jet black, yet alleviated by tinges of blue and pink in the fire of its "stars." Sometimes a comet would appear to rush over, and the salon would resound to little screams and exclamations, as walls, floors and guests were bathed momentarily in brilliant rose or white.

"What a boring novelty," remarked Vyen as, the instant they entered, the apartment blushed violently in one of these comet displays. He accepted a black drink from an airborne Klastu beetle, droning on latticed wings. Vitra had prattled about humanized robots being, in her fantasy, the height of cultural elegance. At least Klastu had spared him that. But here was another comet, and everything cometically blanched. "I must remember to tell Olvia it's her most cunning idea yet, and that she should have been a Fabulast."

But Vitra did not upbraid him. Vyen glanced about and saw why. Her attention was totally engaged by the presence of Casrus Klarn at the far end of the room.

"Now usually he shuns such social events as Olvia's," said Vyen. "Maybe Fate, in which we, in our sophistication, no longer believe, has brought Casrus here for the sole purpose of having me confess to him your crime."

"What crime? An image called Ceedres—"

"You should not," said Vyen severely, "stare at the man so fixedly. He hasn't any time for you. You know it. Your gorgeousness and unsurpassed wit somehow evade the mark. Of course, you put him in your drama in order to indulge yourself. Love-sick, dear sister?"

Vitra jerked about like a spitting cat, the last of which species was otherwise long extinct from the Klave. This was not the first duel between them concerning Casrus, whom Vyen viewed with a jokingly maleficent dislike born of old unadmitted envy. Vitra, attracted and unable to gain a purchase on the cold outer slope of Casrus' regard, viewed him

25

similarly, her feelings, however, tempered by a wish to ensnare and a constant surprise that she could not.

"Oh, snarl away," said Vyen. "I suppose, in the story, Ceedres is also love-sick for your Val Thaidis, who closely resembles you, and is patently a sublimation of yourself. But in reality, we all know he prefers his little Subterior girl, the interesting Temal."

Vitra extended her silver-enameled nails, and raked Vyen's hand. His drink slopped and his mouth twisted for a second in the ugliest of lines. Then he had seamlessly unpleated his rage, and appealed with smiles to bystanders, those aristocrats as inquisitive and prone to vitriolics as himself. "My sister has the Fabulast's inventive temperament," he said.

"Vitra the cat," remarked Shedri Klur, manifesting at her side. "What should we do to make you sheath your claws and purr?"

"Vitra is full of her hours as a storyteller," said Olvia, soothing Vyen's injury. "She isn't yet aware that no Fabulast is ever original and therefore has no right to temperament. The talents of the Subterior, now, the actors and creators who entertain *us*—they have some right to it, and display none."

"Ultimately," said Shedri, "the rabble are always far better mannered than we. But perhaps we should ask the depressing Casrus about it."

Eyes, gilded or painted or pasted with glitter, darted toward Casrus and away.

"I can't guess," said Olvia, "why he accepted my invitation. If I had realized he would, I would never have sent it."

"Of course," said one of Shedri's female cousins, leaning weightlessly upon Vyen, "the Subterines are definitely healthier than we. The rigors of their existence pluck out the weaklings, the remainder are tough and enduring. While we—"

"Live into our three hundreds," said Vyen, and drew off her earring with his teeth.

Vitra turned her back and stole instead upon Casrus, still in a cat mood. As she approached she eyed him disdainfully, assembling her defenses in readiness, for it was true, he had never had much time for her or those of her persuasion. Among Vitra's acquaintants, Casrus was scorned. He would not waste a Jate, but must *use* them all. Yet he had offered nothing to society, beyond peculiar acts carried out on behalf of the Subterior. No, he would not waste a Jate, but he would waste his robots and the machines of his house and his entitlement, laboring to ease the Jates and Marams of the

26

working rabble. A hopeless enterprise, plainly. As was his absurd employment of mortal workers rather than machines in the Klarn palace, which was only an excuse to feed and clothe them. It was said he strove to educate them too, tutor them via mechanical tutors as only the children of the aristocratic matrixes were ever tutored. What good could such teaching bring the rabble? As for Casrus' ward, or mistress, or whatever she was, a girl rescued from the Subterior when the Law had sentenced her to exposure on the frozen airless planetary surface as punishment for murder—

Despite his eccentricity, Casrus Klarn was a tall, unusually well-made man, handsome, and with beautiful hair and eyes. To girls of Vitra's mold, therefore, fair game—which had proved allusive.

"Happy J'ara, Casrus," said Vitra.

Ensid Klastu, to whom Casrus had been speaking, had moved off. Casrus stood alone by a mosaic wall, whose tones were like the chips of a rainbow never seen but in pictures. Frankly, Casrus had been the exact model for Ceedres Yune Thar, all but for coloring, expression and Ceedres' trick of facial mimicry. This last Vitra had borrowed from an occasional knack of her brother's.

"May your J'ara also be happy," said Casrus gravely, looking at Vitra from impenetrable blue eyes.

*If you knew*, she thought, and for a moment felt a false power over him, because she had made him one of the puppets of her dance.

"How are your adopted worms?" she asked now, deliberately sparring.

"The men and women in my house are well enough."

Not a hint, not a clue of anger or embarrassment to guide her, for her to fasten on.

"And the luscious Temal. How is she?"

"Your concern for my people is most affecting."

The edge, unexpected, stung.

"*Your* people, Casrus? The workers exist to serve all the princely houses. How can it be you're able to abduct so many from their ordained duties? Has no one ever complained of you to the Computers of the Law?"

"Not yet," he said. But now he smiled a little, amused by her threatening tone.

How she wished this man were accessible to her. She would like to lead him about by a chain of finest steel.

"And you have disturbed poor Ensid," she murmured,

27

smiling also to demonstrate an unreal camaraderie between them. "What did you say to him?"

"We were dicussing the Subterior."

"Of course. Casrus, you have no tact. But such breadth of thought. You should be a Fabulast, as I am."

"I don't consider it my role," said Casrus slowly, "to pour soporifics into the brains of the working class of the Klave. They need to understand why they are in pain, not to be drugged against feeling any."

Vitra was affronted by his scathing reference to her new skills. And suddenly alarmed.

"Their destiny is to labor. If they refused—"

"I imagine we might be somewhat inconvenienced."

"Are you suggesting that the princely class should toil in their stead?"

"Why not?" he inquired. "But no, that's not precisely my aim. I conclude our machines might undertake such work. At one time, I'm certain that they did, and that no human was forced to break his back, his lungs and his soul in this way. Our technology has slipped, I'm not sure why, some oversight in the past, or merely our own laziness."

Vitra was not flattered that he offered his theories to her. He would offer them to anyone. She wished she might fascinate him. She wished he would speak to her of herself and not of others. She had been in love with him, a sort of love, selfish, but nevertheless desperate and quite hurtful, for some years. Other men laid themselves gracefully at her feet. Casrus, who was perhaps four years her elder, glanced at her as if at a troublesome child.

"You know none of us will listen to you," she said softly and winningly. "We're all too mindless and too afraid of losing what we have."

She was pleased to see he seemed puzzled by her insight and her abrupt veracity. She was not a fool, but she was young.

"I asked Ensid for the loan of a machine," said Casrus. "A tunnel has collapsed in the Nentta mine. My own robots are there, but not enough. I was there earlier myself."

"The Subterior," said Vitra. "Do you speak only of that to Temal?"

"I try not to speak of it to her. She grieves sufficiently for her people."

"Yet doesn't, I assume, desire to return to them? Nor you. Your sad worms are trapped in a tunnel. And here you stand,

28

waiting for Olvia's probably very silly dinner. Oh, forgive me, Casrus. But why should I want to give up what I have to help *them*? I shall help them much better as their story-maker."

There had never been an instant when his eyes had revealed anything to her beyond courtesy, even the inner vehemence of his beliefs was visually held in check. Now he said calmly, "You are quite right, Vitra Klovez. I should not be here but overhead in Nentta. Thank you for your reprimand. Happy J'ara."

And he went by her and across the salon, his black clothes seeming blacker than any others in the room. At the door he paused to salute Olvia, who fluttered, holding up diamanté hands. Then he was gone.

A burning fury filled Vitra. Her mouth became ugly as Vyen's had been. Casrus asked too much of her, too much of them all, and worse, never asked for those things which they would freely and gladly have given. "Marry me," he should have said to her. "Be my wife, entertain me; I'll forget my madness."

She hated him, and she hated the worms, and she hated Vyen's smug blandness, his vicious romantic eyes upon her face, watching the fury and the hatred bite deep in her heart.

A comet passed. The room screamed into crimson.

The beetles brought in Olvia's silly dinner.


Vitra's personal dreams during the dregs of that Maram were swift and ferocious. Vyen had remained at Olvia's palace, a thing which Vitra neither queried nor approved.

Next Jate, about the thirteenth hour, she would return to the Fabulism chamber on Iu and begin work again upon her drama. Next Jate, there should be passion and upheaval enough, if only on a screen.

Angrily she blew out the coldly golden light that burned by her sofa (in the dark, she needed no Maram-chamber). And she remembered how Casrus had left her, had not wanted her, thinking her purposeless and worthless.

*But I am not.*

# CHAPTER TWO

## Part One

At the seventeenth sun-blazoned hour, Maram commenced, the customary Time of Sleeping.

To designate periods of sleep and wakefulness had, eons before, been considered necessary to the Yunea, over which the sun was fixed forever in the green sky. No sunrise, no sunset, no phase of darkness intervened. Maram was marked only by the singing clocks of the palaces, the striking clocks of the Slumopolis. Aristocratic sleepers retired to their shade-producing Maram-chambers, others kept wakeful J'ara, remaining active by the golden light of eternal day.

The inhabitants of the Yunea knew no other style of life, and if their forebears ever had, the knowledge had been mislaid. The static-seeming sun remained, and the world turned, always face to face with the solar disc, so that geographical direction itself constantly altered, traveling onward in a circular motion. The palace of the Hirz, for example, was located during the first hour at the ninth station of Ne in hest, or hest-Ne. At the fifth hour, the hour Vel Thaidis had waited by the lake shore, the palace had moved into the thirteenth station of Dera, in the hespan half of the globe. Hest and hespa were the two circuitous directions of the planet. Otherwise, traveling inward meant toward the zenith, that area over which the sun directly stood in perpetual high noon. The center of the earth was inevitably a desert of classic, unrelenting barrenness.

The vast Ring of the Yunea and its own inner ring of the Slumopolis ended well clear of this waste at the Zenith perimeter.

Conversely, retreating outward six hundred to seven hundred staeds beyond the great estates of the Yunea, the Fading Lands, farthest from the eternal sun, sank away, uncharted and unvisited save by machines.

At the seventeenth hour, the first hour of Maram, the Hirz palace entered the first station of hest-Ume; the palace of the Thars, twenty staeds away, had correspondingly entered hest-Aite.

Soon, the beautiful aircraft of the Hirz, like a slender jeweled insect, glided up into the lower atmosphere and headed hespa.

Seen from below, the craft moved swiftly. Seen from the craft, the ground appeared to drift by with a deceptive smoothness that suggested leisure. The short dry rain had fallen in the fourteenth hour; now the sky was clear almost as glass. The tawny green veldt of the Hirz estate alternated with its lush moss plains, dabs of heavy foliage and the glittering channels of aqua courses, the mineralized, glaucous man-fashioned near-water of this world. The lake itself, the glory of Hirz lands, presently drew away. Stony hills marked the boundary of the Thar holding.

On the other side of the hills decline was already quite evident. Tracks of sand had encroached on its plains, a dusty, scabby undersoil pushed through rise and valley alike. Many aqua courses had evaporated, their previous positions indicated only in thirsty slashes where forests of cacti had feverishly rooted. Here and there were patches of dead plantation, wizened and shriveled from lack of moisture, all leafage and fruit long vanished. On a slope, a sapphire-colored machine, uncorroded, glinted in the sun, but did not perform any function. Technology had perished at Thar decades ago. Now year by year, moment by moment, even before watching eyes, it seemed, Thar died.

Velday did not speak of it. That his sister viewed the wreckage beneath must be sufficient—it did not need words: the whole country displayed its plight with one desolate pleading nakedness. And Vel Thaidis did not look away. She had not traveled to Thar since she was thirteen, Ceedres seventeen, which was his coming of age. The same year old Yune Thar, Ceedres' father, drank a painless drug in order to

32

kill himself. Old Yune Thar had not been able to bear ruin. He left it instead as a legacy for his son.

It was difficult for Vel Thaidis, however, to dwell on these things impartially. She looked at them with her new eyes, enlightened now, and rather than grow tender, she resisted, pushed compassion aside. If she loved Ceedres, she could not afford compassion for him also. So she thought of Ceedres and Velday as young boys, riding along the great Hirz beach, laughing in the sunlight, which gleamed on their bronze mechanical mounts and their bronze human bodies. And of herself, shut up to learn to play upon the Chame, in the house, her eleven-year-old fingers clumsy with resentment and the first intimations of loneliness.

After an hour, the aircraft skimmed above a marsh, where giant shade reeds speared from pockets of debased mud, aglow like bloody gems. The marsh had been a river once. On its bank, the palace climbed in the traditional Yunean arches and pillared blocks of plastum marble and metal.

The house had not lost it grandeur. The gardens were overgrown, yet still fresh and vivid, while beyond the shoulder of the bank stretched the last staeds of decent ground. But it was not much. And what there was had been kept vital merely by the spasmodic help of the Chures, the Onds; mostly by Velday's passionate help which flowed into Thar unceasingly. Indeed, Velday stinted Hirz in order to salvage the dregs of Thar. Even now, two or three Hirz machines were visible at work on the land.

The aircraft dipped down, flaring its gossamer-like wings and letting out its insectile legs. In the humming aftermath of flight, Vel Thaidis heard the tinny rattle of the marsh reeds in their slots of blood.

Other craft stood about on the bank. She absently took in the insignia of Ket and a regular flotilla of Yune Ond air vehicles, Omevia's butterfly among them. The robots and hunting equipment Velday had sent would already have arrived.

At the fourteenth hour, as the dry rain had dusted against the lake, Vel Thaidis had had her hair re-tinted: black. It had been an instinctive gesture of war. Now she regretted it, plainly too late.

Thar's large lower salon echoed to the sounds of conversation and crystal ware, but not to the unmistakable tread of house robots. Ceedres was forced to serve his guests in person, which he did skillfully, as if it were his choice to do so, and not necessity. The ancient furniture, heavy and sullen,

33

pressed against the walls as if it had withdrawn in disdain. Frescoes and painted windows had faded, and their colored reflections were dim. The fountain played into its marble basin, though no gilt mechanical fish wriggled any longer across the basin's floor.

Yet there were still wine and spirits in the cellars. Vel Thaidis stood between two columns, watching Ceedres move about from group to group, easy, gracious, bearing the flagons. She saw him also with her strange new sight, his unique profile against the zenith windows, the flex of the muscles in his arms as he poured drink into the antique smoky crystal cups of Thar. Everything was alarming to her. She braced herself in perplexity against his advance, as before she had only braced herself in dislike and irritation.

Then suddenly he was in front of her, his arm lightly and briefly across the shoulders of Velday, as he extended to her the open formal hand of princely greeting. She took the hand, as she had done on frequent previous occasions, and was astonished that no tactile shock passed from his flesh into hers.

"I observe the proprieties this Maram," he said to her, "to disarm your fury, dread lady." He had put down the flagons before approaching them. Velday had taken them up and poured for all three, with a movement as tactfully gracious as Ceedres' own in serving the others. Bitterly, she acknowledged a quality that her brother gained in Ceedres' vicinity, as if together they invented some extra dimension of manhood and nobility.

"Did the tracking robots bring back good news?" Velday said, bridging her silence.

"Antelines, fifteen staeds over the outer border of Thar. A generous herd, seven or eight hundred of them."

"Good hunting, then."

"Very good. And will you accept the role of hunt master, Velday?"

It was a mere courtesy, since the hunt robots were from Hirz.

"Not I. Give it to Naine Yune Ond, he likes to labor."

"Hunt mistress, then, to Vel Thaidis, if she will accept. One level head at least, for the love of life." Ceedres looked at her directly for the first time, and his eyes, darker than her own, seemed to lift her forward and actually from her body. His gaze was intense, open, and therefore menacing. She felt he understood her dilemma quite well, for only the victor of the combat would dare to throw away his shield.

"I accept," she said.

"Oh, but you hate to be in at the killing, Vaidi," Velday protested.

Ceedres assumed an expression that was his own. She wondered that Velday could miss its scorn, the utter assurance. Then the expression melted into a replica of Velday's, merely slightly taken aback and amused. "Forgive me if I offended you *again*, Vel Thaidis. I haven't seen you at a hunt since you were a child. Don't let good manners impel you to agree."

"I said I accepted. After all, half the hunt machines are mine."

Velday turned sharply from her. She saw Omevia, drifted close on her gauzes, had overheard, and one or two more besides. But Ceedres' eyes remained candid, remained the eyes of victory.

"And does it," he said, "insult you also to drink my wine?" She held the cup toward him.

"Excuse me, I'm not thirsty." He took the cup. By clipping and lowering her voice, she was able to control it. "Put the wine back in the jar, Ceedres. You can hardly afford to be wasteful."

She had not expected a particular reaction. It was virtually the same insult as twice before. Yet for an instant his candor faltered. Thus she perceived the candor itself was the shield.

"I should have been warned by your hair," he said, "shouldn't I?" Then her heart jumped for he said generally to the gathering: "Naine, be my Hunt Master. Choose any female partner you wish, but this one. Vel Thaidis Yune Hirz has consented to be Mistress of the Hunt, and will therefore ride with me."

The hunting chariots of Hirz, unlike the toy chariots for exercise, were not beast-drawn. Hollow, brazen bird forms, they rose up on sensitive, long-clawed feet and jointed legs, almost two and a half yards clear of the ground, to stride, kneel, leap and run in response to the relevant touches on their boxed controls. From the arched bird necks and the gilded rails the riders looked down across mathematically spaced lines of pedestrian robots, faceless metal men, inexorably advancing, seldom varying position or pace. Half a staed in front of these, and utterly noiseless, darted the vanguard of

35

the hunt, the flying midges of spy kites, threading like needles through air and plants, their hair-fine fringes—nostrils, eyes and ears—flicking this way and that.

The machines were capable of hunting alone; the presence of man was not essential. Men, indeed, provided an element of uncertainty, the risk of lost game, botched kill, imperfection and inefficiency. Yet men hunted in their striding vehicles behind the army of machines, as if afraid to be left behind, superfluous and unneeded.

It had taken about two hours to reach the outer border of the Thar estate, the birds running at full speed. Even so, the desolation was grimly apparent. Black chasms empty of liquid, and the spilling powders of dust and sand. They had passed, racing, between the craning pillars of a dead plantation, a petrified fretwork against the sky whose talons raked the plum-green canopies of the chariots. And once the hunt strutted over a bone-pale bridge of ornate design, with a rusty swamp around its ankles.

Nobody commented on these sights, or on the use of Hirz equipment. Naine whooped encouragingly and flagons were tossed, racer to racer, as they galloped on.

The boundary came in a sudden cascading over of the land, a rocky cliff tumbling into luminous valleys. The hunting veldt beyond the estates was a wilderness. Forests had seeded randomly, tall cacti and curious mutated flora. There was little liquid, but here and there one of the antiquated shining aqua-towers would be revealed, a pool spreading over its reservoir in a flat green apron.

The bird chariots bounded wildly, almost recklessly, but with faultless safety, down the cliff.

Yet Vel Thaidis felt a momentary horror—more a premonition or an allegory of her own confusion than reaction to the descent itself.

"We're traveling too fast for your enjoyment," Ceedres said, touching the box. It was the first thing he had said to her since their ride together began.

"Don't trouble," she said.

They had entered the shadow of the cliff, and glancing behind, missed the sun, for it had gradually dropped below the midpoint, half down the sky, and here, at the outer ring of the Yunea, for a few moments, the cliffs would hide it altogether.

Ahead, the other chariots, the robot men and the kites, like bright waves which never ebbed. Below and beyond, fourteen staeds away, a rosy cloud rested thirty feet or so in the air. It was the marker left previously by the scouting hunt robots, the giveaway of the anteline herd roaming and feeding nearby. She thought: *So everything hunted is betrayed by some marker, some trace, high in the air for all to see.* She visualized her emotions, a crimson cloud above the chariot.

"This contest between us," Ceedres abruptly said, "it's not of my devising." She did not answer, staring back at the hidden sun, whose dazzle was gradually reemerging over the rock as the ground leveled behind. "A truce, Vaidi—pardon me, Vel Thaidis. What should I do to retrieve your good opinion of me, assuming you ever had one?"

She said: "Why assume that?"

The sun reappeared and struck at her with a knife-edged splendor. She looked away and saw, along the bowl of the valley, the gleam of a temple, and all the three bright hunting waves approaching it, far distant.

"What then did I do, as a small child, to anger you?"

"We've lagged some way after the rest," she said.

"Never mind. Won't you answer my question?"

"You made me Mistress of the Hunt. The hunt is almost a staed ahead."

"I slowed our vehicle on the cliff in deference to your concern."

He touched the box idly, and the bird chariot ceased to move.

A vast stillness seemed to come down with the slanted sunlight, the cliff shadow folded under it. The sandy plain of the valley was freckled with musk-clovers, lending the stillness its own peculiar scent. The hunt was now remote, the far side of the gleaming temple. She felt the hugeness of the valley, the cliff. All things seemed to be drawing away, as the hunt had done, in slow glimmering, unebbing waves, leaving her at the center of an empty beach. So she found herself magnetized toward the one sure point of reference: the man beside her.

"Deliberately you have kept me here," she said. "Why?"

"To settle our differences, Vel Thaidis. For some years, this inexplicable venom has been on the boil between us; Vay is like my brother."

"Nothing need worry you then," she said. "Let's get on."

The green canopy colored his skin and fair hair. She had started to analyze his face, rather than look at it too thoroughly.

"You're anxious to attend the kill, the slaughter of the an-

37

telines by superior robots and careless, inaccurate men? No, you'd rather talk, even to me, perhaps. Set me a penance," he said, "as the auto-priests used to do, with transgressors of particular laws. For I've transgressed some law of yours, lady, for certain."

She turned and gazed along the valley. The hunt had disappeared. She thought of the maimed antelines stumbling in their career of terror before the killing rain of the guns.

"We'll go to the temple, then," Ceedres said. "Speak to the priest. You can ask him to punish me, whichever way you choose, for whatever it is I've done, or what you think I will do."

"Don't—" she said, and paused, unable to grasp what she had intended to ban.

"*Don't?* Pleading isn't for a daughter of Hirz. Is it?"

Ashamed, she recognized her fear as marvelous, and that she did not want it to end.

"Do as you wish," she muttered. Disgusted at herself and the betraying hovering marker, and her surrender to the maiming shot.

Velday laughed, as he caught the flagon Naine threw to him.

Naine's companion, Omevia, watched Velday under whitely nacred lids.

"Such laughter, and your sister left behind."

"It's a game," Velday said. "I knew it would happen. We intended it."

"Oh wise-as-a-priest," Omevia said.

"Mevi is envious," Naine remarked. The two bird chariots stalked neck and neck. The crimson marker was now a mere staed away, and the pace had slowed. Seen through the lines of the marching robots and the stands of cacti, a fawn animation poured gently to and fro on the swell of the plain. Unaware of the coming of death, the anteline herd browsed among the mosses.

Omevia smiled.

"Ceedres is handsome, but I'm not the head of House Ond, nor ever will be. I don't expect to claim all his attention. You perceive, Velday, I can be as outspoken as your sister."

"I take no offense," Velday said. "This business goes deeper than that with Ceedres."

"He told you so."

Velday tossed the flagon to Uched Yune Ket.

38

"Rein in," Naine called—a tradition, for no reins were attached to these vehicles.

The robots had halted, and light flashed on the narrow mouths of uptilting guns.

The three round domes of the temple were supported on three cylindrical towers, fifty feet high, twenty in diameter. The towers were linked together by pillared walks below, pillared walkways above, woven between countless doorways. The cool and creamy brass of the buildings shed flakes of sunlight onto the ground and into the flowering moss trees which foamed about their bases. Structurally, the outer temples resembled each other in every respect. The same domes and parapets and links, the same carpet of luxurious lawns. All were situated just over the border of the Yunea, at the brink of the hunting lands beyond the great estates. All emitted the same uncanny sound, a tinsely whispering on the air like the breathing of obscure and abstruse gods.

The bird chariot kneeled before the pillars.

Ceedres descended, and held out his hand to Vel Thaidis. But she ignored the courtesy and stepped unaided from the bird on to the emerald turf, into the deep fathoms of the god sound.

They walked, unspeaking again, up the burnished avenue, and as they approached, the door in the nearer tower slid open to admit them. From the lawn they could make out the priest standing ready in the place beyond the threshold.

It was a circular chamber, the foot of the cylinder, columned, otherwise bare and without decoration or window, lit only by the soft false sunlight of the temple which flooded from walls and ceiling. The priest itself, entirely manlike in presentation, except for the poreless plastum skin and hairless skull, opened its flexible hands in a token of greeting.

"Welcome, Ceedres Yune Thar."

"Thanks," Ceedres replied to the priest, nodding as if to a human. Above all, the Courteous Address was used before the robot priests, not by law but as a code of etiquette among the princely houses. Generally, though, the priests did not speak the names of visitors. Ceedres apparently expected her surprise. "He recognizes me since this temple relates to Thar lands. And yes, I'm frequently here. Did you suppose I had no need of solace?"

"Not the solace of priests," Vel Thaidis said.

"Do you seek the Room of Prayer, Yune Thar, or the upper room?" the priest inquired.

"Both, my priest."

The inner circle of the floor, on which they stood, began to rise; overhead, the effulgent ceiling folded itself away. The floor of the lower chamber presently became the floor of the second chamber above. They were in the Room of Prayer.

In common with the majority of her class, Vel Thaidis had come to such rooms most regularly in her childhood. Because of this, they had for her always a tenuous, transparent aspect of holiness, almost of magic, which was the ghost of her childish awe overlaid on adult perceptions.

The walls, painted with the symbols of a science intelligible to robots but not to mankind itself, the yellow globes on their marble stands, a hundred facsimiles of the eternal sun. In order to pray, one should cross to such a globe, embrace it between the palms, rest the forehead against the satin texture of it. In this posture, saffron waters would seem to fill the brain, until at last awareness swam automatically into the invincible aura of the gods, those protectors of men.

Unease was dissolved in this bath, if it had ever existed. Serenity and security proliferated like streams over the anxious soil of the mind.

It was not rare for the vision of a park or garden to enter the spiritual eye at such a moment, a scene of forests, waters; a sky of flying beasts, set over with panes of shade. This dream or revelation of paradise, discounted as optical illusion and childish myth, lost all credence with maturity, and was not often seen past the fifteenth year. Inexplicable, it was frequently explained, until quite explained away, yet another casualty of growing up.

Ceedres was watching her. They were children of the same world and the same social echelon. He, too, would be primed to this chamber and its meanings, the naïve romance of childhood, despite everything, never quite dispelled.

"Whether we credit it or not," he said, "our religion comforts us. Do you understand, Vel Thaidis? I don't need to believe the ancient myths of our culture to find peace here."

"A seeker of solace and peace," she said. "*You.*"

"My priest," said Ceedres, "please tell my companion the truth—that I keep J'ara in this temple one Maram in every five."

"It is true," said the auto-priest.

Vel Thaidis pressed the tips of her fingers to one of the

40

yellow globes. Its light shone up through her flesh, negating it, leaving only the lattice of her bones. This too was truth, the skeletal framework within the skin, the framework of lies which supported the skin of innocence.

"I accept that you pray, Ceedres," she said. Her voice trembled but she continued. "You have some reason. Did you bring me here to impress me with your sad and noble condition? You failed."

"I brought you to show you a mystery of the temple. The upper room."

"The upper rooms of the temples contain their energies. Only the priests go there."

"Here, the priest is generous."

"You mean you've found some way to override its function. But I've no interest in a storage chamber full of mechanisms."

"Beautiful Vel Thaidis, always your eyes firmly bandaged and your ears stopped. One Jate you'll stand in such a room as this for the gods' blessing on your marriage. Blind and deaf then, as now, no doubt."

She had an impulse to escape him then, more intense than all the impulses—to escape or to linger—that had assailed her before. But his timing was excellent, and he had caught her hand before she could speak or retreat. "Upward," he said decisively to the priest, and immediately the floor rose again. The ceiling opened overhead and her heart lurched thickly at what she saw—an incredible blackness, into which the ascending floor was carrying them.

*What has he done?* she thought. *And how has he done it?* Few could intellectually interpret, let alone actively tamper with the fundamentals of machines. And a son of Thar, a house ruined due to the collapse of its technology—surely, of all men, he would be the least capable of such a feat. As for the blackness, the arcanely accursed blackness into which they went, it opened like the mouth of uninvited death. The idea of the blackness overwhelmed her, and she shrank.

"After the peace, the domain of panic," Ceedres said to her.

She turned to him as she had turned to him in the silent valley, as to an unavoidable reference point. And with the utmost cunning, it seemed to her, again he mimicked her face, her expression. Thus she beheld her own furiously controlled and staring fear grimacing at her. But then it came to her

41

that the strong hand which remained clasped over hers, was cramped like a vise.

"Yes, I'm afraid as you are," he said to her. "Fear of darkness is common to our race, Vaidi. And fear is a harsh teacher, though better than the wine of peace and reassurance. Why else do the priests keep it from us? Why else do I explore this dark? To know my fear."

*"To be afraid. Let me go,"* she rasped. Yet she clung to his hand, and now all the black poured down over them, over their heads, their eyes; into their mouths and across their bodies. She shut her lids almost at once. She could barely keep from screaming. But their handclasp held her from it, that, and her desperate anguish that here she must betray herself totally, and that on this assumption he had brought her.

"Priest," she faltered wildly.

"He won't answer you, not in this room," Ceedres said. Then his fingers came lightly to her eyelids. "Have I misjudged you, Vaidi? Are you such a coward?"

"Don't call me by my familiar name."

"A coward has no right to honor, or to names."

Eyes shut, she heard his breathing in the blackness, matched identically to her own. To orient herself, to dismiss her ambience with the ambience of the dark, she raised her lids.

It was no longer black. Above her, and all about, as if floating in immeasurable vistas of jet-black air, white brilliants blazed, bright as the sun, surely brighter. As if the solar disc were blanched and broken and scattered, in specks and streaks, chains and powderings of white fire, a petrified rain—but fallen where?

She began to shudder, but her fear had passed.

"What does it mean?"

"Truly hell, perhaps. Or death. Or a shadow. Always I fear to come here. Always the fear dies quickly. But you've shared it with me. And you've seen me afraid, Vel Thaidis. Not many can say that."

"How brave of you to return to your fear with such diligence. And to include another in the game."

"Now," he said, "we stop playing."

His voice ran through her in a sudden current, and as suddenly she realized that he told her no more than she knew. The darkness had stripped her of fear and apprehension, and so she had nothing left with which to deny him. She stood under the white fires and waited for his words, his touch.

"Beautiful girl," he said to her, "exquisite girl." The fires swarmed in his eyes, so that the fires became his eyes. His face was sketched in bold outline on the black, brow, lash, cheekbone, the carven nose and lip, the jaw with its silver cleft, the muscular tendon in the neck even, the hollow of the throat.

Fascinated, she gazed at the miracle of him, waiting.

"Truce, then," he said. He let go her hand which seemed dismembered by the loss. But his hands moved, warm and living, to her shoulders. "We fight no more."

What did it matter if he had discovered her, found her out? He had found her. What was more valid? She acquiesced.

Some feet away, in the glittering black, the priest. But again, she could forget the priest.

Ceedres leaned toward her and the sprinkled fires seemed to swirl and shatter, and tumble like leaves, and gutter out.

Held by him and against him, and his mouth on hers, she relinquished herself instantaneously. As sugar dissolved in wine, so she was dissolved in the essence of what he was, becoming a flavoring, an accessory, no longer with identity. Initially, the delirium was wonderful to her, to dissolve, to sink, to become nameless.

But when he let her go, as her hand had seemed dismembered, her whole body now seemed anchorless and bereft. She stared at him in shocked bewilderment, aware of what every parting, of flesh or mind, would be hereafter.

"I asked you stupidly before, Vaidi. Blame my pride and forgive me. Be my wife."

He spoke very low, to disguise his indifference, perhaps.

He had overwhelmed her. He could not have done it if he similarly had been overwhelmed. Of course, she knew, even as she knew the hour of her surrender. And of course she would give in to him, float nameless and obliterated, delivering her reason to him as she would deliver her reason to the gods in prayer. Ceedres was her god. To be happy, she must worship him, and let him destroy her, and take pleasure in it.

He was bringing her back, lifting her again into the new landscape of his arms.

She noticed the cleverness of that hold, supporting her, encircling her, so she should sense a flawless completion, like positions in a skillful dance.

"And the priest is to witness me," she said, from a throat that did not want the reality of speech.

"What better?"

"What indeed," she said dreamily. "You have genius, Ceedres. It would be fitting to adore you. To bring you the gift of half of Hirz. To grudge nothing."

She saw his mouth smile. He had cause, she supposed, for some amusement. He leaned to her and kissed her again, and she let herself lie deeply in the kiss, the last kiss.

When he raised his head, she spoke.

"My answer is no. And your priest can witness that."

An interval of no sound and no movement. Then: "Vaidi, the game has finished. This is in earnest."

"So it is. So is my answer. No. And no and no. Forever and always, no to you."

"Eyes bandaged, ears stopped," he said. "You can't hear your own self crying out to me."

He released her, to let her hear, every artery and nerve, calling after him, through the dark.

Tears spilled from her eyes, amazing her; it was not yet the hour for them: she was not ready.

"Wed Omevia," Vel Thaidis said. "She can bring you something."

"Not what I want."

"All my property, and not much of myself."

There was a second quietness, and in the quiet the air seemed to change, to solidify and harden, and when he spoke again, she saw the battle was over, ashes, and the very fluid of her blood seemed to become dust, and her veins like the dry chasms of Thar.

"You lack one incomparable talent," he said, "the ability to lie. Not to others, Vel Thaidis, but to yourself. Do you have any conception of what that lack has cost you? I think not. Enjoy your ignorance while you can. Descend," he added to the priest, and the floor staggered and drenched them in unbearable light.

She had won the battle, and might never be happy again.

"A poor shot, Naine. A hunt master should do better."

The anteline buck lay on its side. Its three-year dappled hide, a shifting kaleidoscope of fawn, umber and pale olive, was further spotted by blood. Its eyes, under the polarizing membrane, were wide. The fountain of five-pronged horns had scraped savage furrows in the moss, as, at Naine Yune Ond's profligate shot, it had crashed down in agony. The energy bolt had smashed its spine, it could only kick spasmodically and rake with its horns. Everywhere about it, dispatched by the robots' swift and unmistaken missiles, its kin had slumped motionless. The sky and the slopes were curtained off by dust, the fume of trampled moss, the after-charge of the guns. Not for some while did the hunters come by and note the anteline, neither living nor dead.

Naine had produced a dispatching knife from his chariot, but Velday pushed the blade aside. He whistled. One of the metal men loped forward, took Naine's knife and went to the beast.

Its eyes fluttered. Perhaps it looked for help, or simply worse and more prolonged torture. Then the steel sheared through its throat.

Compassion had stirred in Velday. His own shots had been accurate. The vast kill for food he had no qualms at, but this unnecessary individual suffering he shunned. Yet, with the beast's slaughter, everything was tidied for him, the J'ara spontaneously cleansed and restored.

His thoughts returned with affectionate malice to Ceedres and his sister. He foresaw, with the optimist's tunnel vision, the conclusion of the quarrelling and a new era of good will ahead. Beyond his declaration—I knew it would happen. We intended it—he had offered no explanation of Ceedres' and Vel Thaidis' absence, nor *who* had intended, or known, nor precisely in connection with what. That he and Ceedres had devised the scheme, certainly he had not mentioned. That Ceedres had formulated the scheme alone and Velday merely agreed to it, Velday did not remember.

The hunt robots were gathering up the kill.

The slain antelines lay piled on gilded sleds. They had had no omen, when they grazed among the mosses, that this would be the end of their J'ara. Nor had Velday any notion as to what would be the end of his.


Vel Thaidis came from the temple and glanced about her at the world, which was the same. The lower sun, the shimmering valleys and the rocky boundary of Thar ten staeds to the zenith.

She was dizzy and faintly nauseated, her physical person no longer seemed to possess any center or wholeness—a whirling planet robbed of its gravity. Yet the tears had dried on her cheeks and behind her eyes. She had recalled she walked, not with friend or lover, but with an enemy.

45

They went to the kneeling bird, and Ceedres handed her in, stepping up after her.

Over the outer rim of the valley, five or six staeds away and to hest, the rose marker in the sky had been replaced by yellow parasols of dust and after-charge.

Ceedres stood looking at this sigil of the hunt.

At that second, a resonant music came filtering from one of the domes of the temple: a singing clock telling the time to the wilderness, the twenty-second hour, Maram, the sixth hour of J'ara.

"They hunt will be over," Ceedres said.

She could not assume he meant to begin another conversation with her, and she said nothing. The dust parasols to the hest had a transparency now, a dilution, the fume settling as no further shots were fired. If she chose to remain with Ceedres here, the returning vehicles would intercept them, very likely in a matter of minutes. Perhaps Ceedres would take sour delight in that, in her discomfort. She did not remonstrate. She had assessed herself as beyond the triviality of discomfort and embarrassment. She had plunged to the depths, that was, the lowest nadir of misery and unreason she had yet known.

"Well," he said.

A metallic snap came with the word.

She turned. He held the driver-box in his left hand, in the right, one of the knives of dispatch, the traditional mercy killers of the hunt, carried always within each chariot. Already he had released the catch, and the sheath had unpeeled, leaving the blade free. The two-foot length of white steel extended between them, horribly apposite projection of hatred and spoiled ambition. The tip was a razor, the sides could cleave the neck bone of a full-grown buck or lionag.

Apparently Ceedres was about to murder her. His face was set, the brain nerving the hand to its task. Vel Thaidis' attention was riveted in absolute belief. She could not have said if she were terrified—for terror implied a logical response, and logic had no relevance to this act.

He poised there, letting the moments stretch, chords tautened on a chame for the master stroke that would commence, or finish, the song. Patiently, it seemed to her, he paused, that she should scent and taste this thing. (The god in the macabre jest—what had he said to the women he cast into a hell of blackness and white fires? You requested it. Now you have it. *Savor.*)

46

And then he grinned at her. And then, as swiftly, his face again was the replica of hers, the blank mask, the darting polarized eyes, the lips parted as if in readiness to cry out, but incapable.

The lethal blade flashed.

Ceedres extended it to her once more, but reversed, the grip toward her hand. And unthinking, unperplexed, she took the knife from him and held it.

Her gesture had been docile and slow, everything for her had run down, become sluggish, tranquil and without motive. The explosion of violence which succeeded dragged her helplessly with it.

Parody of their former clasp, his hand wrapped itself over hers, grinding her palm and fingers closed on the hilt of the knife. Exerting most of his considerable strength—unnecessarily, since he had allowed her no margin in which to summon resistance, or even to be aware of his intention—he jerked her arm forward. Her body followed, impelled against his. She half lay against him, foolishly stunned, appalled and not yet understanding why. Then he pushed her aside, and dropped back, out of the bird chariot. She saw him fall on the lawn before the burnished pillars, and insanely, the next instant, the bird chariot started to rise from its kneeling position.

To the full height of the jointed legs, the bird rose, seven and a half feet, and then, as nonsensically, started to walk back and forth along the lawns.

The driver-box had gone from the chariot in Ceedres' left hand. Inadvertently, or deliberately (deliberately), he had activated the chariot to a pointless and repetitive walk.

She clung to the rail, and the blood stained her dress a rich somber russet, in a design like a torn flower.

The hilt of the knife was also rather like a flower, jutting from the upturned petals of the retracted sheath. The blade was some inches deep in Ceedres' breast, where she had thrust it, under his guidance, her hand locked irretrievably to the grip, beneath his.

He did not move. Only the bird chariot moved.

A small hot breeze was siphoned through the valley, sifting the perfume of musk-clover and fresh blood.

Five staeds away, the dust had entirely settled. The hunt would have turned back toward the valley. Trapped in a situation of madness, she could only look from the chariot for the coming of her accusers.

Events were plain. She had murdered Ceedres Yune Thar—yet she had been the victim, he the instigator of the crime. Already, they made a horrible sense to her, these unholy facts. But she could never explain them, although, in a few minutes, she would be called upon to do so. To Ceedres' devotees, the Yune Kets and the Onds. And to Velday, her brother, who had loved him.

The J'ara hunt spilled back into the valley.

The hunt robots and the kites were stationed now to the rear among the sleds of anteline corpses. The capering bird chariots in the lead came strutting and swaying across the rise and down onto the plain.

Velday, expecting the end of all quarrels and the commencement of good will, beheld random glamour and comfort everywhere. In the distant pleated cliffs, which had taken on a sort of orange blood color when seen zenithward against the singing green of the sky and the dipped sun. In the plain itself, brimmed with a honey glaze and sweet with its musk. In the three warmly nacreous domes of the temple, adrift on the surface of the glaze, and the emerald wash of lawns and foliage beneath. In the strangely humorous parading of the solitary bird chariot, that marched about there, up and down.

Patently, it would be Ceedres' chariot. The idiotic perambulations implied a mind wandered elsewhere, or that the two occupants themselves had wandered.

The man lying on the ground failed to attract Velday's attention for some while, simply because he did not fit with Velday's preconceived ideas of what had come to pass.

When he eventually interpreted what he saw, it was like a sudden intense hurt. It stifled him, prevented brain and limbs from operating. Naine shouted, and Omevia, their cousins and the Yune Kets took up the yell. Velday shouted nothing, did nothing.

Then the chariots ran onto the temple lawns. Velday shut off the bird's motion and set it kneeling. Before the chariot was down he was scrambling from it like a terrified small boy. Time had slipped: he was nine years old, perhaps, and Ceedres fourteen. They and two others had been hunting lionag, without robots or machines, for a dare. In a gulley, coming on a nest of seven sepia cats, which sprang up snarling, the boasting had shriveled and the unveiling of danger broke like a scalding rain. That day, it had been Ceedres who fired, straight at the king cat as it came bounding down on

48

him. The ophian head, with its dripping ruff, had gone spinning one way, the body another. The six cat kindred skulked flat among the stones. Save for the king, the nest was as young and boastful as what hunted it; luck and Ceedres' marksman's aim had saved their lives. But in the seconds before, Velday had predicted Ceedres' death. That day, and later days. And now the day was here, not predicted in any form, but nevertheless actual, irrevocable.

Velday was alone. He did not recollect the other vehicles and the men and women springing out of them or nervously hanging back. They were plants or airs of the valley, nothing more.

He had reached Ceedres now, bending, dropping beside him.

To his everlasting shame, he might have begun to weep, but then some god breathed upon the world. One of the gods who had constructed the sky, tempered the waters, fashioned the mechanisms to serve and heal. The gods who kept harm and sorrow out of the world, at least, the world of the princes of the Yunea. Ceedres raised his outer lids, and looked at Velday.

The polarized lids beneath had turned extraordinarily black, a black almost opaque with pain and shock, but under them the eyes focused on Velday instantly.

"I'm alive," Ceedres said. "That surprises me. You also." Only the quietness of the valley permitted him to be audible. But they all heard, as they clustered near. And they all heard what he said to them next. "Her strength didn't equal her ferocity."

The god who had breathed on the world, now crushed Velday under his hand.

"What? What, Ceedres?"

"Your dulcet sister. She thrust for the heart and missed it. My fortune held, Vay. Just."

Velday could not speak, stifled as in the chariot.

It was Naine who once more shouted.

"You're sick, Ceedres. Don't talk of the impossible."

"How else could it happen?" Ceedres said, his opaque agonized glance now settling on Naine. "Any of your machines can read Vel Thaidis' patterns from the knife, which is still lodged in me."

"The priest from the temple will help you," Omevia hissed. "And any of the robots of Ond. Naine, you're a clod."

Velday glanced up, and saw the priest already gliding to

49

them over the lawns. Between the priest and Ceedres, the crazy bird chariot still paraded. Velday stared up at it and straight into the face of his sister. Framed by its ornately combed and black-tinted hair and the green light behind, that beautiful golden face was the most terrible thing he had ever looked at—as if the sun had faded and gone out and her face was the mirror which showed it. Even Ceedres' blood spattered on her dress was not more ghastly to him. Even the shrill sound she uttered, or what she said.

"He's lying to you!" she screamed to Velday. "Whatever he says, he lies. Believe me, not Ceedres, Velday! Vay— Believe me!"

"My sister," Velday said. He stood up slowly, shaking and yet curiously psychically immobile, as if his heart, or his heart's soul, had stopped.

"Take the box," Ceedres said from the ground. His voice had no emphasis. "Let her get down."

Uched Yune Ket said, "Why did she stab you? For what reason? And how could she come at you and best you?"

"Ask her," Ceedres said.

"Something against honor, perhaps," Naine blustered. "Hers, and yours."

"Mine, certainly. Ask the priest, too. I'm done with this. Velday?"

Velday shifted, and peered down again. Ceedres had shaded his eyes with his hand, and the polarized lids had drawn up a little way. "Velday, I don't wish to bring blame on your sister. I spoke rashly. I absolve her, and I'll say nothing else."

Velday touched the driver-box and the mad bird ceased walking and delicately kneeled.

Vel Thaidis leaned against the rail, her petrifying mask still turned to them. But her whole figure conveyed the bizarre stigma now, its beauty revolting, dressed as it was in the raiment of something cursed. Either their instinctive judgment had cast the illusion on her with the splotch of blood or her guilt, or her fright, had woven it. Whatever, she could not protect herself from what she had become in their sight, nor could she undo the malady. And this, obviously, she knew.

When she got out of the chariot and started to walk toward them, they drew aside. The response was primitive, but unchecked.

The auto-priest was bowed, with two or three of the Ond robots, above Ceedres. The knife had been plucked free and

50

lay on the turf. As she approached, Velday asked distinctly, "Whose patterns on the hilt?"

The Ond Voice robot replied, "The pattern's of Ceedres Yune Thar. Above them, the patterns which were used in striking: those of Vel Thaidis Yune Hirz."

"Yune Thar," Vel Thaidis said. She hesitated, and said, "Yune Thar held my hand on the grip and directed the knife to wound himself."

She did not anticipate belief. Possibly, Ceedres might laugh. She had not reckoned on Velday, reeling about, both lids snapping back from his eyes in an excess of rage.

"Don't slander him, or yourself, any further, Vel Thaidis."

She shut her own outer lids and said, "The priest is my witness as to what happened in the temple. I think, if you question him, the scheme behind all this will become apparent."

The Ond Voice Robot moved over to her, and stood between her and the group about Ceedres. It was like every robot of the princely houses, aesthetically pleasing, lustrously haired and mineral eyed. It filled her with intuitive, illogical despair. Perhaps because its exterior, a copy of life, yet unhuman and unbreachable, suddenly represented how her fellow humans had become for her, doors that would not open, minds forever shielded, blind optics.

"Vel Thaidis Yune Hirz," the Voice said, "a crime has occurred among the aristocracy of the Yunea. You should say nothing at this time. The Law prescibes that you should return to your house, and make yourself accessible there, for a phase of correct and proper questioning."

Two of the robots had lifted Ceedres. The wound had been sterilized, sealed and bound in silken web. His face had paled, the odd, high-colored pallor of a metal-skinned people. His head lolled on the robot's arm, toward Vel Thaidis. For a moment then, he smiled at her. He had not been able to resist the indulgence. It was safe enough, no other could see it, translate it, it was for her alone. It was the wine he spilled, as in the ancient formula, into her funeral urn.

She thought of the Domm hunt Velday had mentioned, when, with the pain of the cracked ribs, Ceedres had joked to ensure his host's admiration and kindness. The collapse of Thar had brought metamorphosis. But where old Yune Thar, the father, had warped like the plastum, crumbled like the plaster, Ceedres had become stone and steel. These closing

51

events of the J'ara had been almost easy for him to conduct. Maybe not so easy as to bind a woman by love, to marry into what he required of her. But in the long view, this method was cleaner, and ultimately ensured more freedom. Rather than amalgamate a wife into his plans, now he need only rub her from the map of their lives.

She stared into the vista of her future, powerless. Without being able to determine it, or credit it, she saw destruction in her path. Abstract as yet, but unavoidable, sharp as a white bone piercing the side of a dead animal, as the varnished nostril of a gun, a fire upon a hill.

She nodded to the Ond robot, Courteously, turned and went to one of the Hirz chariots. Her head averted, she remained until Velday stepped in beside her. At the fifth hour, that Jate, she had concluded she might already have lost Velday. If she had desired proof, it had been given.

Through the embers of Maram, in the tall bird of the jeweled aircraft, unspeaking, the last two descendants of Hirz went home together.

The period of Jate elapsed, and another Maram, and the compulsory interview had not been asked of Vel Thaidis. At first, she held herself sleepless and in taut readiness. The happenings of the J'ara were definite in her imagination, and she had an almost passionate need to recite them aloud to a listener, preferably human. No human was yet prepared to listen, however. Velday had gone, either to his apartments or from the palace itself. Weary and disconsolate, she made no effort to seek him. At length, in the last hour of the second sleeptime, exhausted, she entered her Maram-chamber. She had become sure by then that she had been absurd to linger, that the summons would not come, perhaps, for several Jates.

The Maram-chamber, windowless, without angles, poured down on her its turquoise shade, and began to play to her its gentle melodies and its rhythmic sighings. Vel Thaidis had remained receptive to these slumber inducements. She stretched on the divan, her tensions relaxing, and slid, breath by breath, asleep.

She had set the room to carry her Maram forward some hours into the new Jate. But at the sixth hour, when she lay drowned deep in a womb of viridian blue silence, dreaming incoherently of the garden of heaven, and unprepared as only a sleeper could be, the summons of the Law was relayed to her.

52

She bathed swiftly in aqua-mist. In the outer room, as the robot attendants dressed her, she drank a cup of wine to steady herself. All her nerves had been jarred by her awakening. She felt a dreadful nervousness, which interfered with reflexes of sight, even of speech and coordination, causing her hands to tremble and the inner lids of her eyes to flutter. The five hundred and five gates of paradise were far away.

She had known in the temple valley, with an awful absence of doubt, that somehow her life had foundered and could not be put to rights. Now, wildly, all her resources seemed to gather that she might save herself, and, in gathering, revealed their inadequacy. She could not choose but fight for survival. And the weapons were broken in her grasp.

There was, too, the dim phantom of a second dream dreamt in the Maram, surfacing, as profound dreams were apt to do, some while after waking. The details of the dream eluded her, but the central figure had been Ceedres Yune Thar, and the memory revolted her. She was still in love with him, so much was evident. Some imbecile part of her was still alert and longing for rescue at his hands. rescue from this predicament he himself had calculated with such ruthlessness.

Prepared, and quite unprepared, she went to the main salon.

All the while she had thought about the interview which the Law of the Yunea would demand, she had not properly visualized its form. Or its officers. Naturally, she had not anticipated a purely human agency, for though the princes might convene a council, ultimate judgment for justice's sake was rendered by machines. In the Slumopolis, where crimes of theft and brutality were not uncommon, small bands of robot Lawguards patrolled the thoroughfares. At moments of greater public instability they would issue in large numbers from their brown metal precincts. Those aristocrats who amused themselves in the Slumopolis, generally to sample the gaudy and uncouth J'ara entertainments which the Slums offered, were accustomed to the sight of Lawguards. Vel Thaidis was not, nor had she reasoned that they would be the sole directors of her interview.

They stood by the wall which faced the zenith window, three of them. The gorgeous tracery of painted light which the window hung over the room, shone on their carapaces, but did nothing to modify them or reduce their ugliness.

The Lawguards were unlike the humanly shaped palace robots, not aesthetic, and not pleasing. They served the Law be-

53

fore they would serve men. Eight feet in height, each was a smooth copper pillar, impervious and almost featureless. A slight rounding of the apex implied the skull-shaped electronic brain-vase within. Endless sealed dottings of plates along the armor gave evidence of the tentacle-ropes, all reportedly a staed in length, which could be unwound from the interior to catch, to bind and to restrain. The bases were currently flat on the floor, but would rise when the propulsion air jets were reactivated. By tipping themselves over horizontally and parallel to the ground, apex forward and jets at the rear, they became rockets and could far outrace all traffic of the Slumopolis, though perhaps not always the chariots of the princes.

There was no face to address. The voice, when it came, would be a voice of metal dials and turning cogs, that took no pauses of pretended breath, that had no pretended expressions. The voice of impartial probity.

Haphazard nervousness changed to horror in Vel Thaidis.

Then the voice came, and her skin stiffened and her hair crawled under its jeweled combs.

"Vel Thaidis Yune Hirz your pardon that we roused you from your Maram but it is Jate and we assumed you would be prepared for us seeing you have been the perpetrator of an injury."

She filled her lungs as the Lawguards had no need to do.

"I was ready yesterjate. No summons came."

"Again your pardon some hours are permitted the princely houses in such a case that they may prepare a suitable defense."

"I have no defense, except my innocence."

"Vel Thaidis Yune Hirz will you please listen for the chime which indicates our receivers are tuned to impress your voice and you will then recount to us your version of the wounding of Cëedres Yune Thar leaving out nothing that may assist us or yourself."

"Before that, will you tell me if you've taken a statement from Ceedres Yune Thar?"

"We have done so."

"And from others?"

"Certain others."

"My brother—" she said, but her heart almost choked her.

"Velday Yune Hirz has offered no statement. Procedurally he would be disqualified as biased and now please listen for the chime."

54

"One other thing," she said. "Tell me if you have questioned the auto-priest at the Thar-boundary temple?"

"All persons and mechanisms whose presence was approximate to the wounding of Ceedres Yune Thar have been questioned and now please listen for the chime."

She lifted her eyes for relief, to gaze beyond them.

She tried to draw comfort from the fact that the priest must have revealed to them her conversation with Ceedres in the black and fiery room of the temple, the occult room where he had asked her to become his wife and she had refused him. Whatever act he had implicated her in, the testimony of the auto-priest must show that she had no cause to harm Ceedres, only the inclination to avoid him. That *he* was desperate, not she, for restitution of honor and wealth.

Somehow, no comfort came to her. Her agitation increased and she could not smother it, though it was important that she should. Not only that she might render a coherent account, but that her patterns should be readable. Absolute detection of human lie or truth was not possible to the machines of the Yunea, the human faculties being too complex and the mind too random in its process. Nevertheless, some conclusions could be drawn, which would bolster, or prejudice, the subject's case. Yet the more crowded by fear the patterns were, the less open to analysis. Indeed, fear itself was weighed against the subject. In a world where Law was dispassionate and judgment rarely in error, the guiltless had scant need to be afraid. You came to the machine blameless and therefore calm. The electronic brain, perfect in its logic, absolved you. But if you came uneasily it was because you prophesied your crime's discovery by that same perfect logic. Fear was damning. And Vel Thaidis was afraid. So, when the chime sounded, she said at once, "First let me admit to being afraid. Not because of guilt or because I doubt the ability of Yunean Law, but because I utterly mistrust Ceedres Yune Thar himself. I suspect he has indicated me under a pretense that it will be hard for me to tear aside. I don't know how he has done this, but I'm apprehensive of it. That said, I place myself at the mercy of the Law."

Her voice unsteady, here and there faltering altogether, her hands clenched, she gave her story. As she did so, her eyes were nailed to the colored window tracery reflected on the wall above the Lawguards. She spoke of Ceedres, the temple, the upper room like a mythological hell, the marriage proposal, the denial, the knife he had used to stab himself with

55

her hand locked under his against the hilt. And all the time, she saw the crimson, gold and mauve light-ghosts of the flowers on the white plastum. Somehow she understood her words entered the recording device of the machines, and adhered there as the reflections adhered: colored, visible—but still ghosts. Why look at the flowers on the wall? For the truth, look at the original picture painted on the window. *Ceedres'* painting of the truth. She did not doubt he could lie far more convincingly than she could present her words in frightened honesty.

Her heart stammered, and the Lawguards registered its stammering.

His heart would be stone and steel.

"Vel Thaidis, your brother is coming," the blond robot attendant said.

The sentence struck her, its familiarity. How often this must have been said to her. Your brother is coming. Coming back from J'ara, from hunting, from a dinner at the Yune Chures, the Onds, the Domms. . . .

How often she had inquired: "You are certain that it's Velday?" And his patterns—those fascinating fingerprints of the human life-force, unique in each—had been checked in order to reassure her. A superfluity, for robots were seldom optically mistaken, even at great distances. Her demand for certainty, then, must be yet another part of her insecurity, her dread of losing Velday. Already lost.

She did not ask for the check of patterns now.

She watched the jade platter of the lake, veined with white gold by the sun.

The Lawguards, having recorded her recital of events, had departed four hours ago. It was now the thirteenth hour of Jate. The palace of Hirz stood directionally at hespa-Ule. Vel Thaidis' spirit stood at the gate of chaos.

The Lawguards had not threatened her, nor indeed informed her of anything, except that soon a second summons would be accorded her. They left in her keeping a darkened title which would come alight at the chosen instant to reveal this summons to her. She did not know when. She did not know what Ceedres had told the machines. She did not know anything. Save that chaos was before her. Only that. Now she would bear the dark title with her everywhere, like a vile toy, touching it, examining it, rigid for the moment of communication.

56

Velday had ridden on one of the bronze beasts, across the pale sand from the hesten area into which the estate of Thar was moving, and in which Chure and Ond lands already lay. He had returned from Ond, she deduced, where Ceedres had been taken, the convalescent guest of Naine and Omevia.

Velday was some way up the slope, but he had halted the beast, and sat there, looking down at her. She saw them, the robot mount and the young man, gauzily redrawn on the fluid of the lake. She did not turn.

Suddenly he shouted to her. "Ceedres is alive!"

It startled her that he should shout that. Of course Ceedres would live. It had been her hysteria to think him dead even for a second.

She did not turn.

Velday smote the button panel of the bronze beast angrily, and galloped away along the slope.

At the sixteenth hour, the last hour of Jate, the dark tile of the Lawguards glowed and whispered in Vel Thaidis' hand.

"Vel Thaidis Yune Hirz, from the collective evidence of yourself and others. and from the reading of your patterns and those of others," the tile paused. It whispered. It softly said, "By the Law, you have been found culpable. But, finding you guilty of a murderous act, the Law does not sentence you. Your peers will do that. A council is to be convened at the seventh hour of the following Jate. You must open your house to this council and present yourself before it in fitting manner. Do you have anything to say?"

"Ceedres," she said. Abruptly all inhibition deserted her. "Ceedres lied!" she shrieked. "Whatever he has said, he lied!" It was virtually what she had cried out at Velday by the temple. And she flung the tile from her. Astonishingly, it smashed to pieces against one of the columns of her apartment. Perhaps it had been designed to break. Perhaps all those who were found guilty in this way had flung their tiles from them, and the final mercy of the Law was that the tile should shatter, a sop to their frustration and their terror.

# Part Two

Vitra Klovez was startled; her eyes had flooded with sympathetic tears. She blinked her silver lids, and the tears spilled. She glanced at the screen, but naturally, the stupefied workers on their cushioned platform were not weeping at all, and now the screen faded into blankness.

The rabble were incapable of finer feelings. Or their finer feelings had been sandpapered from them by the rottenness and hardship of their lives. They would find it fruitless to weep for themselves; why spare tears for another? Yet they had been enthralled. Glimpsing the screen now and then during this long Jate's Fabulism, Vitra had thought she detected a certain avidity shining behind their mesmerized masks.

The machines which relayed Vitra's fantasy through onto the screens in the Subterior recreation centers, and thence into the part-hypnotized brains of the watchers, were now quieting in the dome chamber. Above, space kept up its pitiless stare. Some Fabulasts were intimidated by this stare, and would press a switch to mist over the transparent vanes of a dome. (Recalling the Thar temple's upper room, Vitra frowned with pleasure—that had been a brilliant touch, a marvelous joke—though quite where it was meant to lead her characters she was largely unsure.)

As she rose, she was still indignantly sorry the worms had not wept, for Vel Thaidis' story was very moving. The screen revealed selected areas of the watching platforms in all the centers, merging them into a whole in the Fabulast's screen. Later, other shifts might climb onto the watching platforms and replay for themselves the pre-recorded dream. Vitra had a sudden urge, alien to her, to return in an hour or so to Rise Iu, activate the screen and observe how other sections of the rabble received her story—but, no. That was foolish, and most unsophisticated. To *care* what reaction her genius had evoked! In any case, she guessed the *truth* of the matter. The worms thrilled to see the destruction and fall of an aristocrat, even in a make-believe country on the uninhabitable desert of the planet's solar side.

Of course, Vel Thaidis must fall, a panacea to their viciousness and jealousy. Princely tragedy was not an unusual theme for Fabulasts to tackle. Yet Vitra wondered if any others had dared probe so near the sore spot of envy as she.

"How daring of you, Vitra," she mused, half self-mockingly and aloud, product of many hours alone.

Vyen had not come to meet her. He had lost interest already in her vocation, and was most probably still at Olvia's scented palace in the Residencia's Eres sector.

As for Casrus . . . curiously, she had almost forgotten Casrus. Having transformed him into the villainous and electric Ceedres, and in control of him therefore, making him perform all the acts her fantasy suggested, his counterpart had lost importance. Until she remembered him. Sharp as acid, then, the memory of her anger and her failure, making her wince. Ceedres was her toy. As inspiration poured invigoratingly through her, he obeyed her implicitly. But Casrus— she had never, in real life, been able to handle him.

She supposed he was yet toiling in the Nentta mine, working with his robots and machines and with the awful Subterines themselves to unblock the collapsed tunnel. Then he would tend the hurt. Then he would go home to Temal, the worker-murderess, whose hair was the soft ashy black of cinders, and whose feet were shod in gold and platinum. Damn Temal. And damn Casrus. Vyen also, who had not come to meet her.

But she had no need to be alone. Many would be glad of and delighted by her company. She would choose companions.

A great weariness overcame her as she emerged onto the Iu terrace above the city, and beheld the chariot car waiting on its pneumatic runners. To create dreams, though exhilarating at the time, took its toll. Other Fabulasts had not seemed to experience this enervation, but then, they were not so creative, so artistic as she. Her talent had drained her. If she meant to keep J'ara again this Maram, she must first go home to Klovez and sleep an hour or so.

(She thought of Casrus in Olvia's salon, come straight from labor in the freezing, poisonous intestine of a mine—yet apparently untired, alert for more. *Damn* Casrus.)

The chariot car started off with a jolt that matched Vitra's snappish mood. She stabbed at the button panel and the car swirled to the left at the bottom of spiraling Iu road. The Klovez palace lay in Uta sector—or sector thirty-one. The geographical directions of the inverted Yunea were circular and transitory, but the underground cold-side world had no directions at all, and told its areas purely by number.

As the car sped between glacial heights and toppling grottoes, Vitra opened her chronometer. It was midway through the fourteenth hour.

Presently, the chariot passed under Rise Uta. Uta's crowning complex was of air-making devices, which emitted delicate irregular pulses of frosty light. Sometimes, by Maram, these lit the ceiling of Vitra's sleeping chamber. As a child, her parents long dead in their three-hundredth years, (shades of Vel Thaidis), she had occasionally turned off her robot guardian and climbed to high windows to watch Uta's mild glows strike the rock-sky of the Subplanetary city, attempting to predict when each would come. When she was thirteen, she had seen Casrus Klarn racing a flimsy steel chariot at Uta's exercise arena in the shadow of the Rise. Vyen was learning to fence there with the fire-sword, and detesting it. Foppish even at twelve, he preferred to make bystanders laugh rather than himself learn anything. Vitra and Vyen had been the pets of the Residencia, then. Both so alike, such serpentinely pretty and quick-witted adolescents, their slim feline feet already on the path to manhood, womanhood. But Casrus, a remote and impressive seventeen, had never approached.

Fantastic in the intensifier lamps, the palace of Klovez stood on its hill of rock. Pale green fungyra trees, the only sort which the cold-siders had ever persuaded to grow outside a tank, leaned against the crystalline walls, webbing them with the white tongues of their leaves. In the rounded hump of the roof, a single window, shaped like a flying bird and set with leaded blue glass, burned a shrill light. It was the unmistakable outer window of Vyen's apartment, bird-formed to amuse him, for birds did not fly here, save in sculptures, books or ancient screened pictures of other actual or invented places. (Why had she not thought to add birds to the scenery of the Yunea? Perhaps she might.)

Vitra dismounted from the car, which took itself off. She spoke to the door, which opened. A single robot appeared in the shadowy, unilluminated foyer. Unlike the sun-side robots, this machine was simply a box on noiseless wheels, equipped with a myriad dextrous devices that could be extended or retracted as necessary. In height it was a mere three feet. Beetles and such-like Klovez left to its neighbors.

Vitra brushed her fingers over a panel, but the foyer remained in darkness.

"Robot," said Vitra, "why is there no light?"

The robot sizzled and spoke to her in a dry metallic voice.

"Your brother wishes you."

"Answer my question."

"Your brother wishes you."

"Stupid thing," said Vitra. The instruction Vyen had left it seemed to be overriding all other demands. Possibly the absence of light was connected to some new sinister game of Vyen's. Faintly intrigued by the fancy, Vitra ceased scolding the robot, and entered the lift.

She rose three floors, then stepped out in a corridor above and hesitated. The robot had not accompanied her and she could not see her way. Windowless and unlit, the space was pitch black, nor did any of the spontaneous lamps activate at her arrival.

"Vyen!" she shouted.

At once an aperture gaped along the passage, and the electric blue glow of his apartment ran out over the corridor.

As Vitra entered the big room, her eyes went cursorily over Vyen's individual decor. Weird lizard-like forms (again modeled from the memory banks of machines rather than true life) gamboled grotesquely but statically in the transparent floor. A figure of ice-green glass danced slowly on a pedestal, waving its arms. Vyen sat in a black chair, among a litter of books, before the bird window, his hands engaged with two or three fiddle-toys of plastivory and silver. His white face, turquoise in the room's eerie glow, was infuriatingly obtuse.

"What are you playing at?" Vitra demanded with loving dislike, "I supposed you were with Olvia."

"Well, I'm not."

"So I see. What have you done to the lamps of the house, oh most horrid little brother?"

"*I*," said Vyen gently, "have done nothing. I thought it was *your* notion."

"What? Why should I do such a thing?"

"To reward me for my sojourn at Klastu. You hoped I'd break an ankle in the dark and be confined to the house."

"Then why should I stumble about in the dark myself?"

"I don't know," said Vyen. "Why should you?"

61

Vitra took from the silver chain, which passed as a girdle, an alcohol stick, and bit off a piece of it nervously.

"Can it be," she said, "the lamps of house Klovez have failed?"

Her eyes became gradually very large, and she sank down on the book-scattered cushions opposite Vyen's chair.

"What's the matter?" Vyen inquired. "It's easily remedied." He pressed a knob on the arm of the chair. A panel in the blank wall swung open, and one of the boxes on wheels rolled out. "Go and see to the lights," said Vyen.

"What is amiss with the lights?" asked the machine.

"They are *out*."

The robot rambled across the floor and into the corridor.

"Have you," said Vitra, "ever heard of the lamps of a house failing?"

"I'm sure," said Vyen, "if anyone told me such a thing, I'd be far too bored to listen. Therefore, no."

Vitra threw the empty holder of her stick upon the floor, and put her palms to her cheeks. Vyen observed her with relaxed surprise. Only his eyes, enlarged and dark as her own, gave him away. The lamps of the princely palaces of the Residencia never failed, even for an hour, even for an instant. The event was ominous by nature of its uniqueness, if for nothing else.

Suddenly the black corridor, pressed against the open door, fluttered into a chilly lemon sheen. All the art objects, metal tapestries and iridescent carvings of Klovez burst into their accustomed relief.

Vitra sighed and put down her shaking hands. Her jeweled forehead was clammy and her heart drummed. Vyen, too, appeared to be breathing, though he had not appeared to be before. Like scared babies rescued from the frigid black night of that nether world, they smiled their predatory smiles at each other.

"Now tell me," he said, "why you were so afraid?"

"Now tell me," she said, "why you waited so long to rectify the fault?"

"I thought if it was your joke, you'd want to enjoy it fully."

Vitra watched him narrowly. Vyen began to juggle expertly with the three fiddle-toys.

"I don't believe you."

"Don't you?" He looked down his nose at her and said, "Well, I did send a robot to attend to the trouble previously, but it never came back and the lights never reappeared—except in this room, which is illuminated differently, as you know. So then I sent a robot to intercept you below. Have you noticed," he added, "how cool the house has grown?"

Vitra shivered involuntarily in her gauzy dress, and at that moment a robot, either the first, second or third Vyen had dispatched, rolled back into the chamber. It was emitting, quietly but unmistakably, a curious bubbling noise.

Halfway across the glass floor it faltered, spun about, began to retreat, faltered once more and finally froze.

Vyen tapped knobs in the chair arm impatiently.

"Go back into the wall, fool."

The robot took no notice. The bubbling noise decreased. Suddenly one of its dextrous attachments shot forth from it, becoming unattached as it did so. The metal rod landed with a clank on the floor.

Both Vyen and Vitra started to their feet. Never in their lives had they heard of, or witnessed, such a bizarre happening.

After a few seconds Vyen went forward to examine the robot with distaste. Not that Vyen possessed any of the minor technical skills, as some of the aristocratic houses did. The phenomenon of the stalled machine was to him quite impenetrable. It was really a sort of scared awe that drew him closer, the same emotion which kept Vitra away.

Eventually, Vyen kicked the robot with a white plastavel shoe, and the thing skidded and revolved across the room before crashing into the farther wall.

"Whrrp," said the dry metallic voice. "Whrra-prr."

"Be quiet!" shouted Vyen.

"Whrra," said the defunct robot, in an amazed tone, and was silent.

Vitra covered her face with her hands and moaned.

"Now what is it?" demanded Vyen, paler even than he had been.

Vitra, her eyes shut, was seeing visions of the ruined estate of Ceedres Yune Thar, the encroaching dusts, the swamps, the motionless machines glittering like dead blue flies in the eternal sky.

"I," she whispered, "somehow, I—"

"Somehow you? Speak logically."

"The technology of Klovez is about to collapse," Vitra cried in a thin high wail.

Vyen swallowed.

"Insanity."

"No—somehow my Fabulism has caused this to happen— Ah!" This last scream erupted as once more the lamps in the corridor extinguished.

In panic, brother and sister glared at the midnight beyond the door. Unlike the more primitive culture of the invented Yunea, they had no gods to pray to. In such minutes of terror, they were therefore forced back upon arcane obscenities and vague inner howlings for help to some faceless blank niche which had once been occupied by a religion.

For Vitra, the panic was, if anything, worse. It truly seemed to her that her fabulism, the scope of her imagination, had brought this upon them. Was there a remedy? It appeared unlikely. No princely house of the Residencia had ever lost its means of mechanical support. Theirs would be the first. What would become of them? Would the computers of the city, when appealed to, spare precious energy and machines to correct the lapse? Or would they be cast destitute on society, having to beg for shelter, food, clothing—or, more dreadful yet, *unthinkable*, would Vitra and Vyen themselves be forced to enter the Subterior, to join the ranks of the slave-workers, the worms? The Slumopolis should ultimately have been the fate of Ceedres, a fate he was fair set to avoid in Vitra's story. But this was not a story, a fantasy of a dome chamber. This was *real*.

Shriveled of spirit, the heirs of Klovez crept together and held each other's cold hands. In a trembling mutter, Vitra told Vyen all the plot, so far, of her Fabulism. When the corridor lights were once more abruptly resumed, the pair merely glanced at them, as if at artful deceivers.

Finally, Vyen announced, "I still say you're mad, to think your invented world could in any way influence this one. Maybe this is yet some joke another house is playing—Olvia, perhaps. She could be empty-brained enough."

"No, no. My talent's overrun the bounds of my mind. Brimmed through into reality."

"Don't be so vain," said Vyen peevishly. "It's only some extraordinary coincidence. And everything will resolve itself. Even that fool of a robot can be repaired." He shot a look at the corridor. The lamps beamed on. "There's to be a theatrical performance at Derle," he added nonchalantly. "Will you come? Shedri Klur asked for you especially."

"Yes, I'll come," said Vitra quickly.

She did not wish to remain either in her ancestral home, or by herself.

The theatrical drama at Derle concerned princely love and violent death, the only form of death to be feared among the long-lived aristocrats. As a Fabulast, convinced she was capable of inventing better romances, Vitra scorned the performance. The actors, who had risen from the ranks of the Subterine workers, to be fêted for talent and good looks, she scorned equally. Shedri Klur's mistress was currently an actress. Her hair was streaked with cobalt dye, proof of a worker's continued obsession with bright colors, and she was not included in the supper party at the Klur palace.

Vitra strove to fascinate Shedri, who was already fascinated by her. She strove to fascinate others, and succeeded, since they too had long been attracted to her mercurial, one-dimensional magic. She was exactly what a woman of her class in the Residencia should be. Brittle, sharp porcelain, glittering with spangles.

All the while, scornful, fascinating and busy, the spike scratched at the back of Vitra's soul. What of Klovez? What of the technology of Klovez?

Sometimes the thought would come to her distinctly clear and restorative: a fantasy of the mind could never bear upon the events of the animate world. But then again, a doubt would nibble at her. Suppose, it said. Only suppose. Then she said to herself, with friable humor, *But if that is the case, then surely everything must soon be rectified. Ceedres Yune Thar has incriminated his hapless victim by mysterious devices. He will gain her estate and all will be well, for him.* If Klovez had incredibly linked itself to the fortunes of Thar, then Klovez also would shortly be well again.

In the first hour of the new Jate, J'ara burned to ashes in the lamps and wines and filigree drug-inhalers, Vitra and Vyên returned to their palace and entered the shadowy hall, where no lights lit, and no robots came. And despite the frantic cawing of brother and sister, their running about on modishly shod feet, and thrusting down of buttons and switches with their tastefully jeweled fingers, still no lights lit, and no robots came.

There they huddled in the black, the lift before them which suddenly would not work, the whole house, this house which had been so familiar, so friendly to them since their infancy, dimly echoing like a mournful and deserted cave.

65

"If this *is* your fault," said Vyen, "then damn you."

At which Vitra slapped his face, and an iota of their equilibrium was restored.

Sometime after, having manually ascended to the third floor by a ramp the robots used—or had used—they found Vyen's apartment also in darkness. So they fumbled a way into Vitra's rooms. Here, in her bedchamber, the gleams of Rise Uta occasionally struck. There were, besides, a collection of self-igniting flame-lights, curios given her long since by an admirer.

The flames winged up, violet, gray and rose, bathing the exotic chamber in an attractive twilight. Vitra sat on the silken divan and caught sight of her face, petrified and small between its black leaves of hair, in the mirror of her cosmetics table.

Her genius appalled her. Her genius which had undone Klovez. Nevertheless, it *was* genius, was it not, to activate such a miracle of destruction? Then she began to cry neurotically. The room was freezing. Only the ambient warmth of the city preserved them now, all self-generated heat had gone out of the palace. Even the air was stale. Unlike Thar, the collapse had been instant and utter. Like Thar, it seemed irremediable.

"Well, wise sister," said Vyen, striving to control his shudders, "what shall we do next?"

"Oh, how can I tell?" exclaimed Vitra.

"Since you say all this is your doing, I'd hoped you might."

Vitra wept, and Vyen paced about, fiddle-toys awhirl and eyes staring at nothing.

In a short while he and she forced open the windows of the room to refresh the air, and heard the stir of city Jate traffic on the thoroughfares.

"We shall have," said Vyen at last, "to approach the city computers. I don't credit your belief that that will mean immediate exile to the Subterior. Such a thing would be ridiculous."

"The whole structure of the Klave is carefully planned," sniveled Vitra. "We were taught about it in our adolescence. The population is controlled, and the balance is finely maintained between the workers and the aristocrats. Nothing can be spared to aid us."

"Then if the balance is so fine, how was Klarn able to take a condemned worker girl to himself?"

66

"Because Temal was accounted dead. She was about to die for having murdered another—but was exonerated."

"If a murdering clot of a worker can be protected, I'm sure you and I are secure enough," said Vyen. But he was not sure. Temal, the girl Casrus had rescued from death, had had several witnesses who swore she had slain her attacker, a man from the Subterior, to save herself from a brutal assault. In fact Casrus himself had been partially involved, having been in an adjacent Subterine alley, his machines shoring up some of the sagging hovels there. Temal's assailant had begged wine from the prince and Casrus had permitted him to drink. The subsequent attack upon the girl could well have been a result of this act. That Temal was beautiful, in the thin tubercular fashion of the Subterines, might also, it was conceded, have prompted Casrus' defense of her.

All these items, together with Vitra's complicated Fabulism, smeared through Vyen's febrilely exercising mind, restless as the fiddle-toys. And then, all at once, coalesced.

"*Vitra*," he breathed.

Vitra raised her head.

"What now?"

"A solution, now."

"Oh, some madness of yours won't do—"

"Yes it will. Attend to me. The inane tale of your unintelligent princess—Thel Vaidis—"

"Vel Thaidis," Vitra snapped automatically.

"Their laws being based upon our own. As your Ceedres is based on our adored Casrus."

"Well? Don't you think the Fabulism has damaged us sufficiently?"

"That," said Vyen with a lofty about-face, "I'm not certain of. But this I do know. Ceedres' plan, or what you told me of it, can be very ably adapted to suit *us*."

Vitra gazed at her brother, mouth and eyes stretched.

"Firstly," said Vyen, "take me to the dome chamber and play me the recording of all the Fabulism so far. And then I will decide how the strands can be rearranged to fit our needs."

"Vyen, you've taken leave of your senses—"

"Hardly. Ceedres wanted the Hirz estate and tricked the blind Jaida-Vaidis into the semblance of a criminal deed so heinous the Law will deprive her of her property and render said property to her victim. Am I correct? Well then, Prince Klarn is just as blind and hopelessly uncunning as your

67

Vaida. Could we not trick him as subtly, and won't our Law be as harsh, or more harsh, than the Law of the invented Solar side. There are two of us, never forget, one of Casrus. And we were always witty children, weren't we?"

Vitra sat gasping.

Presently she sat gasping in the chariot car, which, to their mutual relief, still ran efficiently on its runners. Not until they were hurtling up the spiral road of Rise Iu did she protest again. But Vyen gave a feral grin and would not answer. The city was far warmer than the house had become. She foresaw a future of beggary or terminus, and as the terrace loomed, she ceased to argue. With congealed eyes, she slunk before Vyen into the complex, and let them both into the Fabulast's chamber with a narrow, trembling, resolute hand.

Temal, the former Subterine, was arranging her hair, ashy dark with one broad streak of palest vermilion lying to either side of the central parting and mingling thereafter with the many slender braids she was weaving. Temal spent much time attending to her hair, as she spent time in bathing, enameling her nails, perfuming herself. All these activities had been denied her in the Subterior. There she had frozen and toiled and groaned with fatigue and hunger along with all the rest. Even now, she had confessed to dreaming of such years, while even as she indulged herself with clean hair and scent, she would admit guilt swam in her heart like a tiny tireless animal.

She had been a water-carrier. Every Jate, and much of every Maram, she had borne empty pitchers to the great machine-supplied cisterns of her sector, and then borne them back, up and down the enclosed, icicle-strung alleyways, to the doors of hovels, kitchens, and in at the gaping jaws of mines. Her mistress, an Upperling of the Subterior, that is, one of the profitless lower class who had yet managed to profit somewhat by putting others to work in their stead, had a chain of such girls and young men. Water was limited in the Subterior. All who labored were allotted a ration each Jate, but never enough. Mostly the inhabitants made up their allowance with boiled ice, and risked sundry viral infections. But for those thirsty ones who had saved enough to buy, there were the water carriers. The master or mistress of each pitcher chain leased a cistern, the chain plied its wares, and brought home the plastic chips that passed for money. In exchange, the members of the chain were rendered scraps to eat, a hole to sleep in, a few of the precious chips for pay.

One Maram, Temal was abroad late, staggering as if half dead from lack of sleep and all else, when a drunken man, dreaming of some Fabulism he had just experienced, set on her. Her wares were spilled, and she spilled after them on the dark stone of a long and winding alley, scarcely wider than the width of both their bodies. Other persons, drearily abroad, saw, but paid no attention to the girl's plight. Some indeed stepped over the struggling pair. Temal herself did not scream or cry aloud. It would have been useless, a waste of action. Instead, she had found one of the horrible iron-stiff icicles at hand, and wrenched it free, even as the man beat her and tore at the layers of her rags. The ice burned her hand terribly, and when she came to pluck it from her grasp later, her skin went with it. But before that had occurred, she had stabbed the man in the eye. It was a vicious dreadful blow, but one which she delivered without pause, for this was the education the Subterior gave its inhabitants. Survival meant, quite simply and on all occasions, some kind of violent triumph over others.

Thereafter, Temal lay on the stone, awaiting the robots of the Law who must surely come for her. A crowd had gathered and stared at her, as if at a screen of Fabulism—for such was only to be expected. But then a man came through the crowd, dressed not in gaudy rags like the rest, nor swaggering and plain as an Upperling. He had not been one of the watchers. She might dimly have comprehended that if he had been present, he would have helped her. Then, in her dazed state, she recognized, she afterward said, a prince of the Residencia. She had heard of him. Casrus of house Klarn, who ministered to the Subterines where he could, ignoring their jibes, fawning, treachery and despair, himself quite ruthless and single-minded in his acts of clemency. A strange man, an unlikely man. And so she must have found him.

For a year and a fortyjate she had lived here, in his palace, (wondrous to a Subterine, mystic as Kaneka-heaven) as sometimes the favored of the Subterior might come to live, under the good auspices of an aristocrat. Casrus was gentle, generous and considerate, and yet it was hard to discover, really, anything of him at all. She might have hoped to be a consolation to him, but she could not seem to talk to him. Despite his attempts to educate her, and all of her class who dwelled in Klarn, they were slow to learn, and slower to adapt.

69

It was not a matter of intelligence, merely that their intelligence had long ago been twisted to a particular shape and hardened in it, and was now unable to reform. She demonstrated that she loved Casrus, but as one might love a god. It was not her humility or his remoteness which caused it, but apparently her need to worship for her security's sake; Casrus was elected her religion. And she for him? A fine tapestry, perhaps, reclaimed from the cold slime of the Subterior.

Her hair bound ornately, Temal rose, crossed the room and descended by one of the several non-moving staircases of Klarn. Soon she was entering an unusual salon for the Residencia, for it was filled with intense golden light. This, Casrus had told her, being an emulation of sunlight, a softer equivalent of the fierce unceasing solar fires of the planet's far side. But Temal had shied away from the notions of the planet's roundness, talk of its black night side, its bright day side, and the twilight zones that partitioned each from the other. Her world, she had explained, was only the city. Its extraneous environs had for her, too, the nature of a myth, even though, unlikely Kaneka, she said, she believed them to exist.

Translucent amber fungyras grew from urns of whitish pewter. A thin jet of water played into a tank—*wasteful*! her Subterine conditioning surely insisted, even though the water constantly recycled itself and scarcely evaporated at all.

Casrus was seated, entering notations on a writing machine. He had returned from the disaster at the Nentta mine four hours ago, having kept J'ara, if so it could be termed, assisting in the collapsed tunnel there. Ten men and three women had perished in the tunnel. A further thirty had been freed, largely due to the use of Casrus' machines and robots.

In the Subterior, Casrus had earned many names, of which most were jeering, but no one had jeered yestermaram, nor this Jate. Temal had greeted him at the porch of Klarn, he covered in the filth and mulch of Nentta, from which phospher was dug. She ordered food for him while he bathed. Yet here he was now, tirelessly at large once more. She knew him to be young and strong, yet who could quite credit his calm fanatical vitality. She doubtless understood this much, his prince's guilt was worse than her own. Once acknowledged, it had not let him rest.

Seeing her, he closed the machine and came to her side.

When he lightly stroked her cheek, her bi-colored hair, she

70

glanced aside as if she imagined that perhaps he saw the averted faces, torn hair of dead women, dragged from a pit by mechanical claws.

"I'd thought we might spend this Maram together," he said quietly, "but first I must deal with this." He showed her a metallic bead, a message capsule, such as any of the thousand or so princely houses might send to each other, either from a palace or from a relay post upon the street. "House Klovez."

"But they're your enemies," she said at once. Her judgment was plainly instinctive, based upon the tutelage of her origins.

"No," he said, "there's no closeness between us, but they're very young. Not enemies."

"Casrus," she said. He had trained her from calling him "lord" or "prince." "Casrus, all I've heard of the Klovez house is bad. Admittedly, my sources are Subterine gossip--"

"Admittedly they are." She lowered her eyes, immediately silent, and he said, "I don't discount your warning, Temal. But I've known them since my boyhood. Two brats, two parasites, as all the aristocrats are, myself included."

"I heard things of their parents. These two are conspirators, whispering together, enjoying little jokes together. And she is a *Fabulast*." The title was spoken with something approaching hatred. "What can they want of you?"

"Surprisingly, my help. For some reason."

"That which you can never refuse. How clever of them to know as much."

"Children," he said dismissively.

"I was a child," said Temal. "I was a child in the Subterior. And things I did there don't fit your vision of a child."

Casrus smiled. Almost delicately he brushed a smoke-fine tendril of hair from Temal's forehead. Sliding his thumb across the bead, he activated it that she might hear. It was a girl's voice which spoke, the voice of Vitra.

*Casrus Klarn, I require and entreat your assistance. I don't ask idly. My brother and I are in desperate anxiety. For the sake of your own goodness, which we know you possess in such great measure, please visit us before this Jate is ended, at Klovez.*

Looking puzzled and perturbed, Temal said, "Some ruse. Beware of her."

"Oh," he said, as lightly as he had stroked her face, "Vitra has some propriety and some sense, for all she pretends otherwise. I think I shall escape alive." He was still smiling, a fraction amused, a fraction moved by Temal's concern.

71

"I can't prevent your going," said Temal.

"No, not on this small matter. Suppose I can aid them in some way. I may then enlist their aid in turn."

"Such as *they* would never loan so much as a lamp to benefit Subterines."

"We'll see," said Casrus. For a moment his face was shadowed, very nearly wicked, very nearly evil with its determination to use all in his power to alleviate the guilt of the princes, the pain of their slaves.

Temal watched him leave the house, walking not riding the thoroughfares, striding across the gray, glinting city. Anticipating, she looked toward the spot where Rise Uta distantly tossed its glows against the sky of rock. Temal could never have seen that other upper sky of blackness and white starfires. Certain of her class toiled beneath it, in the wake of great mechanisms, their bodies encased in coffins of oxygen. Temal had been condemned to die under it, before Casrus spoke for her. Now it was nothing. Here she would live long, maybe reach her hundredth year. Her ashes might lie, as did the ashes of aristos, in an urn, although theirs were of silver.

But she touched her forefinger to her tongue—a defiant gesture of the Subterior, meaning: *Life lingers.*

It was the seventh hour of Jate, yet when Casrus reached the portico of Klovez, the palace was in total blackness. If Casrus' preoccupation was stern, even grim, yet it was factual, and controlled. He felt no foreboding, and hazarded on some jest of the girl who had invited him. Thus he announced his presence to the door with continued tolerance.

Then, standing by the door, receiving no answer, he did perceive the slightest crackle on the air that served to suggest an infantile prank. He had half swung away, when the door sawed wide, and Vitra herself stood before him.

He was not impervious to Vitra's beauty, but to him, her attraction had been thoroughly overlaid by a veneer of inanity; tiresome, pointless and prodigal. Nevertheless, this was not exactly the Vitra he recalled. Crescents of shadow lay under her eyes and her hand trembled, holding up a barbaric contraption of rose-red fires.

"Casrus," she whispered, "it is so good of you, so good—"

Pale in her smoky white against the interior of the black house—not a lamp anywhere—and framed in roseate flame that accentuated her pallor, she seemed about to faint. Casrus reached by her and took the torch branch away from her grip.

"What has happened?"

"*Oh*, what has not?" She put her palm over her lips as if afraid to speak, then removed it, and murmured, "The door won't open except when operated from within. Nothing will do what it's supposed to. The lifts refuse to move—the lights—" She raised her arms like a wraith in some absurd theatrical drama and backed away, and the gloom seemed to swallow her. Casrus went after her. The door did not shut.

The house was cold, deadly cold as the streets of the Subterior.

"Bring the light, and please follow me," said Vitra rather primly from the dark ahead.

He did as she asked, and she led him swiftly up a service ramp—Klovez had no actual stairway of any sort—and through black corridors, and at length into the anteroom of her apartment.

Here, other firelights were burning, serving both for illumination and to thaw some of the depressive chill from the air. The feminine chamber was otherwise like most of its kind, ornate, adorned with fragile decorations. Of the final fragile decoration—Vyen—there was no sign.

"Where's your brother?"

"When I had sent our message to you, he himself went to Klastu on a similar errand. I'm afraid we will need the kindness of all our friends. But it was to you we turned for advice."

"You flatter me."

"Oh no, I'm beyond that. Look about you. Do you see what's become of us?"

The electric crackle in the atmosphere had resolved itself for Casrus as the surplus energy of another's fright. He guessed what had occurred. Some years before, such an eventuality had been the subject of a theatrical in sector Dera. The drama had caused a furore of alarm and had been declared in bad taste. The unlucky dramatist, a worker Upperling currently living on his talents in the Residencia, had come close to relegation to his former home. But that was theater. In reality, the princes had been spared such an event: the collapse of a palace's total technological foundation. Till now.

"What caused this?" Casrus inquired.

Vitra covered her face with her hands, a familiar gesture, apparently now genuine. He did not know she was struggling with the impulse which shouted: *I!* I caused this!

"Neither Vyen nor I," she muttered at last, "know what caused it."

"You've been very unfortunate," said Casrus. "I will, of course, help you in any way. Do you need transport to a computer complex?"

Vitra stared at him, hands removed, shocked.

"Do you think we can beg help of the computers?"

"What else?"

"The Klave is geared," said Vitra, glaring at him with something very like abhorrence for his obtuseness, "to assist only the facets of itself which independently support themselves. The Klave's technology is finely balanced. It will spare nothing to Klovez—how could it? We will be exiled to the Subterior. I suppose you'd think that fitting for us?"

"This is an old argument. No, I don't think that fitting for you, since neither you nor Vyen could survive it. Nor do I think the city computers or the Law of the Klave would demand such a thing. You're confusing life, I believe, with a drama."

Vitra started wildly.

*"What?"*

"The infamous Dera theatrical five years ago."

Vitra gave a vulgar, terrified little laugh.

Casrus put down the torch branch on a table, went to her and took her icy quivering hands.

"Even if such an impossible demand were made, it would then be the duty of your neighbor houses to loan you sufficient machines to repair Klovez technology. If repair were unobtainable, the loan would be extended to support you indefinitely."

"Oh, our *neighbor houses*, our *friends*," she sneered, her large eyes bleak, "Do you imagine they'd care? Olvia, the Klurs, the Klinns—they might take us in for the novelty a Jate or so. But once they were weary of that, they'd put us out, then turn away and let us die."

"If you rate your friends so low," he said, "you should not call them friends."

"But you," she said suddenly, melting, her eyes becoming great pools of gray. "You, that we never dared to call a friend, you wouldn't desert us?"

74

"No. Whatever I could do for you, I would."

"Which is strange," she murmured, "when you despise us."

"You mistake me. But to offer assistance would be, in any case, common courtesy, no more."

"Oh Casrus," said Vitra, and lowered her head, with its brief wave of black satin hair, upon his breast.

He put one arm about her, and as she heard the steady beating of his heart under his velvet shirt, Vitra was amazed its rhythm did not falter. If he would only warm to her now, both might achieve salvation. But if he did not warm, then his punishment would be awful. And while she quite frantically trusted that at this moment she must win him to her, yet some depth of awareness warned her she would not. That being so, all softness must leave her; in disappointment she could become as rapacious as her brother in his piquant envy. This love of hers for Casrus, which had hurt and inconvenienced her with its passion, was after all utterly selfish, though utterly ingrained, irrevocably a part of her.

"If I begged you," she said, in her light musical voice, "begged you to offer me your protection—"

"Vitra, I've said I will do everything I can."

"I mean," she said, "would you take me under your own roof? Nothing could harm me there. I would be safe."

"No, Vitra. I can't make you my ward."

"But—" she said. *I mean,* she thought, *make me your wife, you fool. Or do you realize I mean that, and are you playing with me?* His heart kept up its sonorous even tempo. It was hers which scurried. "How—how can I live here?" she stammered.

"For the sake of your own honor," he said quietly, instructing her. "And for your comfort, too, you'd do better in a household where there are women of your own class."

"You mean, if I were to live at Klarn, I would annoy you with my chatter and my silliness. You don't know me, Casrus. Don't judge me by my public face. When have I ever had the chance to be serious or profound? It must mean something that the computers selected me as a Fabulast—" She broke off, remembering the outcome, coincidence or curse, that had evolved from her Fabulism, was evolving. As she lay daintily against Casrus, willing his body to notice hers, she inadvertently visualized Ceedres Yune Thar drawing Vel Thaidis into his brazen arms, drowning her with a kiss, and how, despite her dizzy hunger, she had said to him in a

75

voice of adamant: "No and no. Forever and always, no to you."

"That you're a Fabulast should encourage you. You perform a task the computers register as necessary. Therefore, why should they cast you out of the city?" Casrus' voice was level. He was being kind to her. He considered the Fabulisms dangerous drugs, derogatory rather than healing in their effect on the workers.

"Casrus," she said. And she put back her head again and looked at him. The living flames made her very lovely indeed, and this she knew. Generally, she had had her own way with the men of her class, leading them where she would, denying them what she had no mind to give, and exacting obedience in everything. "Am I," she said, "so revolting to you that you put me off in this way?"

"What exactly are you asking me for?" he said. The directness unnerved her. She cried: "What else but sympathy, your strength to depend on—"

"That you have."

"But you are—so distant from me—"

"No, Vitra. You are distant, not I."

"In what way? I don't wish to be." Too shyly she added, "I feel I am almost your sister, Casrus. I've known you since we were children."

"I meant a distance in terms of your preoccupations and desires." She heard the impatience then in his voice, and his arm was abruptly no longer about her.

"If you find me wanting," she said, "teach me to be better."

"Vitra, this isn't the hour for lessons. I'll take you to the computer complex."

"No!" Lacking other persuasion, she folded herself against him once more, and said very low, "I'm afraid. Be my brother, Casrus, and put your arm about me again." And from the corner of her eye, she saw a flicker of movement at the edge of the open door behind Casrus, the door to her bedchamber—another man also growing impatient with her delay: Vyen, waiting on his cue. She had had a difficult time convincing him that any of this extravagance was essential. "If we can gain what we wish peacefully," she had argued, "it is far better." "But Casrus," Vyen had said in an unliking tone, "will never offer you marriage. We won't get access to Klarn *that* way." "But let me try," she had insisted. "Belittle

76

yourself then," Vyen had said. "Lick his boots and crawl to him, and see what it will get you." Now she saw. And now the somber side of her love was already turning its face to her, darkening the landscape of her thoughts. That Vyen heard everything only increased her shame, as both had known it would. And clearly Casrus would not be her brother, or hold her to him, or cease to be fraternal suddenly and draw her into his arms as Vel Thaidis had been drawn and drowned in the arms of Ceedres. No. Casrus had stood aside from her, leaving her shipwrecked on the air. What now? If she fainted, would he catch her? Probably not. Could she weep? No, her frightened tears had dried.

"I am wretched," she exclaimed feebly, "and you are cruel to me."

"When will Vyen return?" Casrus asked, on a note so ironic that for a moment she suspected he understood their game. But only a moment.

"I don't know. Do you mean to leave me here alone?"

"Not if you insist I should remain," he said, resigned.

"I am this horrible," she cried, "that to stay with me is a punishment to you."

He did not reply.

And now the dark star of disappointment and fury rose to the zenith of her brain's sky. It was true. She could not influence him. If he considered her fair, it was not a kind of fair that he wanted. Not as a companion, let alone a legal partner to be mistress over Klarn.

Let him be confounded then, he deserved it all. He might have had her and the joy she could have brought him, instead he would have her bane, the double bane of herself and Vyen. Let him revel in *that*!

She turned and walked directly to a crystal table and took up from it the jeweled dagger lying there, artistic heirloom of Klovez, sharp enough to kill. Raising it, she flung around on Casrus, letting the firelights pour down the steel blade.

"You are not my friend," she said. "I can trust no one. I don't intend to die in the Subterior. I shall kill myself at once."

She perceived instantly he doubted her. A mild exasperation went over his face.

"Vitra, your histrionics—"

"My histrionics are the prelude to my death. Wish me Kaneka." It was the name of paradise in the old legend.

She had been schooled to a pretense of wounding herself, but at the final second, either a divination of his perception warned her to be thorough, or else sheer rage took charge. She slashed the knife across her arm, tearing both sleeve and flesh. The gash was slight but spectacular. Blood oozed forth, a sable red, appalling her. Her sight blurred and, stupidly, she almost let go the dagger, before she recollected she must not. Then Casrus had taken the weapon from her grasp. She listened as he said something to her, that she had only scratched herself, that she had lost her reason. Although he held her wrist, she did not heed him, nor the shining blade with its magenta smear. Instead, her gaze slid beyond him, next downward, to conceal what she had seen. Soft and agile, Vyen was prowling across the room, coming at Casrus' back, his hand clenching its silver rings and whitened knuckles upon a box of heavy polished onyx. Vyen made no sound, his feet like silk on the rugs. He moved like the fume of the fires across the airless, heatless room.

*Now it is in my power to save you, Casrus*, Vitra thought. Her lips parted, but Vyen came nearer and she did not speak. And now he was like a shadow at Casrus' shoulder, the shadow of her anger and her spite. The black velvet arm of her brother swung up, the onyx box clutched firmly, ready for the paralyzing blow—

And Casrus, spinning about with a terrifying, cat-like agility of his own, sent the box flying with one sweep of his fist, Vyen with another. Casrus trained for exercise in the art of combat—the two plotters, perhaps, had not been clever in reckoning they could best him.

The male heir of ruined Klovez fell with a small thud and a jingle of ornaments. Vyen's gray eyes were glazed, his head seeming disjointed and his body loose. Casrus, immobile, the dagger yet in his left hand, observed him with an astonishing impartiality. Only Vitra let out a squeak of affront and fear. This was not as they had planned, the brother and sister, when they brooded together in the dome of the Fabulism, Vitra's fantasy replayed before them, and Casrus' indictment in the offing.

Eventually, Casrus said, "I see I was in error. This has been but another of Klovez' dubious jokes. Your aims I don't attempt to guess at, nor what pleasure you derive from such an enterprise. Your jaw will heal, Vyen. I doubt if your wits will improve so much. I assume your technology is as sound

78

as ever it was, and this has been merely a secondary trick of your masquerade. Well, you misled me. I'm happy for you. It will make your friends laugh."

He laid the dagger on one of the tables and began to leave.

Vitra opened her mouth to call after him, but Vyen, floundering on the rugs, somehow was shaking his disjointed head at her. Nonplussed, Vitra attended to this dumb show, and Casrus was gone from the room.

Vitra hurried to her brother, and cradled him protectively. Vyen rested against her, soothed by the contact. Each derived abrupt solace from the proximity of the other. They would scratch each other with their claws, but the link between them was genuine and indissoluble, unlike all other links they formed, or strove to form, with the rest of their kind.

"Our plan has failed," said Vitra.

"The reverse," Vyen mumbled through a swelling lip. "I should never voluntarily have included my discomfort in the strategy, but really, it's much the nicer outcome. Even that silly slicing you gave yourself will be useful. Our injuries, added to his patterns on the blade—what better? Now help me up. I must stagger to the window and give the alarm."

"Are they there?"

"Oh, yes. Would they miss a drama? Casrus will have quite a surprise when he emerges. I think you should tear your dress now. That vase and that figurine must go—and the drape there—pull it off its rings."

Vitra ran to comply. Her heart thudded leadenly as she did so. Anger, embarrassment and confusion were mingled in her. As the gauze drapery, with its glints of metallic threads, piled around her feet, as her nails, (lacquered the shade of the pink-mauve blossoms of another world), rent open the shoulder and bodice of her garment, a peculiar sadness and regret filmed the surface of her emotions, not mixed, not altering them, yet inexorably there, like oil on water.

Then Vyen was leaning from an opened window, shouting in a thin, cracked voice at the groves of green fungyra trees below.

"Casrus! I'll kill you for this—Shedri—Ensid—take hold of him. Don't let him get by you. My *sister*—"

A muffled noise rose from the trees.

When Vyen had watched her Fabulism through to its most recent point, where Vel Thaidis, wrongfully accused, flung from her the file of the Law, Vyen had said, "And what comes next? Do you know?"

"I think I do. I will know when I return here and activate the machines. My inspiration—"

"Yes, Vitra, yes. Obviously your Ceedres-Casrus has some extra trick to aid him. What?"

Vitra outlined her story, the developments which she had gradually deduced would be revealed, though only when Vel Thaidis confronted her human judges.

"Very well. We've nothing like *that* at our disposal. Once your invented tragedy is complete, I suggest you make a new story, and erase the mechanical tapes of this one, everything to do with Vel Thaidis and Ceedres Yune Thar. The worker-worms don't positively remember what they see, or have the acumen to connect your adventure with the truth. Besides which, the machines have no connections with the computers. But, to be sure. . . . You'll do it, Vitra?"

"Yes," she said. Furtively they had glanced at each other beneath their lashes, and an odd gnawing had registered for a moment under her ribs. That was when she had insisted that first she must try to win Casrus over to her, ensnare him, trap him as a woman but not as a foe.

Then, so much settled, Vyen had elaborated on their plan.

It was a simple one, and old as the history of mankind, in whatever clime or planet they found themselves.

Vyen would send messages to Klastu, Klur and two or three other neighbors. He would tell of Klovez' collapse, and plead that they come to his palace. Since the doors were outwardly unmovable, the princes must wait outside, and he would presently come down to them and let them in. He would ask them to be discreet and quiet—they were his friends, but he did not wish the entire Residencia to learn the plight of Klovez. Appended to his message would be the fact that he had also sent to Casrus Klarn, who, though a stony man and no friend, might offer sound counsel.

That done, Vyen would hide himself in Vitra's bedchamber, until the cue of the acted self-wounding, when he would come out. Once Casrus had laid hold of the dagger, Vyen would stun him, thereafter rushing to the window to summon the mob below.

It would see that Casrus, taking diabolical advantage of Vitra's presence in the empty palace of her distrait manner, had attemtped to assault her. Stone, apparently, might crack, given sufficient stimulus. Like many another enigma before him, Casrus would discover his unsociability explained as a

80

locking away of perversity and brutishness. Do this and this with me, and I will save you from the demise of Klovez, the brutish Casrus had declared to the panic-stricken girl, alone, unprotected by kindred or machine. When she resisted, a blade had been picked up and employed to threaten her—the hot humor roused, the stone changed to lava, it must have satisfaction. When Vyen (fictitiously returning to the house that moment) came upon them, he had been forced to strike Casrus unconscious with an onyx box snatched from a table.

This, the plan. Yet the unforeseen had not undone it. The story required few alterations. It was indeed improved, made more credible.

In his frenzy, Casrus had inflicted the cut to Vitra's arm—a token of worse disfigurement if she did not surrender. Vyen, a child of peace rather than a fighter, had been easily slung aside. But by this time, Casrus' fire had cooled from so much argument. He strode out on to the rock hill that led from Klovez, his face set in displeasure, his clothing somewhat disarranged, a smear of Vitra's blood upon his sleeve, the pattern of his hand left behind on the incriminating dagger.

And now, in reality, Casrus stood among the green-white fungyra trees, among the pale snarling faces of the sons of Klur, Klastu, Klinn, and heard the accusation rendered shrill and furious from the upper window.

He knew no protestation was just then possible. He was an outcast of the dully brilliant world of the Klave, shunning its social concourse, frowning at its sports, a thorn in the side of its buried conscience. Like dogga, hunting a clockwork toy so the princes might gamble on the outcome, they had wanted simply a chance to pull him down. A single stumble, they would have him. And he had stumbled. There was no denying that.

House Klur took them in, the two wronged destitutes.

Shedri Klur was passionate in Vitra's defense. White-lipped and silent, he had wrapped about her a rug of smooth synthetic fur.

As Vitra entered the portals of Klur, the central salon with its frescoes and silverwork, Shedri's hand guiding her, his intense eyes blazing, it occurred to her that there was a prince who, despite youth, Law and any number of mistresses, with the slightest of urgings would gladly have made her his wife. True, it would have been a sharing rather than an assumption

81

of sole rights, and for Vyen something less. Klur had twenty heirs in all; the place was a sprawling conglomerate of many apartments, libraries, inner courts, a ceaseless coming and going of robots and men. But need that little crowding really have proved so distressful? Certainly, Vitra had no feelings of love for Shedri, yet neither had she any feelings of hate. Nor did Vyen hate him. They would have been three of one kind. And Shedri, with Vyen's help, she could have ruled.

Why then had it been spontaneously necessary to them to destroy Casrus in order to gain his goods for their own losses—an exchange, indeed, not even legally sure? Were vengeance and spite so vehement in them?

And when she was permitted to escape the Klurs, she lay upon a divan in the palace of Klur, and regret and fear lay down beside her. What had they done? What would be done to them?

It was not exactly the process of the Law which she dreaded. Jurisdiction in the Klave had none of the awesome intransigence of the make-beileve Yunean variety. Penalties were seldom as harsh; where they were, appeal was possible. But this in itself made her uneasy, for suppose Casrus were to defend himself ably enough so that the fabrication of lies was deciphered? And if judged guilty, what penalty would be imposed on him? How had she and Vyen dared rely upon mere chance that it must be the same penalty that Vel Thaidis would presently endure? And if it were, how should she, Vitra, endure the knowledge that she had brought Casrus to it, blameless?

She scarcely slept, dreamed murkily when she did. The twittering, fascinated princesses of Klur, Shedri's companions and sisters, would be upon her next Jate, eager for details of the failed ravishment. Perhaps she could escape them by nobly resuming her duty at the chamber of Fabulism. True, Vitra would now suffer with Vel Thaidis in earnest. The narrative would take on a fresh dimension of misery.

*I wish I had not. If it were to do again, I would not. Klovez might have righted itself. The computers might have rescued us, as Casrus told me. It is Vyen's fault.*

All at once it seemed to Vitra that, rather than invent a story to entrance the rabble of the Subterior, she had woven her own self into it. She had created a situation which was in turn creating her, coercing her. She had become the slave of a mirage.

The long Maram faded, the Jate lay in wait outside her new Klur apartment. And caught in the Jate, a golden young woman seemed to be calling to her of anguish and pride.

This Jate, Vitra would send Vel Thaidis to hell.

To what hell was she sending herself?

# CHAPTER THREE

## Part One

Vel Thaidis heard them arrive and seem to fill the house, their sounds blowing like vapors through its chambers and along its colonnades, its passages.

They would assemble in the lower salon, where blinds of golden vitreous had been lowered across the oval window spaces. In a thick gold light, the machines would offer their knowledge and their judgment and the princes of the Yunea would deliberate and pronounce sentence. On her.

A murderous act. What punishment for that? In the Slumopolis, those found out in a killing were themselves slain, in the way of immemorial tradition. Not a hand was raised against them, and no machine dealt them any blow, for logical justice utilized the logical means. The condemned were taken over the perimeter of the Yunea, into the central desert, the inner lands of the Zenith. There, the sun boiled their blood, soon frying them alive, a prolonged and harrowing execution.

But Vel Thaidis was not accused of murder, merely of a murderous attempt. Her aristocratic felony invited a human council and a human decision.

Were their murmurings, their solemn noises, concerned only with Vel Thaidis, as they filed into the palace of Hirz? Or did they grudge the time they might have spent on sport and music, on the esoteric literature of their class, or its contests of physical skill?

She had sent a message to Velday with one of her attendants. *If you have already determined I am to blame and hate me for it, stay away from this council, for both our sakes.* The robot had returned: "I have left the message in the panel of Velday's apartment. But Velday was not there to receive it."

She knew these were her final hours of life, as she had known life. If death was imminent she could not ascertain. Some sort of death, even if she were spared the extreme penalty, was inevitable. She grasped everything, and yet could not grasp it. She had only her pride left.

So, she dressed to befit her pride as the daughter of Hirz. She put on a dark green dress, richly fringed and embroidered, bracelets of green metal and a collar of sunseyes, the yellow diamonds of her planet. The black tint of her hair had been retouched. Her lids were charcoaled and her mouth painted a delicate translucent red. Her entire concentration settled upon her dignity. She must govern her distress. Somehow the process of Law had been suborned. Helpless, she would not pointlessly struggle or fight any longer, and she would say nothing.

The door to her apartment opened.

The Voice Robot was in the doorway.

"They are waiting, Vel Thaidis."

"Tell them I'm coming, Voice."

As the heel of each sandal met the floor it gave a small bell-like note. The perfume special to her house had been woven in her hair, her garments, dropped into the palms of her hands.

There was no strength in any of her limbs, but she walked fluidly between the pillars, trained walk of the princess, straight into the lower salon of the palace. Straight into the golden glare of the spoiled verdict, the scorn or pity of the eight houses who had been her neighbors and were therefore selected to judge her. She glanced at none of them. At nothing. She went to the chair, set out on its own, unmistakably hers—the outcast's. She sat there. In the stillness, she was the stillest thing of all. *Stone*, she thought. *Steel*, she thought. *And is he here? Of course, Ceedres must be present. But I won't look for him or at him. Stone, steel. This is all I have and all I am and all I can be.*

A man was speaking, the head of house Domm. In his one hundred and fiftieth year, tall and well-built, he was a typical example of his kind, and arrogant as his kind (her kind)

86

were, so she thought, now. Yune Domm. She knew him. She knew every one of them, though not well. Never so well as now.

"Vel Thaidis Yune Hirz," he interpolated in his oration occasionally, to identify her, or to attract her attention. No, she would not turn to him, to any of them.

"Vel Thaidis, it's hard to believe in this deed of yours. But the Law has verified your transgression. It will be proven before us. We will be fair to you. But expect no favors."

*Ceedres*, she thought. *His eyes are scorching me, his malevolent interest and contempt. But I won't look about for him. They love him, as Velday loves him, and they care nothing for me. Why should they? He's taken trouble, for many years, to amuse them, to make them wise, generous, honorable and lordly in their own eyes. And I have shunned them, hidden from them, by which they knew they were unnecessary to me. They would always put Ceedres before me.*

"A young girl, you are yet the head of the house of Hirz. . . ."

*Velday, I'm certain, has kept away. I thank the gods—if there are gods—for that.*

Yune Domm, the spokesman, had finished. Yune Chure would be seated near, Kewel's father. The heads of Ket and Ond would be present, of Lail, and the old lady of Tu, and the sad younger woman who ruled Zem and whose husband had recently died on a lionag hunt. For sure, princess Yune Zem would have no sympathy to spare. But Vel Thaidis would not search for her tear stains or her corrosive sneer.

From the corner of her eye, Vel Thaidis caught the movement of a Lawguard, and heard the brush of its jets across the mosaic.

The obnoxious, unbreathing, monotonous voice began.

*I must listen to this*, she thought. Then: *Why? I can alter nothing.*

But she listened.

"The testimonies of Ceedres Yune Thar and of Vel Thaidis Yune Hirz have been mechanically impressed and will now be broadcast to you please attend carefully."

Then the tone came, as she had heard it in the main salon, yesterjate.

She schooled herself, and did not start as Ceedres spoke from the recording machine.

"I have no desire to make this statement," Ceedres said within the copper tube of the Lawguard. There was a pause,

87

during which, presumably, the recorder had reasoned with him. Again the tone, and next: "Then I will make the statement in the interests of the Law, but under protest. Nor have I any wish to reveal the whole matter. Subject to assurance that I must, I comply. But this procedure isn't of my choosing."

*So clever*, she thought. *Yes, you have genius. Not to protest before the tone of the impression, but* after *it. So we should all hear your recorded forbearance, your noble rejections.*

"For some years I have considered Vel Thaidis as kindred," Ceedres' voice continued. "This was an error on my part, but not perhaps inexcusable. Her brother, Velday, and I have been close since childhood. But in the error of my assumption, I've been lax in my treatment of Vel Thaidis, discourteous and rough, forgetting myself. To which, I might add, the lady generally replied quickly and saw I smarted for it. One Jate I made an ill-conceived remark, a jest that she should marry me and so rescue the Thar estate from its ruin. I should not have done so, and I regretted it. I later strove to make amends. This was on a J'ara hunt, when Vel Thaidis was my companion in the chariot. I apologized to her at once, and asked that our relations be less abusive in the future. Vel Thaidis agreed to this. I had slowed the chariot in order to talk to her. She disliked hunting—I was surprised she'd come—and now suggested we enter the temple in the valley instead of going on with the rest. I was determined to fall in with her whims, to end, any way I could, the bad feeling that had festered between us. We went into the temple, and there she told me she had taken my joke of marriage seriously, hence her confusion and anger. Must I explain all this?" Another pause. The tone. Ceedres resumed. His voice was clipped as if with embarrassment and reluctance. "Vel Thaidis swore she loved me. She frankly demanded I should marry her and thereby take half the Hirz estate. She's beautiful, and knows, as who does not, the condition of my fortunes. The proposal could have tempted me, though I'll admit such bluntness from her amazed me. It wasn't the Vel Thaidis I recalled. But I put her off at once. How could I, for the sake of my honor, marry her? Thar's decline and my resultant poverty precluded such a match. Despite her loveliness, who would suppose that I'd wed her for love? I've lived by courtesy of the kindness of my friends some while. But to marry one of them for her property, which is what such a joining would seem, what indeed she seemed to hold as her premise, that road was not for me. And so I informed her. At which—she begged me. At which, once more, I put her off. The situation was now inflammable between us. Worse than ever in the past. At first she was quiet and I persuaded her to return to the chariot. I was preoccupied. She would have sold herself so very cheap to me. I'd had foolish ideas concerning her, which had been undermined. Then, in the chariot, the words flew. I'd never had to handle such a display in a woman of my own class. I made no move to guard myself when she took up the knife. Partly in order not to hurt her, partly because I still reckoned her incapable of such crude barbarism. My mistake, for which I paid. She missed my heart by a finger's breadth. That minute, she must have wanted my death very much. But—may I say one other thing—her hysteria possessed her. The creature in the chariot was not Vel Thaidis. On my side, I want no recriminations, no insane sentences passed on a woman who temporarily forgot herself."

Vel Thaidis screamed—but mutely. She clasped the scream, bricked it inside her, with the truth.

How could they accept these lies? To love Ceedres and be indifferent to her, that was not sufficient. The auto-priest at the temple had been a witness. The priest would show—must already have shown—that barely a phrase of Ceedres' testimony was accurate.

Not a sound in the salon. They waited.

The tone. Now Vel Thaidis' own voice came from the machine.

How defenseless it was, that disembodied voice, lost in its electronic wilderness: "First let me admit to being afraid," it said damningly.

They all heard it, Domm and Chure, Ond and Ket, Lail and Tu and Zem. And Thar. *Thar—*

What was the girl's voice saying now? (Not her own voice, surely, fragile, trembling, tiny flickering motes adrift in the wide chamber.) She was telling how he had taken her into the temple, and they had risen up into the bizarre black place ablaze with white flowerings of fire.

An indistinct mutter about her. She did not need that to reveal to her the idiocy of what the voice said. No temple had such an upper room, a room like hell in a myth.

The blood pounded against her temples and her eyes. Had

she gone mad? Had she dreamed the black room in Maram, as she had dreamed of heaven? Had she dreamed it all?

"He said he didn't understand the room's purpose or what it symbolized, but that he went there often, to conquer his fear of it," the naïve girl said in the recording machine.

Vel Thaidis felt her mind swirling against her skull. Shame and nausea flared in her stomach. Her eyes were filming over and she was ready to faint in order to escape—from the salon, her voice, and from herself.

But somehow she had held herself immobile. And suddenly a cool acid flowed through her, and she was sane again, appallingly so, in possession of herself, mind and body. At that instant she saw the depth and height of Ceedres' plan and comprehended why she had known she could not fight him, that item she had been instinctively aware of but unable to reason out. For Ceedres *had* taken her to the upper room, hidden from others. Ceedres had overridden the conditioning of the auto-priest. Ceedres, whose estate had been wrecked by a failing technology, experimenting perhaps in ways to salvage it, had hit instead upon methods of robot control, which, like the black room itself, no others had ever encountered.

And so, not only did her testimony appear deranged, but the priest—

The priest (denizen of the Thar boundary: "He recognizes me . . . I'm frequently here . . .") would not necessarily speak the truth.

In a world where machinery was incapable of falsehood, a machine which Ceedres had learned to control could be the exception.

It could say that everything had occurred in the temple as Ceedres had avowed.

It could say Vel Thaidis was the liar.

And no one would doubt it.

She would not laugh or weep. She would not faint. She would remain immobile, looking at nothing and at no one.

The voice in the machine was done.

Yune Chure broke out: "The girl's story is a ludicrous fabrication. An hallucination caused by an unstable temperament and muddled wits."

"Pure madness." That was the old lady of Tu, dry as rain.

Yune Domm said heavily, "We have yet to hear from the priest who witnessed the dialogue in the temple."

"The priest is here," the Lawguard said.

The door slid open. The priest was walking toward her. Vel Thaidis did not look. She did not need to see it, nor to hear. The priest would repeat Ceedres' testimony in its own words.

It was like a white gleam on the periphery of her vision. The drapery to ape human clothes, the large hairless skull to ape intellect, the poreless complexion of the non-man. Unobtrusively, the sentences dripped into her ears. "Yune Thar and Yune Hirz came into the room of prayer. She began to suggest to him that they become man and wife. He said nothing, and her speech grew more ardent. He rejected the proposal politely, though with some self-consciousness. . . ."

It was over. It was as she had known it would be.

Yune Ket asked if he might question, and was invited to do so.

"There's been talk of an upper room, modeled like hell in the myth. Is there such a place, and did Vel Thaidis Yune Hirz go into it?"

"The temple energies are stored above the room of prayer. No one enters."

"Thanks, priest." The Courteous Address.

She was utterly discredited. She had invented a fantasy about the temple. Ergo, everything she had uttered was fantasy. She had begged for Ceedres' love and he had refused her on the grounds of honor. In spite and humiliation, she had lashed out at him, and he, too thoughtful of her weakness, had enabled her to stab him. His tale was plausible, realistic and gallant. Hers ridiculous.

"Will you deliberate?" the Lawguard said.

Domm answered at once.

"The bulk of the facts were already with us before we formed council. There's no need for deliberation. Subject to this proof, we had our response in readiness. Precedents for such business are rare, but they have been set. Shall I still speak for us all?"

The others acknowledged, thus affirming his role as spokesman. Their calls of assent were like the scrape of metal blades, cleavers parting the sinews of anteline carcasses, wheels grinding pebbles at the wayside, the gears of clocks striking together.

That was fanciful. Too much so. They were condemning her for a fantasy.

"Then," Domm said. He paused. He was stern in preparation for her stare, her crying. She did not stare or cry or look

at him. "By the Law, no criminal can go unpunished, whatever rank he occupies. Similarly, restitution must be made,
where possible. Our decision is based on others to be read in
the statutes of Yunean legality. Vel Thaidis will be stripped
of her title and her holding, and this portion, half the estate
of Hirz, shall be awarded to Ceedres Yune Thar. She herself
thereafter to withdraw to the Slumopolis, to live by common
labor. Her act was without honor. It's fitting she should become a daughter of the Slum, which has no honor even in its
name. There is our decision. There the matter rests."

"No. The matter can't rest there."

Vel Thaidis' wrists jerked and her head almost lifted. But
she snatched herself away from the brink. It was Ceedres
Yune Thar who had spoken. No longer from the machine,
but from the hollow of the room. His voice was like velvet,
and serene. It embodied restraint. It showed the council that
they must reassess their command. The very slice Ceedres
had carved for his plate he now pushed gravely aside. His
wickedness was wondrous. It had a high gloss, an intricate
patina.

*He plays them all like chames. I wasn't alone in that.*

In fascination, she heard Yune Chure say loudly, "Ceedres,
you're misguided to plead for her. Even her own brother has
avoided the council."

"I won't turn thief against Hirz," Ceedres said.

"Let the girl talk for herself," said Yune Tu in her wry
cracked drawl. "Let Vel Thaidis ask for clemency."

"Vaidi," Ceedres said, swiftly, intimately, across the
crowded chamber. "I can try to protect you only so far. For
love of life, say something to them."

Words seethed in her mouth. She bound herself in a vise.

*How different it might have been,* she thought. *They might
have convened council to marry us. Maybe he would have
been kind to me, as Omevia is kind to her pet cat. Kinder
than now.*

"The sentence stands," Domm said.

"It stands," said Yune Tu.

Each repeated the ritual.

This time Ceedres was dumb.

The Lawguard moved again. It glided to Vel Thaidis, and
then her space was filled with gliding. A fence of copper
columns, twenty Lawguards shut her in. At last she could focus her eyes and turn her head, for she would see only
machines on every hand.

92

"You must come with us."
She rose.
She was dead.

They told her she might take nothing with her from the palace of Hirz. Of course not. The dead took nothing with them. In ancient compliment of the eternal sun, they were cremated in golden ovens, their dust mingled with wine and stored in golden urns. The Lawguards, being primed to human frailty and requirements, even gave her a sip of wine. A sip of wine to mingle with her dust.

They walked down through the gardens. How soothing the lawns under her feet. She had never properly appreciated them before, they had simply been part of her. And the slender gemmy spikes of the fountains, and the extraordinary trees. This was her home she was leaving.

As they crossed onto the sand of the shore, another of the dry rains had started. The pale green flakes, scales of the sky, slanted across the air, dissolving without moisture on ground, fabric or flesh. One brushed her mouth, and she tasted, appropriately, its bitterness.

Near the margin of the lake was a vehicle. It resembled no living species, it had no decoration, no team of robot animals reined in front. Brown metal; the transport the Lawguards had brought to conduct their human passenger.

The sight of it was unbearable. It was the funerary urn. Suddenly, the leash on which she had held herself slipped from her fingers. Her knees gave way, and she dropped on the sand with the dry rain dappling her shoulders, the nape of her neck. Then something was firmly wrapped about her upper arms. She stared dazedly, and beheld the unfurled tentacles of the Lawguards elaborately binding her, as they eased her upright.

Her mouth gaped maniacally to scream. She thought, with great clarity: *Begin, and you'll never stop. They'll pick out your screeching from the palace. The Lawguards will bind your lips, or pour some drug between them, or under your skin. Don't scream aloud.*

Supported by the Lawguards, she regained her feet and walked on. She did not scream.

A section of the vehicle folded aside.

Within was a rectangular area. A nodule of automatic controls bulged at its center, inartistic divans of plastum were

93

fixed to the floor against the walls, from out of which a narrow aqua-closet jutted. There were no windows.

Into this blind box Vel Thaidis stepped.

"You must relinquish your clothing and your jewels."

She made no protest. She had known how it would be. The Lawguards had no humanoid digits with which to unfasten the seals of material or of necklaces. Yet the Law demanded she renounce everything. All she had had belonged to Ceedres now.

She undressed herself and let the drapery fall (maybe he would gift it to Omevia), the tissue-fine undergarments, removed her sandals, the bracelets, the collar, the rings. She stood at the heart of a second dry shining rain, and hypnotized by it, overlooked an ornament in her hair. A tentacle came and plucked it away, and the up-combed pilings loosened. Skeins of silk, danger-black, shawled her shoulders and her breasts.

"Your hair," the Voice Lawguard said.

Perhaps by custom they must hack it off. But her moment of abjection had gone by.

"Your hair is tinted. This tint cannot be matched in your new condition of life. At the Instation it will be molecularized to conform with its natural color. This is in your own interests. Now please dress."

They would undye her hair in order to disguise her. How curious. The gray tunic with its metal-link belt would not disguise her. Her body proclaimed her origins. Full-breasted, small-waisted; the apple curve of the hips, the rounded arms and long legs, the slim wrists and ankles and the high-arched feet. In the Slumopolis, the women were as lean as lionag. Their breasts were shallow, their hips no broader than their waists. Their limbs were bony, their hands and feet huge and overgrown, their faces regularly deformed. Or were these stories also lies?

The Lawguards were leaving the vehicle, bearing her jewels and clothing with them.

She watched the door shut. She was enervated. She did not care any more.

The vehicle twitched and raised itself on its jets of air.

Too late now. Too late to protest, to cry out for mercy, to scream and beat with her hands, to take up a knife and cut her veins. Much too late for any of that.

She had begun to speak again. As the vehicle whirled over the sandy shore and presently across the surface of the lake

94

itself, Vel Thaidis discovered herself lying on a divan, and praying to the gods of her childhood. Her words were incomprehensible and had no passion. She did not, in her incoherent and lusterless frenzy, suppose they would be listened to. Apparently they were not.

Pollinated by the dust, the sunlight streamed through the main salon of the Thar palace. Motionless and brief, the wine-red shadows hemmed the old furniture, the carven benches, the gilded message panels. The fountain pierced the fishless aqua of its basin. A little sand blew about the floor, as it usually did, unswept.

Velday stood on the threshold woodenly.

"It's Maram," he said to the man seated in the tall chair beyond the fountain. "I waited, but you didn't come."

"Did you think I would? Stride into Hirz as your sister was dragged out of it?"

"She didn't speak at the council. There was nothing she could say."

"She should, nevertheless, have spoken," Ceedres answered.

"My sense of shame," said Velday, "is insupportable. The princes have urged you to take your portion of the Hirz estate. It's due to you. My sister—I believe she kept silent because she acknowledged the justice of her punishment."

"Oh, you believe that, do you?"

"Ceedres," Velday muttered. He hung his head. He became a child, offering the childishness that Ceedres should master him, and remove all grounds for independent concern, all trace of doubt. For Velday felt doubt, keenly. His blood tie with his sister hurt him like a bruised nerve, yet Ceedres had come first. It had been intuitive, the brotherhood of gender staking its claims before the shout of blood. Where Velday had been all-important to Vel Thaidis, Ceedres had been all-important to Velday, and for not dissimilar reasons. Each of the Yune Hirz was young and desperate for a hero, an anchor, some wondrous essence to love, which would make him more than he was. But after the battle which Ceedres had easily won in Velday's soul, Velday knew the sting of conscience and an alarm at the random forces which had reshaped his life. He had prophesied for himself Ceedres' and Vel Thaidis' marriage, or had thought he had. That Ceedres would shirk such a union, deferring to his poverty, had smitten Velday with unfathomable pangs of excitement, admiration, misery. That Ceedres had not come to Hirz to comfort

95

him, to fill up the gaping void, smote Velday more deeply. "Ceedres," he said, "my sister's holding is yours by right of Law. Accept it. For my sake."

"Vay, the process of the Law is perfect, but harsh. We're human."

"The council told me of your reluctance. I gave my word I'd persuade you."

"I'm to trample on your grief."

"Yes, I grieve, but what she did—was intolerable. I thought she'd killed you."

"You were not alone."

"I remembered the lionag hunt—I suppose Ermarth Yune Zem's death may have reminded me—you were fourteen. You fired when the king cat was almost on top of you. I dreamed that hunt over and over for a year. I thought then you'd die. We're brothers, Cee. We swore that before the gods, do you recall? Ten years ago, in a room of prayer."

"You recollect it all excellently. You realize Vel Thaidis was also important to me? I've curdled my brains trying to find some way to approach the conclave of the Law on her behalf. How is it machines can order our lives so thoroughly?"

"The council is human, and passed the judgment."

Ceedres smiled. Until that moment his face had mimicked the dark melancholy of Velday's own. Motivated by the psychological cue, absurdly, Velday found he too was smiling.

"You're too good to me, Vay," Ceedres said. "You won't rest till you take the burden from my shoulders."

Velday's head went up. A whisper of his own virtue had reached him. He was refreshed, as if by strong drink.

"I won't rest till you assume your residence at Hirz."

Ceedres rose. He glanced into the smoky aqua of the basin. Only the liquid saw his eyes, black as danger, fixed as the Zenith.

"Very well," Ceedres stretched. The knife wound was long-healed by an advanced science. The athlete's body, male token of the princely line, moved fluidly, raced with golden lights on muscle, armlets, draped tunic. The sun combed over his hair. Aureoled, godlike, he turned to Velday, dazzling, but gentle: "In any event, we could work together more successfully, to gain her pardon. To undo this inappropriate sentence."

Velday's heart broke.

He felt himself borne up into new spheres of radiance and

96

optimism. Ceedres lent him bright wings, showed him a glittering mountain where only a pit had yawned before.

Ceedres plunged his arm into the minerally chilled basin, drew up a watertight flagon, cracked the lid.

He walked to a table where cups were stacked under their protective plastum, the old graying glass of Thar.

"Let's drink then, Vay," he said, "to a fair solution of our troubles."

The sun had seemed to follow him, to worship him. It sparkled on the long-stemmed glasses, and through the thin colorless fermentation that trickled into their bowls.

"Violent liquor," Velday commented. "If it's the draught I take it for."

"It will do us good. I meant to sample it alone and put the sun out with it. But this is better. You've given me back hope, Velday, and my self-esteem. Thanks. My brother."

They drank.

It was the white-berry caffea Velday had suspected, a whirlpool brew of the Slumopolis. This disturbed him briefly. But at the second glass, no more.

Presently they went out, and strolled the edge of the marsh where the indigo shade-reeds rattled and the blood pools rippled to some subplanetary rhythm of their own.

They were keeping J'ara, as often before. As often before, Velday, drinking deeply and assured of friendship, gave himself over to an innocent delight in all things, and a belief in all miracles. This Maram, Vel Thaidis was an outcast. But next Jate, might she not be freed?

He thought of all their parents in their death urns, ash forever, while he and Ceedres lived and the sun burned with their youth.

He did not see that Ceedres' first glass was never emptied. He had never seen this. There was much he did not see.

When at last, in the twentieth hour, Maram, the fourth of J'ara, they mounted the lion-dog Hirz chariot to ride across the hills, Velday saw instead white-berry phantoms crowding the landscape, air-flowers, rogue fires, the psychic arteries that ran along the earth, and a hundred rivers pouring up into the green sky.

Ceedres set the chariot leaping. He threw his arcane crystal cup away, and did not watch it bounce from sight, unbreakable glass, among the rocks and rusty drifts of Thar that need no longer bother him.

97

# Part Two

The process of the Law. . . .

The room was spacious, pleasing, lit with a soft and pearly light by the frosted intensifiers in the ceiling. No machinery was visible, beyond the silken ovoid of highly glossed platinum which rested motionless in the air about two yards from a couch of pale cushions. Beside the couch, on a small table, a blue glass thimble ready to be filled from either or both of the two flasks of incised silver, and a tray of inhalants and alcohol sticks. Here in the computer complex of Uta, everything had been thought of to provide comfort and equanimity. Those giving evidence, accusers and accused, were all treated identically. When the voice came from the metal ovoid it was courteous and mild, encouraging even.

Vitra sat on the pale couch, much paler, and twitched a jade fiddle-toy. Nonsensically, as she waited for the voice to begin, she found herself thinking of the dry rain which had fallen on the neck of Vel Thaidis as she was carried from Hirz. The rain, of course, was a waste product of the converted atmosphere of the solar side, a flaking off of gaseous scales smelted to a sort of consistency by their fall from the ether. She had been incredibly intelligent to devise such a detail. Incredibly.

If only she could maintain that intelligence now.

The silvery ovoid spoke in its silkiest tones.

"This machine is prepared to receive your statement, Vitra Klovez. Please speak in your own time, withholding nothing."

"Will you—" Vitra hesitated, "will you record what I say?"

"Naturally, but the statement is for the computer's assessment alone. No other human will hear it."

The computer complex lay even farther below ground than the Residencia, and was reached by a series of moving stairways. Quite suddenly, and with no warning, Vitra experienced a sense of smotheration. She mastered it hastily and plunged into the tale she and Vyen had so meticulously rehearsed. Vyen had already spoken here. Also the princes of Klur and Klastu. Casrus' statement would most probably be called for last.

Vitra tried not to gabble. Luckily, if she appeared distraught and anxious, these emotions were readily accounted for by her supposed ordeal. For the lie, no machine could delve in her mind, and she was word perfect as any reasonable actress had to be. She had called for the help of Klarn, as she and her brother had called for the help of all the neighboring princely families. Finding her alone, unprotected and despairing, Klarn had sought to violate her.

The machine spoke to her.

"And you had no feelings of liking for this prince?"

The question had been anticipated, Vyen had predicted it. Cannily, he advised her to offer, where possible, the truth, even in the midst of the deception.

"Yes. Since childhood, I—had admired him."

"Would you, if circumstances had been other than they are, have consented to become the wife of Casrus Klarn?"

"I am ashamed to say I should have consented. I didn't know then that, rather than remain an ideal, he could become—"

"Pardon my interruption," said the machine blandly, "but did you, during your interview with this prince, act within the bounds of Klave propriety?"

Vitra flung up her head.

"Yes," she flared. "How dare you ask me such a thing!"

The machine did not reply to her virtuous outburst, and Vitra suffered an apprehension that she should not rail against it as she had against her house robots.

Presently, the machine prompted her to continue with her statement, and Vitra told of Casrus' threats with the knife, and displayed the thin lilac seam along her arm, which deliberately she had left unrepaired. Then came Vyen's return, Casrus' blow that felled Vyen, and last of all Casrus' departure from the house in stony rancor, only to be detained by the Klurs and the Klastus and the Klinns, at Vyen's cry, a few paces from the house.

The machine remained silent awhile, assimilating her sentences. At length, it said, "This incident was brought about by the failure of the lamps and other gadgets of the palace of Klovez. If Klarn had not attempted assault, what were to have been your plans?"

Again, well rehearsed.

99

"We were unsure what to do, which is why we appealed to our friends, and to Casrus—no friend of ours, but reckoned to be grave and trustworthy. Ultimately, I believe we must have come to this complex, or to another computer elsewhere in the Residencia."

"Did you tell Klarn of this plan?"

"I did. He responded that the computers would refuse us aid. I declared he was mad, that the computers would restore Klovez' technology in full, and that therefore I had no need to sully my honor, with him or with anyone."

"In part, you are correct. But I regret that Klovez would not, nor will, be completely restored. The collapse of the life-system of an entire house is so rare as to be virtually unprecedented, which is fortunate. The Klave is perpetuated on a most finely balanced scale. To draw off sufficient power to replace the whole support pattern of a palace would tilt that scale precariously. Certainly, Klovez can be made livable again, but no more than that. For your luxuries and aesthetics, you would need to depend on the generosity of your peers."

Vitra looked startled. It had been essential to appear to think Klovez could be restored, hence removing from herself and Vyen all whisper of an ulterior motive for the charge against Casrus. Now, within herself, Vitra sizzled in anger, at the patronage of the computer, the dismal half-existence it offered. Through no fault of their own, she and Vyen had lost everything, and were to be awarded the life of Subterines and beggars in exchange. That portional help was forthcoming seemed insult rather than alleviation.

"I'm sorry to distress you, Vitra Klovez," said the machine. "But your friends, surely, will be thoughtful."

"Oh, I suppose they will. Only Casrus has shown himself a monster—the one allegedly most upright and conscientious among us. What a parade he's made of his sobriety and charity! What a mask it has turned out to be. I can only assume," she added bitterly, "that spending his hours in obscure connivance with the Subterines, he's learned their manners."

"Vitra Klovez, I thank you for your statement. You may now leave the complex. You are a guest in the house of Klur, but this Jate, Klovez has been made livable, should you wish to return there. Should your charge against Klarn be found proven, you and your brother will be entitled to recompense. At this stage, its substance has not been decided. You will be

100

informed of the computerized verdict in four Jates, when all evidence has been collated and perused."

Shedri Klur waited for her at the arched portico of the complex, and behind him his coal-blue chariot car. Strung taut as a wire, Vitra took in the earnest bejeweled young man, the gleaming functional vehicle, and burst into tears.

Shedri comforted her with a tender, almost a smug enjoyment. For a long while she had fenced with him, flirted, and turned him coldly aside when she grew bored. Now, in her reduced circumstances, afraid to lose his good will (in case the plot foundered), Vitra was very gracious, and her vulnerability soothed him, toned up his self-esteem, making him irresistibly a little cruel. When he said, "I hear Klovez is restored. Would you like to see?" he was paying her out for six years of indifference. He understood, as well as she, having himself made inquiries of the computer during his statement of evidence, what Klovez had been restored to.

"Very well," said Vitra bravely. And so they rode there.

The first sight that greeted her was that of all the funygra trees dejectedly dying on the rock around the house. Naturally, no sustenance of the impoverished palace could be spared to nurture flora.

They left the vehicle and went into the foyer—the door having been opened, not by Vitra's command, but by the wrenching of a handle. There were no lights. Then two of three insipid globes came on, giving an unattractive pallor to a scene already redolent of neglect. The lift worked, but grudgingly, slowly. The upper rooms, the lower, the salon, the bedchambers, each was the same. Vaguely lit and barely warm, augmented with an array of dreadful functional heaters, like squat stones, that gave off a raw sear when activated, drying the air, which itself smelled overused. Three robots were in evidence. They did not speak to anyone and, horror upon horror, their wheels creaked and squealed, as if on purpose to fray the nerves. Dust was gathering on the furnishings. At the corner of a court where a fountain had played, but played no longer, white mould had begun to colonize. Tepid water came from gold and silver faucets. Books in a cabinet showed already signs of mildew, a steel firesword, an edge of rust. No alcohol of any variety could be obtained. The rare rich dishes that had been brought to the breakfast and supper tables would be brought no more. Viands were basic now, uncolored, unspiced and undecorative. Washing of utensils and garments must be performed by

101

hand. (Obscene things, these, events never before contemplated.) One robot in particular had developed a distinct list to its right-hand side. When Vitra, clenching her fists in abject fury, shouted at it to stop, it paid no heed.

"Are we to endure this!" she screamed, and the house echoed, as now it consistently did.

Alarmed, out of control of her once more, Shedri blustered that his home was hers, she need fear no loss of dignity or opulence.

But Vitra, scarcely hearing him, struck her fists upon a table of fine mosaic.

"It must," she hissed, "It *must*. I will not suffer this. It *must*."

Shedri could not know to what she nounlessly referred, or that, extraordinarily, it abruptly seemed to her that Casrus had been the cause of all her trouble, even of the fall of Klovez. That she had shaped the villainous Ceedres from him was no more than just. Indeed, in that moment, she believed the lie she had spoken in the computer complex. For in a way, Casrus *had* attempted a rape—the rape of her personal world—when he recommended that she live like this.

Vyen sat in Olvia Klastu's heated chariot, upon a bridge if silvered rock, in a grotto of green and blue ice pillars.

Moodily, he stared across the ice and drank wine clear as water from Olvia's flask. Olvia, in a robe of synthetic gray fur, chattered archly, unaware she was no more than a background to his thoughts. Not that his thoughts were in any way meaningful or progressive. Like Vitra's they went in an endless circle of uneasiness, anger and biting concern for self. The ovoid machine had made no unpredictable comment when he rendered his statement. His bruised lip and jaw would have been noted. And Vitra would have been as faultless as he in performance. On the whole, he might congratulate himself on both the scheme and its perpetration. Nevertheless, sudden horrors assailed him, at the knowledge of the vast sequence he had set in motion. The abhorred Casrus was yet a fixture. To topple him was, all at once, a strangely disconcerting achievement. Added to that were the bad dreams of discovery of the truth, plus great rollers of appalled realization that everything had been drunkenly based on Vitra's ridiculous Fabulism.

Olvia was stroking his hair. If he wed her, or one of the several girls of Klur, there was a way out of technological deprivation. Probably he would have to take it. A dismal cogitation. Of course, Vitra might enchant Shedri or another into a union. That, Vyen supposed, would do. But with fraternal possessiveness, even that did not satisfy him, any more than had her pursuit of Casrus.

"And I trust Casrus will be packed off to live with the nauseating Subterines he's so fond of," said Olvia, coming near enough Vyen's thoughts to interrupt them.

"Oh, I doubt that," said Vyen, and, before he could resist it: "It wasn't, after all, an attempted murder."

"To threaten with a dagger; it might have come to a beating and a near murder if you, you handsome, courageous boy, hadn't burst in on them."

"He loves the Subterines," said Vyen gloomily. "He should be happy to dwell with them. I don't know why he stayed in the Residencia when their company was preferable."

"So everyone says," said Olvia.

Of course, however, everyone knew why Casrus had remained a prince. While he was Klarn, he kept hold of the Klarn technology, whose machines and robots he constantly set to work in the Subterior.

"But in any case," said Vyen, "the computers are just."

He could have wished them less so.

"Ensid remarked the other Jate on how great a voice our machines have in the Klave. Unavoidable, but absurd, he said. We're fashioned from our parental genes in the computers' genetic matrixes. Our names are chosen by the computers when we're delivered to our parents at birth. We're raised and nursed and tutored by robots. Thereafter our security rests on mechanical diligence."

"The machines obey us, not we them."

"Will you say that, if the punishment given to Casrus is a light one? Ensid says," irritatingly droned Olvia, "that the computers may call for a council of Klovez' neighboring houses to decide the punishment. The records of Klave Law refer to such an event." Vyen's heart had jumped. The similarity to Vitra's story shocked him at last. He said nothing, and Olvia finished, "If the punishment were to be selected by Casrus' peers, he wouldn't escape. It's become quite fashionable to detest him. He could expect small leniency."

Casrus, Prince of Klarn, delivered the only real truth to the ovoid machine in the computer complex. The single flaw in this truth was that, robbed of the motive of villainy, his

103

deeds at Klovez seemed inconsequential. And though, undoubtedly, he had reasoned Vyen and Vitra's perfidy by now, and the aim of their accusation against him, he said nothing of it, nor did the computer ask him for any conclusions on the matter. He assumed it could divine their impulse for itself; if he failed to add a pointing finger they might receive less censure.

It was not necessarily only the innocent and the naïve who looked for justice from an ostensibly perfect Law. The just might also rely on it. In fact, Casrus had observed the ruthless efficiency of the Law, following countless tumultuous crimes of the Subterior. But in the instance of Temal, never had the Law been executed so fairly.

Serene and unemphatic, therefore, Casrus gave his statement, and went home to await the verdict. (He even had some notion of attempting to mitigate whatever sentence should be passed on the two liars. He viewed them with sympathy and some tedium. As with the Subterines, loss had incited transgression.) He was therefore surprised to come on Temal weeping in the falsely sunlit salon of Klarn.

"What is it?" he said to her gently. "Not this Klovez ploy."

"Their hate," she said. "It hovers over your house like a cloud of smoke."

And then, for the first, though why he was uncertain, a positive foreboding came to him. He did not let her see it. But after he had comforted her, and they had spoken of other things and drunk caffea together, he went to his apartments. There he began, coldly and meticulously, to put his affairs in order, as if he were in his third century, and felt death approaching, the calm death of ennui only the aristocrats knew.

Such a death had removed Casrus' father ten years before. Most of the aristocratic houses did not consent to create heirs until the end of their span. Physical and mental stamina being of such high standard, this lateness had no adverse effect upon the extracted gene cells. Rarely, however, did any child gain much from the presence of a parent, or live long in company with one.

The old prince of Klarn, in common with his fellows, thought nothing of the Subterior beyond its undoubted usefulness. The Subterines he considered, if he considered them at all, were beasts of burden, animals permitted to draw breath that they might serve and entertain the Klave, as the dogga did. On the Fabulasts, those picked from the sons and daughters of the palaces, in order to serve, in turn, the workers, old Klarn had looked with mild disgust. "If the computers deem it important, let the computers see to it," he had said. On one occasion, to the child of a brother aristocrat picked in this way, he awarded the single injunction: "Refuse." The refusal had been effected. The young man was released from his duty immediately, but another Fabulast was chosen to replace him.

Casrus was in his fourteenth year, the year before his father died, when he became aware, quite shockingly and in a succession of minutes, that nothing was so simple. With two other princes, of Klinn and Klef, he had visited a Theatrical in Eres sector. The drama was a comedy, covering the myth of the garden of paradise and a prince turned there into silver; trivial stuff, unmemorable. Save that, some way through the action, during a piece of buffoonery, one of the clockwork slabs of scenery depicting Kaneka slipped from its moorings, rolling a little distance to mocking calls from the audience. Errant motion was quickly halted and things put to right, but not before one of the small brass runners, the weight of a quarter of the slab upon it, had gone over the foot of the leading actress.

The sight of the blood her foot was now slippered in, enthralled the watchers. Even Klef and Klinn, who had been squabbling over a board game while they intermittently eyed the stage, grew dumb and intent.

As the girl moved across the platform, her foot left everywhere a blue-red print. Her face was almost blue with pain, but somehow she had mastered herself, somehow she adhered to her fatuous role, not stumbling on her lines, somehow not even limping. Casrus, horrified, could not imagine why she should suffer in this way, and for some while, combined with his horror was an admiration for her valor, her nobility.

Then, when the drama ended to savage applause, and credit chips hailed on the stage with the jeweled flowers, the answer to the riddle, sickening and undeniable, came to him.

She was a Subterine. She had not dared absent herself. If she spoiled the Theatrical, the aristocrats would not forgive her. If, on the other hand, she suffered before them, fascinated, they might laud her. And she must keep princely approbation at all costs. Why? Because if she did not, they could return her to the Subterior. Her agony and her steps of blood had been preferable to her, beside that alternative.

That was how Casrus learned the nature of the Subterior,

and the nature of those who came from it. It was a lesson apparently only he did learn, but he never mislaid it afterward.

He suffered then, inside himself, the first bouts of his adult illness: guilt. To old Klarn, astutely, he did not apply for a remedy. Nor, in the wake of the father's death, did a remedy suggest itself. For three years, Casrus brooded. He went to the libraries of the city, to its computers, seeking the very soul of it, questioning, trying to tear out the answer. He went among the Upperling Subterines of the Residencia too, the artists, artisans, actors, dramatists and the household pets, attempting to uncover in them the cause of their destiny, and the destiny of those others left behind in hell. But he gained no more than elaborations on his original discovery. For the Subterines, they fawned on him, elicited favors, and, he was positive, scorned him, laughed at him, his callow overtures to their warped self-disliking cynicism.

Then, when he was eighteen, a prince of Klef, Bermel—not the boy with whom he had watched the actress bleeding—came to a supper to which Casrus also had come. Bermel Klef entered, leading a man by a collar and leash—a Subterine. He was supposed to be a dogga, and was obliged to crawl over the floor. Casually, for Casrus had observed the casual approach was generally the best, Casrus asked Bermel Klef if he would barter ownership of the man. Bermel, with some amusement, named an item of the Klarn wealth. "It's a lot to ask, but then, this dogga is a very good dogga. And you don't have to accept if you'd rather not." "It's yours," said Casrus. "I'll have it sent to you by one of my robots next Jate. Will you do the same with this man?" "Have him now, if you want," said Bermel, and tossed over the end of the leash. The dogga man was the initial Subterine to be installed at Klarn. The usual rituals of fawning, scorn and two-facedness occurred, no more than Casrus foresaw. Nor did the relationship ever substantially alter. It merely became duplicated in other, similar relationships, the other Subterines with whom Casrus peopled his home. Not till Temal was genuine concern fleshed out by the response of a genuine belief, even then not totally; for Temal had never agreed to being his equal, a kindred human. He was the god, and she the acolyte.

At nineteen, Casrus was already growing familiar with the ways of the Subterior itself. He went there often. To rebuild, to insulate, to assure medicine, food, clothing to those in greatest poverty, to make safe the abysses of the mines, to service the faulty machines that might lead to death on the

106

outer surface of the planet. These forays were always greeted in the everlasting spirit—fawning, scorning, the hidden jeer, the barely muffled glare of envious hate. Casrus expected nothing else. His mission was not to win love but to ease an impossible, unreasonable, inexorable state of things, which in itself had no hope of ending. That the Subterines loathed him, just because he was a prince and because he struggled to relieve them, did no more than occasionally rouse his impatience, and only then when their loathing prevented improvement of their condition. That his own classes, the princely houses of the Residencia, also loathed him as a sting on their carefree skins, was likewise no amazement, and caused him no pangs.

To live forever spiritually alone was something he had grown accustomed to at an early age. It did not make him afraid. His one unique dread had been, and remained to be, that some unprecedented happening would intervene, stripping him of his means to salvage where he could. At twenty, he had had dreams of this intervening happening, this weird stroke of fate. In the dreams it was some malady that defied the computers, some disintegration of the brain itself. Dreaming, he beheld himself staggering about Klarn, a witless imbecile, unable to remember what must be done, or why. But such dreams had passed. Only the haunting dread, faint as a far-off call, still lingered. Lingered until this Jate.

And this Jate the dread had taken on a form, a substance. Exile.

Such a penalty would be extreme, but not unheard of, for he had plumbed the depths of Klave Law along with its other cultural issues. A thousand years ago, a prince had been condemned to give up half his estate to a house he had wronged. The shadings of the case were dim but the outcome explicit.

Deprived of the technology at Klarn to expiate a crime he had not committed, how could Casrus thereafter deal with the Subterior, what use would he be to that upper nether place? Therefore what use to himself?"

Four Jates after the statements had all been given, the computers sent their judgment, separately and in five silver capsules, to each of the five houses directly concerned: Klovez, Klur, Klastu, Klinn and the palace of Klarn. The words from the capsule were spoken, in a soft and reasonable voice, unlike the human, beyond humanity.

"From consideration of the evidence and logical assess-

107

ment, the computer of the Uta complex, in conjunction with the other computers of the Klave, confirms this verdict: that Casrus, prince and heir of the house of Klarn, is guilty of all crimes and charges laid against him, namely: threat of violence with a blade, act of violence with a blade, attempted assault against a woman of his own class, second act of violence against a man of his own class, though without a weapon, false statement rendered to this machine. The verdict attained, it is not open to appeal of any sort. However, the felony did not result in a mortality, and the assault was not concluded. A death penalty is inapplicable. In accordance with ancient custom, the computer therefore gives over Casrus, heir of Klarn, to his fellow princes, his punishment to be decided by them, recommending only that it be severe and complementary both to the crime and to the plight of its victims. The punishment shall be chosen and evoked from the computer by the thirteenth hour, this Jate. At the seventeenth hour, Maram, the machines of the Law will visit palace Klarn in order to enforce justice. Klarn must hold himself in readiness. We repeat that no appeal is, at this time, possible to him."

The effect of this message was to galvanize. Like magnetized filings, the elected judges rushed together to symbolic Klovez to make their play at jurisdiction. Great-eyed, alert, primed by their sudden authority, they perched like predatory birds in the chill dismal salon, watching Vitra, watching Vyen. A veiled discussion began. All knew what was intended, had indeed been speaking of it quite frankly throughout Jates and J'aras. Now, it was abruptly coy, hinted at, toyed with merely, as if to give some semblance of genuine debate to the proceedings. But of course they had sentenced Casrus long ago. Presently Olvia Klastu spoke the actual phrase: "Justice is only this—let Casrus lose the technology of Klarn, and let Klovez be given it."

Agreement dashed into the breach.

"The very computers themselves seem to suggest as much—*Complementary to the plight of its victims*. What could be more clear?"

"He's never acted as a prince. Why should he remain one?"

"He loves the Subterines. He'll thrive on being with them." And slyly, "The Klarn palace has much to recommend it."

Vyen and Vitra said nothing. Stark white, perching like the rest, shivering from the cold house and with nerves, they stared at their dangerous friends who were brilliantly protective of them, offering them now what they had planned for and schemed so recklessly to get.

Though the princes would, naturally, round on Klovez as readily, given sufficient cause. Anything for a drama.

And Vitra, in her shivering thoughts, heard Ceedres Yune Thar say, "I won't turn thief against Hirz." Much more polished in his wickedness than she. Then, horrifyingly, she had cried out, impelled by hysteria! "No, I won't—I won't turn thief against Klarn!"

A silence fell. She was aware of Vyen, his eyes flaming on her. Then Ensid Klastu said to her, "Vitra, the only thief in this business is Casrus himself. Your generosity is exquisite but misplaced."

"Yes," she blurted out, "how true—" Turning, she ran away, out of the salon, into her decaying apartment, soon to be exchanged for accustomed luxury. "What have I done?" she whispered to the walls, the ceiling, on which the beacon of Rise Uta's lights randomly came and went.

You *know* what you have done, the lights said to her, the room said to her.

By the thirteenth hour the computer had been informed. By the fourteenth hour, Casrus had also been informed. At the seventeenth hour, Maram, the ovoid robots of the Law came gently into Klarn, and gently, politely, took Casrus away with them. No one spoke, no fuss was made. Even Temal, motionless among the other rescued Subterines of Casrus' household, (everyone of them understanding that their time of security in the Residencia was also about to end) even Temal made no outcry.

After Casrus' departure, the hours of Maram wore, but the new owners of palace Klarn did not appear. Despite success, perhaps, putting it off.

Vyen was suitably at a gambling stadium in Eres, with Olvia, Shedri and others.

Vitra stood in the Fabulism chamber of Rise Iu.

She had come to erase the tapes of the Fabulism, to wipe Vel Thaidis, Velday, the Yunea, most of all the plot of Ceedres, from the machines. But it seemed to her, standing there, that to do this would also be to blot out all their lives, to blot out the residue of life which Casrus might jettison easily enough in any event, in the Subterior to which she had condemned him.

109

Thus, one hand on the keys, she sank into a sort of vegetable state, unable to proceed with her intention.

And on the inner screen of her brain, the images began again to form. Vel Thaidis, as Casrus, sent into hell, alone, comfortless. But beside the freezing cold, a furnace heat, by the deadly blackness, a petrifying light. . . .

Day by night, night by day, yet malevolence and anguish in both of them.

# CHAPTER FOUR

## Part One

Slumopolis—Slum City—that had not always been its name. The original title was gone, wiped out by generations of descent from a past all but forgotten. Whatever the Slumopolis had once been, now it was a slum. A glamorous fluorescent slum in spots and patches, a rickety bawdy slum in others. In some hot, bone-dry, bleached-out, chemical-stinking subsidences, lower than a slum, more a garbage-tip, a charnel house: the sink. The grave.

The aristocrats of the great estates played about in the Slumopolis, getting their hands dirty, because that made it more fun to soap them afterward. The young princes purchased their prostitutes, their unnatural wines and their slum dinners here with the tech-credits that were worth more than jewels and metal. To attract the aristocracy, the Slumopolis prettied itself and evolved its entertainments. But for its own, mostly it had a sour and ugly face, an unwashed body, a foul tongue, and an illegal knife or a gas-gun in its sleeve. Even the sky was not the same as the sweet jade roof that overhung the estates and palaces farther out. The Slumopolis was closer to the Zenith, closer to the perimeter that marked off the interior circle of the planet. Here the sky was paler and more desperate looking. The sun, a ball of white howling matter, raged almost directly overhead. Inward from the perimeter, where the ring of the Yunea ended, stretched the unspeakable desert, less a land than a method of execution for murderers. While outward the Slumopolis was girdled by desert of a milder kind. This outland, which divided the Slum from the inner boundaries of the great estates, was turned over to a back-breaking parody of agriculture. Sprawling crop fields were cut through by occasional fluid courses and tufted by plantations. Domesticated beasts were in evidence. Emaciated herds of antelines, wretchedly roped neck to neck, browsed from plant to plant at the canal sides, searching always for shade as they nibbled the acid stalks. Bands of humans toiled under movable shade roofs, sorting the powdery soil by hand or with plastum plows hauled by teams of dogga. To see an automatic machine was rare. The technology which sustained the palaces by ancient right extended only thinly into the Slumopolis and its adjacent staeds. In order to survive, men were reduced to primitive measures. They hated it, but spared small vitality to recrimination. They fleeced the aristocrats where they could, and spat after them and fawned on them, and somehow understood it was the correct order of things. Some twisted dream from the unremembered past still chained them. Some dream in which this had to be, and where the world kept its course only while the unjust order obtained, the broiling sun in its sky, the gods in their temples, the princes in their palaces, the slum dwellers in their brightly lit hell on earth.

The journey, undertaken at varying speeds and elevations to suit the terrain, lasted five hours. No vehicle, even the insectile aircraft of the palaces, was capable of lifting to any great height—technology's provision against disrupting the upper layers of an erected atmosphere. For the most part, the transport of the Law traveled five or six feet clear of the ground, rising to twenty when the way was rough. No halts were made, not even at the boundary of the estates, where a wavering wall of electronic impulses was strung between columnar steel pylons. This wall ran in an irregular circle, (as ran all the rings of life on the planet's sunward face), describing for thousands of staeds the outer edge of the Slumopolis and containing it. The pylons marched through valleys and, in the perpendicular, up cliffs. Rarely was the geography itself so coarse that the barricade had been deemed superfluous. It was a prison wall, naturally, and no mistaking it. But, like every prison wall, it would open itself to permitted traffic. The aristocrats came and went as they pleased. The transport and its escort of horizontal rocket-formed

Lawguards were also reflexively recognized. The wall neutralized itself to form an entry point. They passed through (Vel Thaidis unseeing in the windowless enclosure) and on to the baked plains of the Slumopolis outland.

Here, metal roads ruled fiery lines across the veldt. Lowering itself almost to the earth, its speed tuned from a hundred to a hundred and fifty staeds per hour, with a hissing of its air jets, the shining cortège streaked zenithward.

Along the verges, the herds of tamed antelines shied away, dragging each other by their ropes. Men and women, scattered in crawling groups on the crop fields beside the road, squinted briefly through their polarized lids and beneath the rims of wide shade hats. The firework-fast movements of the Law touched them with a mixture of frustrated curiosity and dread. The racing chariots of the aristocrats going slumming had a better reception. They stirred the more refreshing emotions of avarice and dislike.

After two hundred staeds, the transport shot on to a road which angled to the hest, where the land began climbing steeply. In minutes, a building appeared on the ridge above. Matt steel glinted dully, a group of block-like structures and several rod-thin towers, naked on a brown rock where nothing grew, against a white-green tension of exhausted sky. The Instation of First Hour hest-Uma.

As the transport approached, slowing as it came with a thick sizzling of depression, a sphincter pulled open the steel wall nearest to the road. Vehicle and escort dove through. The aperture squeezed itself tight.

The unalterable landscape lay once again heat-blasted in stasis, framing the empty road.

The door section of the transport had slid aside.

Beyond, an iron hall, windowless, lit by an inner sunlight, similar to that which permeated the temples, but harsh, cruel as the light of the solar disc on the plain.

Vel Thaidis saw her own hands bathed in this artificial glare. Her skin seemed hard, its metallic quality intensified into a new substance—the gleaming covering of a robot. The air itself had a brittle glow. Each movement and gesture seemed to separate and groove it, like motions made through liquid.

She got to her feet and waited for some order to be given her by her escort of Lawguards. Now once more vertical, they stretched from the transport along the hall, a colonnade.

113

But no unbreathing voice uttered. Then Vel Thaidis saw a figure, walking toward her along this copper fence.

This was the first denizen of the Slumopolis Vel Thaidis had confronted. Confront was the applicable word. A female, she glanced in no direction but one; her gaze fixed on Vel Thaidis. The features were overlaid by a strange enamel, a plaster of pallid make-up, even on the mouth. A scarlet cloth concealed hair and much of the head. The gray tunic was draped, a haphazard and ungraceful drapery, and bordered with untranslatable scientific symbols, red on a white ground. In the dry fluid of the light, blank-faced and immutable, the woman looked too much a robot to be one.

About three yards away, she came to a standstill. The white lips unseamed. The dark eyes never shifted.

"You are called Vel Thaidis, formerly Yune Hirz. Don't answer. I'm stating a fact for our records, not questioning you. Now come out, and follow me."

Vel Thaidis complied. What else?

Near the end of the hall was an escalator on which the woman stepped, and Vel Thaidis after her. The stair spilled itself down, through a tunnel of floury white, reminiscent of the woman's coated face. The woman did not turn to see what Vel Thaidis did, or if she had obeyed. Presumably obedience was inevitable.

Vel Thaidis, numbed and wrung of all prayers and all hope, felt the ache of humiliation and horror yawn again in her vitals. Her pride had disintegrated. She could no longer brick herself up in protective silence. She longed suddenly for any hint of comfort, at an hour and in a place where comfort was not to be had.

"I—" Vel Thaidis said. And fresh humiliation deluged her at her weakness, her compulsion to speak.

"You may talk if you wish," the woman said, not turning. "Expect no reply."

Vel Thaidis sank against the rail of the moving stair, weary almost beyond endurance, and effectively gagged.

At the escalator's foot, a succession of cubicles opened one from another. The woman went through, Vel Thaidis a few feet behind. She noticed gleams igniting and going out along a variety of panels, and heard the faint humming and muttering of hidden mechanisms. Eventually, the cubicles gave on a round pale room, awash with the awful light.

The woman indicated a bench.

"Sit."

114

Vel Thaidis sat. The woman went to a panel and read from it. Presently she also seated herself, in a broad plastum chair. The chair had an air of studied authority about it, as did the woman's clothing and manner. She resumed her stare into Vel Thaidis' face.

"You aristos," she said at last. Something had amused her slightly, though her mouth did not reveal it. "Even in such an extremity of loss, you look at me as if at a tiny beetle that has crawled onto your plate of candies. Such unwinking hauteur, little girl. But your hands betray you, and your stiff spine. Well. The machines report you have attained your twenty-first year and have faultless health. But then usually, you know, you aristos are healthy. A life of mild solarism, nutritious food, relaxation and unforced exercise makes for strong specimens. But I forget. No longer an aristo. For a crime unstated, you've been relieved of your title and your rights to service. Now you're a plain Zenena of the Slumopolis. *Welcome!*"

"What will happen now?" Vel Thaidis said. She was not sure why she asked.

The woman nodded and said flatly, "Let us have this straight. I'm here to tell you things, but not to answer questions. We have no leisure for such niceties. Time only for orders related and orders carried out. Dawdling could entail the failure of crops, the lowering of production—the means of existence, in other words, dashed from our hands. Here we survive by bone-tearing labor, and by luck. Your luck's run out, lady. You'd better decide on labor."

The woman paused. Vel Thaidis said nothing. The woman nodded complacently. She said, "I am Dina Sirrid. I am, you might say, the matrix mother of what you're about to become, what in Law already you have become. Zenena Thaidis. Unremember title, frills of cognomen and rank. In the Slum, you'll be free to take whatever work is available to one of your sex, physique, health and aptitude. No slum work is attractive or particularly inspiring. The criteria are simple: Will this put food in my belly? Of course, it will be doubly difficult for an aristo. Not only because you are so far good for nothing, but because it will be impossible for you to conceal what you are. Your looks, your attitude, defy camouflage. Some advice. Your safest employment would be that of a prostitute. Why? Because you'll need to know little at the start. Your customers will derive their prime delight in sleeping with a woman of the estates, a princess. They'll exhaust

115

their antagonism toward you during the pleasure act, exulting in the disgrace you will obviously experience. You may subsequently grow adept, or discover a protector with access to tech-credits. Tech-credits are, patently, the most precious commodity of the Slums. The luxury of robot service you received as your due in a palace. Ours is restricted and mostly unavailable. Only tech-credits can procure robot service or mechanical aid of any personal sort. If you have ever been slumming for enjoyment, you'll know about all that. If not, well, you'll learn, girl. The Instations are the stopover points to which vagrants are brought, or, in your case, exiles. That's tradition. The Instation's function is to direct and to place. But who listens? The Zenens who visit us want new employment in another portion of the Slum, or to exchange the urban hell for the farm hell on the outland, or they require medical attention perhaps, or have broken the Law and fear apprehension. Even they don't accept much of the advice offered them. While an aristo—" The woman made a yapping sound. It was not really a laugh, more a coda to her scorn. It was also deliberate and false. She too was deriving her pleasure from the downfall of a princess.

Vel Thaidis met her stare, burned in it, suffered it. She wondered how much longer she must control her wounded writhing, and how much longer she could. Would there be any privacy for wounds in such a spot?

"But," the woman, Dina Sirrid, remarked, "I had better mention something at this juncture. You see, dear lady, your special plight, your—fallen—condition, is very unusual. The last aristo cast into the Slum—that was many tens of years ago. And before him, a few men, but not many. I speak of those who were exiled, owing to a crime of some sort. Now and then, a prince has joined us, because the technology of his estate has failed—but of these, not one for many years. You have, you see, no kindred here. Probably you knew all this. Your education in all things, I'm sure, is complete. The ignorance which prevails in the Slums is deplorable, but you will have had your robot-tutor and your instruction machines. . . . But I wonder if you know of the single consolation the Slumopolis is able to offer to those of your kind?"

Dina Sirrid pressed the arm of the plastum chair, which opened a partition. Within the hollow thus revealed lay a black metal tube attached to a bulb of black flexite.

"All weapons are technically illegal in the Slumopolis,"

Dina Sirrid said. "But a certain number are ethically necessary, and the Law permits them. This, for example. A gas-
gun. Very easy to operate, children could use it—and have
done so. Do you wish to look at it more closely?"

"Now, I am to speak?" Vel Thaidis asked.

"Oh, I think you might. Do you wish to inspect the gun?"

"Why?"

Dina Sirrid took the weapon from its recess and held it of-
fensively, daintily, in her large hands. Her nails, long but
squarely cut across their tops, were possibly also a mark of
her authority. Vitamin deficiency in the Slums would reduce
the strength of bones, hair, teeth and nails. In this handmade
world, weak nails would snap. The nails of Dina Sirrid explained that her position provided better food, and that her
fingers were not familiar with mechanical tools, acids, excess
of aqua or farm implements. Even here, a hierarchy persisted.

"Why?" repeated Dina Sirrid, playing with the gun in a
mimicry of aristocratic refinement. "I'll tell you why. The
idea of the gun is that some Jate you might wish to end your
life with it. This is allowed. Not many of your class can face
what lies ahead of them at this stage. Most accept the gun instantly. I wonder if you will."

Vel Thaidis recoiled. She was young, and though she had
counted herself as dead, her youth told her otherwise. Her
reaction was animal, however, virtually abstract, when she
answered: "I will not."

"Won't you? The procedure is minimal. Put the tube between your lips and compress the bulb. I've seen men die
from less efficient application; still very swift. And, I'm assured, painless."

Less abstract now, stronger: "I will not."

"You say that this Jate. Next Jate you may think otherwise. But come back at any time. The gun is always here,
ready for you. It's a kindness, you understand. Our sensitivity
to your grief, your inability to bear the ways we're bred to,
what we come out of the matrix wombs anticipating. Our
*only* ways. Dirt, toil, tedium and unloveliness. *We* die young.
A hundred, a hundred and ten, these are celebrated ages
here. Not everyone reaches those. It depends how long you
can keep working, once symptoms of aging set in, around the
seventieth year. Yes, you'll note old age in the Slum. Skins
puckering and hair dropping out. The sun dries us and nothing restores what the sun steals."

"There's always a position like yours," Vel Thaidis said, shocking herself.

"Mine?" Dina Sirrid yapped twice. "It's better than some, I grant you. But you won't get where I am. There'll be too many wanting to witness your dust. What crime, by the way, did you commit to put yourself among us?"

"Am I obliged by Law to answer?"

"No. Besides, all you aristos, you always claim, according to the records, that you're innocent."

"Then I'm innocent."

Dina Sirrid widened her mouth, and yapped silently on this occasion. The white make-up sun protection—Vel Thaidis would come to see a lot of it—made the woman's teeth into dark yellow fangs, the cavity of her mouth much redder than her scarf.

"Little girl," said Dina Sirrid, "I like you. I will look forward to the hour you disintegrate. I will take vast interest in considering you, wondering when it will happen. And at the end, when you come to me to ask for the gun, I'll treat you with courtesy and gentleness, out of thanks for all the entertainment your agony will have given me."

At an Instation, one meal was awarded, without charge of credit or labor. One meal, and, at Maram, a pallet in a Maram-dormitory. Like the meal, the dormitory had no pretensions. The light was dimmed to a murky monochrome. No music murmured, there were no sleep-inducing sighs. In the Slum, tiredness replaced ritual aids. The pallets were ranked close together. A communal aqua-closet, with sketchy partitions, ran along the wall. The dormitory was deserted. The aristocrat had her privacy, and could not use it.

Hunger coupled with despair had tangled the sour salad of plants, the spongy bread, in Vel Thaidis' stomach. Needles darted through her skull and behind her eyes. She lay on the pallet and slept and woke and slept and woke. She dreamed of Ceedres Yune Thar, his failed estate lost to him, Slumopolis the only alternative, placing the gas-gun economically between his white teeth.

In the twenty-first hour, the fifth of Maram, she rose. In the washing stall of the closet, only a trickle of aqua would come. Aqua, like everything, was dispensed meanly in the Slum, for there was not enough to go around.

Later, she went to the door of the dormitory, which would not open. A round eye pulsed in the door. A voice said: "It is

118

not yet Jate return to your pallet at the first hour there will be an alarm."

Vel Thaidis returned to her pallet. She lay in the muddy dark, wishing she could shed tears, but no tears flowed. She feared she would weep instead in the presence of her enemies, the water, somehow held back as if behind a door, bursting from her irresistibly at some unforeseen moment. Then she found herself reciting snatches of songs and rhymes from her childhood, shaping the obscure mannerisms of a guessing game she had played with Velday when she was eight and he seven. Then she began to doze and wake, doze and wake once more. She dreamed she had married Ceedres; in the formal tradition of the princely houses, he was carrying her in his arms into the nuptial chamber. The dream was very real. His strength, his human warmth, the great attraction which she felt for him, were all faithfully represented. Even the scent of flowers and wine, the texture of his skin against her own. Then a terrible shouting broke out.

She woke, and the door of the Maram dormitory was shouting at her, standing open, letting in knives of incendiary sunlight.

She had been crying in her sleep. She had just the space to rinse her mouth and her cheeks before Dina Sirrid came for her.

Over the ridge where the Instation stood, the land folded down toward the Zenith. A sparse plantation of iron ferns straddled for a staed or so below, brown claws throwing a litter of shade from the sun. The metal road passed through the ferns, and on downhill into the urban development of the city.

The view, seen initially, was startling.

In width, the ring of the Slum fluctuated between five hundred to one hundred staeds. Here, under the Station of First Hour hest-Uma, the stretch of the city was broad, and seemed to go on forever into the blazing rim of the horizon. In color it was rainbow, but a rainbow that decayed. Where distance added its tinge of atmosphere, the buildings blended into a kind of emerald stew, out of which threads of smoke and vapor constantly filtered. There was indeed a haze over the whole vista. Chemical smoke from the giant chimneys of manufacts, char and steam from sectors where automation had sunk to its lowest ebb and power generated from the

119

cores of furnaces or hydrobanks, or ultimately the action of blindfold dogga harnessed to wheel and pulley.

This was the aspect of the city. It also made a noise. A growling, gushing, pushing noise, sometimes underlined by vague hummings, distant thuds, whistles, engines, alarms. At each hour the hour-clocks struck with a monotonous roaring of notes. Generally, the cacophony was subdued, choked almost, as if some huge animal were slowly and eternally strangling in a pit of colored fumes.

Progress from the Instation to the urban belt took an hour.

They traveled at a jogging unreliable pace. The expedition was made on an iron-plated high-tired sled, boxed by a rail, backless, frontless and without sides, and with a wooden slat fixed over as a canopy. The contraption was drawn by six dogga, shackled two by two. Hard-muscled yet otherwise thin to the skeleton, each sandy dog loped, pointed muzzle down and jaws slack, the hackle crest of bare leathery skin purposelessly erected. Across the lean backs whipscars were carved in a white intaglio on the beige pelt. This Jate, Dina Sirrid carried the whip, looped idly on one knee as she drove the sled. Dogga had been known to run wild or turn and rip out the throats of teammates. The whip, with its drugsacs readystrung against the steel prongs, provided a savage but efficient sedative.

Vel Thaidis was seated beside the woman driver. To the rear, uncommunicative and subtly menacing, glided a solitary Lawguard, vertical, restricting its speed to accommodate that of sled and team.

In this fashion, they moved down the metal road and into the smoke and smell and mood of the city.

Buildings formed up behind each other on either side of the way, some on one or two levels, some in piles of eight or nine stories. Here and there a chimney, a funnel or a tower poked forth, as if attempting escape into the sky. The smogs gathered, violet, cream, rust, umber and lime. Metal streets radiated in all directions. Bridges arched overhead, rattling and thrumming with unlikely improvised vehicles. There were people and beasts. A thousand momentary glances hit the sled. Vel Thaidis felt them like the fangs of dogga, the pangs of the whip, and flinched at them. Her hair had been stripped of its aristo tinting. A heavy silk of fine fair brown, it was not like the hair of the women on the streets. Their hair was frequently concealed beneath scarves against the bite of the sun. Where it showed, it seemed shriveled, like burnt grass.

120

And their bodies, scrawny, flesh like the leather crests of the dogga. There, one leaning and crippled. There—another, and another. The men who slouched or trotted along the streets were similarly seared and knotted. A crowd of men perched on a low wall, resting from some enterprise. Their bare torsos were horrible, the spines bent, the chests narrow, their shoulders blistered and scarred. Vel Thaidis could scarcely bring herself to look at them. Pity and revulsion sickened her. But they looked at her. She imagined they guessed it all. She, an exile from the great estates, tossed into their midst. A bit of meat thrown to starving felines, like those she had seen three turnings back, fighting together in a porch while the humans bellowed and laid odds on which would win. They would maul and rend her. She was a victim they must have prayed for, if ever they prayed in this place. Despite the Law and its edicts against violence, she could never be safe.

She would hardly need the gun.

She would not live long in the Slumopolis.

"Thinking of your own murder?" Dina Sirrid suddenly remarked. It was not telepathy. An aristocrat's meditation, under these circumstances, was predictable. "They won't kill you. It will be more insidious than that. Things the Law can't punish them for. Things they can prolong. Indefinitely."

The sun screamed a handspan below the apex of the sky.

No covering had been given Vel Thaidis. Her head throbbed, even beneath the wooden slat canopy of the sled. She put her palms over her eyes and sat stupefied till Dina Sirrid called to her.

"Here we are at your new home, little girl. Rejoice."

They had reached higher ground, and thus left most of the smolder behind. The residential areas of the Slum—if so they could be termed—were usually situated in this way. Ancient customs of habilitation persisted. Here and there, trees had been planted and still grew, mutated into odd shapes and shades by the environment. Vel Thaidis lifted her lids and saw two such trees, tents of limbs, with thick flags of mulberry-red hanging straight down. Between, stood a public cistern with unrefined milky aqua in it, to be gathered in jars or plastum buckets, and purified by boiling. Men and women queued there, as they did all Jate. Buildings of three, five and six stories went up round about. Washing was pegged on ledges, already dry, apparently abandoned. A streamer rose from a solitary brazen funnel a few hundred yards beyond the hespan roofs.

121

Vel Thaidis had never seen sights like these. The unreality was anesthetizing her, making her vacant and languid.

The sled had halted. Dina Sirrid locked the reins and swung onto the stone yard. She beckoned peremptorily and Vel Thaidis also swung down. The Lawguard remained stationary, behind the sled, and those queuing about the cistern averted their eyes from it nervously.

Dina Sirrid led the way into the hespa-side building and into a metal cage-lift. They were borne up the five stories at a swift, soundless rush.

"There's a cubicle to spare here," Dina Sirrid announced as the cage jerked to a stop.

They went along a narrow passage, painted at short intervals on both sides with door markings. At a space marked with the number Nentem-Nenta (one hundred twenty), Dina Sirrid touched the hidden door, which drew aside.

The vacant cubicle was large enough only to hold the pallet, when horizontal, which was currently stacked against the wall, and a pillar-slim closet. A slit of window, polarized dark as ale, looked out onto the mutated trees, the cistern, the aqua queue. The closet was chemical, judging by a faint antiseptic odor. There were no arrangements for Maram, beyond the polarization of the plastum pane, which—when fully closed—would make the room into an oven.

Dina Sirrid threw a bronze chip onto the inner ledge of the window.

"That chip proves your right to this cubicle. Don't mislay it, lady. The Law allows you three Jates, three Marams, in which to obtain employment. You will do so or the cubicle will be given to someone else. You'll think it poor, doubtless, but many live less nicely than this and would be thankful to get it. Regarding employment, I shall presently take you to a point of labor allocation. Unless you've decided to follow my earlier advice. I mean, prostitution. No? Only consider. That way you might renew old acquaintances from the estates. I'm sure they'd be glad to tip you with several tech-credits. . . . Never mind. Pick up the cubicle chip. There's a sealed pocket in your tunic. If anyone is unwise enough to rob you of the chip, or any other credit, report it at once to any Lawguard on the streets."

Dina Sirrid crossed to the chemical closet and touched open the sliding panel.

"The facilities are functional merely. In order to wash or to drink, you'll draw water from the nearest public cistern.

122

Two buckets or three jars are your Jately ration. The cistern will recognize your hand on the faucet and supply or withhold accordingly. Should you attempt to gain extra aqua from another cistern, you will inevitably be found out. The process is illegal and some fine will be imposed—indefinite loss of food credit is the normal reprisal. Drink no aqua that hasn't been boiled. Boiling must be done by hand, there are no appliances to spare for it. Bucket or jar and a brazier for boiling will be your most urgent purchases, and your most valued possessions. At your first period of employment you'll receive enough article credit to buy these items. You must tell your employer you were robbed in sector hespa-Ia. Sector hespa-Ia, you see, is the area of the Slum you're supposed to have left, in order to enter this one—sector hest-Uma. You grasp the notion, do you? You're an itinerant. The Instations try to place your sort. Perhaps it was a failed liaison that drove you from your former sector, or lack of work opportunities for your particular skill—better devise a story to fit, Zenena Thaidis."

"You've implied my identity will be discovered in any event," Vel Thaidis said.

"It will."

"Why bother, then?" Vel Thaidis listlessly turned from the polarized window. "Why not reveal the facts instantly?"

Dina Sirrid grinned, showing her yellow teeth.

"If you wish. And will you inform them of your crime, too? You'd better tell me what it is, after all."

Vel Thaidis picked up the bronze chip and dropped it into the pocket of the tunic. She said drearily: "I think you know it all. You simply want it from my lips."

"Such pretty lips. Such smooth, pretty, healthy lips."

"You mentioned employment. Please take me there."

"Oh," Dina Sirrid grinned more widely, "*don't* give me orders, madam. I'm not your robot-maid for you to offer Courteous Address."

"I'm sorry," Vel Thaidis said, without expression.

"Too easy," Dina Sirrid answered. "You still reckon me as something beneath you and it costs you nothing to apologize to me. When you see how small you've shrunk, how huge I've become, then it will cost you dear. Now. Memorize your route from this hole. You'll have to make your way back here alone."

Outside, the queue about the cistern had changed in content, but not in length. Nor had its nervous aversion changed

123

to the Lawguard behind the sled. The dogga lay snarling softly in their harness. Unattended, they had not fought each other, as if they, too, were conscious of the machine at their backs.

Reseated in the sled, Dina Sirrid removed a plastum jar from a hatch under her feet. Uncorking it, she drank.

"Will you give me some liquid?" Vel Thaidis asked.

"Will I? Yes, I think so. By Law, I'm required to tend you, this Jate."

She passed the jar, and watched Vel Thaidis intently.

Vel Thaidis automatically wiped the muzzle of the jar and tipped it in her mouth. The fluid was aqua, mixed with some pale dry alcohol.

Dina Sirrid unlocked the reins.

"Up, stench of the gods!"

The dogga rose and loped back onto the thoroughfare.

There was a sector market half a staed down from the apartment blocks. Metal sheds squatted on a flat-topped plateau. Awnings stretched between poles. Beasts were shut in transparent pens open at the top to let out their noise; ante-lines for meat or field work, dogga for carriage, cats for hunting. A gang of dull-green incs jostled in a gold-plated cage. They would be going to the J'ara mansions of the Slum, having been captured at the edge of the central desert. They were creatures of the Zenith, good for nothing but to learn weird, occasionally ghastly, tricks to intrigue princes. Vel Thaidis had seen a pet incs once, at the Yune Domm's. Its skin reminded her of hard green cactus. The slot eyes, shielded by the curving half-umbrellas of its brow ridges, the tiny 0 of the mouth and the ten-inch-long sticky filament which could extrude from it, had filled her with dismay. She had been twelve years old. The incs had looked five thousand.

Beneath the awnings, and among the sheds and pens, business transactions were going on. Barter—a pair of botched sandals for an equally botched tunic, a basket of wall-grown berries for a stoup of anteline curds brought in by a dogga wagon from the agricultural belt. There was an iron arch with a crimson jar hung from it, and a man was framed there, ladling from a barrel of poisonous-looking scummy wine. A pink fluorescent lamp on a pillar indicated a credit mart where one type of credits might be exchanged for another.

Hespa of the plateau, a public kitchen. To such a building

you brought your food credit to receive sustenance. Another public cistern stood nearby, larger than the former, with fifty faucets.

A two-story building of orange metal ran hest along the plateau. Countless arched doormouths led inside, and round them milled a turgid crowd. (There were such crowds, it seemed, grouped about every edifice, slowly moving, or waiting, queuing, for food, for drink, for work, for such pleasures as the place afforded.) This was the house of labor allocation, and fluorescents glared up on the façade, showing assorted symbols of hammer, loaf, cart, jug, basin, stylus and many more—the sigils of the trades of the Slumopolis. They also conveyed, by their nature, another message: that few in this city could read.

The throng of people parted like sand to let by the sled and its gliding Lawguard.

Inside the archway was a yard, with escalators going down from, or up to, the second story. More human groups were in the yard. A large party of men and women crouched in a circle, engaged in some curious throw game. Two or three children were earning tips of some kind by bringing in plastum cups of the scummy wine from across the market, and handing them to the players. These children were the first Vel Thaidis had seen in the Slum. The Slum aqua (even boiled) had abortive properties, she knew. The entire planet-wide city could support only so many persons. Children here were matrixed on random selection. Those mechanically elected to be parents would find a Lawguard at the door. Conducted to the medical cubicle of an Instation, the relevant generative tissue would be procured from them. Half an hour's local anesthesia and a modest bonus of credits were all that marked parenthood. The resulting offspring were the property of the Slum. They were raised carelessly and institutionally and sent out to power the city with their working capacity. They replaced the dead, nothing more. The odd natural birth was treated in the same manner. Few knew their mothers or their fathers; fewer were concerned to know.

Seeing the children, irrationally, for Vel Thaidis had not yet come to any special emotion for the very young, a passionate melancholia swept over her. Then, shame. At what she had thoughtlessly been when protected from this awfulness. Worse, that she had joined its awful ranks.

Her heart seemed to beat too sluggishly to enable her to live.

A mechanical voice called from the walls, spelling out names, next forms of work and the titles of streets and blocks where these employments were to be found. Men and women got up from several portions of the yard and went off. They displayed neither relief nor anxiety.

Dina Sirrid had seemed to linger, sadistically, allowing her charge time to take everything in, every speck and atom of the squalor. Now she tapped Vel Thaidis' arm, and pointed at one of the up escalators.

"Ride those. At the top, turn into the right-hand corridor. A panel will ask you questions. Answer with what lies or truths you will. Officially, as I told you, word has gone ahead to the human personnel of this house that you are from sector hespa-Ia, seeking new employment. Well. Go on."

A stab of panic lanced Vel Thaidis' apathy.

"You are to leave me here?"

"Yes, I'm to leave you. Pine for me?"

Now the maleficent yapping laugh was genuine and sparkling.

Vel Thaidis got off the sled and began to walk across the stone yard toward the escalator. A terrible physical insecurity had gripped her, so the ground seemed to sway and the sky rotate. But she kept on, propelled by that joyful hate at her back. When she was almost to the escalator Dina Sirrid shouted after her: "Be happy, princess!"

Vel Thaidis fancied a great wave of adrenalin burst over the yard, heads raised, nostrils dilated, dark-lidded eyes scanning. She stepped stiffly onto the escalator, not looking around. She was close to vomiting with terror. She drove her nails into the little crescent wounds she had already made in her palms. Despite her fatalistic phrases in the cubicle-apartment, her drugged sense of inescapable death, now, publicly revealed as the hunted thing in the midst of the hunters, she was ready to deny anything, to compound any falsehood.

Nobody ran after her.

Gradually, as the escalator bore her up, her fear subsided. Perhaps she had imagined the reaction in the yard. Perhaps "princess" was a term of mockery from Zenena to Zenena, a jest in the Slum, as a hideous girl might cruelly be called the beauty.

But she did not venture to glance over her shoulder.

She reached the top, moved to the right-hand corridor. Already, involuntarily, she was plucking at her tunic, making it bag over the link-belt; she was untidying her hair, which she

126

had absently combed to silk at the Instation. Already, she was altering her gait, slouching somewhat, bending somewhat. She would learn to keep her eyes down and her diction slurred. Deprivation, lack of fluid and food, the scorching sun, these would soon camouflage her looks, her textures, her loveliness. Soon, she would be as much a hag as any of them. Shrill-tongued and creeping. Her breasts would sag and her teeth rot, her hair would become burned grass.

She stumbled into the corridor, which amazed her by being empty. Some yards down it, a wall door awaited her.

Also involuntarily, Vel Thaidis started again to weep, but as the wetness of the tears dropped into her bleeding palms, suddenly she knew she must not ever cry here. You might spit in the Slumopolis, but not weep. It wasted too much moisture. Tears would be rationed, like the aqua.

As she went on toward the wall door, a panel lit itself and spoke to her.

"Give name and reason for approach."

"Thaidis," Vel Thaidis said. "I seek employment."

"You are not of sector hest-Uma?"

"I am from sector—from sector hespa-Ia."

"You have registered at the Instation for this sector?"

"Yes."

The panel went out and the door slid aside.

A small room appeared in which two women sat facing her across a table. Tablets of paper were laid out and styluses. A blue metal gadget rested between them. No other machinery was evident. The women themselves wore orange scarves and the same inexpert, humanly achieved drapery Dina Sirrid had affected.

"Zenena, I have your record here." One indicated the blue gadget. "You wish employment in this sector. Tell us why you left hespa-Ia."

Vel Thaidis lowered her head. In her skull she heard the tones of Dina Sirrid.

"A failed liaison."

"Oh," the woman chuckled, "it must have been a good one, before it failed. You look well-fed and healthy. The record from the Instation agrees. Did he have access to tech-credits, your lover?"

"Yes."

"Then you're a fool to have left him. You know your application for labor will come second to any application from a native of this sector. What can you do?"

127

Vel Thaidis felt the room tilt. *What can I do?*

The woman scribbled irritably with a stylus, providing a clue.

"I can write," Vel Thaidis whispered. Caution seized her, making her tremble. "A little."

The second woman spoke.

"Come here, then, and write down what I say to you."

Vel Thaidis went to the table. She took up the stylus and wrote, as the woman recited to her: "Was there ever such a stupid mindless slut as I, to leave a tech-credited man. I should be whipped and put onto the Zenith to fry. Or maybe he slung me out because he was bored with my silly face."

Her hand shook and left damp marks of sweat and blood. But consciously she misformed the letters, misspelled a number of the words. The dictated insults barely registered.

The women pored over the result of the test. They laughed and made much of the errors, repeating over and over that *little* was the proper description of her skills. They alluded to every mistake several times, all but two. These they consistently missed, obviously words they also were unable to spell.

Vel Thaidis remained immobile, and at last, the entertainment finished.

"We have your request and will pass it into the machine. If you've tried to mislead us—if you've committed a criminal act in your previous sector—rest assured the Lawguards will pursue you, even here. To change sectors is no deterrent to the Law. Now. Go wait in the yard. Your name will be called in the normal way if, and when, you can be placed."

Vel Thaidis understood she was dismissed, but as she turned to retreat, the second woman said, "Have you thought of doing what you did before? Whoring, I mean."

Vel Thaidis could take no refuge in silence, for the Slum demanded vocal affirmation through all its strata of wretchedness.

"I won't do that."

"Oh, you won't, will you not? You might be glad in a Maram or two. I see the Instation provided you with a cubicle. You're lucky. But you only keep it three Jates without payment."

"Yes."

"Out, then. Wait in the yard."

Vel Thaidis went out and through the corridor. She found a descending excalator and rode on it to ground level. By a square column she hesitated, afraid to reenter the yard after

128

Dina Sirrid's shout. But no alteration seemed to have over-taken the crowd there. The throw game was continuing. The other groups sprawled or conversed or plodded about. No party had been established, apparently, to snatch her on her return. The dogga sled and the Lawguard were gone.

Presently, the voice called from the walls again, giving names and areas of work, and certain people went away in response, as they had before.

Vel Thaidis sat by the pillar. Sick and spent, her hands loose on the dusty stone, bound in the heat as if in a scalding bandage, she seemed to metamorphose and to die.

*So I shall die. Let me die. I am glad to die.*

She thought of the proffered gun and the surge of survival within her, and felt no surge any longer.

The wine was still coming in, and boiled aqua; and later some food was brought from the kitchen on the hespan side of the market.

Now and then, the voice called names and places.

*If it calls for me, how can I discover the street?*

But she did not really believe it would call for her.

Every hour clocks all over the Slum clanged and roared simultaneously.

Eighth hour of Jate. Twelfth. Fourteenth.

Was she asleep or awake? Alive or dead?

Was she Vel Thaidis Yune Hirz? Had she ever been?

Abruptly she knew what the throw game in the circle en-tailed. They had prized some small insects from the cracks between the paving of the yard, and were throwing shards of pottery or rock to try to hit them as they scurried, betting on which would be struck, and whether killed or only maimed.

The wanton viciousness was a predictable product of the vicious treatment fate had meted out to the Zenens of the Slum.

Vel Thaidis shut her outer lids.

At once Ceedres Yune Thar stood two hundred feet above her, and mountains flew from his hands to smash her spine.

Not a mountain, but a shard, flung lightly in the sixteenth hour, caught her shoulder and roused her.

A man was grinning at her from the insect-game circle. He was like all the rest of the men, burned-looking, unattractive, ragged, dirty, thin as sticks. Raw stripes showed on his naked arms—memento of a recent whipping, the legal penalty for minor theft.

129

"Zenena!" he cried, as her eyes opened. "Go and get me some wine."

She stared at him blankly. Her mouth was parched, and no speech would come, even if she had any prepared.

"I can't go," the man assured her. "These next throws are mine, and I'm winning." Then he pushed out of the circle and came over and stood above her as Ceedres had. "Stinking gods," he said, "you're nice as a J'ara girl. Here's a credit for the wine," he spun it, a tiny tag of red plastum, into her lap. "Take a sip yourself, if you like."

It was like another dream, for truly he did not seem real to her. Once more he misinterpreted her quiet.

"I'll listen out for you, if it calls you. Though it's nearly Maram; there won't be many calls now. What name?"

Perhaps the voice had called her while she slept.

"Thaidis," she said.

She looked at the red tag, and at his skinny blistered legs. Obviously he would not go until she obeyed him. She wondered if he had been present when Dina Sirrid shouted "Princess!" And if he meant to hurt her.

Then he leaned down and yanked her to her feet, almost pulling her arm from its socket. Impatient, he scolded: "Pretty but slow-witted, eh? Can you remember? The wine pitcher across the market?"

"All right," she said.

She recalled she must slouch and lean as she went.

There were fewer people about on the plateau. Many of the awnings were being dismantled and the sheds closed with unmechanical bolts and cage structures of steel. The pens of beasts were vacant. Of course, the man had said it was almost Maram. Areas such as this market would not keep J'ará. She crossed over and went to the iron arch from which the jar-symbol hung. The man with the barrel was still there. He grabbed the tag from her without inquiry, ladled the wine into a plastum cup, and thrust the cup, slopping its mauve scum, into her hand.

The drink, disgusting as it appeared, caused her parched throat almost to close with its thirst. Ignoring the film and the shade of the wine, she swallowed a mouthful. Then had to fight to retain it, as it gnawed into her empty stomach. After a moment, the nausea faded, and she was stronger. She swallowed another mouthful, then bore the cup back to the yard of the house of labor allocation.

The man was already throwing his shards. Each throw was

130

a killing hit. Curses went up, and tags were thrust into the man's hand. He turned away, brown teeth still showing, saw Vel Thaidis and ran over to grab the cup and drain it.

"I thought you might have stolen my wine tag," said the man. "I was thinking of going for a Lawguard. I yet might. You drank half my wine."

"You told me I could drink," she said.

"Sip, I said. A sip."

"It's vile."

"It's all there is. Was it better in your sector, then?"

"You know I come from another sector?"

"Oh yes. No Jate girls that look like you in hest-Uma. I'd have spotted them. Got to know them."

The wine fire was going out inside her.

She had been trapped into the company of this man, through fright and confusion.

"Did it call my name?" she asked, not meeting his eyes.

"No. No work this Jate. Maybe next Jate."

"Thank you," Vel Thaidis said. She turned to walk away, and the appalling blistered hand she had been dreading fastened on her wrist.

"Where are you off to?"

She faltered on the words *cubicle, apartment, home*. She could not even recollect the way.

"I've got a lot of credits," the man said. "Let's share a J'ara, you and I. I'll buy you food—you haven't a credit to spit on, I think. Yes? And then you might come to like me."

"I'm not a prostitute," Vel Thaidis said. Absurdly, she was angry; in the midst of fear and uncertainty, fury made her glare at him.

"You look like one," said the man. "You can always tell a whore by her looks. A haughty J'ara girl, that the aristos go with."

"If that were the case, I wouldn't be here, seeking common labor."

He smiled rather foolishly.

"I heard what Dirri yelled after you."

"Dirri. . . ."

"Dina Sirrid, the old Instation doggabitch. She said 'Princess.' which means you had a lover who had techs, or you had them—everyone knows that. So I suppose you won't sleep with me for the fee of a meal."

"Release my wrist," Vel Thaidis said.

"Go to hell then," the man said. "Fall in the jet-black land."

131

Conjured by these terms, the upper room of the Thar border temple manifested itself in her brain. The black air, the white flame, and Ceedres' face, drawn by that flame.

Then she was lying on the ground, and the man was kneeling by her, sadly stroking her forehead. He stank faintly, as the whole Slum did, of chemicals, sweat and live cooked flesh. But his eyes were astonished under their polarizing lids, and the hand was surprisingly gentle.

"I didn't mean it, girl," he said. "I said fall, and you fell."

"Leave me alone," she said.

"No," he said. "I want to give you a meal. Not for a fee. Just—I'll just give it you. I can't force you, girl. You'd tell the Law, wouldn't you? I've had one whipping this tenjate. No more, I thank you."

"Why?" Vel Thaidis said. She had been taught an important fact. No human aided another without a reason.

"Because I'd like to watch you eat," the man said, strangely. "I'd like to watch you, that's all."

Weakly, because she was denied tears, she laughed.

He bought another cup of wine and made her drink half of it. It gave her the vitality to climb up a long street with him, out of the smolderings of the lower city, to a building of many-colored brick. It was a J'ara eating house, gaudy but rough, for the patrons were natives, not aristos. There were no windows. Inside it was a hot somber box lit by irregular batches of anteline tallow candles that burned from the ceiling in a sour greenish drizzle.

There was no choice of menu, unless you were in credits and could afford a steak. The man ordered steak, fruits, and bloodale, another of the potent fermentations of the Slum. His name was Sherner. He had worked in a series of manufacts, tanning leather, molding buckets, preparing chemical substances for the creation of aqua, and at a plastum still. This last job had terminated when his blisters from the always splashing white-hot plasta had forced him into a medical cubicle of the Instation. Out of work, he had foolishly stolen meat from a kitchen. The Lawguard came for him before he had done digesting it. The resultant fifteen lashes had laid him up again. He was still waiting for work, but the insect-killing game had won him enough credits to live gratis for three or four Jates and Marams.

All this information he awarded Vel Thaidis, first as they toiled up the hill, and next as they sat on a bench under the

132

greengage drizzle of candlelight. Vel Thaidis listened. His voice became the anchor she had needed. His voice, riddled by the coarsenesses and slovenly accent of the Slumopolis, erected a screen against chaos.

When the food came, she ate slowly and not very much, for her weariness swept over her, and she drifted asleep, her shoulders on the grimy wall, beyond abashment, the lullaby of Sherner's voice in her ears.

She woke when the clocks of the Slum screamed the nineteenth hour, the third of Maram.

"There, she's awake," said Sherner, and put the wooden beaker of bloodale to her lips. She drank the alcoholic gravy and coughed, and drank again.

They were no longer alone.

Vel Thaidis protested to herself with horror that anything might have happened, anyone might have arrived. A gang of Sherner's less gentle cronies, enemies of all sorts. Fortunately, the newcomer was solitary, and female, though she had, undeniably, an enemy's countenance. Startlingly attractive, narrow, sly, uncommunicative. The eyes slanted slightly at their outer corners, and the lids were painted with gold. The mouth was red and full, and the teeth were white. Nor was her hair the withered grass general in the Slum, but profuse, though dyed a hard raw yellow. The girl—she was about seventeen or eighteen, maybe younger, for here it was difficult to be sure of age—wore neither the faked drapery of officialdom nor the soulless tunic of the herd. Instead, she had a dress of golden tracery. She did not smell of manufacts or dirt, either, but of some floral scent. Her nails were each an inch long, and each had a tiny picture enameled on it, miniature flowers, minuscule cats, tinier chariots. There was no doubt as to what she must be—a girl from the J'ara mansions. Improperly awake though she was, Vel Thaidis looked up and beyond her, and sighed with a bizarre and desolate jealousy. For, standing a few feet from the J'ara girl was her attendant—a humanoid, aesthetically feminized robot.

"You see," said Sherner, "I have friends who move in exalted circles. Here is Tilaia, and, as you note, she has access to tech-credits. Look at the robot woman, Thaidis. Isn't it fine? And it will do whatever Taia says it must."

Tilaia's face realigned itself. The steely watch she had been keeping on Vel Thaidis was put aside. Majestically, she smiled.

133

"Sherner sent me a message. It cost him ten tags. He must think a lot of you, Thaidis."

Stupidly, Vel Thaidis said, "How would you send a message?"

Sherner grunted. "By public runner—how else? One drinks here."

"Don't you want to know why Sherner contacted me?" Tilaia the J'ara girl said, arching her gilded brows. She played the aristocrat as only a Slumdweller could, to perfection, and a fraction beyond it.

"Thaidis guesses," said Sherner. "She's so pretty. She guesses."

"Sherner," said Tilaia, "trusts that I can find employment for you in the J'ara mansions. He assumes that in your gratitude, you will then support him from your tips and possible service credits. As to how he and I come to know each other, we are two of the few natural births, unlike twins—how unalike you perceive. But we grew in the same childhouse. It gives him some claim on me, I suppose, though not all the claims he wishes. I won't keep him myself, you see. You can, if you're sufficiently brainless."

"Then you'll find her work?" Sherner demanded.

"Perhaps," said Tilaia. She examined the picture on one of her nails.

Vel Thaidis struggled to collect herself.

"I have said I will not—"

"Won't lie down with men. I know. He told me. There are other employments in the mansions. You can wait on tables, if you desire. But the women who do it must be lovely. Sherner says you are. He's a man, I hear. He should know. Certainly, you're rather better than most of the crones in hest-Uma sector."

"Oh, Taia," said Sherner. "My sibling has a tongue which bites sharper than her teeth. Take no notice."

Tilaia yawned. All about, the people in the eating house gazed at her, malevolently envious and intrigued. Presumably, the Law and the robot servant made it secure for her to go abroad to such a rendezvous as this. The high heels of her sandals chimed as they brushed the floor, as Vel Thaidis' sandals had done on the palace floors of Hirz.

"This revolting food shop is boring me," said Tilaia. "Does Thaidis say yes or no."

"Why," Vel Thaidis said softly, "would you help me?"

Tilaia's features, features of an enemy, sly and beautiful,

closed upon themselves as certain blooms of the veldt closed upon moisture.

"If my house likes you, I will receive a bonus. If you're grateful, I might be able to exact some errands, some support from you later on. One never knows where an accomplice may be of aid."

Vel Thaidis glanced aside from the hauteur of the enemy.

It was pointless to debate. There seemed no other door but this.

"Next Maram," the girl said, "at the stroke of the seventeenth hour, come to the Basin, to Mansion Seta, the Black and Gold. I, or someone, will greet you and conduct you inside. Or, sit in the labor accommodation yard and listen to the voice and lose your apartment."

"Aristos," Vel Thaidis said. She had to drink a mouthful of bloodale before she could conclude the sentence. "Do aristos come to your mansion?"

"Of course," Tilaia said. "How else do you think I got my maid, there? The mansions exist to please the aristos, or those who have their credits. The Yune Meks are our current patrons. Are you nervous of the aristos? Yours will be kitchen tasks, you'll hardly see them. And even they must abide by the Law."

Yune Mek was a family Vel Thaidis had never had connection with. Even if a Domm or Ond or Chure were to enter the mansion, he would ignore her, possibly not actually recognize her. Or she might hide herself, behind a wall, behind paint and behind demeanor. Or yet—it stole over her that this venue, which could afford her the most trepidation and danger, also enticed. One Maram, might Velday come into the Black and Gold mansion? It was not one of the J'ara houses he had ever mentioned, but then he had mentioned to her little enough of the city or what he did there.

To see him, in the distance. To be recognized after all? She might be able, now, to make him accept the truth—

Perhaps they might meet often.

Perhaps.

"Maram, the seventeenth hour," Tilaia said sharply. "Or else don't trouble yourself."

Vel Thaidis was hallucinating, half asleep, Velday holding her hand. *I know it was a lie, my sister. We'll prove it to them. I will get you free of this. Hirz will be yours again, and Ceedres will pay the price of his crime.*

"Come," said Velday, in Sherner's Slum voice.

135

Vel Thaidis raised her lids. The green lights were sinking, dim, these were the last hours of Maram, and Tilaia had gone away. Drunkenly, Sherner murmured of a pallet in a shed.

"No," she said.

"You are a doggabitch," he informed her. "I'd only look at you."

"No."

"Maybe another time," he mumbled incongruously. He lowered his head among the beakers of ale and snored.

Outside the windowless restaurant, the eternal sunlight gouged her eyes.

Smokes and steams still flooded up from the chimneys of the lower city, but not many people were abroad, and most of these were drunk or drugged. Here and there, persons lay huddled at some angle of a building, thick cloth set up haphazardly tent-wise for a Maram chamber.

Across the top of the street, a single copper Lawguard passed, patroling vertically on its jets, sinister and inimical.

Vel Thaidis could not begin to assemble the route she should take to regain her apartment cubicle. She could reconstitute only the way to the plateau market. So she went back there, walking lamely and exhaustedly, and reaching the spot, seated herself in one of the deep-porched entries of the locked kitchen. Pulling a fold of her tunic over her eyes, huddled in the static, inadequate shade, she slept. No one intruded on her. Others slept as she did. The Lawguards prowled. The market place was otherwise deserted, save for rustling dusts and scraps of paper and plastum cups kicked by localized atmospheric winds.

But as the first hour of Jate sounded, one of the ubiquitous queues began to form at the public cistern. A couple of dogga sleds rattled across the plateau, awnings slapped and sheds were unbolted.

Vel Thaidis was conscious before her own shelter was despoiled. She rose and stared at the useless cistern whose fluid she had no means to boil. Her pride had prevented her from remaining with Sherner; Sherner who was food and drink, Sherner who demonstrated sympathy, for whatever selfish motive.

With a toiling heart and a mouth dry as the blown sand she trod, Vel Thaidus went to the arches of the house of labor allocation, and waited there for them to be unsealed and for the voice to commence in the yard.

All Jate, she waited in the yard.

People came and went. Sherner was not among them.

Rain flakes floated down in the twelfth hour, tinted strange colors from the smokes of the city.

Her mouth became a brazen cup, her throat a cistern of dust. Her belly clenched and unclenched like a fist.

The voice spat many names into the court, and none of them was hers.

At the sixteenth hour she got up. Dizzy with fatigue and dehydration, past scruple, she approached a woman and asked her: "Which way to this sector's J'ara mansions?"

"Outward, and hespa," the woman grated. "And may the gods frizzle you before you get there."

The smoke of the city seemed to have penetrated Vel Thaidis' skull, and she staggered through it, and here and there she asked the way. On a narrow street, she asked a man, who struck her casually across the head. She fell back against a wall. Then there was a sound she vaguely recognized. Two copper pillars went by on their jets of air.

"Pardon me," the man said. He took her in his arms and stroked her hair and she had no strength to resist. "Don't tell them I struck you."

"No," she said. "No."

The man gave her a drink of boiled aqua from a flask on his belt.

Everything came suddenly clear, focused and exact. So clear, so exact, she almost retreated. Then the man shouted: "Here's Sherner."

"I've been chasing after you for three staeds or more," Sherner grumbled, panting, seizing her arm. "Why didn't you wait for me? I'd have guided you, you anteline of a girl."

She was glad to see him, glad he had followed to enmesh her in Tilaia's weird promise. The focus of the aqua seeped away.

When Sherner picked her up in his arms, she was dully surprised at such strength from the stick-like muscles. She did not struggle and her hair brushed the ground.

*I lost home and rank,* she thought, *kin and kind. All security, all rights to security. My silence I had to give away. Now I have lost even pride,* she thought. *I am finally one with the Slumopolis.*

But Sherner was carrying her to Mansion Seta. Velday might come, a companion of the Yune Meks, having been

137

told by them: Your sister is here. How many J'aras would pass before Velday came, and clutched her to him, and cursed Ceedres, and vowed she should be vindicated?

She was feverish and began to be afraid she would say aloud these dreams, and give away beyond doubt her aristocratic origins.

"Sherner," she gasped, "how far is it?"

"We're there," Sherner said.

Somewhere, time had evaded her on their route. Minutes or more had elapsed, streets and byways with them. A peculiar thing had happened to the sky, to the odor and the noise of the city.

"Let me stand," she said.

"Oh you," he said. "Always giving orders, like a lady from a palace. Your tech lover learned you such ways, I suppose?"

But he swung her to her feet, and supported her, amused at her weakness, her reliance on him.

They were high up again, the Slum a lake of jewel-like mists below, its pollution made, as always, glamorous by distance. And ahead there was another lake, a sheet of true fluid, though not the aqua of the canals, not the green of the wonderful lake at Hirz. This lake was like red wine. It filled a huge basin stretching for two staeds or more, and on all sides there piled extraordinary edifices, built in cones, in cubes, in steps, in craning spikes and needle towers, sheer-walled or overhung by decoration. A hundred stages and balconies stretched out over the crimson liquid, supported by columns and pylons, carved, incredible and festooned with fluorescent lights of rose and tourmaline, purple and iron-blue. In turn, these glows ribboned in the lake, which all the while gently rippled and simmered. The air did not smell of chemicals but of perfumes, and there was a confused guttural of music on it. An ultimate strangeness beyond scent and noise, beyond the appearance of Basin or buildings, overlay the scene. A giant parasol, over a staed in diameter, of polarized flexiteglass tinted with a deep olive tone and mounted on pillars of bronze, roofed in the Basin and all its mansions. The grimace of eternal day was transmuted to a walnut-green blush which thickened the atmosphere, blurred the edges of metal, plastum, wood and stone alike; tinged everything, skin or hair, soothed, disoriented, inebriated.

"There's beauty," Sherner remarked, indicating the parasol.

"Is it aqua in the Basin?" Vel Thaidis inquired. Her awareness had crazily centered on this. Its very unnaturalness

138

seemed to mark a period, a gateway. As if for sure, beyond this point, her fate could be changed.

"Not aqua. Plasta, kept blood-heat by a furnace beneath to prevent its solidifying." Ego burnished by his wisdom, Sherner added: "There is nothing better in hespa-Ia, I'd guess? Those J'ara mansions there had nothing like these."

Vel Thaidis did not know if this were so or not.

The winy plasta lake, the tiny suns of the lights, all in the soup of the parasol shade, set her eyes swimming. Then the roar of the Slum clocks, hoarse and pitiless, drowned the music and invaded her trance. The seventeenth hour: Maram.

Tilaia's words: "At the stroke . . . or else don't trouble."

In sudden alarm, Vel Thaidis cried: "I shall be too late!"

"Not quite. We're at the door."

# Part Two

Casrus Klarn entered the Subterior of the Klave by means of a slow-flying transport. The entranceway, a smooth and unpretentious hole, led into a tunnel and thence upward. For the Subterior was lower than the princely palaces in personality alone. In location it lay mostly above the Residencia's thick sky-ceiling of rock, and thereby closer to the frozen surface of the planet. Only at its edges, far beyond those of the Residencia, did the Subterine complex fold down into abysms of the world, to the deepest mines, the most obscure shafts, pipes and channels of itself.

Traveling, there was at first no light. The transport glided through a bath of ink. But this was hardly novel to Casrus. He had come so many times, and by so many similar routes, into this place. Nevertheless, the symbol of the dark was not entirely lost on him. When he had come here before, he had had the option of returning.

Presently, lights tore down the black, mechanized yet uncosmetic. (The makeshift fires the Subterines themselves were forced to ignite, lacking mechanical illumination or heat through great stretches of their warren, offered a strange by-product of color and flamboyance—perhaps resembling the gaudy dyes they daubed upon their walls.) The transport halted and its side pleated open. Clearly, Casrus was to leave, having arrived at his destination.

The bitter cold struck him like a series of well-aimed blows. But again, he was prepared, had anticipated nothing else.

Before him lowered a gray, featureless mass of building, part freely contrived, part hewn from the rock at its back. The savage lights hovered forty feet up in the air in front of it. As Casrus started to walk forward, a section of the wall hissed back. It was a center of mechanized management, in his case, of induction. Here he would be given clothing suitable to his new life, instructions, warnings, also suitable. Within the door, he found he had stepped straight onto a moving ramp which bore him farther inward. The atmosphere was warmer, and smelled of certain of the ubiquitous Subterine smells: disinfected oxygen, electricity, darkness, freezing, and insulating materials of all types. Also of despair? Maybe not, for Casrus had not yet despaired.

Not that his attitude was based on any sort of blind optimism. That a future appeal to the computers might be available was a slight chance, and he did not depend on it. Nor did he expect miracles, gods leaping forth from the machinery to save him. Rather, he was dependent upon himself. As ever. And, as ever, he did not feel he would necessarily fail himself. Indeed, he trusted himself to do as well here as he might, given the impoverished means at his disposal.

Altogether the mood of dread that had assailed him at Klarn, when he had gone to set in order the affairs of his house, had passed. First into swift shock, not softened by preknowledge, then into black anger, a desire to rail against the shortcomings of so-called justice—equally swift and passing, and of course, not put into practice. He had been, as usual, calm when he went from Klarn, though a different calm, obviously, devoid of most of its grounding. Then, a new structure had arisen in his mind to support him.

Almost all was lost to him, but not everything. While he lived, he could strive. Now on his hands and knees, where before it had been a sweeping act, entailing robots and technology, but still there would be things for him to do. It was pointless to bemoan past wealth, and easier for him than for most not to bemoan it, since he had only thought of it in terms of its use to others. Now *he* must be used instead, must give himself, since he was all he had to give. Not from altruism, for it had never been that, but from the awareness that the Klave was a balance out of true, and a disturbance in him at the sight of human adversity, those things he invested together with the name: my guilt.

And he need feel no guilt at last. He could work in liberation. He had become one with the Subterior.

The moving ramp ran into a brightly lit room, saline white as the lights outside. Machinery in the walls ticked and whined, investigating him, finding him sound; the physique of the athlete, the tutored intellect and skilled brain of a prince.

No human being inhabited the building or at least, none appeared.

From a chute, clothing jumped out into the chamber, the dress of the Subterior, but not yet dyed, nor ragged as a Subterine's clothes invariably became, cold rotting the fibers of cloth, rough edges, fights, knives tearing it, live fires scorching. A thousand severe types of labor, the mines, the installations, adding their damages. Replacement clothes meant saving credit chips or suitable barter. Rags were the mode.

Casrus dressed himself. Undergarments of insulated weave, several layers of shirts and breeches, bundle of top garments, linings, a long coat with wide sleeves to be tied close at the wrists, insulated thin gloves, thicker top-mittens. Footgear of plastomil, soles three inches thick, wadded with insulated foam. An outer shawled half-cloak, equipped with head wrapping. Shields for the ears hanging ready from a pin, shields for nostrils and mouth, curved visor to cover and protect the face. There was also a knife, for cutting the wedge-shaped blocks of compressed food, for slashing down icicles, for defense, and for attack, too, though this was against the Law. No gun was carried in the Subterior. (Nor, for that matter, in the Residencia, where guns were the property of the arenas and stadiums, for sport only, shooting at targets, or clockwork animals fashioned from the computerized memory banks.) The color of the new clothes was umber, patchily diluted to white along the insulated areas. Subterines would dye their clothes, even their rags. The alleys abounded with raddled scarlet, yellow and green figures, as they abounded with spitting crimson fires, and leaning hovels and apertures in rock streaked and bannered in a score of shades. He knew it well. It was his second home. Except that, in the past, he had not needed such clothes, such weapons,

141

such fires or such a hovel, as now he would need them. Before, plain velvet, equipped with its own heating apparatus as small as a chip. Before, another world to go back to, to rest in.

Yet of everything, in that moment, he regretted only those he had rescued, now condemned to flounder, those Subterines who had shared his house. He understood he had the strength to persevere. But had they, having been taken from this pit, the strength to return? What of Temal?

A panel buzzed. It fed into his palm the polished iron tab he recognized as the key to, and proof of ownership of an apartment, or such apartments as the Subterior afforded. The panel spoke.

"Casrus, formerly prince of Klarn. You know the way things are done here. You are fortunate in that. Your accommodation is off main thoroughfare Aita, near to the entry to the Aita mine, the passage termed Aita Slink. Go there, and someone will come to inform you of employment. You are, of course, known in the Subterior. You should be wary. Respond."

"I'll be wary," Casrus said. "And I have the tab."

"You have transgressed the Law," said the machine. "But, despite that, the Law here will take your part if you are wronged. You recall the Stare-Eyes? Respond."

"I recall them."

"Go then. The door will open now."

The Aita mine lay over and around deposits of copper, calvium and fosscoal, which latter the Subterines grubbed for their own furnaces. Other minerals, fuels and gases went to power the life-supporting mechanisms of the Residencia. Near to Aita, across the main thoroughfare, a vaporine funnel arose, sheer black steel, ending in a conducting box against the overhang of rock above. Icicles formed at intervals on the edge of the box, during periods of inertia, when the gas rose sluggishly from the vents beneath. Then, when the process quickened and heat came from the box, the icicles snapped off and clattered dangerously on the street, or such street as it was. The heat, however, was approved of, and Aita was a popular byway, and crammed with cells of living, some of piled rocks, some of mine sludge hardened by cold, some scarcely bigger than each individual occupant. On intermittent tall poles of white metal, trellised with ice, the Stare-Eyes duly stared, as they did in most quarters of the

Subterior. Each a milky sphere, three or four inches in diameter, motionless, all-seeing, only aggression committed off the street escaped them, and then not always. Aita Street itself was a strip of smoother stone between tumbles of rough stone, where the accommodations huddled like groups of atrocious warts, lit in pockets by fires. Aita Slink was one of those indigenous alleys, mostly unlit, prolonged and twisting, hemmed in by grotesque walls or by rock face, around two feet in width. Now and then, advancement was limited to the sideways motion.

Casrus' new home lay about two-thirds of the way along the alley, close to the mine, and so received some of the light from the lamps above the mine entrances. A stone stair, rough and much trodden, led to a terrace that overhung the passage below, and supported two or three bulges with rents in them—dwellings. Thus far, Casrus had gone unchallenged, for it was Maram, and not many persons were abroad. Nor did anyone approach now.

In the way of mechanically allotted tenure, the third hovel was ludicrously barred by an iron mesh, only to be penetrated with the suitable tab. Casrus operated the tab, the mesh drew itself aside, and Casrus entered.

The room balanced atop the Slink was about seven feet by five, with a variable ceiling, in spots a few inches from Casrus' skull. The walls, thickly plastered with insulating material, were daubed vermilion and pale amber, apparent even in the dark, and on one there was a crude drawing of a catlike animal pouncing, presumably remembered from a Fabulism, for books of any kind were unknown outside the Residencia. An insulated pallet rested upright in the wall, with a stash of coverings, mainly in tatters. There was a scoop in the floor for making fire; black from previous coals. Beyond the door screen of thin plastomil, a roofless latrine let down into the usual hygienic, naturally available sink of ice. Ice fringed the walls of the latrine also, and pointed in spikes from the roofless opening.

Casrus had seen many such apartments. He had tried to restore and to replenish them. But there was little to be done, for what a robot would install, want could barter or let fall into decay.

There were, of course, no coals left. Despite his garments, Casrus had remained keenly aware of the cold. Not a cold which necessarily killed, but which produced physical torpor and mental depression, a cold to be resisted. After a glance,

143

unsurprised, at the room, Casrus turned to leave. Aita had deposits of fosscoal, theoretically free to all who could dislodge them.

But before he reached the open door, another figure darkened and filled it, coming in.

With the gray twilight of the mine lamps behind him, the figure was momentarily indiscernible, revealing itself only as male and tall, tall as Casrus which, for the undernourished Subterines was stature indeed. Then he moved a fraction and was minimally described. An Upperling, not in rags, nor affecting the raucous colors of the unprivileged; instead, unrefined nuggets of copper and silver fringed his shawl-cloak. One ear was pierced, and from it depended a bright yellow credit chip on a ring of stainless steel, the message obvious: *I am well-off and can spare this chip for ornament which the rest of you would need for clothing, food, and drink.* The face itself was thickly bearded, for warmth rather than for fashion, and amid and above this sable forest, a mean mouth and narrow teeth, a bony flattened nose, broken and healed long ago, eyes of a pale brown like mud mixed with water. Upperlings were not loved, by reason of their success, yet some earned their unlove more thoroughly than others. This was a man Casrus had not come on before in his excursions to the Subterior, yet the type he knew—the needlessly callous chip earring, the smell of something that feeds on its own kind. A smell strangely missing from the Residencia, which should have reeked of it, as if, disclaiming the Subterines as their own kind, they had made it so.

"Welcome, mighty prince," said the Upperling. "Welcome, heir of Klarn, famous Casrus, aristo and master."

It was the sort of greeting Casrus looked for from any of them. He said nothing, merely waited.

The Upperling bowed, hands over face, arcane worship for a god, learned from some machine of memory.

"Let me introduce my humble groveling self," said the Upperling. "I am Dorte. I have charge of three gangs of men, strong men, who can work planet-surface. You must be strong for that. I know. I did it, five years. Then I was blessed by the clever machineries. They let me pick men suitable for the work. The ration of food is better for surface workers. I was able to get recompense from the ones who begged to be chosen. Now I'm where I am. But you, you're where you are. Think you're strong enough to work surface, your elegance?"

144

"If," said Casrus quietly, "the induction computer had registered that I was not, then you'd hardly be here."

"Ah, true. Perceptive of you, your elegance. However, you
know, I never trust a machine to think a thing all the way
through. How should I? Did you hear, there's another piece
to the Klave? I mean, apart from the Subterior? A lovely location, by all accounts, full of warmth and light and entertainment. And princes live there. They live in palaces. They
eat sweets and lie on silk and fight simply for pleasure.
Would you believe it? It's so. And that being the case, and
the machines keeping it the case, us here, them there, you'll
comprehend, your elegance, why I don't trust a machine always to be right."

Casrus was an aristocrat, looked one, and knew he did,
and he did not attempt to alter his inbred demeanor. That it
would provoke, that it could enrage, he grasped perfectly.
That he made no effort to avoid such provocation and such
rage was not arrogance, but an understanding of himself, and
others. He did not scorn to hide, but to hide would be useless—still, they would find him out. It had to be. The soonest
faced, the soonest done with.

"Well," said Dorte the Upperling. "Too proud to talk to
me, eh?"

"What would you wish to discuss?"

Obviously, it sounded of sarcasm, even in Casrus' level
quiet voice. But Dorte did not react, or seemed not to.

"Nothing, now. You're to come out with me. I've my own
ways of testing your mettle, if you're worth taking on my
gangs. After all, we wouldn't want the work on the surface
skimped by a weakling. The princes might suffer. Couldn't
have that."

Outside, beyond Aita, a bell was faintly clanking. Four
bells were rung from the various mechanical centers of the
Subterior, to mark the first and mid hours of both Jate and
Maram.

Casrus reckoned on probable trouble in the alley. When
none came, he knew it was just trouble deferred.

Dorte led the erstwhile prince, now and then making courteous remarks, like a guide. Those things which the Upperling
indicated—a mechanical transport rail high overhead, torches
ablaze at intervals along slim uneven streets and main con-
courses, vaporine towers, the distant bulk of a center, cold-
gleaming its metal—all these things or their twins, Casrus had
seen often. They walked for perhaps half an hour after the

145

mid-Maram bell, Dorte taking them via deserted byways, or crossing through thin crowds in open spaces, here and there stepping over those pathetics forced, by loss of their dwelling, to curl together on the bare rock to sleep, potential prey of any who passed. At one point, a knot of three or four little girls sleeping, crammed into a crevice, having tried to warm themselves at a low torch there, drew Casrus' attention. Few children were born in the Subterior, and mostly of computerized selection, a sought-after function for the parents, since it entailed a brief stay at a center with all its facilities. The occasional natural birth generally died, uncared for by the machines which nursed only programmed infants into their sixth year. After the sixth year, they were sent to labor in any event, and again, frequently perished, from the industry itself or the hardship of their world. On the whole, a percentage of forty survived each hundred, more than sufficient to power the Subterior.

The little girls, exhausted, asleep, did not notice when Casrus, shrugging off his shawl-cloak, left it to them to wake up under at the Jate bell. His act caused predictable obscenity from Dorte.

"You oaf of an aristo. Now they'll part kill each other for it, while you freeze."

"Don't be concerned for me," said Casrus. This time his tone was not absolutely devoid of shadings. "I'm hardier than those children. And it gives them some chance, where they had none."

"Always ready to help us," sneered Dorte, "even when you're brow-deep in the muck with us. *Noble* Klarn."

Above, the Stare-Eyes watched. At the ends of streets, smoky red and flimsy yellow, fires burned on rods, in iron tubs or scoops of stone. They gave off small heat, being maintained for light rather than warmth on the minimum of scraps, coals, driblets of gas.

Somewhere, streets away, a pair of dogga barked and fell silent. Breasts of burden this side of the Klave, whipping posts for the frustrations of humanity, they had slight incentive to make a noise.

The two men had left Aita by now, and the domestic huddle about the mine and vaporines. An irregular square spread out, sprawled across by erections of haphazard and negligent building; the barter shops and taverns that lay about the Subterior. Dorte made for the nearest, a one-story windowless shack some sixty yards long, put together of

146

hardened muds, slushes and rubbish slapped over a frame of rusted iron mine joists.

Dorte pushed through the patched curtain, its metal weights jangling, his hand suddenly firmly clapped on Casrus' sleeve.

Visibility inside was murky. One intensifier lamp had been rigged in the asymmetrical ceiling, other light soaked out from a central firescoop. Customers sat around the floor on frayed dogga hides that lent the enclosure an extra stink. A brew bubbled in a pot over the fire, alchafax, a potion of pure alcohol mixed with various dregs, primarily the ice-diluted lubricants the machines used on themselves, and which the workers stole to intoxicate, slowly to rot their bellies. Three toughs kept watch over this precious liquor and the boy who ladled it. Everything here must be paid for, even poison.

The room was not crowded, however, not even full. Nor did the Stare-Eyes of the Law reach into it.

"My friends," Dorte announced to the place at large. "Here is a being from a story, come to enthrall us. Have you ever heard of Klarn? *Prince* Klarn? Have you heard how he came here and learned our ways and tried to act them out in the princes' city?" There was some vague, automatic, yet quite malign laughter. "Well, Klarn's back among us now. Without a robot or a machine to help him. It's all up to us, at the last, to make him feel at home."

Men were getting up, three of them. They were big men, though not quite as tall or as fully fleshed as Dorte. Doubtless members of his surface-working gangs. Their employment offered better food, more water, sturdier accommodation, and more credit chips, even after they had paid their dues to Dorte. Also, danger, and dread—even though subconscious, probably, by this time—of the large and appalling sky of space.

They came over and stood, smiling at Dorte, and at Casrus, exiled prince of Klarn.

"Now then," said Dorte, "I was just saying to our lord, here, since he's been allocated to our line of work, that I like to be sure that my gangers have the muscle for the job. A weak link in the chain would be detrimental to all. So I brought him along to see what my boys thought."

This was illegal, naturally, but the Law might wink. Indeed, literally did so, since it could not see into the tavern. To report the beating afterward would be to incur other

147

beatings, besides which, brawls were a lately happening, as were rape, robbery, crime of every sort and nuance. Only inexcusable murder was rewarded by death. And besides, punishment and death were already inherent in the Subterior; while those who dealt on the surface, close as a skin to annihilation—such men could be accustomed to dreams of mortality.

Dorte stood aside, grinning, disdaining a ladle of the poison drink as he went; he could afford better. The other occupants of the tavern, perhaps hand-picked by Dorte to be privileged spectators, and maybe even for a fee, settled themselves, unblinking. The theater waited.

"Well, Klarn," said the shortest of Dorte's gangers. "What will we do now?"

"Let's," said another, "play a game."

"The game is harmless," said the first.

"To us," added the second.

The third did not speak. He flung himself forward, his arms flailing. His knife remained undrawn. It seemed he thought his hands and feet, and the great bound that propelled them, would do.

His boots should have caught Casrus in the ribs, the arms descending, the gloved fists hammering shoulders and neck. But as the man soared, Casrus dipped one knee, only very slightly. He took hold of the man, who, rather than colliding, abruptly found himself passing over. In the smooth dance rhythm of the trained fighter, Casrus threw the man on the way he was already going. It was faultless, so much an ideal union between what the man had begun, what Casrus finished, that it appeared almost as if they had planned and rehearsed the moves together.

With a rush and a thud, the unspeaking man fell to ground among the hides on the floor. His padded clothing cushioned him, all but his uncovered head, which met one of the naked, rusting iron joists that formed the frame of the walls. Bruised and articulate at last, though beyond curses, into an animal growling, he rolled up again, and in that moment the other two ran for Casrus.

One aimed a blow at his face, which Casrus deflected with no hesitation; while he was so engaged, the second crashed against his legs. As Casrus rocked back, riding the impact, the first man swung in again. But Casrus' fist to the side of the jaw sent him staggering, even as the third ganger, yet growling, landed on Casrus' back.

148

They had him now at all vital angles, the legs, the throat, and one man to come reeling in to try again for torso or head. But Casrus was as strong as they, stronger. And now they realized that what a prince practiced for exercise could make him a better fighter than they, who tussled in earnest. Schooled, the prince was ahead of them. The long-instilled trick was not to register or accede to those points where the enemy had attached himself, but to note and respond to those areas of the enemy's own person left unprotected by that adherence.

So Casrus, noting everything instantly and spontaneously, allowed himself to plunge forward almost bonelessly. As he dropped, both his fists smashed down on the vulnerable skull of the man who kneeled, jailer of his legs. The blow was sufficiently accurate that the man toppled aside, soundless and senseless, out of the contest. Meantime, the sideways attacker, who had trusted to the hands of the man on the floor and the man whose fingers were locked on Casrus' throat to keep the quarry static, staggered into the tumbling mass Casrus had engineered, and went down with it.

The third ganger was still firmly fixed to Casrus' back and windpipe. Only the powerful muscles of the prince's throat had kept strangulation at bay through this maneuver. Now the muscles of his arms came into play. Reaching around even as he tilted floorward, he had secured his own hold. Next, bowing to the ground, Casrus heaved the ganger up for the second time, and for the second time cast him irresistibly overhead. The locked stranglehold disengaged voluntarily as the man found himself once more in flight. His roar of fury altered to a continuous shriek as he saw where his flight would take him, and that he could not prevent it. His impetus bore him straight through the scattering ring of toughs, and against the pot of boiling alcohol above the fire scoop. The pot tipped sideways on the coals. There was a big *whuf* of ignition and the light in the room grew very bright.

The man who had aimed from the side and consequently gone down was striving to drag Casrus over from behind. Casrus moved, almost as if in courtesy not to omit him, and slammed the battle's ultimate blow against his mouth.

Freed, Casrus was on his feet, turning about now to confront the new light which brightened the tavern—the light of a burning man.

The third ganger, himself drenched in the inflammable liquid, had attracted the explosion of alchafax in the scoop.

149

Writhing and floundering, cries ripped from him, a meaningless cacophony of fear and maddened agony, he dominated the room with his wings of flame. In such a place, fire, so unavoidably essential, was dreaded once uncaged.

Casrus was across the intervening space in seconds. He threw the man down as if he finally intended to murder him, and flung the stinking floor hides upon him. In a pall of smoke, the human lamp was extinguished and lay whimpering.

The rest of the room stayed voiceless. Even Dorte, his jest ruined, had nothing to say, and stared vacuously.

Klarn had proved himself a surprise. What would he surprise them with next?

The surprise came when he stooped, again hoisted the man he seemed to have been casting hither and yon more or less at will, like a great doll, and slung him over his shoulder. The ganger gave a pitiful, imbecilic wail of pain, beyond all argument, virtually beyond sanity.

Casrus went toward the door.

"You, Klarn!" Dorte bawled. "Where are you taking my ganger?"

"To the nearest center," Casrus replied. "Medicine is free, even here. You'll agree, this man needs it."

There was a mutter.

"He'll kill him," one or two said audibly, "in some cranny out of sight. Law or no Law."

One of the toughs bellowed: "This spilled alchafax—you pay for it."

But Casrus and his burden were gone.

Flinging a couple of chips ungraciously to the guards of the cauldron, Dorte lurched out into the street, in the prince's wake.

The Mechanized Center of Kaa was alike to all the rest, gray, gleaming, faceless, lit by white glares floating in the atmosphere. Within, ramps and moving corridors led to various chambers. There were also amenities which several centers possessed, but which hardly any but Upperlings could afford—baths, gymnasiums, halls of food, drink and sport. There was, however, at Kaa, one of those recreation areas that contained a Fabulism screen. The Fabulism, though not gratis, demanded fewer credit chips, and was therefore available to the masses of the Subterior. Even as Casrus approached, Dorte a stride or two behind, a crowd of would-be

150

dreamers was squatting on the rock outside the blank wall, waiting for admittance when a previous crowd would file out. It would be a recorded replaying they attended. No aristocrat kept J'ara at a Fabulast's duties during Maram.

The crowd peered at Casrus, less interested in real life than in the illusion they had saved their credit for.

Within, the ramp deposited the three men in a chamber. This asked them what they required, then checked them with gadgets before passing them into a cubicle.

The burned man Casrus set face down on a padded bench. He had lost consciousness. Dorte, glowering, having remained silent during the walk, now spoke: "Don't think you'll earn my favor by acting nurse to Hejerdi, there. If you're trying to prove your strength, I've seen it. I grant you the job."

Casrus said nothing, but watched a red glow which flickered in the wall.

Presently, a medical apparatus slid from below the light, examining the prone man, Hejerdi, soon stripping him and attending to his atrocious hurt. Implacable, Casrus stood by. Dorte, with a fastidious grimace, turned away.

"He won't love you for that," said Dorte. "Either for inflicting the injury, or for striving to amend it. You'll be employed, and you'll be paid in rations and chips. He'll get nothing till he's mended."

Hejerdi came to with a sudden cry and began to struggle in panic. Casrus reached out and pressed his head gently back to the bench.

"The machines are attending to you," said Casrus.

Hejerdi lay still, and only cried as the steel delicately probed him. No anesthetic was supplied. The treatment was basic, yet efficient, despite its sparsity. No human had charge here, which was perhaps as well. Human sadism and desire to exert power were obvious enough elsewhere in creatures such as Dorte.

Dorte now thrust his face nearer to the sick man's.

"See, Klarn's reputation is well-founded. Throws you in the fire, then tends you, sweet as a girl with credit chips to make. But don't you forget, your wage is going to be his. And you won't see the surface again for five Jates or more. If ever."

Hejerdi rolled his eyes, one cheek stuck to the padding, tears running in spasms, keeping pace with his pain.

"You set me on to it, Dorte," he croaked.

"If you'd been as much a champion as your mouth is, you wouldn't be lying there in your own baked blood."

151

"The others?"

"Sore heads, no more. They didn't let my lord chuck them in the alchafax. Rot on the princes. And you—you deserve nothing."

Dorte smiled. He produced from his layered clothing a string of ten white chips on a metal ring and handed it to Casrus in full sight of Hejerdi.

"That's yours. Advance on next four Jates' labor, as the Law specifies. I reckon you're fit for my gangs. Be at Kaa exit point at the second hour."

Dorte swung about.

"Dorte," said the burned man, as the steel apparatus sliced through his upper flesh, "I've been a good—a good man to you. I've nothing saved. I'll starve."

"Ah, what a tragedy," said Dorte. "Oh, what a piquant story. Like the theater in the Residencia is it, my prince? Don't put blame on me," Dorte said to the man, from the doorway. "I can't afford to keep you. Blame that one, that fallen star there, with the pretty manners."

The door slid shut.

A fine frost was poured upon Hejerdi from the machine, and he let out a mild sigh at its abrupt soothing. Something touched his face. Opening his eyes, he beheld five of the white chips, still clasped on the ring.

"Take it," said Casrus, "it's yours. I think you've earned it."

Hejerdi snarled.

"And have you say I stole it from you?"

"The mechanisms in this room will witness half my wage was given you freely."

Hejerdi's face was clotted with hate, but he moved his lips, seizing the ring of chips between his teeth, dogga-like. No one could get it from him now.

He watched Casrus out of the opening door, as an end of his pain began temporarily for him like a huge pale silence.

There were two hours left of the Maram. Casrus walked directly to Aita, through the slink and to the entrance of the mine.

A couple of men kept guard. Sometimes the mines were mechanically guarded. It would not always be necessary to tip, but usually, and this time it was. For a white credit chip each, they let Casrus through to crawl on the slides of foss-coal.

152

The slides lay downward, though most of the galleries of copper and calvium rose above the Subterior. In a tube of rock, men and women together clawed and picked at the somber slopes. A single electric bar gave light, touching the proceedings to a dismal sheen. The coal came away in little avalanches after much slow prizing. All worked noiselessly, with a noiseless desperation. Only the coals made any sound, rattling free, and the steady mindless chiseling of knives, stones, fingers.

Cloakless and lacking the usual plastomil sack for transporting coal, Casrus bore away his spoils wrapped against him in a fold of the outer long-coat. In the narrow alley, occasional wanderers scraping by took note. Once a thin skeleton of a man came prowling from a doorway, only to be drawn back by the words of an unseen mutterer: "No, leave him alone. He's too big to tackle."

Then, at the rough stair leading to his new dwelling, hearing a soft pattering, Casrus turned about and found four women behind him. They were almost identical, melted into one mold of deprivation, long matted hair, loose and uncovered, fire-colored tatters, faces gaunt white as if carved from slender bones. One held a stone in her rag-bound hand, but at his turning all four backed away. She with the stone it was who spoke, lifting her head to stare at him.

"You've gathered much warmth there, man. Let me share it with you. I'll see you enjoy it, too."

Another of the women punched her on the shoulder.

"Take me," this woman wheedled. "I'm better than she is. I've known fewer men."

The other two lowered their lids dully, waiting on fate, past outcry.

Casrus went toward them, and again they flinched, but the woman with the stone and the other who had cried kept their fierce eyes on him.

"Do you have a coal sack?" Casrus asked.

The woman with the stone unbelievingly stared on. The other with the voice, more flexible, said at once: "The skirt of my coat will do," and held it out. Casrus dropped into it immediately two handfuls of fosscoal. Then, as the others slowly followed suit, spreading the coats or the threadbare liners of their clothes, Casrus awarded them each the same measure.

The woman with the stone was ready the last. As the coal fell into her grip, she said, "Do you want all of us, then?"

153

Casrus ignored the question.

"Have you far to go?" he asked her. "You may be stopped for the coal, now that you have it."

"Not far. We'll keep together. And stealing is lawfully punishable, if the offender is caught."

"So it is," said Casrus, with the faintest smile, and turned once again to climb the stair.

The nearer of the speechless women whispered, "Look, he has only three or four coals left for himself."

"He's a fool," said the second woman loudly and sniggered.

She with the stone said, "It's Klarn. Can be no other."

They hung there, grown quiet, and observed the stupid hated benefactor go up to his hovel, activate the door and enter. Then they ran for home.

Even in the two hours left him, he could not sleep, but lay on the insulated pallet, watching the drawn leaping cat and the pale tired flame he had kindled in the scoop by striking sparks on the coal with his knife. His insomnia did not unduly trouble him. He had long ago learned to sleep little.

Beyond the hovel, vague sounds of Jate commenced instantly with the bell. They were not the sounds of the Residencia by any means, but a clamor of machinery and human discontent. Dogga barked, wheels argued with each other, a woman wept. Presently Casrus rose, and smothered the fire to save the coals.

In a bartering space, in one of the streets below the Slink, a white chip bought him a square of the concentrated gluey food and a plastomil cup of sour processed water tasting of disinfectants.

It was a cold Jate, extra cold, for the temperature here fluctuated, either as certain forms of heating—vaporines, fires—were left quiescent, or as some intensification of the surface temperature far above gradually sank into the bones of the planet. Ear shields had been donned, and the shields for nostrils and mouth. It was not extreme enough this deep into the Subterior for the entire face to be covered.

Casrus, huddled at a low communal fire with others, was distinguishable only by his superb physique, which, bundled as it was in layerings of garments, might be mistaken for the gaunt bulk of the surface worker. His face, however, gave him away. Good looks were not common, or, if they were, were totally submerged by want and anxiety. Besides, the aristocratic caste to the features alone betrayed them.

154

Word had spread. Three-fifths of the warren had learned by now of the fall of Prince Klarn. Those who had not learned would shortly do so. His crime they had not heard, and so invented crimes, the crimes of the Subterior, often sinisterly apposite to the lie which had condemned him. Other tales were also rife. Casrus had given away the stuffs of life, careless, princely still, and unforgivable.

No one approached him as he sat at the fire, but when he rose to seek the Kaa exit point Dorte had exhorted him to reach by the second hour, in trios and quartets, members of the bartering crowd got up and followed him. At first with stealth, amazed at him and his unprotected advent among them, conscious too of the milky, all-seeing Stare-Eyes on their poles.

The initial vocalization was raw, half wary of itself, but soon enough others joined it. Even the Law would not intervene in an affair of taunts and insults. Ane there were alleys between here and all other places that might be his destination. The Law had sent him to them. Perhaps the Law welcomed their assumption of its task. And there were many of them now, too many for the blame to fall squarely on any individual or group, if they proceeded well short of murder.

Casrus, knowing most of the main thoroughfares and linkways of the Subterior from five or six years of coming and going in them, knew that to gain the exit point he must presently traverse a part-buried gallery, scanty of light. If he had needed reminding, last night, Dorte and he had trodden there, en route to the tavern.

The mood of the crowd, perhaps now thirty strong, had increased. It was close to attacking him, regardless of the Law, driving itself into a fever of viciousness.

He was a street away from the gallery when he turned and faced the crowd. They had not expected it, or the absence of unease which he displayed—they might reasonably have anticipated his terror.

But Casrus, a fatalist, a cynic even, understood them, and felt neither anger nor alarm. He was that unusual entity, a man assured of self if not of his world and the deeds of that world. Actually, he was unafraid—not from blindness, but from true sight. Fear was superfluous and unhelpful. To erase it was instinctive, an act unfelt by him, or those who gazed at him.

The abuse had slackened. Now a single voice yelled from the midst of the crowd.

"This is the man who gives away fuel and clothes. Give us your coat and top shirt, Casrus Klarn!"

Then other voices took up the howl.

"Give us your boots!"

"Give us your quilted vest!"

"And your gloves."

"Give us your breeches."

Spurts of laughter went up, and suddenly a man came running to Casrus. His face, shielded at ears and nostrils but not across the mouth, was a grinning cypher for the entire crowd, as was his advance. His hands were already out to rip and snatch some fragment of Casrus' gear when Casrus struck him one felling blow across the head. The man whirled and went down, bleeding from the left brow, barely conscious, yet his protective facial shields unharmed. The blow had been chosen at the instant it was delivered, to save him that.

Again, the crowd was hushed. The spoon they had used to taste the broth had broken in it. They hovered between the impulse to rush upon Casrus in a body or else to leave him be.

In this interim, Casrus appeared to scan the crowd. His scanning was leisurely and thorough. His eyes came finally to rest on a youth with a crippled shoulder, result of some accident of natural birth or unnatural industry that had gone unhealed—for though the centers would treat the sick, during treatment employment and wages were lost. The young thin fingers, ungloved, had the blueish tinge of bloodless bitter cold.

The crowd was again checked. Casrus, rather than back off, stepped across the felled man and walked forward.

"I am willing," said Casrus, the first time he had addressed them, his voice clear and steady, "to give up what I myself can spare. Therefore, you take these," and he drew off the upper and the lower gloves from his hands and extended them to the young man with the frost-nipped fingers.

The gesture was imperious, but not offensive. As a surface-worker, Casrus would receive sufficient credit to obtain other gloves. The youth balked only for a second. Then he reached out and grabbed. And from his lips, unbidden, absurd, yet quite audible, came that phrase least often heard hereabouts, the fumbling sentence in which he made his thanks.

At the same moment, another in the crowd laid hold of Casrus' coat, and moving like a piece of oiled machinery,

156

Casrus spun about and struck this one also across the head, sending him crashing down. (All violence having been self-defending, the Stare-Eyes would ignore it.)

Casrus walked away.

The crowd, defused and irresolute, hovered murmuring.

Only two men pursued Casrus into the gallery, risking the Stare-Eyes that marked them go. Their imaginations did not stretch to the idea that Casrus could have looked for something of the sort, and waited for them. As they jumped down into the gloom, he seized the foremost in two gloveless yet immaculate iron hands, and rammed him first into the rock and next into his companion.

Alone, Casrus proceeded to the Kaa exit point.

A flying craft, similar to that which had brought Casrus to the Subterior (a plain sphere of white metal, equipped with windows and elevating motors) took the gang of ten men to the surface.

Dorte the Upperling rode with them, lounging on a padded chair with a drape of crimson and (aristocratic) blue cloth.

"Ah, so they did not eat you yet," Dorte had remarked on seeing the prince. By that title he introduced Casrus to this, his second gang. "His elegance takes the place of Hejerdi, whom he put into a center for medical attention."

The nine men did not speak. Where they were going there would be ample opportunity for murder, but only by endangering themselves. If they reckoned on a score to settle with a deposed aristo, it was doubtful they would try to settle it on the planet's surface, under the eyes of the machines, and under the awesome eyes of space itself.

Dorte, gang-master, would not be going out. His Jates for that were done since he had achieved position. Others took chances, while he lolled in the cabin of the flyer, or returned below to whatever pastimes he affected. Dorte was hated, too, but in the way a man would hate a blemish on his own skin.

The vehicle traveled the intestines of the planet. Through the windows unlikely glints and chasms of darkness manifested and vanished and thrummed. Old mine-shafts gaped, and fresh, deep random openings, like mouths into the night itself. Casrus had a few times entered this region before, as far as the mine workings extended. He had also picked up the crude mythology of the Subterines in respect of the uncharted ducts which poured themselves away beyond the mapping of men or machines. Some, the rumor propounded, pushed directly through the planet to that farther side, uninhabitable and airless as this, yet held in the glare of an unslumbering sun. Untenable, a desert harsher than the harsh and freezing rock of the night side, the sun side was an unthinkable fantasm, dressed in ridiculous surmise. The sun itself fired off flaming missiles into the earth. Inconceivable monsters swirled in the airlessness, dueling with each other. Recently, there had come to be an additional myth—that another race lived under the sun, with complexions of yellow metal and customs which crazily echoed those of the Klave. Casrus had not yet heard this latest legend, a half-dream left over, unrecalled, from the hypnotizing Fabulism of Vitra Klovez.

Casrus, as his fellow princes, had learned in childhood of the desert face of the planet and the eternal sun which hammered on it. He comprehended that life of any sort was impossible there. The beginnings of his own species were baffling, and indecipherable, despite the accumulations of computerized wisdom regarding other times and other worlds. Concerned with his own time and world, Casrus had set aside contemplation of origin, as his peers set it aside from lightness.

Ultimately, the flying craft came to a chamber of rock insulated with plastomil, and with a series of pressurized doors which gave on the nightmare—the naked landscape of the dark side surface.

"Into suits and out," Dorte declared with the jollity of the nonparticipant.

The men obeyed immediately, Casrus going with them to the ready-opened lockers. Each selected an overgarment of slick resistant material, equipped to inflate a bulging transparent skin, that became a great drop of contained atmosphere, forming up to cover the whole of the body and the head but leaving arms and legs outside and therefore mobile. Into the garments the men stepped, drew upon the scarlet cords, and became strange balloon creatures. Only the extremist of pressure changes or the snag of the sharpest object could puncture these air-vortexes. Should such a thing occur, another tug on the red cord would repair the self-reconstituting material.

Casrus knew of such suits, though he had never used one. In the vehicle, he had bound his uncovered hands with strips of lining from his top shirt. The suit adjusted itself to his body. A black knob upon his left shoulder brought him the breathing sounds of the nine men, and would bring the orders of the machines and robots outside.

The door of the flyer was already folding aside. The men plodded clumsily out on the weighted soles of their overgarments, jumped down in the cavern and went toward the series of pressurized doors.

There were three in all, and beyond the third lay the land of everlasting night.

Dreamlike, yet only beautiful in abstraction, the scene flowed across their eyes.

Slender pointed rocks rose all about, and away in colonnaded lines. Far distant, an upcombed tier of mountains, curiously tall, with crests crystalline and thin to the brink of translucence. There was a sense of glitter, specks of brilliance cloned in the dry wet-shining ground, in the pinnacles and shatterings of the rocks, and all across the sheer black membrane of the sky.

It was a sight absolutely of terror. Underground, all vistas were limited, and this, seemingly limitless. It was an alien country to which those who came frequently never grew accustomed, before which the stranger had been known to throw himself, as much as his suiting would allow, face downward. But Casrus, prepared by education if not by familiarity, took in the prospect, and put it from him. Its grandeur and its ominous message of danger he recognized, but his preoccupation was with the internal scenery of men. The scenery of the planet touched but did not subdue him, never would.

Robot machines moved slow and gliding, colorless beetles on the colorless climbing, glowing plain that ran between the nearer rocks. The purpose of their comings and goings was ill-defined, as was that of other gangs of men, all clad alike and moving, unlike the robots, with a weightless, graceless lolloping, restrained only by their conditioned soles.

Now a robot approached. It came to Dorte's ten men, paused, and said by means of the microphone knob: "Follow."

They followed it, out onto the wild plain.

On the surface there were many types of employment. The heads of subsurface mines to be maintained, crevices to be sealed, and new crevices capable of yielding ores to be opened and driven inward. There were also units which fed upon the outer nothing, isolating from it vital elements. Even in airlessness protoforms were obtainable, flecks of gases,

159

moistures and other ingredients available only with machinery. Yet these machines needed in turn to be served and constantly restored. Meteors crashed from tails of luminescence against the unprotected waste—bringing new riches, and sometimes damaging equipment. Among all the gadgets, globes and little towers which freckled the surface, there stood on the high places the barren vents of ancient volcanoes and the satiated, paved cliffs, the mirror bowls of the intensifying lamps. These sucked at the pulses of light the stars wept on the planet. From millions of miles away, the tears were falling, from sources grown old, or cold now, or dead. Yet the mirror bowls licked up the ghosts of the tears, and concentrated them downward into the clear, still radiance that lit the undercity of the Klave.

Dorte's second gang of ten were first to visit the far cliff line and there work on some of these bowls.

The journey was of nine or ten miles, but accomplished in less than half an hour in the great leaps common to surface travel.

A ditch of light dust lay under the cliffs, produced by a long ago grinding away of their skin, now caged in the vacuum. The dust smoked up whitely as the men and the machine went through it. Suddenly one of the men spoke to Casrus, "Like walking through your mistress's powder box, eh, Klarn?"

Then they were scaling the stem-like knotting of the cliff, arriving in a depression about a mile in diameter. On a stalk of white metal, the flower cup of an intensifier bowl reared, wide open to space. Gradually, throughout each Jate, each Maram, the bowl would turn itself in pursuit of the brightest stars as they wandered down the sky. Yet the turning was infinitesimal as the star-movement itself.

And this bowl was to be cleaned, and was now shutting off certain of its cells, fading from silver into a pearlized opacity.

The men swarmed up the metal stalk, aided by magnetized rungs. At the lip of the bowl, each swung and tipped over like an insect into a dish.

"Here," the man spoke to Casrus again. "You must take one of these."

Along the edges of the apparatus, small wands could be pulled loose on lengths of rubberized coil. A dry scouring of particles blasted softly from these wands at the thumbing in of a button, to play over the bowl, cleansing it, though from what, save occasional disturbed dust, was not evident.

160

Casrus was acquainted by hearsay with both method and occupation. He knew also to activate the wand delicately in order to prevent himself from being rocketed backwards. The men, of course, had watched for just such a display.

One of them said to the others: "He knows his business. How come?"

"Oh, Klarn knows everything there is to know about us."

Beneath the intensifier bowl the robot machine was glimmering away. As soon as the faint knob-conducted hum of it was gone, another of the men said, "A razor flint would puncture your air suit, Klarn. No Stare-Eyes here."

"He's only to touch the red cord to get the air back."

"Unless we rip the cord. There're nine of us."

They went on with this for some while, as the ten of them proceeded minutely over the bowl, cleaning it. The talk was just that. Eventually, the man who had first spoken of a woman's powder box exclaimed, "Well, what do you say, Casrus Klarn? We kill you and it goes down as an accident."

"I say," said Casrus, in a voice that had never changed, during combat, threats or silences, "that you'd better hope no accident of any sort befalls me. The computers who sent me into the Subterior will be waiting for just such an event as my death."

"You mean they'd welcome it—sentence carried out?"

"I mean that they'd anticipate crimes against me. And whoever was by me in the hour of an accident must be suspect and a scapegoat. Murder is rewarded by death."

"That's so," one of them said. "Sent up here, but without a suit, without any air. Just the stars to watch the lungs bulge out of our mouths. We'd better let this prince live."

"More than that," Casrus said. "You'd better be sure I do."

They went on cleaning the intensifier bowl diligently.

The first speaker spoke again.

"A year ago," he said, "three hovels collapsed in Ni Slink. This man here brought a machine and cleared the rubble. The wretches there survived because of that."

"What about Nentta," said another. "He saved some lives there."

"Why did you?" yet another demanded.

Casrus failed to answer. There was a pause as they cleaned. Then somebody said, "More important, what were you sent here for, into cold hell? Why?"

Again Casrus did not reply, though he glanced at the man

161

through the milky barriers of their air balloons. The glance was grave but uninformative.

"Someone hated him, why else?" the first man supplied. "Hated him because he came often to the Subterior. Those stinking aristos. That's it, isn't it?"

"Is it?" said Casrus.

A couple laughed.

"He can fight, I'll tell you that," said the first man. "Rotten-bone Dorte set three gangers on him—one was Hejerdi. And we all know where Hejerdi ended. Klarn slung him in a fire scoop at the drinking shop." The man took a couple of bounds. He struck Casrus mildly on the arm. "I'm Zuse. I'll see that you don't die. We might have some bets on you in the alleys, who can beat you in a brawl."

"I think not," said Casrus.

"Live anyway," said Zuse. The others had stopped working to look. "It's hard enough, without us making it harder."

"My thanks," said Casrus, without a trace of mockery, prince to prince, on the offer of truce.


Besides dread, and the frozen dripping of stars, there was on the surface a measure of freedom. The form of travel, in large bounds, an effortless almost-flight, was not unpleasing when understood and in control. Yet they worked throughout the Jate, unrecalled by any bell, told by machines when to attach a tube to the facial area of their air balloons and sip a gruel that gave strength but tasted of diluted plastomil. Even without gravity, the muscles of the spirit began at last to ache. To cleanse the mirror bowls, to haul equipment in the tracks of the machines, to apply force-drills to unspecified vents in the ground. That was the Jate. Repetition and unchanging vistas of black and white. The cold, too, pressed against the air suits, quietly coming in, so that by the end of his stint, each man felt the threat of freezing half an inch away beyond his suit's skin, leaden mouth breathing at his flesh as if through a window. The false staling air in the bubbles that shrouded them, drugged them with inexorable fatigue.

By Jate's end, Casrus, with the rest, knew exhaustion. But they were worn to the shape of their fate, and he, indifferent to it as he might be, not yet worn. The rigors and the soullessness of this time jarred on him, body and mind, on those parts unworn, unshaped. That the next ten Jates would be all the same was no consolation.

162

The ovoid transport took them down to their cheerless home. Dorte had come to see how the prince had fared. All were too enervated to pay much heed. Sneering, Dorte walked Casrus to his hovel in Aita Slink. For a while, Dorte stood in the alley, joking, pointing out to those who went that way by Maram the royal residence of Klarn. At length, a woman came and Dorte rolled off with her.

Later, a woman came also to Casrus' sealed metal door, begging for coal. Word had apparently spread fast. Casrus gave her one piece, all he could spare. Then, like the dead, insomnia and all else vanquished, he slept.

The Jate bell woke him, as it was intended to wake the sleepers of the Subterior. Those who overslept would lose their work, and maybe starve, or maybe worse than starve.

To work the surface was hard but profitable labor. The computers had been just in selecting it for Casrus. If he retained his stamina, in a few years he might become an Upperling like Dorte, finding others for the work, taking dues from them, living as well as he could, given living's low shape in the Subterior.

Casrus warmed a cube of concentrated food in a small pot of water rations he had been mechanically awarded as he left the surface, along with the other men. The light of the two coals had become greenish, for they were low. About to quench them, Casrus heard a stone rattled along the metal mesh of his locked door.

He turned. Hejerdi leaned there, peering in through the net of iron.

"I lost my cave," he said at once. "Someone took it while I was at the center. I tried to scrap with him for it, but with my burned back I couldn't." Hejerdi's face was greenish in the coal light, dark gray beneath the eyes. "Dorte put me up to beat you," said Hejerdi, "but you treated me fairly. Will you shelter me, now?"

"Yes," Casrus said.

He unlocked the door with the tab, and let Hejerdi crawl inside. Plainly, his illness was not theater; fresh blood had trickled, despite the cold, through the liners, mottling his coat and cloak where they were worn enough to be absorbent.

Casrus indicated the pallet.

"Lie there, and sleep."

Hejerdi flopped down with an agonized grunt.

Casrus drank from the mixture of food and water, then

163

took the container to the sick man. Hejerdi drank greedily, breathing in gasps.

Then he lay on his side, staring, as Casrus prepared to leave the room.

"You're a madman," said Hejerdi. "When I'm better, I might steal from you. There's the Law, but I might evade the Law."

"I doubt it."

"You doubt it, Klarn, because you wouldn't, and you a prince."

As Casrus reached the door, Hejerdi said: "Quench the coals. Don't leave them for me, they're almost gone."

"I'll bring more at Maram."

"Yes, and give them to half Aita. I've heard. And not even taking traditional payment from the women. Do you want to ruin the social structure of the Subterior?" Hejerdi grinned. "You," said Hejerdi, "why are you helping me?"

"Why did you come to me for help?"

"Because you're mad. I knew you would. You've been groaning for our trouble since you were a boy."

Casrus had paused in the doorway.

"I must lock you in," he said. "For your protection and my own, I keep the tab till I return."

"Agreed." Casrus was locking the door when Hejerdi said, "Those others, Subterines from your household in the fine city. Will they be coming to you here?"

"Not if they're wise," said Casrus.

"Not even your woman? Oh, I heard about the woman— Temal, the girl you saved from the Law. Not even her?" The door was secure. Casrus had gone down the stair into the Slink. "You mudskull!" Hejerdi yelled after him in an excess of gaunt passion. He went on shouting this, and other epithets, until the pain in him forced him to be quiet. He sank back on the insulated pallet, and into much the same deadly slumber as that of the man who had lain there before him.


Temal, clad in a brown robe—brown, the seldom affected color of Subterine lament—stood at one end of the gold-lit salon of the Klarn palace. Vitra Klovez in black and silver, with ear clasps of calvium-sapphire, stood at the other.

"We're to have an auction," said Vitra daintily, twisting one of the aristos' fiddle-toys, matching sapphire, between her long fingers. "An auction of Casrus' human slaves."

"They are not slaves," said Temal.

"What, are you daring to talk to me?" Pale and haughty, Vitra added surprise to her repertoire of looks.

"Excuse me," said Temal, "I merely sought to enlighten you. The small tasks Casrus allotted to his household were only a pretense to ease their pride. They were here to learn and to better themselves."

"You're mistaken. No Subterine has any pride. Except, possibly, you. But then, your status was different, was it not?" Temal said nothing. Vitra smiled and inhaled a mild perfumed drug from a little filigree lozenge. Vyen's idea was to give away Casrus' pet Subterines to interested friends, who would pay Klovez token barter—some ornament of racing dogga in recompense. Vitra had noisily applauded the notion, but she was not quite herself, not quite as Vyen had anticipated. Edgily, catching her mood, he had asked of her: "Did you destroy the Fabulism tapes as I told you?" "Of course! Do you take me for such a lunatic? How dare you question me this way. Nor do you issue me with orders. If I had not erased the tapes of Ceedres' plot, that would be my affair." "But you *did* erase them?" "I *did*." But, of course, her vehemence sprang from defensiveness. Strangely, she had been unable to do as Vyen suggested. Incriminatingly whole, the tapes of her Fabulism remained—indeed, had been added to. A weird picture of a slum, as bad as, yet different from the squalid Subterior, had begun to haunt her reverie in the chamber of the dome, thrusting through her brain onto the screens. . . .

And now Temal, Casrus's woman. A slut—defying her.

Vyen had suggested that Temal should be the last and most celebrated item on the agenda of their amusing auction.

"Now Casrus has gone," said Vitra to Temal.

"Now you have made sure he has gone."

Vitra stared in disbelief.

*"What did you say to me?"*

Again, reticence.

Vitra flung the empty lozenge against a wall.

"You insolent nonentity. You should be on your knees to me. What do you suppose you can do with yourself now? Be an actress, perhaps. Flaunt your shamelessness in some entertainment. But you're not pretty enough, not striking. The princes wouldn't be interested in you. What's left to you but to beg aid from Klovez now that Klarn's sunk in the slime."

"I can go to my lord," said Temal.

Vitra gave an actual shriek of mirth, overdone, silly, yet quite corrosive.

*"Go to your lord?* You mean to the Subterior, where he's been sent?"

"I mean that. I was matrixed there, and grew up there. It won't kill me to return."

"Return, and do what? He can't keep you there. Casrus won't welcome another mouth to feed, another human body to support *there.*" Temal stared at her. Maybe she had not considered this implication before, that Casrus would feel bound to support her, and could not. That she, meaning to assist, would be merely a burden. To follow him could have been her single beacon in a darkening landscape. Her eyes showed her thought. Doubtless accustomed long ago to gazing on desolation, they revealed that once again desolation was all they saw. "Casrus will be hard put to it enough to support himself," Vitra continued, ruthless and unnecessary. Also, oddly and invisibly, slightly afraid. She could not have said why, as she could not have said why she had not wiped the tapes of the creatures of her imagination, or why these creatures obsessed her. Long before she confronted Temal, aware she must confront her, Vitra had been uneasy. The only liking Casrus had ever awarded a woman had come to Temal, and not to herself.

"Everything you say," said Temal, "is wise. Will you permit me to leave you?"

"Do as you wish. Possibly it will be the last time you can indulge your whims. My brother wishes you all assembled by the fourteenth hour. See that you're there. Wear your best garments, not that brown vileness. And put on your jewels, if he gave you any."

Temal bowed. Her subservience was now faultless; and, peculiarly, also her dignity.

Alone, Vitra seethed. Almost instantly, the balsam for her nervous fury presented itself. The Fabulism—

She knew what came next. It exhilarated her. She could not help it. Though she could never again see Casrus in the flesh, yet she could conjure him on the screen in the person of Ceedres Yune Thar. She could maneuver all of them, and work out her neurotic impulses on them—even on Vyen. Even on Temal.

And perhaps also, on her guilty self.

Vel Thaidis, the innocent. Vitra, the serpent. Interchange-able.

As Temal, with a soft footfall, climbed the stairways of the Klarn palace, Vitra vacated the house, and dashed, in her vehicle of bells and ribbons, toward the dome of Rise Iu.

# CHAPTER FIVE

## Part One

Mansion Thirty-Seven (Seta), the Black and Gold, was a four-stepped pyramid, of ebony columns and sable brick, which framed a façade of two hundred and seven windows of saffron glaze. The entire structure was built out along a pier and towered, a shining mountain, on the surface of the wine lake.

Undeniably, Seta had the look of a palace. Which intimated that once, maybe, it had been one, a princely house raised close to the Zenith perimeter, before the borders of Slum and estate were established. Probably these ancestral undertones had given the place its extra fillip of arrogance, and chosen its first danger color of black.

A girl in transparent black satins thick with gold, stood on the outer stair. The stair was non-moving, also the girl. Neither was she Tilaia. She waited for Vel Thaidis to approach, having beckoned to her desultorily. Sherner, she waved away. At her back, the door, veiled only by clear glass, blazed forth its yellow light. Indeed, all the windows and lamps of the J'ara Basin blazed under the thick green olive shade of the parasol. It was an uncanny phenomenon, unlike any other.

Vel Thaidis, having found the strength, went up the stair.

Sherner, left behind, bared his awful teeth moodily.

The girl was comely, yet not so arresting as Tilaia, nor so over-polished. Her hardness had a brittle quality that matched the brassy hair.

"The princess," the girl announced, "sent me to bring you in."

Vel Thaidis' heart hammered from the short exertion of the climb and her eyes blurred at each beat.

"Princess?"

"Tilaia, who but? She has techs, didn't you notice?"

"She spoke to me of kitchen work and service to the tables," Vel Thaidis said hoarsely.

The girl paid no heed. She climbed the last two stairs and pressed one finger to a black marker on the glass door. The door lifted away in petal sections, into lintel, sides, floor. It seemed the J'ara quarter, like the Instations, had certain benefits of technology at hand.

In a golden foyer black flowers trailed from a lattice on the ceiling. A living cactus squatted on a pedestal—an incs. Vel Thaidis recalled, with a pang of retrospective premonition, the cage of incs at the plateau market. A thin red metal chain secured the creature, but it appeared docile, basking witlessly under the effete artificial sun of bright lights, perhaps fantasizing to itself that it was at home in the Zenith desert. Apart from the door, no absolute technology was in evidence. Where there were no windows, the lights were the fire-and-fuel sort, ignited behind yellow panels. There was, however, a lift. The J'ara girl led the way inside and held depressed a lever. The lift rose with the heavy lilt of hydraulic pressure.

"At another time," said the girl, "you'll take a more modest entrance. You were admitted frontward since no patrons are due for another hour."

"May I drink?" Vel Thaidis said.

"Possibly."

"I mean, aqua."

"The girls of the house may take one bucket or two jars a day from the cistern on the roof. There's also a bath. Even for the kitchen sluts."

"I mean, I must drink now."

"How long since you drank?"

"A sip on the street. Before that . . . last Maram; ale not aqua."

Floors had glided by. They were now at the fifth. The J'ara girl let the handle slide upward and the elevator flowed to a halt. They were in another kind of foyer, hung with gauze curtains and tinsel ornaments. The smoke of music audible outside also haunted Seta, but was at its slightest here. Passages threaded from the foyer, and women occasionally came and went along them, clad in the somber gilded garments of the mansion.

The J'ara girl stepped from the elevator. Dina Sirrid-like, she did not glance back to see if Vel Thaidis followed.

"Please," Vel Thaidis said. She put her hands to the wall to steady herself as they turned into one of the passages.

"What do you want?"

"I want aqua. I must have it. In the name of the gods—"

"Oh, the gods. Excrement on them," said the girl casually. "Boiled aqua is more precious than wine. Tech-credits more precious than metal or gems."

*I cannot bear it,* the cry came from within Vel Thaidis. But she must. She had borne so much already, she could bear this. Truly, she would. And suddenly, she could. It was as if the gods, the sophisticatedly accepted gods of the estates, the reviled gods of the Slum, spoke in her ears. A strange confidence went through her. She could bear it all. The revelation lasted only a moment. The corridor was turned, and there a basin jutted from the wall, a bright faucet, the girl mocking her before it. "It's allowed you. Drink then."

Vel Thaidis went to the basin and pressed the faucet and filled the little drinking thimble repeatedly, and drank and drank the ready-boiled aqua. All the while the gods seemed at her elbow, yet as the cool fluid put out her fever, the gods also drew away. It appeared they had rewarded her valor, yet not allowed her to prove herself. Later, she searched for that sudden moment of self-reliance, and felt only a dim residue of religion, of childish myopic trust.

She did not see Tilaia, the "princess," that Maram. Instead she saw a succession of women, the gilded objects of the house, who mocked her, taunted her, but did her no positive harm. Also she saw an older woman, with lines cracking the thick plastum of her cosmetics. She was ninety years of age, she informed Vel Thaidis, and mistress of Seta—indeed, that was the name by which she would be called: Zenena Seta. The master of the mansion did not trouble himself with the hiring, upkeep, reward or chastisement of his J'ara girls. He dealt only with the credits they brought him. He was to be called the Princes' Friend. (Many mansion zenens along the Basin were so self-styled, due to constant patronage by the aristos.)

Before Zenena Seta, Vel Thaidis must disrobe. Shamed, affronted, Vel Thaidis nevertheless obeyed without fruitless protest. Something of her former strength had come back to her, the strength of silence, a refusal mentally to take part.

Zenena Seta pronounced Vel Thaidis a fitting acquisition for the mansion. Fifteen gold bracelets collided on Zenena Seta's bony arms as she magnetized her index seal to a bronze tablet, and fed it in a small machine.

"Give me the possession chip of your apartment," said Zenena Seta. "From this Maram until and if you are dismissed you'll sleep here."

Vel Thaidis handed her the bit of metal which she had never been able to utilize, and the chip was tossed into a chute beneath the table.

Zenena Seta wore a wig of blond spinning, like a robot. Probably the creeping in of age coupled to the near Zenith sun beyond the parasol had crisped her bald. Vel Thaidis had observed bald women and men about the streets.

One of the dark-tunicked women took Vel Thaidis to a huge communal bath chamber, currently empty. A flush of aqua sped from the faucets, and as the woman did not leave her, Vel Thaidis bathed in her presence. When the woman brought a sachet, broke it, and began to knead its contents, the saffron dye of the house, into Vel Thaidis' hair, she swallowed down her objections and her allergic anger. Such a thing was unimportant; she might be thankful later for its disguise. Vel Thaidis asked, "Is it difficult or simple to serve the tables here?"

"Both," said the woman.

Dumbness came between them again. Vel Thaidis sensed a peculiar combination of resentment and indifference from her companion.

When the dye had been set and the bath was finished, the woman handed her charge a loose black robe to wear, then took her to a cubicle room. All the living chambers were situated in clusters along the spiraling, twisting corridors, but the woman had indicated panels at intervals which had picture-symbols of baths, closets, foyers, lifts and so on, and pointing hands painted underneath to reveal their direction. The cubicles of the kitchen workers were squeezed together at the rear of the building, and were windowless, yet ventilated by shafts let down from the roof. Enameled fans were set in the ceiling over these shafts, to cool the air on entry; they whirled continually with a relaxing insectile sound. Men and beasts toiled

172

in circles in the cellar, dragging around the wheels which powered the fans.

The cubicle was a few inches larger than the room in the apartment block, though the pallet was stowed against the wall in the same fashion. Another wall was a mirror, and before it stood a small table of plastum-marble, with combs, brushes, slabs and sticks and pots of make-up and a vial of Seta's individual scent. All these items were obligatory of use, the woman proclaimed. By the mirror, a rod hung with one of the long, light black, full-skirted tunics, a belt of gilt links, gilt sandals.

"Each Jate after J'ara, before you sleep, wash the tunic in the bath chamber. That's the rule of Seta. The ceiling fans will dry the garment."

The woman demonstrated (Dina Sirrid had not bothered) how an upright bed was lowered by a lever. Another woman, twin of the other, entered with a jar of anteline milk and a platter of bread, herbs and cheese paste.

"Next Jate, you will be summoned," the first woman told Vel Thaidis.

To what? Vel Thaidis did not inquire as she crammed the bread into her mouth.

*Even this pittance is luxury to me now, and I devour it like an animal, so low have I been brought.* But she no longer felt it keenly.

The women went away.

In the milk some of the dry alcohol was mixed, the same as had been in Dina Sirrid's aqua jar. It drugged Vel Thaidis. She fell on the pallet, on its black sheets, her newly yellow hair on the yellow pillow. She sighed and slept and dreamed of Velday.

She woke once or twice in the Maram, to loud floodings of music from below. She slept through Jate to the fourteenth hour, till a bustle in the passages outside alerted her.

Someone had entered while she slept and left for her a square of paper held on a metal frame. The paper was scrawled with written instructions and bore the seal of Zenena Seta. Perturbed, Vel Thaidis wondered how they had ascertained she could read, then recollected her testing at the building of labor allocation. Doubtless, information had been passed concerning her.

The instructions offered her the facilities of the mansion, including an upper kitchen where she might break her fast.

At the kitchen one would come to her and take her for training in her duties.

Vel Thaidis, a princess of Hirz, felt a spasm of nervous fear at the thought of this lesson. But she put the fear from her, and did as she was bidden.

Her reflection had mansion Seta's hard saffron hair. And presently Seta's face, lacquered in cosmetics, in rose dusts and gold coarse powders.

The painted pointing hands guided her to the upper kitchen.

Vel Thaidis entered on a gallery, above a wide and steamy area, where great braziers throbbed between the pillars. There seemed few pieces of machinery here, most of the work being done by hand and foot. The toil was basic in the extreme and entailed much physical exertion. Vel Thaidis understood little, as formerly she had known only of the kitchens of the palaces, robot-operated and hidden under the foundations.

But this much she understood. These human menials were a broad step below her own new station. One, dressed in a sleeveless, colorless shift, scrambled to the gallery immediately, to serve her boiling caffea, a cake of the inevitable rough bread and green honey, the delicacy manufactured mechanically from the distillations of flowers.

The hand which settled on Vel Thaidis' shoulder was timed so perfectly to accord with the end of her meal, it occurred to her she had been watched some while. There in the overheated and urgently laboring kitchen stood the J'ara girl who had first admitted her.

"The princess wants you."

"I'm to wait here for training in my tasks."

"The princess will arange your training."

"You mean Zenena Tilaia."

"I mean the Princess Tilaia."

There was revealed to be some spurious justification for the title. For one, Tilaia's chamber was not a cubicle. She was the foremost courtesan of Seta, and lived to suit her position, in an apartment rented from the Princes' Friend at the apex of the building. No ceiling, but a dome of pale amber crystal which stood open to the parasol sky. Beneath, all was silk and bead-sewn gauzes. Divans poised on many tiny lionag paws of rose metal, prisms glittered and smoking pomanders elevated incense.

In the midst, Tilaia, wrapped in a robe like fiery glass, her nails in the process of manicure, her hair in the process of

174

being dressed by two robot attendants. Princess Tilaia. She looked long at Vel Thaidis. *See where you are,* her look said. *See where I am.*

"Are you happy, Thaidis?" Tilaia eventually said.

Vel Thaidis returned the look. Her face was patrician in its silence, though she did not know it, had not calculated its effect.

Tilaia's mask twitched, then smoothed.

"Are you going to thank me for my kindness?" Tilaia murmured. "My kindness, and the generosity of my Slum-dog brother?"

"I thank you," Vel Thaidis said. Now, even she herself caught the glare of her own comportment. She must be wary. And yet, more than the coming of amorphous hope with the aqua basin, more than her scornful obedience to her instructions, such as the painting of her face—those acts and attitudes which had followed a renewal of her inner strengths—more than these had made her bold before Tilaia. What was it, then? Tilaia's absurd title of princess? Tilaia's pretended aristocracy? No. Another thing . . . which had, as yet, no name.

"Well," said Tilaia. She glanced at one of the attendants. "Wine," she said. No hint of Courteous Address. The robot woman moved elegantly and brought her a goblet of thin yellow jade. Tilaia sipped. "This Maram," said Tilaia, "the prince who is my master, to whom I am mistress—Yune Mek—is to keep his J'ara here, from the eighteenth hour, with certain companions. I intend the nicest girls to amuse him by waiting on us. You shall be one."

So even the strongest-seeming tower can shake at a planetary tremor. A gong of brass seemed to strike in Vel Thaidis' breast. Shattered by this immediacy of a meeting, even with a house unknown, she was once more afraid.

"I have no experience. I shall be awkward," she said. Her voice again betrayed her. Its regal arrogance was astounding. *If I am awkward,* that voice said, *yet are you honored by my lack of skill.*

Tilaia threw the jade goblet to her second robot.

"You're too modest," said Tilaia. "To carry a few dishes, a flagon, to stand behind a prince's chair—what is that?"

"You judged rightly in the beginning. I don't wish to have contact with aristos."

"Oh, that was your lie in which I humored you. Who in the Slum wants otherwise than to fawn on rich technocrats?

175

Someone may tip you. It may be enough to buy a sumptuous garment. Better, an hour's use of a robot maid. I should be lost without my robots, Thaidis. But then, I'm extravagant—my prince is generous." Her eyes narrowed, narrowed, became impenetrable slits. "And he is handsome. Virile and handsome and magnificent. And has many friends."

Vel Thaidis guessed Tilaia's power in Seta. She could not dare defy her.

"I beg you to excuse me this," Vel Thaidis said humbly, lowering her head—all too late. The bow after the regality before was inflaming as acid on a burn.

"I will not," said Tilaia, her pleasure blatant.

Vel Thaidis thought, *she has planned this, intended it. I believe she guesses what I am, have been. But the Yune Meks, if they have heard of my exile, won't expect me here, won't know me, a rouged kitchen slut. If she'd prove me that way, she may fail. Or if they learn, then I shall get word to Velday. I have only to survive. And murder is forbidden. I, of all women, should remember that.*

The incorporeal gods at her back, Vel Thaidis said quietly, "Since you are a princess, then, I accept your command."

Tilaia started as if she had been scratched.

"I'll see to it," Tilaia said, "you don't forget who I am. Now, out. Fressa at the door will teach you how to carry a dish."

Fressa at the door. the J'ara girl, waved Vel Thaidis again to follow.

Vel Thaidis was grateful for an awareness of gods; the very air of the mansion seemed to have grown hostile and electric.


At the eighteenth hour, second of Maram, Seta, the Black and Gold, officially opened itself for business. To advertise this event, a spire upon the topmost parapet of the roof was activated and began to give off fluorescent pulses of topaz neon.

A scatter of some two hundred or so customers began to fill the first and second floors. These were the lesser patrons of the J'ara mansions, the scum who, by good luck or lucky villainy, had risen to the surface of the city and gained thereby sufficient credits to visit princely haunts. (Possibly, too, they were the bread by which every mansion lived, the aristos being its sweetmeats and its wine.) Overseers of manufacts, masters and mistresses of Instations and other crea-

176

tures of the Slum's human governance. Any, in fact, whose job was equivalent to that of a machine, and who, a few hundred years before, would have had no position in that former era, when mechanisms had care of all work of consequence, however slight. But technology was melting from the Slum, gradually, degree by degree and inch by inch, and men necessarily took up the roles of machines. Computers, those enormous brains which had been the core of the sun-side world, had split into little units to tell time, add sums, effect justice, supply air and feed the millions of mouths. And human hierarchs replaced the lesser computers, and unowned and malnourished slaves replaced the lesser robots. Which had benefited some, those at the surface, or had seemed to. The process, besides, in the long run, was subtle, covering countless decades. Each generation scarcely registered how the vast wheel was running down. Only when some great estate collapsed, abrupt dramatic disaster, did the heads turn. Then, merely in a baying joy to see the favored topple. Not to decipher anything from it of their civilization's fate.

The third floor of Seta held its lower kitchens, far worse in appearance and frenzy than the private kitchen which served the women's fifth floor above. Between the third and fifth floors, the fourth and broadest, which was portioned into a series of dining salons and adjoining chambers—the aristocrats' playground.

On the threshold of this floor, at the eighteenth hour, Vel Thaidis stood, one of ten superficially identical icons.

Having gazed in the mirror at the stranger she had become, Vel Thaidis had secured comfort from her anonymity. To her own eyes, she no longer looked anything like herself. No one could recognize her, unless she determined to reveal her identity. So it had seemed.

None of the J'ara girls, not even Tilaia, had yet arrived. Presently doors of beaten copper slid aside and the kitchen women, Vel Thaidis taking the cue from the rest, moved forward to the brink of a brilliant salon. Intimations of heaven. Pillars of black plastum-marble upheld a roof of sunglobes fired and scented. Flowers bloomed in sculptured urns about the individual tables. Wine stood cooling in jars of mineral crystal. A tank of fluid at the room's center was continuously, but spasmodically, smashed by three jets of white vapor smoked from the golden nostrils of fish. Gilt fish swam also in the tank, robots.

Unavoidably, immediately, Vel Thaidis thought of the ruined salon at Thar, its basin empty of mechanisms, and claws seemed to fasten on her.

Just then, Tilaia entered by another doorway.

A moment came, which stepped between the measurable shortcomings of the present and a future of trackless, teeming vortexes. It was the moment which separates the final leap, out over the precipice, from the screaming wind, the agony and irrevocable terror of the fall. The moment which divides sanity from unreason. And in that moment, as Vel Thaidis saw Tilaia, garbed in a dress of dark green richly fringed and embroidered, bracelets of green metal on arms and wrists, a collar of sunseyes at her neck, in that moment Vel Thaidis was enabled to gaze at Tilaia, nonplussed, bemusedly seeking—but not yet answered. For a moment, Vel Thaidis could retain her reason. But then the moment was done.

The inchoate questioning within her, the macabre familiarity, all grew sharp-edged and undeniable.

The dress was Vel Thaidis' own garment, even to its drapery. The dress she had worn to face the council gathered at Hirz, the dress in which she had heard Ceedres' false evidence believed, her verity disqualified. The dress of which she had stripped in the Lawguard's transport, along with her bracelets and her jewels, every iota of what Tilaia now carried on her body.

Even then, as reality coursed over Vel Thaidis with its madness, she did not grasp its meaning. She did not have to. The ultimate answer was upon her.

A gilded lattice flew aside, a risen elevator filled the opening revealed. From the elevator emerged a lean sinewy man, a typical zenen of the Slum, but with a bag of belly slung before him which the richer years had added to his frame. On this frame, black silk in the coarse Slum drapery was bordered with jewels, and he was otherwise jeweled at ear, wrist, finger joints and throat, for all the world like one of his girls, for he could be none other than the establishment's master, the "Princes' Friend." His skull was shaved and buffed to a brown and varnished nut; skipping aside, he lowered his skull to his very vitals, a mark of honor to the man who came from the elevator behind him. The man who was Ceedres Yune Thar.

The elegantly draped tunic was pure white, the blinding white of solar heat. A white suncloak, figured in dull gold, hung negligently, held across the broad shoulders by two crossed chains of polished bronze. Vel Thaidis consciously

178

saw none of this. Only afterward did she recall his clothing in such detail it seemed she had labored to memorize it. Neither did she see his face. Rather she felt it, a shock wave, a current which passed through her, fierce enough to kill, somehow only stunning her.

He was smiling and contemptuous, yet there was about him an aura of enjoyment, gluttony almost.

Tilaia wasted no time. She went straight across the length of the salon and kneeled with the lithe grace of a dancer; leaning like a snake, she kissed Ceedres' sandaled foot. It was a gesture of total abnegation, performed with the utmost pride. *It is no shame to honor a god*, it said. And, in parentheses, *If he is a god, look which mortal he has chosen.*

The Princes' Friend, not Ceedres, courteously assisted Tilaia to rise. Ceedres watched their actions, contained, entertained. Gently, he lifted the collar about Tilaia's neck, weighed it lightly, let it fall.

Throughout this prologue, Vel Thaidis remained rooted to the floor. There was no escape. The copper panels had joined at her back, to release their seals would be to draw attention rather than evade it. So far, she was still thinking in terms of a monstrous coincidence. A coincidence which had brought her to take refuge in a resort Ceedres frequented, in which he kept a mistress, to which mistress he had given apparel from the spoils of Hirz. Reacting in this way, she had forgotten Tilaia's story of the Yune Mek patrons, the unnamed antagonism that had fired between Tilaia and herself.

"Your companions, Prince Thar?" the Princes' Friend inquired.

"Give them a while longer, I think," Ceedres said. "They're somewhat—occupied."

The Princes' Friend gave an unctuous growl of understanding.

Ceedres began to stroll through the salon. Tilaia moved at his side, subtle and unspeaking. At the waiting kitchen girls no one cast a single glance.

"The dinner you ordered, Prince Thar," said the Princes' Friend, "stands ready. Shall it be served?"

"Why not? Let the others have the leavings when they arrive."

"Oh, Prince," said the Princes' Friend lovingly, "as if my house would serve leavings."

Ceedres, head partly turned, had been fluidly matching the man's expressions, virtually smirk for smirk. Vel Thaidis, the observer, had followed the old trick, paralyzed. And now, Ceedres' face abruptly flattened, grew bleak and unliking, terrible by contrast. He said nothing; from the gaze alone the Princes' Friend recoiled. Hollow-cheeked, he lurched into motion, beckoning to the ten female waiters.

"Not all," Ceedres said then. "Leave one girl to serve the wine."

"Thaidis will stay," Tilaia said from beside him, inevitable and soft as a leaf falling through the air.

"Thaidis?" Ceedres asked. He did not look about him. His voice was very bland. "I don't recall that name. She must be new."

Thus, completely, the fantasy of coincidence deserted Vel Thaidis.

The other kitchen women left the chamber and passed away through a side door, in the wake of the Princes' Friend. Vel Thaidis remained alone with her two enemies. And, alone, she tensed as if for an executioner's blow.

"Well, Taia," Ceedres murmured, "where is the wine?"

"You, girl," Tilaia said, also looking nowhere in particular, "pour wine for my prince. She is very slow," Tilaia added to Ceedres. "Please forgive her."

"I remember a princess of the estates," Ceedres said. He seated himself on one of the divans, his eyes half-lidded, the smiling mask replaced. "She served the wine and told me to swallow my tongue and die of it."

"Such a woman should be made to suffer," Tilaia said.

Ceedres, lolling, unlooking, said like velvet: "Pour my wine, Vel Thaidis. Though I can't promise I'll choke, you can pray for it."

His utterance of her name—her full and exact name—fixed the seal upon her horror. And simultaneously, strangely, released her from her paralysis. She went to the table nearest Ceedres, uncorked the flagon and drew it from the cooling mineral crystals. Fressa had given her sufficient lesson in this art. The cups stood ready. And then he said again, "Pour the wine." And she knew at last his eyes were on her.

She barely foresaw what she would do, did not foresee enough to prevent it.

She turned, and dashed a stream of the glaucous liquid on the tiled floor.

"It's poured," she said. Her voice was husky, but audible. "Now lap it, like the other dogga."

But then she shrank, and when he got to his feet, she

180

scarcely held her ground. If he was angry, she could not tell, could not, in fact, bring herself to meet his eyes or scrutinize his expressions any further. But he only came for the flagon, which he removed deftly from her fingers. He took a cup and poured for himself.

Tilaia, naturally, submitted no word. This was her master, and she would do nothing without some sign from him.

Ceedres drank. He said, "This new one, I like her, she has originality. She'll be my steward through dinner, but keep a watch out for her. I don't want the gravy down my neck."

At that, Tilaia ran to Vel Thaidis. She whipped back her hand and swung it forward in a striking action. Vel Thaidis, still unused to physical violence of any sort, shied away inadequately, but the stroke was never finished. Noiselessly laughing, Tilaia had stopped her hand at the last instant. It was a warning, no more.

"Taia has a brother," Ceedres remarked, resettling himself on the divan. "Taia's brother is one of the Slum rabble. At my suggestion, Taia sent the fellow to hunt for you at the labor centers of hest-Uma. How did I locate your presence in this sector? Because it's adjacent to your estate. The Law is direct, and never wastes unnecessary staeds. Sherner did his work well. He discovered you an hour before Maram. Taia invited you to become one of Seta's glittering company. How could you resist?"

Strains of a music had detached themselves from the general melodium of the mansion and were coming close.

"Don't be afraid I or Taia will reveal you as a disgraced aristo. We are discreet. Though others, of course, may know you and betray you."

The side door opened.

A procession, music, food and fire, came through and filled the chamber.

The nine women served Ceedres. Not even Tilaia ate with him. A man of the house stood by to carve the meat, another to decant the J'ara's wines. Musicians played upon the chame-sett, the horizontal baritone extension of the upright chame, upon treble pipes and basso, bell-drums and liondrums. Two girls danced, one to the rhythm of the drums, one to the meandering of strings and pipes. Black beads and gold dripped from their bodies and their brass hair. When the meal had passed through a scarlet course to a white course, a porcelain thimble of white caffea was offered to Ceedres by a child hardly more than eight or nine years of age, beautiful,

181

spangled, clad in the bleached skin of a lionag cub. The dancing girls faded away. Fressa came to dance with a golden knife and dressed in a black armor out of legends; breastplate, thigh guards, armlets, a helm with a trailing violet plume which licked and sipped at the scattered flower petals and beads left behind on the tiles. Fressa's partner in the dance was the incs. It too was armored and bore a knife of gilded wood. It had been trained to rear on its hind limbs, and imitate the coilings, cuts and retractions of its opponent. The result was mirror image rather than mock battle, each advancing on the other as one, aiming, retreating as one. The girl's skill was in her judgment. Too vehement a cut would mean the incs also slashing too vehemently, a bruise to ribs, hands, ankles. Brilliantly, yet mindlessly, the almost mechanized creature copied Fressa's dueling. When the dance was done, negligently Ceedres threw it a coin of meat. To the girl, nothing.

He seemed indifferent to them, these lower humans who tended him so diligently. They might have been robots. With self-absorbed countenance and lazy eyes, he sat through the proceedings. Of only one person might he have been aware, the young woman stationed at his left shoulder. She who must receive those plates intended for him and set them down, those wines, and pour them. He neither spoke to her nor turned to her. Nor was he in any way apparently alert or eager.

And yet, as he exacted service from her, Vel Thaidis told herself that, of all the life in the room, she alone mattered to him at this hour. Her thoughts were a confusion, she was in an agony of uncertainty, amounting to fear. But still she responded to her place in his awareness with a ghastly vibrancy. For the same reason Tilaia had abased herself, Vel Thaidis steadied herself to endure. *See whom he has chosen.*

She shivered and imagined the table knives, within her reach, snatched up and put to use. She imagined her death from sheer dismay. But it all sprang from him. An electric chord, like one of the pulsing chords of the chame-sett, stretched singing between Ceedres and herself.

She had heard stories of Slum J'aras. These things of food and dance were tame: she divined that he had picked them for their worth as a background. To demonstrate orgy before her would not achieve his aims. Like him, she must note only one other in this room.

182

Even the dance of the girl and the incs was like the games of mimicry Ceedres played.

She balked at her own logic, which seemed coordinated by the power he exerted over her, the net he trapped her in.

The incs had gulped its piece of meat, and Fressa, taking up the bit of chain at its neck, led it off.

A course of sweets was being brought before the next savory. As the platters approached Vel Thaidis, she beheld the lattice which veiled the elevator pull aside.

"My tardy companions," Ceedres said.

Two of the manufact hierarchs advanced into the chamber. Their clothes were festal and of token princeliness. Between them they supported a man drunken or drug-sodden to the point of clownishness, but who was a prince in title and in fact. The three laughed together idiotically, and Ceedres raised his cup in greeting.

"Ceedres! Ceedres!" they cried back at him.

"Be seated, gentlemen," Ceedres called. "You have missed a duel-dance, Vay, between Fressa and an incs."

Supported between the hierarchs, Velday Yune Hirz frowned in sad delirium at a world he could no longer fully see.

Golden Vel Thaidis had changed to stone.

Her spirit seemed to leave her body and fall upward into the air. From this novel vantage, she stared at her brother, an unknown young man, bright fair hair poured over his wine-darkened face, swollen-eyed, maniacal and boneless in the grip of fiends. (She saw them as fiends, insubstantial yet malignant, from the same arcane mythos as Fressa's dance armor, and a black occult room ceilinged with white fires.)

This was not her brother.

She had never seen him like this. He had never actually been quite like this before, quite so reduced. Ceedres had had three Jates, almost four Marams, in which to work upon him in the confines of Hirz, the depths of the Slum. But it was a masterpiece Ceedres had begun long ago, Vel Thaidis accepted as much in this minute of revelation. For years, Ceedres had been weaning Velday from the customs of life, from Maram to J'ara and away from sleep, away also from intellect, from abstinence, continence and self-evaluation. In these recent three Jates, a culmination, given impetus by Velday's guilt and willingness to grow blind, his sense of honor long perverted; his basic trust in his adopted brother

183

who, since the commencement of their lives, it appeared, had striven in undetected ways to coerce and eliminate.

Half of Hirz? Ceedres would take all.

So Vel Thaidis foresaw. Not simply destruction of herself, but of her kindred, of her name and house.

Velday could not resist. Had not. Velday, the magical being beloved in her childhood. Velday, youthful, handsome, his open-heartedness altered to the falterings of an imbecile, his gentle sophistry poisoned. Velday, a cripple.

The alcoholic fumes, the fumes of the fuel lights had gone to her head. Despite the rationing of tears, she began to cry, there in that place full of danger and despair. She had believed the dam of her grief would collapse in public and in the sight of foes, and she had prophesied. The charcoaled tears drew furrows in the gilt powders and rose powders on her face. No one perceived, or, if any did, they were untroubled by it, not even moved to jeer at her. While Velday—it had been clear at once, as he careered with his escort among the tables—Velday did not see or recognize her.

Ceedres, not turning, said to Tilaia: "Empty this room, Taia."

Tilaia rose and imperiously clapped her hands, functioning as Ceedres' right arm and mouthpiece. She was submitted to as such. She ordered the musicians out, the carver, nine of the waiting girls, the dancers; they were gone. She wound her body toward Ceedres, for his approval of her authority.

"Also yourself, Taia," he said.

At that, Tilaia let slip her stance. Seconds only, but enough that her lips sewed themselves together as if on a tart fruit, and her tilted eyes burned. Her inquisitiveness, her malice, were to be balked after all. "May I," she broke out, very nearly shrill, "may I not—"

"Not," he said, the man who held her leash. He turned then, and showed her unerringly her own expression on his face, and Tilaia lapsed and folded herself away. She lowered her eyes. Her mouth was smooth and yielding.

"I do as my prince bids me."

"Conduct my two friends here," Ceedres said, indicating the drunken hierarchs. "Select them another dining room."

The two were already slouching up, bowing to Ceedres, groveling, sidling to an exit.

Tilaia proceeded to them and led them away, with a mask of courtesy, even interest and vivacity. She had been, like the incs, well trained.

184

The side door shut.

Velday, Ceedres, Velday's sister were alone in the salon.

Ceedres rose. He walked quietly to Velday, taking up the dull bone jar of white caffea as he went. Velday sprawled on a divan, beside the chame-sett which, with the larger drums, had been left behind. Monotonously and unmelodiously he stroked the strings, and drank between whiles from a leather flagon that one of the hierarchs had brought in with him.

"Well, my brother," said Ceedres, "did you spend your time profitably? Did Ler justify my recommendation or exceed her fame?"

"Ler is a bowl of light, a river of shade."

"Is she?" Ceedres drew the leather flagon from Velday's hand. Velday protested, noted the white caffea, and graciously accepted the exchange. Velday gulped from the throat of the jar.

"Ler," said Velday, his speech barely understandable, "is a pitcher of white caffea."

"And the other things?" Ceedres inquired, enunciating ever more finely, as if to compensate, in order that the third person with them should miss nothing.

"Superb," Velday said. "Now, I have been educated. I am wise."

"There is also," Ceedres said, "a girl in this room."

"A girl?"

"By the table there."

Velday squinted, tried to make out the girl Ceedres spoke of.

"Is she wholesome?"

"Oh, yes. I think you would find her so."

"Bring her then. Let me *find* her. I ask, because my legs," Velday laughed wildly, "refuse to bear me any farther."

Ceedres glanced at Vel Thaidis. He nodded to her, politely.

"Come here."

"Won't she do it?" Velday asked, fascinated.

"She'll do it."

And Vel Thaidis, a puppet, began to walk toward them, dragging her limbs of stone.

"She's been weeping," Ceedres remarked. "Tell her not to be afraid."

Concerned, Velday assured Vel Thaidis: "Don't be afraid."

"Perhaps," said Ceedres, "she has had some contact with your sister."

"My—sister—" Velday's face crumpled. His youth, with his intoxication, combined to make him look younger even than he was. Almost with a child's face, horribly sottish, a child's sick sleepless eyes, he wavered his attention to his friend and brother. "We made a vow," he said, "a pact, Cee. Not to talk of her, not to think, until some solution could be—some plan—and the Law, the conclave of the Law—"

"But perhaps," Ceedres said, "this girl may be able to help us."

"Oh, girl," Velday stammered, "girl—girl—" And huge muddy tears ran also from his eyes, without warning. Deprived of control even as he had been dehumanized, he put down the white caffea, and reached toward Vel Thaidis as if he sank in mire, an analogy vile in its exactitude.

The stone cracked and splintered from Vel Thaidis. She dropped to her knees before Velday, snatched his hands, caught them, held them.

"Vay," she said, her voice breathless but expressionless, for her emotions had been orphaned of expression. "Vay, look at me. Look at me."

"Yes," he said. His eyes swam over her, over and over. He struggled to identify her, as his instinct already had. His whole body writhed, and he jerked their locked fingers, clinging to her. Then, quite suddenly, he knew her. A dreadful stupid astonishment sped across his features. He bent his head, and rested his forehead on her wrists in silence.

In the silence, Ceedres spoke.

"Yes, Vay. A little J'ara slut. In the ranks of the Slumopolis far beneath Ler, your river of shade."

"But, Cee," Velday whispered (yet he did not look at Ceedres any more), "we have found her. Didn't you say, to trace her was everything? That we must attempt to trace her?"

"Well, let us say, I had some part in bringing about this sentimental reunion. And, abruptly, love is flowing like a fountain. Though for three Jates, and more, you've scarcely thought of her."

"I have—thought of her," Velday said carefully, his hair spilling on her wrists.

"Yes. Of course. When we drank and when we rode. When we played suns with balanced dice in Mansion Nu. All through the hours you lavished on shade-river Ler. Each of those times, Vel Thaidis crowded your thoughts."

Vel Thaidis saw her brother's stupid bewildered tears drop

186

like pearls of polished lead, falling straight from the flooded sockets, beyond her wrists, to the tiles of the floor.

"Ceedres," she said, "why are you doing this thing?"

She was surprised to have asked him this. Yet, as her voice, unable to convey her turmoil, had grown level, so this conversation had moved beyond heat or hysteria. Certainly, though she was not calm at all, she could demand his motive. Ceedres, in this environment much more than master, was quite capable of reply.

"Why? If you mean your hapless brother, he has been drinking much and inhaling pavra dusts. By Jate he'll remember next to nothing. What he does recall, he'll think to be a figment of the dream-wash in the Maram-chamber. Or hallucination itself, brought on by guilt."

"No," Vel Thaidis said, "I meant to ask you why you've become a torturer. Your strategy I know, to obtain Hirz. But this. There can be no need for this."

Ceedres had seated himself on the table's edge. His lazy eyes were introspective. She realized that he too was a little drunk. As once before, the realization was terrible, to know he felt himself this secure that he would throw away his shield.

"Well," he said, "well, Vel Thaidis. Why am I torturing you without profit? Let me see." His eyes came to her face and for the first, she met them. They were only human eyes, the eyes of a young man just four years her senior. Yet they were the eyes of death. "Recollect a certain room," Ceedres murmured. "A black room you had never seen before. And I told you I went to the room to know my fear of it, and to conquer my fear and know my conquest. In your obsession with rank, your cringing unappreciation of self, how can you possibly assimilate what I tell you? That I'm intrigued to be alive, enthralled with what I am. That I intend to discover every facet of myself, to open the innermost chambers of brain and spirit. My fear, what pleases me, what amuses or disgusts, these things I explore. I intend to taste what I am to the full. And that includes my capacity for cruelty, if you wish to call it that, the lengths I will go to in order to inflict harm, and how much interest harming another affords me."

"And Velday," she said, "is merely part of your experiment."

"Oh, Velday," he said, "you and your brother, two spoiled brats, two pets kept by robots in a palace and fed off gold plates. I'm astounded you learned to chew for yourselves."

187

"You never cared for Velday."

"Do you imagine that in reality I ever could?"

Then, in the midst of hell, she felt triumph. That Velday, even drugged and half-senseless as he was, had surely heard this admission from their enemy's own mouth. Even if it were to be forgotten a minute hence, still it had been heard. And then remorse dwindled her triumph. For Velday withdrew his grasp from her, stopped touching her altogether, and sat bowed over in his silence, unreachable.

"You, on the other hand," Ceedres said, "have irritated me. You did nothing quite as I anticipated. I reckoned you would be easy, since you were a fool, but not so. You have been grit in my sandal, Vaidi."

She stood up, and an abrupt impulsive solution suggested itself. She began to walk toward the copper doors.

She did not catch his movement, but Ceedres came up with her by the table where he had eaten, encircling both her arms, and holding her there against him. His hard smooth muscles, that pressed on her shoulders, her spine, reminded her of this hour's beginning, Jates before, and barbs ran through her nerves where she touched him.

"Why not," he said, "allow yourself the one pleasure you refused in the temple? Now you're a J'ara whore, you've no reason to deny yourself."

"Grit," she said, and the words rose freely in her, a fount that bubbled over. "Grit rubbing the heel of your *vanity*. You think me nothing, yet you can't bear that I should resist you, that I should be able to. Even now you've shown me my brother as your victim, even now you suppose I'd lick your feet as your mistress does."

"Love is such a curious condition. And you love me. More than your sickly adoration of Velday. So much more."

"A short distance from my hand there is a table knife. I was exiled here for a lie. I can redeem the Law and make it truth."

"Vaidi, Vaidi," he said, "I'm so afraid of you." And he laughed and let her go.

"Pride and honor you would not understand," she said. "You have none. You belong in the Slumopolis. You should have been glad to come here. You will be unhappy in Hirz."

"Shall I? Is that a curse?"

She thought: *I cannot kill him, for then I must die horribly myself. I cannot curse him, since there are, after all, no gods.*

She went swiftly to the copper doors. Ceedres said nothing

further to her, but as the doors unsealed, she heard him say, "Wake up, Velday. It's no J'ara if you fall asleep. And you lag behind. Drink this berry juice, my brother, and tell me more about Ler of the Forty-Ninth Mansion. Was your couch the purple or the red?"

Vel Thaidis was through the doors, which closed.

Above her, on the hind stair, Tilaia stood in the green and gold of Hirz, the sunseyes prismatic at her throat, her own like blots of ink.

"Don't you agree," Tilaia said, "my prince is all I reported him, even though his name isn't as I informed you. Did he send you out? Don't grieve. You'll see more of him next J'ara."

No more were the gods at Vel Thaidis' shoulder. No longer could she convince herself supernatural forces might gather to her aid. She had no personal reserves at all. And so the courage of the damned replaced the courage of the blessed.

She mounted the stair, and as she approached Tilaia, Vel Thaidis thrust her aside.

"I have endured him," she said. "I will not endure *you*."

Tilaia huddled to the wall. Generations of an inferior class had left their brand on her genes. But then she recovered, and at the aristo's back she slung foul words and fouler wishes, like rotten fruit.

The screeching miasma fading behind her, Vel Thaidis climbed intuitively to her cubicle, the only sanctuary she could think of. In her mind the wretched chant went on and on.

*There are no gods. There is no strength. There are no gods.*

# Part Two

Love, the curious condition. . . .

The Klovez auction at Klarn was over. All Casrus' house pets, his subterines, had been apportioned to the friends of Vitra and Vyen. The best-looking went first; only one was too ugly to be wanted at all. He had groveled like the rest, and finally given evidence of a talent for buffoon jokes directed at himself. When the party grew bored with him, they recommended he try the theater in Dera; shivering, the man went. Neither he nor any of his fellows had retained Casrus' teachings of self-pride. Nor had it been reckoned they would. The gold salon, softly aflame with its strange false sun, rang and crackled to princely laughter and wit. Twenty persons hung their "barter" of jewels and curios on the brother and sister hosts. Then, Vyen realized that Temal, the prize of his proxy collection, had not appeared.

Vitra had registered Temal's absence throughout the hour of the auction. She had been irritably dreading Vyen's registering of it. Now she would have to seek the girl, or at least send the Klarn robots to find her. (Vitra had come to the salon bathed in the glow of the unsatisfactory revenge she had vented on Temal, making her, as before, assume the character of the crawling vicious Tilaia of the Fabulism. Vaguely, Vitra was aware Tilaia also bore some resemblance to herself.)

In fact, Vyen's complaint did not result in Vitra's having to send for the girl. Cries of a general willingness to search broke out, and the glittering crowd of aristocrats was already scattering from the chamber when a single robot appeared.

"Instruct," said the robot.

"What is it?" demanded Vyen.

"The woman Temal is dead. What shall be done?"

Inspired by genuine horror and disgust, the princes were impelled to go and see.

The machine led them into the apartment which Temal had occupied. It was modest, yet blazoned with dark rich colors. The richest color of all spread on the bolster Temal had used to soak up the blood from her severed neck vein. Sure child of the Subterior, she had obviously known the swiftest way to die. Sure child of the Subterior, she had never relinquished her knife, or the pessimistic vision that she might one Jate need it. She had caused thereby the minimum of inconvenience to those hated ones who must find her. She had arranged herself neatly. Only the bolster had been spoiled. Bloodless and white as a stone, her face, angled a little into the cushion, was yet composed. Her hands were loosely joined upon the knife. Her oblique dignity, if not her life, had remained intact.

Vitra had never seen death before, actually in front of her.

She had been very sick, and now lay in her new bedchamber at Klarn. Vyen held her hand.

"So much distress," said Vyen briskly, "for a worm of the Subterior." Yet he, too, was white. Mocking at Vitra lent him bravado.

"Casrus taught her to be human," said Vitra weakly. "She died honorably."

"She died moronically. She could have lived at Klef or Klur. I know Shedri would have taken her, if only to annoy *you*."

"She wanted to live at the side of Casrus," said Vitra, and tears rolled from her eyes. It was not remorse, but simply the old guilty fear, coupled to a gnawing knowledge that she too would have wished to live at Casrus' side. A sudden irresistible picture spread through her mind: Vitra, Casrus' wife, and Casrus dead in some racing accident or fire-sword contest. Casrus in a silver urn, and Vitra, her white face dignified and composed, cutting her wrists (but oh, not her neck) and lying peacefully to die on a silken divan, her blood caught tastefully (humorously?) in two matching nacre bowls. The fantasy made her feel quite faint. She thought of the gold faked sunlight of the Klarn salon, like and unlike the sun of her invented Fabulism—why, why had Casrus not loved her as she deserved? None of this need have happened. Or, suppose Casrus had betrayed her, sent her to the Slum of the Subterior, followed her there as Ceedres had followed Vel Thaidis, to be cruel to her in bruised vanity and contempt? Masochistic with culpability, she painfully enjoyed these mental wanderings, as she had bitterly and uneasily enjoyed the latest installment of her Fabulism. But she felt herself compelled to say to Vyen, "Probably Temal believed in the Kaneka heaven. In her soul."

"Confound her soul. Whatever shall we do with the body?"

"Oh!" moaned Vitra.

"Well, but there it is. In the Subterior, those bodies which are found are cremated, and the ashes shoveled somewhere. Unfound bodies presumably rest until detected by their perfume. Or else they freeze."

Vitra snatched away her hand.

"You are detestable."

"Practical. I suggest we order her burnt. Perhaps we could send the ashes to Casrus as a token."

Vitra widened her eyes, as if astounded by his spitefulness.

Naturally, disturbing her, a complementary tug of spite primed her spirits.

"You're revolting, Vyen."

"Detestable, revolting. . . . Why not in a silver urn? He might be able to barter the silver. This is the fifth Jate he'll have been in the Subterior. He'll be grateful."

Vitra stared into space, at Ceedres Yune Thar opening an urn of gold, discovering gray cinders with a tiny scented note on metal-paper. *Herewith, Tilaia. Fond greetings from Vel Thaidis.*

A fresh spasm of sickness contorted Vitra's stomach and face, subsided, and was replaced by a woodenly malicious smile. Why had she not made Vel Thaidis more resilient, more forceful. Her only wickedness was her ignorance. Her nobility was tiresome. She was spineless. An ideal complement, not for Ceedres, but for Casrus.

"I would like," said Vitra, "to see the urn, when it's ready. Now go away, you nasty beast."

When Vyen had gone, she rose. She pressed a gilded button, and a flower cup of platinum, recently designed by her and installed at Klarn, elevated and opened its petals. Vitra chose from the spectacular bottles, flagons and bulbs of liquor—also recently installed—a fortified wine of three layerings of color. She poured carefully into a goblet, making sure the lowest black layer mixed with the transparent rose-tinged middle layer, before running on through the top layer of honey-bronze. The resultant drink was dry, unsickly and uplifting. After three or four goblets, Vitra was herself again. More herself than she had been for some while. More herself than herself, perhaps.

She summoned a robot.

"At the first hour of Maram, I intend," said Vitra, "to visit the Subterior. The machines of this house are quite accustomed to such visits, I believe."

The robot assented.

"I don't mean to go, however," said Vitra, "with the purpose of offering assistance. I shall require merely personal protection from the savage sub-humans there."

The robot assented.

"Oh, and there is no need to inform my brother of my whereabouts. You can tell him I'm riding about the Residencia, may visit the Klurs, or may not."

The Klarn robot assented. It had, of course, no opinions.

192

All house machines were capable of lies, providing they were programmed.

Vitra sampled another goblet of the three-color drink.

She bathed and called other robots to scent and dress her. She chose a plastavel sheath, the secretive white-blue of ice, and had it fitted with a minuscule heating device. Unnecessarily and deliberately, she chose a mantle of white synthetic fur, each hair tipped with dark silver. Blue luminants were combed into her own hair.

Ceedres had dared intrude on the abyss. Why not Vitra? She did not stop to think what she was doing. The way was accessible, and her confidence (a black, rose and honey-bronze confidence) was at its premium. All things seemed possible. Even rescue. Even love.

Only when the robot came to tell her the transport stood at the doors, hurrying herself so Vyen should not see and guess, did she experience a moment's doubt. Her reaction to it was to hand goblet and flagon to a robot, instructing it to bring them after her. Portable good luck and bravery.

The Portables were useful. Abruptly, seated in the transport as it rose through the veins of the planet, taking her to a region she had never visited, thought of rather in terms of a dream-place, barely real (less real than a Fabulism?), Vitra fluttered in a belated confusion.

All at once it seemed to her, as it had now and then seemed before, that Vel Thaidis was possessing her. Vitra had sent Vel Thaidis into hell, and now Vel Thaidis coerced *her* into visiting her own equivalent of hell. Vitra realized she was afraid to see anything. Afraid to look at the rocks passing the windows of the transport, afraid of the selected Subterior opening that approached.

When they were through, coming to rest outside one of the gray mechanical centers, the fear intensified. The transport settled, and Vitra's guard of ten robots (more than needed—she had insisted, on seeing there were only two, that eight others be added) were already arranging for the small closed traveling car to be placed on the rock outside. As the transport door opened, a robot came to her. "You should adjust your heat dial, Vitra Klovez."

She started, fumbled with the tiny dial on the collar of her sheath as freezing air scoured the interior of the vehicle.

Almost, she visualized maddened Subterines rushing at her from all sides, waving stick-like arms, cold-gnawed mouths

193

vomiting curses. She was Vel Thaidis, entering in terror the Slum of her world. Though better protected than Vel Thaidis, but Vitra had forgotten that. She was vulnerable. She seized the ready-filled goblet and drank.

Tipsy, yet still afraid, she stepped outside and into the car. It was small and cramped and capable of lifting fifteen feet into the air, in order to negotiate the narrow confines of the Subterior. But it had windows. As they began to move at a quick yet cautious pace, life came and dashed itself in Vitra's eyes like acid. She had come at Maram, yet even so, there were many abroad, or so it appeared to her. A great pressure of skeletons in flame-bright rags turning to gape. Nightmares shrank away, frostbitten hands and tortured optics and faces twisted in a permanent malady of grief and hurt, now brushed by dull disbelief. The worms. The worms for whom Vitra generously made pretty dreams. Somehow, they had never looked like this as they lay on the platforms of the recreation areas, revealed in the Fabulast's screen. Then they had looked docile, blank, witless yet reasonable, asking nothing of her at all.

What am I doing here?

Casrus, she had come to find Casrus.

She must rescue him from this. She must rescue him, and then he would love her.

She blurred the windows and drank. The robots had discovered the whereabouts of Casrus' lodging and would take her there. That was all that mattered.

After half an hour, the car arrived, registered Aita Slink as impassable from ground level, and slid up in the air above the top of the bulging rock walls. Presently, the car cruised down to rest on the overhanging terrace before the three hovels, two of which were patently uninhabited, having inwardly collapsed. The third hovel had a door of iron mesh, shut fast.

Vitra tottered daintily from the car as it opened. The venue seemed thankfully deserted, no one prowled in the alley below. The ten robots had joined her.

Vitra drew herself up, her fur sweeping the filthy rock.

"Rattle the mesh," she instructed the nearest robot.

The mesh was rattled. Nothing happened.

Vitra went forward. She looked through the mesh, curiosity and an agonized excitement overriding her doubts.

In the murky space beyond the mesh, a dull fire burned in a scoop of stone. Beyond that, a shadowy amalgamated

194

huddle of pallet and apparently sleeping human figure bundled in Subterine protective garments.

"Casrus!" Vitra said fiercely, "wake up and let me in."

The figure stirred vaguely, like one drugged. And Vitra seized the mesh in both her gloved hands, rattling it ferociously.

"Let me in, for love of life. I'm terrified—Casrus!"

There came a sudden awful growling from the pallet, and a vast upheaval of movement, that seemed to come careering straight at her, causing her to start away.

"Get off, you hussy, or—" a guttural voice began, and there ceased.

Vitra Klovez and Hejerdi regarded each other, both with infuriated astonishment. She, galvanized by alarm, recovered first.

"Where is Casrus?"

"In Aita, getting coal. Where are you is more to the point. Out of my head, are you? Fabulism, are you, or dream?"

This odd shot so near the mark, gave Vitra a transitory courage to enhance her arrogance.

"I am a Fabulast, it's true," she said, She expected gratitude. Or thought she did. There was no gratitude.

"An aristo," said Hejerdi. His face said more. "A crowd of robots with you—that's sensible, girlie."

"Be silent," Vitra said. Drink, robots, the mesh separating them sustained her. Hejerdi, inadvertently, sustained her, for, made indifferent by his lifelong aversion to her kind, he obeyed. He was jolted but not intrigued by her arrival. He would not argue with her technological strength, her clean and lustrous appearance. She had come to call on her fallen peer. What else? And Casrus was approaching, for Hejerdi could hear the murmur of voices that seemed always now to come and go in the prince's company. The Subterior was learning fast that to attempt Casrus from behind meant cracked ribs, a ringing head, that to approach with a request was to be helped, never turned aside. In two successive Jates Casrus had gone out early to buy clothing to replace that which he had given away. All the credit chips had been gone a Jate before the new wage was awarded. Of the new wage, half had again been presented to Hejerdi. Hejerdi took it with an oath. Later, when Casrus slept, Hejerdi had crept up on him and replaced two of the three chips in Casrus' pocket slit. Then Hejerdi had been appalled at himself. To survive meant to take and not to give. Yet Casrus gave and did not look to be crumbling. But Casrus, Casrus was—

The noise pushed into the Slink and became hollow and vociferous, in the enclosure. The female aristo raised her sequined head in fright and quavered: "What's that?" Shadows splayed on the rock walls, but the alley bottom was invisible, hidden by the overhang. She was too nervous to peer over.

"A big mob," said Hejerdi, "coming to eat you."

The Subterines were animals. To be eaten seemed possible.

"Protect me," Vitra choked to her robots. "Break in the mesh, and beat this man!"

Hejerdi tensed, but the nearest robot said, "He has offered you no physical threat, Vitra Klovez."

Vitra broke into a drunken tantrum—this was not to be borne—could a robot refuse her order? Then the great noise outside seemed to wash against the terrace, and suddenly sink attentively, and in its sinking she heard Casrus' voice, though not the words, in the alley below the stair. Perhaps the aristocratic car had been spotted, looming over the terrace above.

"They have short memories of what he did for them before," said Hejerdi, "but it's coming back to them. Even so, I don't know why I don't try to kill him. It might be worth death, to get an aristo." He licked his pale lips. "Maybe you."

Vitra had one of her visions—Hejerdi pushing open the mesh, emerging to wring his hands on her throat, Casrus racing up the stair, flinging Hejerdi aside, cradling her—

"Do it then," she said.

"Your robots would protect you."

She had forgotten the robots. Of course, they would protect her from a physical threat. Her head was whirling. She went to a robot and leaned on it for support.

The noises below, muffled by rock, went on. The calm tone of Casrus' voice reached her occasionally. He was not afraid of the dreadful rabble, had never been. Their thinness, their sores, their stink and melancholy. She turned maudlin with no warning. Surely she, too, had a social conscience, which had driven her to explore these pits of unloveliness, as presented in parallel through the shapes of the Sun Zenith Slumopolis. Her compassion was more developed than she had known or admitted. It must be so. It had never really occurred to her before.

Troubled, still inebriated and on the brink of tears, she missed the dispersing of the crowds and Casrus' quiet footfall on the stair.

Casrus had spent the Jate working on the planet's surface, the labor peculiar and monotonous as ever. The first hour of Maram he had spent chipping coal. He had acquired two sacks to carry it, more than one of which he subsequently distributed. The human guard at Aita had demanded an extra tip to permit Casrus to enter. He was gathering fuel for others than himself, and therefore must reward them fulsomely. Casrus refused. Short of combat, the guard could do nothing. Either fear of the nearby Stare-Eyes or of the nearer Casrus prevented the combat. When he reemerged with the coal, a small throng had gathered at the mine opening. The guards ridiculed Casrus for collecting what he would now give away. Casrus ignored them. The machines of Klarn had scrabbled out coal for the Subterior formerly, from countless mines; now he performed the task. The jeers were the same, but from a different quarter. The earlier throngs who had grabbed at the coal had jeered at the prince and his robots, the Upperling guards had fawned on him. Now the guards jeered. The people took almost gently, bewilderedly. They were the destitute, the sick, men and women in the last corner of deprivation. Or if malingerers swelled the throng, he had judged they too had rights to something of his service, skin and bone and rag and disease being also their ultimate lot.

From this he came and found the princess Vitra, in an iridescence of white and silver fur, supported by ten robots, at the entry to his hovel.

He paused, but Hejerdi, locked behind the iron mesh, said loudly: "A sweet gift for a J'ara, Klarn. Pity you'll be too tired to enjoy it. I, on the other hand—"

"Oh, Casrus," whispered Vitra.

Casrus walked by her, took out the tab and opened the mesh.

"Oh Casrus—we must talk—"

Casrus turned, looked at her.

"Vitra, your utter foolishness has no place in this world. It was better suited to the world you came from. Go back there."

"No. Let me explain." He waited, courteously. She faltered. "Send that man away. How can I say anything when he stands there, insulting me."

"I don't recall that Hejerdi insulted you," Casrus said. "Women here have few choices. To be able to offer a J'ara

197

night to a man who can pay them is an envied talent. Most who must are too ill to try."

Vitra frowned. Her giddiness had passed, leaving a sour premonition of failure behind it.

"I didn't come to this foulness to run from it without speaking to you."

"You intended that I be sent here," said Casrus. There was no accusation in his tone or in his expression. He seemed not even astounded at that incredible foolishness of hers which he had named. "I am here. Be content."

Vitra exploded into vehemence, reaching for the first weapon at hand—defense or offense, it was all one to her.

"Temal," she announced, "killed herself." Silence. Stiffly, futilely, Vitra added: "Temal is dead."

It was the face of Hejerdi which fell.

Casrus only glanced aside, and with the same enigmatic courtesy said to him, "Are you fit enough to leave me alone with her, for awhile?"

Hejerdi did not reply, but came straight outside and moved toward the stair.

Contra-suggestively, beyond herself again, Vitra spat at him: "Good. You do as our master bids you."

Neither man acknowledged this. Hejerdi hobbled, grimacing now with discomfort at his healing burns, down into the alley. Casrus stood to one side, for Vitra to enter the new Klarn palace.

She flounced by him, a whirl of synthetics and scent, and glinting gems. She stood in the midst of the hovel, brighter than the fire. Then, she hung her luminous head and pressed her hand to her cheek.

"Vyen means to send you the woman's ashes. In a silver urn."

"How kind of him."

"It isn't kindness—"

"You amaze me."

"Don't play with me, Casrus. You're too clever for me."

"And all the time I thought it was you who had been too clever for me."

She flickered up her gilded lids. His face was only polite. He did not mean to cut her with his abhorrence, merely did.

"Casrus." She tilted back her head, staring boldly at him. She was about to betray the one basic faith she had always kept till now. "It was Vyen's plan, and Vyen forced me to do it, to implicate you in a crime of which you were innocent.

198

I—I wanted to save you, but he—is jealous. We were both in distress when Klovez failed—but now I must absolve you. I'll try to lodge an appeal, to gain you a pardon from the computers."

"A pardon for what?"

"It's the only way it can be done. I can't admit our lie, Vyen's and mine. You're strong, but Vyen would die here—"

"Vitra," he said, "why did Temal kill herself?"

"Vyen auctioned off your Subterines. It was a joke. They were all placed. All but one. And Temal—"

"She could have come to me here."

"Did you tell her so?" Vitra demanded.

"No. She knew she could come to me. If I had said it at that moment, she would have thought I was asking her to return to this place for my sake. She might have found a way to remain in the Residencia. I had no right to persuade her from it."

"No *right*—when you had housed her, fed her, clothed her—"

"You're attempting to turn me from the solution, Vitra. The solution being, I think, that you assured Temal her presence would be unacceptable to me. It seems I was able to teach her nothing of the Klave, or of herself, after all, for she believed you."

"I did not—" Vitra cried.

"The fault is mine, not yours," Casrus said. "I was a poor teacher, and you an excellent one."

The flames sizzled among the fosscoal in the scoop, meeting some imperfection there, a bit of metal or stone. The splash of light showed the lines of weariness in his face which her awe of him had obscured from her before.

Vitra crossed the room. She came near to him and looked up into his face.

"Forgive me all my sins against you," she said. "Let me atone. Let me set you free of this. I can enter an appeal on your behalf to the computers."

"The computers which wrongfully condemned me."

"I will beg them for your liberty. Share Klarn with us. We won't trouble you."

His eyes were bloodshot from the frosts and fumes of the Subterior, the stale atmosphere of the surface air-suit and the mine, and the dust of coal. Reddened, they seemed bluer than ever. heavier, deeper, and far, far colder.

"My thanks, Vitra. I don't want to share Klarn with you."

"Oh, but let me help you. Please, please, let me help."

He took a breath, and waited, as if to quiet some turmoil inside himself, though outwardly he showed no evidence of turmoil. Then he said, "If you sincerely would help me."

"Yes! Only say. I'll do anything."

"Will you? This then. Loan me as many machines as you can from Klarn, to carry on my work here. The work you and your brother put an end to."

Vitra jumped as if slapped. Her features, her stance, merged from the yielding into the hateful.

"No. Ask me for anything else."

"Simply that, nothing else."

"I refuse," she exclaimed.

"Then you intend not to help me after all."

"Help you to escape this mud into which Vyen unjustly cast you. Not help you to linger here." He said nothing. Vitra said, "If you were resident at Klarn once more, you could organize the machines as you wished."

"Vitra, understand yourself, and the circumstances. If you obtained my pardon without admitting my blamelessness to the computers, I should come to the Residencia, not as a prince, but as an Upperling. I'd be dependent on your charity. I'd have no call on any of Klarn's technology, save what you would allow me to use of it."

"You'd be free to use all as you wished."

"All, I surmise, but the machines which would frequently bring me back here."

This truism went beyond even Vitra's powers of self-deception and denial.

"I would be your slave," she said desperately, "I would be your Temal."

"That," he said, "I doubt."

His voice had never changed, yet at last, something within it, or within his eyes, made her draw away. The armor of the fortified wine was deserting her rapidly. She found herself suddenly, as if waking from a trance, alone with her enemy in the belly of premature death. How had she come here? What had she said? What betrayed—and whom? Things which, a moment before, had seemed both inspired and assured of success, were abruptly displayed as mistakes, oversights. And Casrus, for whom she had tried, twice, to sacrifice herself and even her brother, Casrus had nothing for her but dislike. Sober and in dismay, she altered as if she had gone mad.

200

"You won't accept my kindness," she said brightly. "Rot here, then, with your precious dirty half-dead friends. Watch the skin flop loose on your bones, listen to the poisons gather in your lungs and stomach. Fail here and die here."

He said, "Go now, Vitra, you've said enough."

"No, not enough. You imagine yourself so wise, so superior to me. And all this while, I held you in my palm. I held you by strings and made you dance." Her breath came fast, and the words expired outward with it. She could no more stay dumb than stop breathing. A pounding of victory rang in her heart, and yet, at the same instant, there was a clamor in her somewhere, a bell which rang a warning. No, Vitra, no. Tell him no more. But the pounding of victory bore her on, a drum of war from a forgotten era of war. "You," she said, "I made you dance like dolls. Casrus and Ceedres, Temal and Tilaia."

He might have missed it. He was weary and sad, the endless guilt become, for an hour or so and maybe forever, a block of granite upon his shoulders. But he did not miss those two alien names mingled with Temal's and his own.

"Who," he said, "is Ceedres? And Tilai—"

"Til-*ai*-a. And who is Vel Thaidis? And *where* is she? Here." Vitra put her gloved finger to her forehead. Her solitary remaining pride carried her like wings, better than wine, or love. "I have worlds inside my skull, as does any true Fabulast. A world of endless sun. I created it to mock at you, and *her*, and all of them. Your other selves. And from the plot of their lives, I made the plot to destroy you. You who trusted you were a man of such intellect. *You*, my *superior*."

"Go home, Vitra," he said again.

"And you, go to a recreation center. Go and watch my Fabulism, *Subterine*. Go and see the blazing sun, and how I made you dance under it. How I can make you dance, over and over and over, whether you will or no."

She ran to the door, but in the doorway turned for her final look at him. Her face was, for a moment, unsuitably beautiful, then rumpled with distress. And then she had fled to the mechanical car. She knew what she had done.

Already she saw the Rise Iu dome chamber before her, and her busy fingers erasing the tapes she should have erased long since, long since.

Strangely, she seemed to have known she would one day tell him all this, which she should not, and it was as if she had left the tapes purposely so he might then witness them.

201

But probably he would forget her words.

And even if he did not, by the time he had gone from the recreation area, fought off the hypnotic effect which might in any case make him forget, and reached the machines of the Center to register the proof of the Klovez plot against him, she would have destroyed all evidence. If she were quick.

Of course, she was weeping.

She did not see any further unwholesome pictures of the damned through the windows, her tears at least spared her that.

Her social conscience had died before Casrus' reddened and unfriendly eyes.

Another woman came to Casrus' open door some minutes later. She was quite old for the Subterior, perhaps thirty-eight or forty years. She looked a hundred. Though those who lived to a hundred and beyond it, in the Residencia, would not look this way at all. She straddled the door, arrogant as Vitra, yet not as Vitra.

"My man's sick," said the woman.

Casrus rose from the ledge by the scoop of fire, where he had been sitting. He placed two white credit chips in her hand. The woman stared at them.

"They said you would—" she said. "Suppose," she said, "I lied. Suppose I have no man?"

"You would still have some need, or you would not have come to me," he said.

The woman hurried to the doorway; her back to him, she hissed that rare blessing of the abyss, "Live long," before scuttling down the stairs.

Hejerdi came some further minutes after.

"Was the princess nice?" he asked. Casrus did not answer. "There was a crone listening down the stair. She told me your lady was shouting about some Fabulism she made."

"What do you know of the Fabulisms?" Casrus said.

"Nothing. I seldom go there. It enfeebles the mind. And you forget. There's one that some claim to recall. Let's see. . . . A prince who duels with another for a woman—and a great cat of bronze that kills men when they sleep—"

"A blazing sun," Casrus said. Involuntarily, with a gestural drama rare to him, he dropped a fresh coal into the scoop, causing the fire to blaze.

"A sun—*that* Fabulism—Yes. Must be one like that, I've seen sun symbols painted on walls. That's one way the

202

memory comes back. Or we tell a story. The ganger Zuse, when he was drunk on alchafax seven Jates ago, said he'd seen an installation on the surface that was like a dream he'd had. He said the sunside of the planet had women on it with golden bodies and gold tresses and uncanny black eyes. And there were gods there, like yellow globes, inside a house of bronze, or brass. He'd been to Kaa center recreation."

"So must I," said Casrus.

"*You?* Dreaming's not your business. I know a girl—"

"Hejerdi, I have to lock you in again. Or you can take the door tab, if you want."

"You mustn't trust me," Hejerdi barked at Casrus, but Casrus, leaving the tab by the fire scoop, had gone.

Fatigue chewed on Casrus' brain as he walked. Perhaps it was fatigue which drove him to investigate Vitra's insane outcry. Fatigue which said: She has overreached herself, put into your grasp the key to retribution and recovery. She, who killed Temal by inference, and the worthless brother. Children. But such evil children. If they must be eradicated in order that life and duty can go on, then eradicated they will be. *When I am myself again,* he thought, *I will think tolerantly.* Go quickly, said the other within him. See and judge and act before you think better of it, before you tolerate. A hundred may die this Jate or next, which the machines of Klarn could deliver if you had charge of them. Regain those machines. Why cosset two worthless ones, and let a hundred of the luckless perish?

The plot Vitra had boasted of as inherent in the Fabulism, he had fathomed too well, having borne the brunt of it. If the Fabulism could prove the scheme and intention of the plot, the machines could not refuse his appeal. She was sufficiently demented to come to him, his overt enemy. Why not sufficiently demented to reveal where the flaw in her security lay? He pitied Vitra, even then. But a ruthless anger, engendered more by Temal's senseless death than any other thing, goaded him toward Kaa. He was twenty-five, had never allowed himself a boyhood, scarcely a childhood. All at once, the denied ghosts of his younger selves beset him, sobbing and shouting for justice. For revenge. He pushed them down, but he kept walking.

Vitra Klovez went swiftly to Rise Iu in the robot car, the larger transport left behind at one of the tubular, gloomy entrances to the Residencia. And as the coal luminous light of the city salved like a medicine across her agitated nerves, she took several new drinks from the flagon.

At Iu, she dismissed the car, and moved toward the doors of the dome chamber. Her ten robots followed her. She was amused by the picture they must make. Tragically amused. She had become a figure in a drama, Vitra spurned, Vitra in despair. She comprehended that when her sense of theater seeped away, she would begin to cry ignominiously once more.

But she had no opportunity, either to strike poses or to cry. Or to enter Iu and erase the tapes of her Fabulism.

On the twisting road she heard a vehicle behind her, strung in a singing of bells. All at once, Vyen was beside her, clad in pointless somber synthetic furs to complement her own, scowling to compliment nobody.

"What are you doing here?" rasped Vyen.

"My new Fabulism—" her continued pretense to him that the old was wiped from the records was now most important.

"It's Maram, J'ara. No prince conjures up stories for the worker-worms at this time. Where have you been?"

"I was—strolling."

"With ten robots. How extraordinary you must have appeared."

"I was depressed. The Fabulism will make me feel better."

"It usually makes you worse."

"I don't care. I must do it."

He looked at her, cold pale face, cold pale eyes. Colder than the eyes of Casrus, yet not so disconcerting.

"Why?" he said. And suddenly she was disconcerted after all.

Vyen had insisted that the tapes be erased. She had not touched them, but pretended that she had. Now that he might learn of her stupidity—it had been stupid—she feared him. She had betrayed him, and read the innate viciousness of his face, so similar to her own, with foreboding.

"If I say I want to," said Vitra, "I will do it."

"I perceive," said Vyen slowly, "there is unfinished business in the dome. What haven't you done, dear sister?"

"Accusations!" she squealed.

"Did you," he asked, "destroy the tapes?"

Vitra stared at him. "Did I not tell you I had? Of course I did."

Vyen was suspicious. Feverishly, cruelly he played with fiddle-toys of steel and crystal, watching her.

"Then come to Klef. You were invited to dine there. Shedri and three others were clamoring for you."

Vitra set her mouth, her very soul.

"Then I'll come."

She got into the Klovez chariot car and averted her face haughtily from Iu, the Fabulism, Casrus, destiny.

The crowd waiting to dream was just then shuffling into the center at Kaa. A few recognized Casrus dimly, muttered and lost interest.

Chips clattered in a chute, an opening folded wide. The darkened platform, with its shallow cushioning, rose up like a step toward death.

A stir of noises rippled through and through the room.

The crowd, arranging itself on the platform, lapsed, sprawled.

Casrus reclined, staring with the rest at the great curved ominous screen. The others drifted, he must not. His mind, used to supposing itself the servant of his will, though sunken with sleep and gathering hypnotics of the chamber, conditioned itself to remember. Somewhere from the walls, mechanical voices wafted. The maximum request from the crowd, issued and collated before Casrus' arrival, was for all installments of the drama, from the beginning Jates back, up to and including the latest. The fortuitousness of this struck Casrus as bizarre, yet the hypnotics, his struggle against them, took away doubt and all questioning.

The screen flashed bright.

The crowd on the platform sighed.

Casrus beheld a great white star that had burned the sky to a fiery green—a sun, some spans below its zenith.

A columned palace shone above a strand, a green water lay like a huge spoonful of jade. On the pale gold sand stood a golden young woman and her three attendant robots.

She was. . . . Vitra Klovez. But a Vitra he had never seen. A Vitra with large, curiously darkened eyes, warm skin, a depth, like the depth of the strange lake, held close within her face. Even the poise of her, the angle of her head, her burnished slender wrists ringed with apricot metal, conveyed nuances of a thought, a spirit, a training, alien to Vitra as was this sun to a black sky of stars.

"Vel Thaidis, your brother is coming."

The extremely humanized robot had spoken to the golden girl.

205

"You are certain that it's Velday?"

"I will check the patterns. Yes, they are his. There are also companions."

Presently the girl asked, "Is Ceedres Yune Thar among them?"

About one minute following this interchange, Casrus Klarn saw drive across the screen a golden, physically rather different version of Vyen Klovez. Eventually, a golden, physically not so different version of himself.

In the twenty-fourth hour, the last of Maram before Jate, Vitra Klovez paced her apartment at Klarn. She had been mildly scintillant throughout the J'ara at Klef, and had drunk much wine. The young men had more or less knelt at her feet; Bermel Klef had made her First Lady of the Feast, an arcane title of absurd glamour. Three quarters of her mind had been willingly captivated. One quarter remained intransigently in panic and at Iu. But she could not escape Vyen. And Vyen must never discover whom she had visited, what she had done or left undone.

Now, sober again and too late, she came to see that Vyen's frenzy was less important than the proof of their crime left undestroyed.

Yet, she could not, somehow, credit that Casrus would work her ill, or even bring her to justice. No, not Casrus. Not Casrus against Vitra. The very fact that she had not deemed it essential to erase the tapes before was sound evidence of her instinct for Casrus' restraint. Yet, why ever should he be restrained?

When Jate began, she would ride to Iu and make all right. Providing Klarn, who would not hurt her, had not unremembered it by then, she revealed her complicity to the overseeing machinery of the Subterior.

Casrus had come from the recreation area at Kaa in the fourth or fifth hour of Maram. Too exhausted to walk back to Aita, he had sat down leaning on a wall of rock there and slept, along with others homeless or tired beyond mobility.

The Jate bell of the Subterior woke him.

Automatically, he took a piece of the concentrated food from a compartment of his coat, broke off a small square and placed it in his mouth. Sucked slowly, it would gradually soften without water, providing both moisture and nourishment. A whisper at his side, and he had broken off another square and another, to feed the destitutes about him. It was

206

automatic, yet, as he performed the action, he was aware he had reached a hiatus. That now he gave his food away not from guilt but from a sense of divorce. All around, his world, palace or Subterior, seemed to have grown phantasmal.

As Vitra raced her chariot car to Iu, blue hollows beneath her lustrous eyes, Casrus sat by the wall of Kaa center, and noticed Hejerdi pushing a way to him.

"You kept J'ara in *there*?" Hejerdi asked, astonished still by the prince's sudden uncharacteristic penchant for Fabulisms. "And now your head is thick. Don't forget I've an interest in your wage." Hejerdi grinned sheepishly. "Don't lose *our* wage, Klarn."

Casrus said nothing. Hejerdi squatted by him.

"Do you recall any of it? Share."

"I recall sufficient to damn my enemies," said Casrus.

Hejerdi's mouth opened behind its shield—the Jate was very cold.

"Well, damn them, then."

"But I see," said Casrus, "a box within a box."

"What box?"

"A manner of speech," said Casrus.

"Oh, princely talk. What will you do?"

"I must think."

Casrus rose and walked away, to Hejerdi's relief toward the Kaa exit point for surface transports.

As Vitra stood, her ringed fingers darting on the keys in the chamber of the dome, she felt a sort of concentrated regard upon her, and glanced over her shoulder in fright. No one was there. Possibly she had caught the ray of Casrus' inner eyes staring at her through tissue, skull, rocks, plastics and room. His impulse to obtain proof of her treachery had faded. This was not the aspect of Vitra which obsessed him, which had obsessed him so violently there had ceased to be a need to fight the hypnotics of the Fabulism platform. Wide awake and fully conscious, he had analyzed and processed the pictures before him. Presently, as was his habit, he had put aside himself, his wrongs, his rescue; even Temal he put aside, for she was dead, he could no longer help her.

The balance of the Klave, he had always known, and unwillingly accepted, was out of kilter. Now, *now* he saw, amorphous and untranslatable, a mystic answer, written in pictures on a sun-blazoned screen. Untranslatable? Maybe not forever.

Vitra, shrugging off her fears, returned to her work on the

207

incriminating tapes. She did not hear Casrus' inner voice, which asked of her: How could you, Vitra, poor shallow empty child, have dreamed such a world, and such deeds in it? You, who lack the imagination to understand the pangs of the Subterior, to invent a Subterior by another name, burning in white heat under a zenith sun. You, unsubtle, naïve, to create the subtlety of Ceedres, the apathy, nobility and anguish of Vel Thaidis and her inadequate brother? *You?*

Can it be you are not the inventor, but merely the transmitter of another's invention? Or another's actual existence? Their lives, and ours, troubled, disturbed mirrors of each other—but equally *real*.

With a shake of her head, mannered and pretty, Vitra gazed upon the stilled keys. The tapes of her Fabulism were blank. Vel Thaidis, Ceedres, Velday, Tilaia, all were obliterated. Nothing more could happen to them or their ficticious world. They were myth now, like hell and like Kaneka.

It was over.

# CHAPTER SIX

## Part One

At the twelfth hour of Jate, when Seta lay stilled and sluggish after the riots of J'ara, Vel Thaidis left the mansion, and walked from under the parasol of olive glass, toward the roil of the Slum below.

She wore the dark tunic of Seta, the gilded belt and sandals. Over her yellow-dyed hair, to shield her head from the sun, was draped a broad fold rent from the loose black robe Seta had also given her. To destroy or tamper with the property of the mansion was a crime. But it scarcely mattered now. Or at least, it would not matter for long.

Her Maram had been sleepless, somehow timeless. She seemed to have lain on the pallet for a year. To begin with, a million thoughts beset her, of suffering and recrimination. But eventually she thought only of one thing. Not of the failure of the gods. Of her own failure.

Like an inky stain spreading in clear aqua, so Ceedres' guile had spread across her landscape, blotting it out. And now the stain, a huge smoke, smothered against the lips and nostrils of Velday, stifling him. Stifling, blinded, he loved the smoke, trusted the smoke loved him, was not smothering him but nurturing him. But she, knowing everything, had traded Velday's life and Ceedres' death for her own survival. Despite the fact that her own life was now worth nothing, and had ended, in soul or purpose, Jates before. Thus, argue as she might that Ceedres would have prevented her attack on him

209

during the J'ara, his hands, muscles, wit, all too quick and too vital for her blow—yet she grasped only that she had failed in not attempting it. The last door of her destiny she had retreated from. For the ills which accumulated now, she alone would be to blame. This, her constant thought through the hours of Maram.

Then, when the Jate-calmed house grew muffled and sullen, timelessness and self-accusation left Vel Thaidis. The answer came softly, saying to her: It is not too late.

Tilaia had taunted her with the promise that Ceedres would return to Seta the following Maram. Vel Thaidis believed her. Oh, yes, he would come back. Back and back, until he could erode her control, and watch her crawl to him. Which one Maram, eventually she would do. She understood as well as Ceedres that it remained in her to do it. When Tilaia had knelt, Vel Thaidis saw herself, and was chilled. But, lying in silence under the roof of her enemies, suddenly she beheld that what had oppressed her was to be her salvation. He would return. She would kneel. She would abase herself. This very Maram she would do it. And when she rose up, she would plunge the knife she had concealed deep in his breast.

The enormity of her insight shook her through. A gulf of frightened astonishment, a gulf of murderous gladness, rushed together and mingled.

So she rose and went into the city. The final lunacy had made her rational. She already knew the knives of Seta were not sharp enough.

Clad in her sluttish finery, freshly painted to hide her face, she would find someone on the street. She would barter herself and her pride and her fastidiousness for a metal blade of the Slumopolis.

When it was burnished by Ceedres' blood, there would be the space, granted her by the surprise of others, to sever her own veins.

Thereafter, she might rest, in paradise or in nothing. In her weariness, death seemed acceptable, if she could seek it without undue fear or pain.

She had come to a wide street. Blue metal buildings craned to her right. A wall of bricks, stained and scorched looking, went up twenty feet on her left, a pillar of dirty vapor lifting beyond it and straight to the sky. People came and went, crowded in porticoes, spat and drank and brawled, mild scufflings that did not attract the Law. She had passed another cat fight, which had turned her faint and sick, so she had leaned against a doorpost and a man had come out and pushed her aside. There had been games of throw and guess, too, childish and often malignant. There had been open yards yawning on to alleys, full of men and women blotched with filth and scabs and burns of acid or steam or plasta. There had been two girls, twelve or less, faces daubed with the white protective cosmetic fudge, patroling arm in arm, brass rings in their ears, prostitutes not special enough for the mansions, good enough for the streets.

These persons were like another species. It was going to be difficult for her, after all, even to approach them. They seemed now not to see her except as something to be thrust aside.

In a seizure of self-doubt, reaching this street, she had paused to nerve herself to her work.

Her eyes burned, irritated by the high sun after the J'ara parasol and the fuel lamps of Seta. Again, as formerly, her throat was dry, and it troubled her to swallow. She had no strength to bear it any more.

*Go to a man,* she thought. *Any man. The more atrocious the better. The atrocious one will be sure to have a knife about him.* But she could not, had not, and did not.

An example of one of the ubiquitous aimless crowds ever present in the Slum was shambling up and down the street. Presently Vel Thaidis wandered with it. The street gave on to a square on three sides of which the blue buildings lined up their archways, while on the fourth the high wall angled away. Near the square's center a fire was blazing in a large iron pot. A woman tended it, the sweat raining from her heat-bitten face. Buckets swung over the pot on a hook and bar device, boiled, and were removed, and fresh buckets hung up. A queue filed to the pot and away, handing the woman, along with each full receptacle, a credit chip or article of barter. The barter the woman picked over, shaking off all the time her furious sweat. She was an aqua-boiler, to whom unfortunates, who had lost a personal brazier in which to purify the Jate's supply of liquid, had recourse.

Vel Thaidis, pushed to the wall, saw a knot of women coming from the pot-queue with their now-drinkable rations. The fourth woman in the knot was barefoot.

Vel Thaidis edged through the crowd and ran to the woman. Halting in her path, Vel Thaidis pulled off her sandals.

211

"These," she said, "for a drink of that."

The woman looked at Vel Thaidis with scorn as she reached and grabbed the sandals.

"You must be an imbecile, girl. To offer me *both* shoes. One would have bought you drink. Still, you witnessed her, didn't you, friends?"

The women, envious of their comrade's luck, and contemptuous of the imbecile, grumbled mocking assent.

"Drink then," said the woman, and set her bucket before Vel Thaidis on the ground.

Vel Thaidis knelt in the brown dust and scooped the aqua into her mouth with her palms. It remained hot from the fire and scalded her fingers, lips and throat. After she had achieved five or six mouthfuls, the woman drew the bucket away. She was already wearing the sandals, which were a little too small for her. She had tongued off the smears from them, and now paraded their sparkle coyly.

"I trust you came by them legally," the woman said. "If the Law asks me, I can describe you very well."

Vel Thaidis stared at her, and felt heavy remorse. She had learned want and fear, she had learned villainy. She understood, at last.

In that instant, a commotion began in the crowd behind her, in the square. To begin, there was only shouting, a confused bustle of movement and an illustration of speed which had not been there previously. Then a part of the queue seemed to explode. A woman fell, and a man came jumping over her back, his arms and legs pummeling.

Vel Thaidis received the impression of one driven mad, the straggly flying hair and limbs, wide-open mouth and eyes that flashed, for in his extreme agitation the polarizing inner lids were fluttering up and down. This had almost blinded the man, yet he kept running and now his arm struck against the suspending device over the fire pot. Aqua tipped and sloshed upon the flames and gouts of steam arose. Shrieks of outrage at fluid wasted were coupled to the wholesale yelling, as the press sprung aside, to avoid more than the onrush of the demented sprinter.

The crowd had peeled back now to the very walls and arches that framed the square and led from it. Vel Thaidis saw several men burst up the deformed trees in the street beyond.

The running man ran on. No one questioned him, attempted to detain or chase him.

As he raced from sight, so the outcry in the street and square also vanished. No one uttered or moved. Plastered to the walls, tensed, noiseless, they waited.

Half a minute elapsed.

Then the atmosphere sizzled. What the people anticipated was coming.

The air tore.

Two red-brown metal missiles, horizontal, parallel to the earth and five feet above it, pierced into the square. Their jets sent a colorless emission after them, their rounded heads pointed inexorably. The velocity in this populated area was not great, sixty or seventy staeds an hour. Probably, too, power had been reduced in order that the hunt be prolonged, for plainly it was reckoned a public show.

With a hiss and tide of heat, the Lawguards came level, flared by, and were gone. Swerve and battle as he might, they could not lose their target.

Uproar broke out again. Jammed in the maelstrom, Vel Thaidis beheld face after face, identical. Excited, electrified, transformed by terror and greed, the lust to see another less fortunate in this most misfortuned place. New shouts: "The outer ramp! On to the roof!"

The crowd, like a single organism, hurled itself forward, and Vel Thaidis, swathed in its mass, was hurled forward with it.

Her feet almost left the ground. She was borne upward, along a slanting walk that led from the street to the apex of one of the blue metal buildings. Glazed matte though the metal was, it gave off a furnace breath of sun. The plastum ramp sang under the thud of footfalls.

They were on the roof, sixty feet up. The crowd gushed against the railing, climbed on each other's backs, pointed, swore. Through smolders, between chimneys and blocks, they could see him running still, small as an insect now, and behind, a few staeds off, the copper pointers, ever in his wake.

"That's Nesh. It must be," a woman said to Vel Thaidis. She leaned on Vel Thaidis' arm, for they were all brothers and sisters at this minute, bound by their hunger and their sublimated fear. "Nesh—he stole minerals from the manufact where he had worked, and made a gas-gun, and shot his woman's customer with it."

"No," said a man close to them, "not her customer—her employer. But it's Nesh."

213

"Her employer *and* her customer. Also the woman's neighbor,"—another.

"They'll drag him howling to the Zenith,"—another.

"He'll roast."

"His guts will bake."

The small figure was flagging now, as if weighed down by the burden of so much amplified hate. On other roofs all about people had scrambled for a vantage.

The Lawguards gained suddenly, for the spectacle could be prolonged no further, the man was on his knees. Tentacles shot from the pursuers, scores of them, thin as threads in the distance, wrapping and wrapping him, raising him, bearing him. And now the two rockets upended and came vertical and were two copper needles with a knitting between them, and a struggling insect tangled in it. The crowds on all the roofs cheered, and when the cheering died, Vel Thaidis heard his cries, erupting to their freedom as he could not, hitting the walls and blending to a ghastly music.

They would carry him to the nearest precinct of Law. They would not hurt him, only question him, to be sure. After which, the Zenith desert.

*If I delay with the knife on my wrist,* Vel Thaidis thought, *there is my end.* Then, almost a cry within her: *No knife. Here is the means!*

The crowd, deflated, began to disperse. Soon she was alone on the roof, the sun beating on her skull. The revelation was extraordinary. Nesh had killed with a gas-gun. Driven by his madness, (who but a mad or desperate man would commit murder when the process of the Law was virtually inescapable?) yet it had been difficult for Nesh to obtain a weapon— he had to steal and construct it himself. But such an implement was easier of access to Vel Thaidis. Easier than a knife. More certain than a knife.


"You assured me you'd permit me my death," Vel Thaidis said. "I have come for it."

Dina Sirrid had lifted her head, bound this time in a scarf of luminous white that made her whitened face sallow, her teeth ocher bones, her eyes lusterless and black as two holes. If enjoyment or interest touched her, she did not reveal for the moment.

To reenter the Instation had been uncomplex. As Vel Thaidis stood before the steel door, a voice had asked of her, in the manner of mechanical Slum entrances, "Give name and reason for approach."

"Vel Thaidis," she said, "formerly titled Yune Hirz. I seek Dina Sirrid, who pledged she would receive me."

The door, instructed presumably by the Instation's mistress, opened and let Vel Thaidis in, next showing her, by pointing hands which lit on the walls, the way she must take to reach her objective.

The journey to the door, however, had not been so simple. It had taken more than three hours. An initial hour of asking direction through the maze of streets, of following it, in some cases observing she had been willfully misled, turning aside and asking again. The city clocks were raucously speaking the fourteenth hour when she emerged onto the border road which led up to the Instation of hest-Uma. Two hours had elapsed as she walked from the fringe of the Slum, up the steep incline. She had walked perforce barefoot, and before she left the city, already she stepped in her own blood, leaving footprints any might note.

Some way up the slope, she sat by the road and knew she could go no farther. An apple bush grew there, withered and black, yet affording spots of shade. The shade erratically revived her. She told herself that she could, after all, proceed, and must do so. If she would only suffer this, Velday would live and Hirz would live through Velday. She recalled legends of ancient contests before the Yunea had been settled, when ancestors had been glad to die, providing they could pass shoulder to shoulder with a dead foe and providing their house persisted after them.

Half mocking herself, she thought: *Demonstrably, I was weaned on ideas of honor*. But nevertheless, her impetus was renewed.

Somehow she got herself the rest of the way up the hill to the brown barren ridge, the steel building with its thin, thin towers, and so into it and to Dina Sirrid who had formerly said to her: "The gun is always here, ready for you."

Yet now, Dina Sirrid had remarked, "Whatever can you want of me?"

Vel Thaidis had answered, "You assured me you'd permit me my death. I have come for it."

"You disappoint me, Thaidis. I thought, after your display of determination, you'd last rather longer."

"The odds against me were too great."

"True. But I believed you hadn't yet realized as much."

215

Dina Sirrid unfolded to her feet. "The gun is locked away. I'll take you."

"Tell me first—am I to have privacy? No machine to watch my death?"

"If you want, why not? Privacy leading to the ultimate privacy. Are you concerned as to what crematory arrangements will be made?"

"No. But the gun—will you explain the principle of it?"

"Why do you need to know that?" Dina Sirrid inquired. "To know it will kill you is surely enough."

"You told me," Vel Thaidis said, "when I sought you, you would be courteous and kind because you had derived pleasure from my wretchedness. Look at my feet. Be kind, be courteous."

"Have I grown large in your sky, at last?" Dina Sirrid asked. "Yes, I see I have. Hang on my words, then. Touch the activator and direct the nozzle of a gas-gun at any subject, in this instance, yourself. Immediately, the gun will read you. Your chromosomes, atoms, blood, brain-wave, pulse, the very ladder of nerves buried in your spine. Next, compress the gun's flexite bulb. The minerals in the bulb will already have formed a puff of gas inimical to you alone. Use such a device in a crowded chamber, and you alone die. The closer to your flesh, the more lethal and therefore the swifter the dose. But I've seen men fired on by such a gun at a distance of several yards, and the gas marked them down and slew them quite efficiently, though more leisurely, hurtfully. The principle: human uniqueness. As no human, even a twin, is ever entirely identical to another, so our bodily content, the grandplan of our individual survival, is in each unique and can be chemically reversed—the gas—to choke on a breath of unique poison. We rejoice, even in our murder, Thaidis, that we're not part of the huge battery of machines. Better than our robots, which are as alike as one Jate to another."

"How often can the gun be fired?"

"Curious question, Thaidis. Should I suspect duplicity?"

"If I should miss—"

"Haven't I explained there's no possibility of your missing? Generally these guns will fire seven or eight times, rendering seven or eight individual poisons. The gun I offer you has only one charge."

Vel Thaidis had lowered her head. She had absorbed the talk in the street—the murdered persons numbering three— she had assumed this gun also would have several charges.

216

"Yes," Dina Sirrid said musingly. "I'd almost begun to distrust you. Except that, for the murder of another than yourself, unavoidable death is your payment—so what gain? Come, then."

The round pale room was as Vel Thaidis remembered, the panels, voices of hidden mechanisms, bathed in the turgid, harshly shining light of the Instation. The great plastum chair was also present, in the arm of which reposed the gun.

"Vel Thaidis, erstwhile Yune Hirz," Dina Sirrid informed the room, "has come here to avail herself of death."

The panels responded, flashing gold then black.

In the confusion of her plan, which seemed coming unwoven as she took it up, Vel Thaidis nevertheless cowered inwardly. To be twenty-one years and hear of the world's end—for the world was alive only while she experienced, felt, knew of it—she could hardly bear this vocalized sentence. For if she did not die this hour, yet she would die soon. Death deferred remained death.

Dina Sirrid depressed buttons along one wall and all the panels were suddenly colorless and the murmurings silent.

"I've shut off the machinery in this chamber," she said. "Now, neither overlooked nor overheard. The partition will also open in the arm of the chair. Go and take the gun, little girl."

On slow, slow feet—she welcomed their blazing living agony—Vel Thaidis went to the chair. She recalled the partition as if she had seen it operated only moments before. The gun, a black serpent, lay curled within, awaiting her. She put in her hand, and at the contact of flesh, metal and flexite, she felt the breath of oblivion on her neck.

What had been her unwoven plan? To kill the woman with the first charge of the gun. (In contemplation, Dina Sirrid's death had seemed naturally less real than her own.) But the gun, she had learned, held only one charge, that charge her gift to Ceedres—not enough poison left to account even for herself, then. (The blunt knives of Seta would have to serve her if not the man. But she was not so well-armored as he, more brittle, softer, requiring less to be broken. And if it was terror, she must not think of it.) Yet now, in this place where no machine kept track or record to raise an alarm, Vel Thaidis must somehow destroy or disable the Instation's mistress, unaided by the gun.

She held the gun cupped in her hands, like a small animal

217

she nursed. The raised nub, its activator, was tempting, unusable.

*Fool,* she thought. *As Ceedres called you: fool. What now, fool? What will you do?*

Everything was a question. She had no answer, could no longer reason, could not decide.

It would be simple to stand forever, the gun in her hands, her eyes closed, her soul leaking out of her.

"Strange," Dina Sirrid's voice entered Vel Thaidis' head like an iron pin. "You seem less fervent than you said. Perhaps, when I've left you, your suicidal inspiration will return."

"Wait," Vel Thaidis cried. She darted around on the woman, the gun still clasped unweaponlike to her, her face full of misgiving.

"Ah!" Dina Sirrid let out that yap of hers. "Now I see it. You want to take the gun away with you, and I must be incapable of warning the Law of the theft. Well, girl, either you use up the gun on me, or you fail. Do you reckon a Slum dweller in my exalted position knows nothing of defending herself. I'd cripple you, little aristo. Little tender lady. Your snapped bones would rattle under your satin skin." But the Instation's mistress seemed only amused, not threatening. "Despite everything," she said, "you go on performing for me. I've heard some gossip from the J'ara quarter. Let me put it together for you. You had a lover, one of your own princely class, a man you hate since your exile. Would the gun be for him?"

Dina Sirrid toyed with a fold of her white scarf, and with Vel Thaidis' life.

"You see," said the woman, "my predicament, here in this room with its machinery shut off, where nothing records what we do or what we say. I abide by the Law at all times. But the notion of two dead aristos—one slain by Vel Thaidis, Vel Thaidis herself carried to the Zenith to bubble and crisp and fry—how I relish it. How it tickles me. Worth a brief discomfort to allow it, maybe. A handful of lies. For I can lie somewhat to the Lawguards, a talent few possess. Did you see the chase in the streets, the zenen Nesh hunted down by the Law? The screen here shows such things. They freshen all our lives. Shall I let you refresh my life?"

Vel Thaidis did not mean to speak, yet the sentences came.

"I ask only the opportunity. I'll kill him, and must therefore die myself."

218

"But can I rely on you not to disappoint me? Delicate hands flinching aside at the last instant."

"I won't disappoint you."

"You hate him so much?"

"I hate him."

"An extra thing," said the woman. "Shall I?" she queried of herself. "Shall I? Yes. You aristos," she said, "so well educated. I wonder if you know this? But then, you know your world is round, but, in common with all your kind, never needing to, you'd find it hard to visualize as such. And the world's turning; you grasp the Stations of the hours through hest and hespa, but not their significance. No. And the Fading Lands. You know the name. But what are *they*?"

Vel Thaidis simply stared.

"Very well," said Dina Sirrid. "The Fading Lands lie beyond the hunting lands, seven hundred staeds outward of the great estates. Far from the temples and far from the beasts, and far from men, farther than you ever went, riding or in your mind. These are the lands where the sun has fallen low, a burning coal on the horizon, and where the sky's dark as the shade of a Maram-chamber. Where your shadow runs before you, but like no shadow you ever saw, long and black, a phantom on the ground, leading you to the door of hell. These are the Fading Lands, my lady. And were you aware the Law and its guards will pursue a criminal to the edge of them—and *no farther*? What a hideaway, among those long shadows, those cheerless Jates and Marams.

"Why do I mention it?" Dina Sirrid asked. "Because we Slum dwellers like the chase to be prolonged. Kill your lover, and then steal his princely chariot and run. Run for the Fading Lands, little aristo. See if you can get there."

Vel Thaidis' face had not altered. Her eyes were sightless. Dina Sirrid hit her lightly, stingingly, across the cheek.

"Your feet are almost walked to the bone. Can you still reach him?"

"Yes," Vel Thaidis whispered. With one hand she smoothed her cheek, again glad at the reality of her own body.

"Flirt with some man on a sled. He might give you carriage. You won't care what he does, will you? It won't concern you long." Dina Sirrid waved at the gun. "Employ the nozzle to strike me. Strike here," she touched the base of her skull under the white scarf. "Strike as hard as you care to. It should seem genuine to those who'll come to investigate me. You see, I turned to leave you, scornful, and you flew at

219

me. I was lax, but innocent of abetting your crime. Take the right-hand passages—there'll be three—and out of the hind exit onto the path by the road." Dina Sirrid turned and walked toward the door. "Come," she invited, "you must do it now."

Restraint left Vel Thaidis as dry plaster a wall. She moved forward, the gun raised. She hammered the woman across the head with the whole force of her arm. Only when the impact jolted her was she horrified.

Dina Sirrid plunged straight down as though her limbs had disintegrated.

Vel Thaidis sprang over her (Nesh had done the same thing with the tumbled woman in the square) and through three passages, and through the door which opened, and out under the white-green fever of the sky.

A quarter down the road leading to the buildings of the Slumopolis, she heard the clocks shrieking the seventeenth hour.

It was Maram. In another hour, Seta would light its yellow beacon. Ceedres could stroll onto the pier.

How slowly she moved. Had the Jate gone from her? The last Jate of her life.

Perhaps she had misheard the voices of the thousand clocks.

The agony in her feet had mounted into her stomach, her ribs, her breasts, and droned thickly in her ears. Yet she knew the agony, was accustomed to it. The occasional heightening of agony—a stone trodden, or a patch of rougher ground—penetrated the ambience of the hurt like a dull cry, making her start, but that was all. The deep lakes of dust glazed the amber wounds. She did not imagine Ceedres' death, or her own. Or Velday saved. Or Hirz, or honor, or despair. All she visualized at last was the mansion of black and gold, its steps, its entrance: an end to walking.

A minute after she had thought she heard Maram struck, she made out, vague and nearly irrelevant, a noise behind her on the road.

The noise was one of wheels, not the runners of a sled. Wheels which rotated at colossal speed, and the thud of metallic animals bounding.

Vel Thaidis paused, looked over her shoulder listlessly.

Over the crest of the ridges, winged by two huge foamings

of gilded dust, came a brazen shape, leaping formless upon her.

It was a chariot, burnished bronze, the two robot lion-dogs hurtling before it, its velocity a hundred staeds an hour. And all the once the speed strained back, the mechanical beasts upreared and static.

*Ceedres*, she thought. Her knees buckling, heart stopped.

But it was not Ceedres.

A white parasol with a three-tiered fringe of gold nodded its flower-shade above two young princes. Their faces were merry. And known.

"In order not to collide with her," one said to the other, "having sensed her, the chariot nearly somersaulted. Why didn't she get from the way as they usually do?"

"Recompense," said the other, "for the near-somersault. You, girl, keep J'ara with us."

"Oh really, Du, there's better at any of the mansions."

"No, no," Du—Darvu Yune Chure—answered stubbornly. "I fancy this one's looks."

The other, his cousin Kewel, whined in feigned revulsion.

Darvu himself leaned over the rail and grabbed her hair in a cruel and biting grip. "Up, zenena. Think of the robot service credits you might get out of me."

She did not consider saying to them: *Do you not know me?* Plainly they did not. How often had she met with them? Perhaps thirty times during the years of her childhood and young womanhood. She had always thought them stupid. She had not foreseen they could be brutish and dangerous. But then, never before had she encountered them as a girl of the Slumopolis.

Darvu was wrenching her into the chariot, hauling her over the rail, by her hair, her arm. She screamed with the pain, but her mind worked separately, still striving with this problem. Her dilapidated condition, her bloody feet, stimulated the cousins. Psychologically, they were powerless ever to recognize her, or of being consciously *willing* to recognize her. She had passed beyond the pale, and was fair game. And maybe a subconscious glimpse of this stimulated them more than anything else.

And so, detached, she pressed the gas-gun to Darvu's chest. She knew another thing these two did not, that this gun could only fire once.

Darvu dropped back, letting go of her.

221

"Out," she said. "Out, handsome aristos. Out, or I kill you both."

*I have caught the argot,* she thought. But that was good. Under her feet, the rugs of Chure were downy and yet gravel to her ruined soles. Darvu and Kewel were blundering from the vehicle. As Kewel went, she lifted the driver-box from his grip, and the long reins.

"Pathetic zenena," Kewel blustered. "This is against the Law."

"And the Law's already on your bleeding heels, bitch," Darvu added frantically.

Then she felt the talons of destiny close on her for sure. She understood Darvu spoke a fact, and glanced behind her, and saw about ten staeds down the road into the city, sunlight fire on copper.

Dina Sirrid had been afraid and gambled for her life. Under her white scarf—the shock and the jar—might have been any skull-protective covering. She had acted her concussion. She had alerted the Law as soon as Vel Thaidis was from the building. This time, Vel Thaidis' avowed intention to become a murderess would be enough to send her to execution.

For a second, everything was clear, and bright, and terrible before her. Then only panic ruled Vel Thaidis, and panic was her teacher.

A chariot of the princely houses could match, perhaps outrun, the Lawguards on their jets of air. Who had ever tried? And she had seen Velday, and others, motivate the chariots.

She spun the dial on the driver-box. The chariot flung itself about, animate, febrile, away from the Zenith and the Slum. As quite recently she had seen Ceedres do, she thrust the speedometer to its maximum.

The guiding reins unreeled and braced like solid steel in her hands.

The world cracked in fragments, swirled, became fluid, became smoke. Green smoke and gold and white, it was smashed before the chariot and burst away on either side.

She did not think at all. Of the electric barrier about the estates which would open for such a chariot, though for no human traffic of the Slums, of the roads to which the chariot would adhere, the faults and spurs it would jump, of the estates themselves, the hunting lands and their temples, the cliffs, defiles and outer places, of the Fading Lands. Of Dina

222

Sirrid's soliloquy, the sun a coal, the sky a Maram-chamber shade.

A face steamed away through her mind, Ceedres' face, growing distant. She had accomplished nothing, would die for her intent alone.

She ran, as Nesh had run, but better able.

After her, informed of her schemes, programmed to punish them, the copper rockets of justice, that none had ever escaped.

And overhead, eternal, pitiless and unmoved, the sun, the sun.

# Part Two

Dorte the Upperling slumped in his chair aboard the transport. Now and then, as he ran his eyes across the gang of men, he smoothed the festive red and blue drape, or toyed, aristo-like, with the metal nuggets on his cloak. Presently, the transport would arrive in the pressurized plastomil chamber which opened to the surface of the planet. The men sat or sprawled, expressionless, almost mindless, at the prospect. After a Tenjate's labor, they would be awarded one Jate of rest, so the machine of the Klave stipulated, for surface work required, if not invention, at least precision. Long before the Tenjate was reached, however, men began to slacken. Grayly they hung there before Dorte, who reveled in their grayness and in his freedom from it. The only irritant was the aristocrat, Klarn. Klarn alone showed no sign of moral or physical collapse. Indeed, the rumors of the Subterior had altered, become sympathetic to the exiled prince. Dorte, every time he glanced in Klarn's direction, felt a stab of uncontrollable yet unusable hatred. Klarn, who should have come to his knees, succumbed to the poison-drink, to turpitude, abjection, suicide, had remained the same. His face was weary and its hollows and young lines deep-carved, but the basic resolution and strength of the face were not dissipated. In fact, Dorte detected in squirming frustration, a new interest in something seemed somberly flickering there.

The throats and maws of black holes went by. The rock itself, frosted, catching the transport's gleam, returned it spasmodically in blue and white refractions. Occasionally, ice rods like glass, or pipes of rock, dully boomed or whistled at the air blasts of the vehicle's elevating motors.

Dorte turned from these uninspiring vistas—the sub-planet, Klarn—to Zuse the ganger. Nauseated by another Maram's drinking, the man crumpled on his bench, too wise to groan.

"Zuse," said Dorte, "I see you kept J'ara."

"Yes, Dorte."

"You were misguided, were you not?"

"I was."

"If you get sick, I must dispense with you from my gangs, eh, Zuse?"

"I won't get sick, Dorte."

"You're sick now."

"No, Dorte—"

"Don't interrupt, Zuse. Never interrupt me. I had not finished."

Zuse waited. This was a game Dorte sometimes played. If the victim pleaded and groveled sufficiently, as a rule, Dorte gave over, and left the unfortunate his place as ganger. To be ill or drunk was not necessary for the game to begin. If there were no weakness evident, Dorte would guess one, devise one. There were genuine weaknesses enough to be hazarded on, or prophesied.

"I think," said Dorte, "I think, I will award Zuse one Jate's grace. See how he does his work. There are," said Dorte, "many men in the Subterior hungry for your luck, Zuse. Recall Hejerdi—laid off by his elegance here, our aristo friend. Still sharing wages with him, Klarn? He won't get back on my gangs now. Unless you'd care to exchange your place with his. I hear you give up a lot—clothing, coal. Though one Maram, a fine aristo lady came to celebrate a J'ara with you. Or is that a lie? Eh, Klarn? Eh?" Casrus was expected to reply, but he did not. Dorte rose from his chair, and strode to where Casrus sat still on his bench. "Stand up," Dorte said. Casrus did so. "There are no Stare-Eyes here," said Dorte. "Like to duel with me, would you? I never gave you the chance before."

"If I touched you," said Casrus, "I would lose my employment."

224

"Just so," said Dorte. "But if I beat you across the face, what would you say then?"

One of the men said, fiercely, anxious for the fight, for difference of any sort: "Hit him, Dorte!"

Casrus' eyes were steady and unreadable to Dorte, who could divine only the most basic optic emotions. Nevertheless, the blueness, the very construction of them unnerved the Upperling, so that, not meaning to, he swung forward his clenched hand to deliver a blow across the aristocrat's mouth. But the features, eyes, mouth, blurred over and were gone. Without apparent effort or forethought, Casrus had moved aside. Dorte's hand lashed against the padded wall of the transport, bouncing back to him, his own blow recoiling, catching him in the chest. Too wise to laugh as too wise to groan, the gang of men watched acidly from under their lids.

Dorte, at a loss, did nothing, but his face set in an almost lifeless rigor.

Exactly then, the transport grounded. A curious suspension in time seemed to afflict the Upperling. The light of the pressurized chamber doused the windows; the door was already opening, and already the men were scrambling in silence for their air-suits. And Dorte remained rigid, doing nothing, suspended. Suits donned, the men began to file to the flier exit and drop down into the chamber. Casrus, too, had passed Dorte, and was suited, leaving.

Then Dorte recovered himself, and spoke.

"Zuse. Here."

Zuse turned. His invalid's face, trapped in its milky bubble of inflated air, had strangely distorted with foreboding.

As the others trod on their heavy soles to the surface doors, Zuse stood in a pear-shaped cage of oxygen, nausea and cringing, before the gang-master. Dorte's voice came through a little speaker attachment, and so through the knob on Zuse's shoulder. He could not avoid hearing every word, nor avoid rendering audible replies.

"You comprehend," said Dorte. "I'm not meaning you should harm him. That's murder. We don't want that."

"No, Dorte."

"So you must be subtle. Careful. You're sure of the spot? Of course you are, you saw it first. Clever. Just a lesson to him. It's a kindness. No hurt. Just an aristocratic jest. You and someone else do it. I don't mind who. But he's tricky. You've seen how tricky. Do it pleasingly and there'll be a few chips in it for you. Remember, though, I've not told you to

225

do anything. Smear me in your muck, and the whole three gangs will suffer. No one will like that."

"No, Dorte."

"Out you go, then." Paternally, Dorte smiled Zuse toward the exit, and Zuse obeyed.

Vyen Klovez, a male doll dressed in black velvet, with one dull silver streak running from his left temple the length of his black hair, placed a burnished silver urn on the Klarn robot's extended carrying attachment.

"Take Temal, with my compliments, to Casrus in the Subterior." The robot acquiesced and turned to go. "Wait. You have yet to find out from the computers where Casrus is."

"It is already known," announced the robot.

Vyen paused. Curiously he inquired: "How? Because you're Klarn property?"

"Because the exact location of Casrus Klarn was formerly ascertained at the request of your sister."

Vyen's face molded into ice.

"Why would she want to know?"

"Vitra Klovez was taken to the Subterior by a transport."

The ice grew icier.

"When?"

The robot stated Jate and hour.

"I was informed she was riding the Klovez car about the city."

"We were programmed to tell you so."

The ice splintered into a very bestial, dogga-like grin. Vyen for a moment savored Vitra's unawareness, priming the robots temporarily to conceal her activity, but neither to conceal the concealment nor any subsequent anomalies. Brother and sister generally greeted each other's errors with peculiar minglings of fascinated delight and protective alarm. On this occasion, fury and fear were added.

"Where is Vitra now?"

"Rise Iu chamber of Fabulism."

In the minimum of time, Vyen had joined her there.

The chamber of the dome was closed, Vitra the Fabulast safely ensconced to weave dreams for the Subterine worms. Vyen waited two or three minutes, and then began to rain violent blows upon the polished doors. A glow appeared in the wall, and a machine vocalized.

"Please desist."

226

"No. And don't instruct me to again. My sister must be called, and must come out at once."

"This is unusual."

Soaring into a pale and mad-eyed animosity, Vyen altered his tone to become a scream: "Don't argue with me! Do as I say!"

"Please wait. Vitra Klovez will be called."

Vyen paced, a ring of white showing all about his gray irises, and his dogga-white teeth bared. A fiddle-toy of thin plastivory snapped between his fingers, and as he snarled and kicked it aside, the dome chamber doors slid apart and Vitra came out.

Her face was quite desperate, even before she confronted him. Without any attempt at evasion or bluff, she spread her arms and wailed, "Oh Vyen—something dreadful!"

The instant he saw her, the normal reactions took hold of her brother. His basic security was reaffirmed and his spitefulness flared up. In harmony, this spite became a consortium between them, a weapon honed for others. With no outsider to use it on, a special phase was entered, more intriguing and more unnerving, a desire to wound her coupled with an aversion to wounding.

For a few moments, Vyen lapsed into an enraged tirade. Its substance was Vitra's visit to Casrus, and the borders of the substance hinted at plans revealed, strangleholds offered to enemies. Its epilogue was the inference that Vitra was a slut, who ran after a man who had no care for her.

Throughout all this, Vitra seemed to hang there, virtually in midair. Vyen, ranting, waited for the narrow hand to smash against his cheek, the nails to rake his neck, the reedy musical voice to rise into a howl capable of insults worse than his own. And even in doubt and anxiety he half enjoyed this preface to a vast impending conflict between them. Then, as Vitra, unresponsive, only gazed at him with wild dilated eyes, Vyen's clockwork diatribe ran down.

"Well," he eventually demanded, "what do you say?"

"Oh, Vyen," repeated Vitra, "something awful."

And suddenly she seized his hand, and drew him into the chamber of the Fabulism.

"I erased the tapes," she haltingly said. "I did. I truly did."

"What tapes? The tapes of your sun-world? *Life!* I should hope you did."

"No, but," said Vitra. She pointed to the empty air. "It goes on. I can't make it end."

227

"What do you mean?" Immemorial procrastination. He knew.

But Vitra continued her explanation with appalled precision.

"I had a new plot. The story of a prince who invents a beautiful robot woman real as flesh—"

"Unoriginal," drawled Vyen inappropriately, trying to stave off facts.

"But the images refused to come. Instead—"

"Instead? *Well?*"

"Look."

Vitra pressed a key in the tray of keys, and into the air uncurled a cloud of shapes, colors and light.

The chariot, drawn but not powered by its leaping brazen beasts, speared along the sun-stitched metal roads of the Slumopolis outland. The golden girl, dyed hair blown straight back like a tongue of fire, black tunic molded over her body, the material also blown back and held out behind her as if secured on wires; she resembled a statue, though she traveled almost too fast for any to see.

The air-shield, which Vel Thaidis did not understand, or know of, or contemplate, had raised itself from the prow of the Chure chariot to guard her against the flying dusts and missiles stirred up by their speed. The chariot cut the atmosphere cleanly, clearing all obstacles—sand drifts, shallow ditches—automatically. Human obstacles, which would have halted it, also automatically, did not present themselves. If humans were on the roads, they had dashed from the path of the volcanic rocket which the vehicle had become. Its velocity was at the maximum, two hundred staeds an hour. A fraction more.

If she passed unseen (beyond a rush, a flame), neither did she see about her. Tumbling washes of light, unraveling lines of green and brown, were all she beheld, the waves of the lake of air the chariot cleaved.

Even at her back, she could have seen nothing, if she had looked. How near or far they were, those things which pursued her, or how many. But she had passed, for the moment, beyond looking, or thinking. Hunted, she ran. It was sufficient.

"You see," said Vitra.

"I see you're insane. Stop this."

"I can't. As I operate the keys, this fills my mind—and so the screen."

"Then, if you've no control of yourself, leave it. Come away."

"I'm a Fabulast, I must return sometime. Have I actually lost my mind?" she gasped.

"Oh, very probably."

But his fingers trembled as he hesitantly struck down the keys in the tray, and dragged her from the room.

The three round domes of the building were supported on three cylindrical towers, about fifty feet high, twenty in diameter. The towers were linked together by pillared walks below, pillared walkways above. The creamy white metal of the building throbbed softly under the stars, held in the black fluid of space and space-black rock. No sound emanated from the areas. Only the vast silence of the planet's surface came to the men within their air-suits.

No other manufactured thing was visible in any direction. Far away, left behind, the busy machines of the nighttime surface, the clumsily bounding figures of workers. Zuse had brought his two companions, a ganger whose name had not been announced, and Casrus, beyond the installations, saying oddly, "This is a place we were sent to Jates ago. Only I remembered. But it's like an invented building, a god's house in the hot-side Fabulism."

So it was, indeed. Save it was a cold metal rather than a warm one, and set in bleak darkness rather than a musky dusty valley, honeyed over with perpetual sun. Save that it made no noise, stood voiceless under the stars. Zuse partly recollected; Casrus, who had set himself not to forget, recollected all. To him the comparison was phenomenal, yet somehow expected. The third ganger, equally uninterested in all the structures of the surface, stimulated only by Zuse's side-of-the-mouth mutterings, balanced nearby, waiting.

Now Casrus said, "Why should you suppose I'm interested in the resemblance to a Fabulism?"

"Last Maram, I met Hejerdi. He said you'd gone to the screen at Center Kaa."

"I imagine," said Casrus in his habitual quiet, measuring fashion, "that you told Dorte of my interest, connecting it with this edifice. A convenience. What had Dorte instructed you to do?"

Zuse stared, not exactly in embarrassment or strain. More in relief.

"I knew you'd guess it. Dorte's sharpening knives for you."

229

"Attack would be subject to failure out here, where there is no atmosphere," Casrus said, "so presumably we're meant to go inside."

Impatient, yet sluggish, the other ganger said, "Let's do it now, Zuse."

"No. Klarn's right. Out here we'd fly. And haven't you heard how Klarn can fight?"

"This isn't any fire-sword pretty arena," said the ganger, but he made no move.

"This way," said Zuse.

He floundered forward, and as he approached, the door in the nearer tower slid open to receive them, as the door of the temple had done to admit Ceedres Yune Thar, Vel Thaidis Yune Hirz, in the Fabulism. If mere Fabulism it was.

One by one, floating a little in the airlessness, they entered the circular chamber. The door shut, but the ghostly dark was incomplete. A vague illumination had woken to greet them. Even the pillars were there, nacreously gleaming. And above, what? A room of religion and golden globes, a second hidden room of black space and the brilliant mercury drops of the stars?

"Come," said Zuse, absurdly proud to show off the building, whose significance, whatever it might be, only he had noted till now.

Casrus said, "Inform me of Dorte's wishes."

The ganger made his move, untutored, at Casrus' back. Casurs flowed away, the ganger careered on, his great and purposeless leap bearing him up into the ceiling. His yell of anger and disorientation mewed through the microphone knobs, almost amusing.

"There's a room below," said Zuse. "We were to stun you, throw you down, let the floor close. Sometimes men get lost on the surface and never found. I'd say that was Dorte's hope. Or if you should free yourself, or a machine unearthed you, I'm to be his witness and he mine that neither of us meant anything against you, or knew you'd come here. Not many know of this building. The machines seldom come. Last time they took metal from the walls for use somewhere else."

The soaring ganger tumbled to earth.

"You dolt, you clot—" he said to Zuse.

"Shut your mouth. Klarn's a safer bet than Dorte. How if," said Zuse, "you go down in the underroom, and I come here next Jate and I let you out. Dorte will be satisfied. You

230

can say you discovered a way to get free. Then we'll have a hold over him, do you see?"

"I'm to trust you," said Casrus.

"If I don't do as Dorte said," Zuse answered, "I'll lose my post in his gangs. And maybe get a beating in a slink some Maram, besides."

"And you're certain that argument will sway me," Casrus said flatly, and thought of Temal, who, last time he had been betrayed, had used almost these words to warn him—to no avail. "You think my concern for you will outweigh my self-preservation?"

"Look at Hejerdi. You hurt him, and next you tend him. Look at the crowd you give coal to, and food. You put us first."

"Before my life?"

"Let's kill him now," droned the unnamed ganger. "No one would come on him here. No one can see."

"Try to kill me," said Casrus.

And then he caught himself. Beheld himself. Changed. Vitra and the workings of fate had finally engineered an alteration. Because how positive was this world he had been sacrificing himself for? To this question, his thoughts since the Fabulism had led him.

Zuse was running in rocket-like plummets across the floor. Now Casrus stood alone on it, held by his heavy soles, his heavy painful doubt: What am I engaged in, and with what validity? For if a dream is real, this reality may have lost its roots. Life on the planet's hot-side was deemed impossible, yet maybe is not. Does this cold world exist? For the first, he felt the agonized onus of self, the exclusion of all others, the cry of the voice within: I too have a right to live, to be, to remain. That terrible cry, inside the very chamber of the brain. While all other cries, however loud, however piteous, must sound in exile beyond the walls.

And then, Zuse shouted.

"Down! Down! Down!"

Casrus realized simultaneously that he had halted at the floor's center. The floor was now jerkily sinking, and inexorably, unsuspected panels of the room above were closing over. Looking up, Casrus perceived the two men, transfixed as if with the same aimless surprise as he himself, craning over, before the closing panels blocked them out.

Even as he had glimpsed the mirage of self-preservation, the way to it had been barred. No matter. It was as he

231

deserved. With abrupt unanticipated sour-tasting humility, he thought: *Here is my punishment, my wages, attempting to be a god, attempting to steady the toppling world. No man could do it. I have made it worse.*

But ironically the utter blackness which might have been reckoned to accompany punishment, did not come. Instead, slowly, second by second, the under-chamber flooded with a rich red-golden glare.

It was sunlight, simulated but nevertheless accurate. More accurate than the notion of the Klarn salon. Ripe, very nearly raw, burning the backs of the eyes.

Zuse had not seen this light, which came only with incarceration. It could blind a man who, all his Jates, all his Marams, had dwelt in the cool dusk of the Klave. So. It was to be a punishment of flame, not dark.

After a moment, Casrus slipped to his knees. His body did not swim, and it occurred to him that with the light had bloomed a new young air, but blazing and unbearable.

And then another door furled wide in the curving wall of the light. This door was black, a cave of shade, and toward it, bowed over under the burden of fire, instinctively Casrus crawled.

He reached the dark, seemed to slide forward, and then there came another closing over, hemming in, initially merciful, eventually not merciful at all.

After a while, he got to his feet in the darkness.

The support of the air persisted about the bubble of the suit. The cold lay also the other side of it. The rest was black. Impenetrable black after impenetrable gold. And yet, despite this, he sensed a wide way ahead. And then—

And then the ground shook itself.

Vitra, standing on the threshold of the apartment, its doors having just opened before her, felt a distinct misgiving. She stared about her, examining every corner and angle of the chamber. Somber glowing colors stared back at her, objects, furniture, but not, on this occasion, the awful white stare of closed dead eyelids.

Temal, whose apartment this had been, was now merely ash in the silver urn Vyen had intended to gift to Casrus, the urn Vyen had subsequently thought better of sending.

Why was Vitra here, in this gaudy, common Upperling's room, the quarters of Casrus' mistress? There could be nothing for Vitra here but acid to smart in her wounds. And yet, obscurely, it had suggested itself to her that Temal was, in some way, a clue, a key to what had happened: Vitra's failure, both with Casrus and with the bewitched fabulism that refused to stop. But how? Some uncanny Subterine curse, lingering on the air of the Klarn palace? No, it was idiotic to be superstitious. Even now, in the throes of unnatural events, insoluble errors, Vitra must retain awareness of her position. She was a princess, and a genius. Not mad. Not superstitious. Not cursed, not hopelessly at the brink.

Casrus had loved Temal—or at least he had respected her life, her person. And she, for sure, had loved Casrus. Casrus' face, at the news of her suicide, so blank, so hollow. . . . If someone had come to him, speaking of Vitra's death, what would have been his reaction? Polite regret?

Everything was his fault, his and Vyen's. Or Temal's. They had driven Vitra to this wretched pass. She, so sensitive and rare, should not have had to bear it.

She ran into the room. She seized draperies, ornaments, and flung them about. She dashed open a chest and plunged her hands among long scarves and floating shawls, rainbow dyed. The touch of Temal's garments seemed to scald Vitra. She hated the feel of them as she tore them into shreds.

Suddenly, in the midst of ripping material, paper ripped also between Vitra's fingers.

She looked down. She beheld an eccentric parchment, unlike the tablets of the writing machines, and portioned by her violence into two pieces, lying on the heap of massacred shawls.

Quivering with aversion, Vitra knelt and drew these two parchment pieces together. They had been neatly written on with an electric stylus. Probably Casrus had taught the woman to write. Vitra, shrinking, read.

"My beloved, my lord and my life. Every breath I take, every step, every glance, every gesture and realignment of my body, comes about only through the medium of my love for you. My love, which enthralls me, uplifts me. My love which is my universe. How can I be worthy to feel such love? to suffer such love? I would, at any time, have died for you gladly. I would lie down under the wheels of a vehicle, and let them grind me into the earth, for your sake. For your honor's sake, I would offer myself to knives, and to fires. You are my world. I love you. I did not ever tell you this, in words. I may not tell you now. But I do not need to tell you.

233

Nor have I needed to write it here. It is to be written in my blood."

Vitra gasped and let the papers fall again, in bits. Had this ghastly trivial thing been penned in the moments before Temal slew herself? What could be the purpose of leaving it here—almost as if someone had been meant to come on it. Vitra herself? Vitra, who would then writhe at these protestations of selfless and inane adoration, these purely badly written *lines*. (Vitra, who had put herself before everyone, including the man she asserted she loved.)

Temal had sacrificed herself for Casrus' good, the stupid slut. And as the bearer of the ill tidings, Vitra had been ensured of her loss of him for ever. Temal's fault. Temal, Temal.

The princess of Klovez got up slowly, her skin crawling with cold, as if the heating at Klarn had also failed.

The notion of curses no longer seemed idiotic. Temal had surely cursed her. The suicide had been a malevolent masterpiece, the guarantee of Vitra's final false steps.

While, dead, Temal seemed to have become far more vital, far more *pervasive* than ever in her miserable, amorphous existence.

When the ground shook, Casrus had been pitched backward. Even as he righted himself, he touched a surface which was mobile, which ran forward, irresistibly bearing him with it. A moving ramp, like those of the Klave. But proceeding—where?

The burst of solar light, which had flooded the area on the closing of the upper panels, was perhaps an indication.

The simplicity of his thought stilled him. It was an astonishing thing, yet strangely precedented. The conviction had come to him, and would not be shaken from him, that he was to be borne away, straight through the planet, to the golden death of fire that was the planet's opposite side.

Although about him now was only death-like blackness. And before him, eternal, pitiless, the night, the night.

# CHAPTER SEVEN

## Part One

Vel Thaidis had driven the chariot toward the barrier of
energies that divided the great estates from the great Slum.
The barrier which, to an aristo vehicle, was no barrier at all.
The impulses were bound to make a door for her, and so
they did, beautifully, graciously, a crystalline shimmer, a curtain of brightness parting, a crackle of electricity politely restrained.

At the ease of this passage, a kind of savagery broke on
Vel Thaidis. She had reduced her speed to a little less than
eighty staeds, and something of the landscape had returned to
her vision. Beneath her feet, the white Chure rugs soaked up
her blood; over her head, the fringed white parasol immersed
her in shade. It seemed, though only for a moment, that she
had outstripped fate, and she turned, to see if she had.

She had not. Fate was still behind her. The distant hard
sheen of brown metal, the Lawguards: death.

Unshakable pursuit. And yet, not gaining—this far.

Outward from the electronic barrier, where she now meant
to go, across the lands of the princes themselves, the terrain
was more varied. The chariot's progress must grow erratic
there, as it strove to avoid pitfalls which the Lawguards could
evade merely by lifting a few feet from the ground. It was
conceivable, was it not, she might meet death in flight, an un-
negotiable chasm, some tract of treacherous sand. Her brain
seemed to fragment, showing her, in that instant, a thousand

235

possibilities. That she might die before capture, that the chariot might founder, casting her out, unharmed but into the path of what followed. Other scenes aside from death; that she might find the route to the very door of Thar itself, or Hirz, meet Ceedres, emerging or returning, his J'ara curtailed by her gun, the traitorous mocking gun with its solitary shot—or, she might slay herself, not meeting him at all—

Yet none of these vistas of intent or wish could keep a purchase on her thoughts. Savage, she understood only flight. Flight that was more or less senseless, since it swept her from one hell straight toward another. She had no guarantee that she could reach the outmost region, the un-world of the twilight, nor that, once there, she would be protected from further pursuit. Indeed, Dina Sirrid had promised her such sanctuary, and Dina Sirrid had been proven a liar. Nevertheless, Vel Thaidis' vengeance, her ideals, had gone from her in the burst of the chariot's speed. She had surrendered to the animal urge to run, and now, whatever kaleidoscope might flood her imagination, her purpose and her goal had become solely escape. No more than that.

The chariot was suddenly racing once more. She could not recall if she had operated the driver-box. It seemed she had not, but that the chariot had been pushed into momentum by her will, her instinct alone.

Too fast, again too fast to guess where she might be. Pink striations of rock upon green rollers of air, the flash of waters, huge cascades of shadow—cliffs or plantations—all stirred in the whirlpool of bleached dust.

Until, at last, an abrupt reaction, fear or bewilderment, made her reach with hasty fingers to slow the car, in order that, even for a moment, she might see what country she raced through, and that she might look behind her again, the persistent need of the hunted thing. So she learned she had, in her savagery, rushed beyond the codes of her universe, put herself outside the pale for sure. For the chariot no longer obeyed her touch upon the driver-box. Do what she would, fumble with dials, with gauge, cry out, tug at the reins, fling about to watch the world pulled away like a bolt of fraying silk; nothing could check her progress now.

The final shreds of her identity and her role seemed to discard her. She was left, a pebble spun through chaos, no firm ground anywhere for sanity to take a stand.

The first screen, shimmering a clear brilliant gold, revealed all this in its vast oblong, some eighteen feet in height, forty in width.

The second screen, directly opposite the first, and its twin in height and width, glowed by contrast somber as a coal.

Casrus Klarn, retained in the whitish drop of oxygen his suit provided for him, kneeled on the swiftly flowing sub-planetary ramp. The blackness all around had drawn outward, and lightened infinitesimally. Enormous caverns appeared to pile and slope and steeply fall away. Here and there, a pocket of gas or phosphorescence added a brief green or blue or purple lustre. Spears of petrified moisture, arches of glass ice and hollow arcades of stone or mist or illusion arose and were retracted out of and into the dark.

That he had not dispelled the protective bubble, the breath of life from around himself, that he knelt on one knee, the resting stance of the active combatant, demonstrated his caution, and that the sudden and the preposterous had not overtaken logic. Terror, that unnecessary and inconveniencing state, had not been permitted to lay its claws on him. His face revealed nothing, nor did any spontaneous movement of his body, his hands. He was apparently waiting, but whether in unease or puzzlement went unannounced. Physically, that was.

The screen itself, in which the smoky image of Casrus was contained, gave off the same invisible rays as the golden screen which framed Vel Thaidis' chariot. To any who entered, or had entered, or might enter the circle of these rays which emanated from the two screens, the mental condition of all who evolved therein was completely revealed, along with the sensory nuances, the vibrations and the moods of everything depicted.

Casrus, in a cloak of immaculate resignation, reviewed his uncanny journey without flinching. A little anger, perhaps, and a tinge of self-disgust, the only recognition he would give to that knowledge that some large hand had gripped him. That, as Vitra had believed she controlled invented lives, so now some other controlled the life of Casrus, and no doubt Vitra's life, and all lives that existed, under the sun or out of it. Although he did not gnaw on it, he had never dismissed the incongruous failure of the Law to judge him fairly, nor the inexplicable collapse of the technology of Klovez, nor the pointless Fabulisms themselves. Now, the oblique segments joined together in a cogent whole.

237

He must be approaching, with burning death, an ultimate solution.

Here was no pebble spinning in madness. Casrus perceived the chain which bound him, and how it had bound him all his years, leading him like a dogga this way and that.

To a man of such strength of will, to comprehend such a chain about his throat was maybe worse than any perception of chaos.

The slackening of the chariot, the falling of a rain, roused Vel Thaidis from the semi-sleep into which she had dropped.

Waking, she saw at once, through the curtains of the rain, the transformation of everything. When fear filled her, she welcomed it, a looked-for guest, one familiar thing remaining.

She was perhaps eight hundred staeds from the boundaries of the estates, outward, lost on the Fading Lands. Unraveled by speed, great precipices had passed, chasmatic valleys; and lost in unconsciousness, aqua-courses like the green eyes of cats, herds of antelines gushing on their banks, a fawn-white abstract of sunlight on skin and horn and dust. Behind her, gradually, the Zenith had metamorphosed, and overhead, the sky. Now she beheld a plain, unending, every side. No trace of colored vegetation, no galloping fauna. Only the long ropes of the rain drifting down, and the coming of an alien coolness, and of an alien dark.

No prince had ever hunted here, farther than the brink of the hunting lands. Even the tracks of machines had left no mark on this place. Surely she approached the end of the world. And fear, the known friend, turned her head gently, showing her how it was. While the chariot, slower but yet unobedient, incapable of retreat or halt, enabled her to ab-sorb all the details of this nightmare she had sloughed in sleep, regained in waking.

The sun was much more than three quarters down the sky. Its searing blaze was gone. Through her polarizing lids, Vel Thaidis could glance at it. Reddened by its fall, and shrunken, it smeared the atmosphere below it and some way above in rougings of scarlet and brassy green. But the sky only a fraction higher was bled of brilliance and of tint. It was a sky of old brown wood, unpolished, whorled and traced with lightnings that sifted, eddied and went out like pallid fires inside a dirty lamp.

Before the chariot, on the unending plain, a supernatural overflow, the vehicle's own huge malt-dark shadow, pooled

238

and spreading as predicted, copied the taint of the sky onto the earth. While the flakes of the dry rain, rusty scales sometimes the size of her palm, dazzled her nostrils with an electrical odor of burning.

Vel Thaidis shuddered in the tepid cold. Quite without warning, out of doors, the inner lids had lifted from her eyes. In her nakedness, she watched a hill of metal rising in front of her across the plain.

The black rocks shelved up, the ramp running with them.

Casrus sensed the door before it was reached, sensed it like a note of music, part of some song he had often rehearsed in his mind, never before listened to, but which he now heard sung aloud.

The doorway melted at the precise instant he had known it would, and a round sequin of luminescence wept through the rock. The ramp carried him into it, and drained away under the floor, leaving him, stranded on firm ground, symbolically inappropriate to a degree.

He had been deposited in a cubicle, bare of anything, even of shading or texture. At the cubicle's farther end, a stair attracted the eye by moving interminably upward and beyond his view, beckoning. And down the stair, into the cubicle, the charge of alien light and warmth fanned to envelope him. Bearably; not as he had expected.

Backing him, the route in from the rocks had healed itself. Only the stair now would take him from this nowhere, or anywhere. And the unseen implacable hand which gripped him, seemed thrusting him forward to the stair. Go that way. There is no other way to go.

With colossal tiredness, Casrus stepped down the stair. Dark head bowed, broad and durable shoulders bowed, lids bowed over the eyes, no longer in the stance of the fighter, indifferent now it seemed, both to an observer and to himself, he stood and let the stair conduct him into whatever presence had arbitrarily summoned him. And journeying thus, he felt himself a boy, with all a boy's poverty of true ego, and true ego's quietude. And he felt himself, too, an old man, three hundred years, bored literally, in the manner of his kind, to death with the senseless world.

The endless plain had become a floor of cracked and vitrified gray stone. The outer sky ebbed to a black horizon. Here the lightnings met each other in enormous silent concus-

sions of green and white. Against this backdrop, the metal
dome of the hill reflected and returned the snarl of the red
and shrunken solar disc, the hill itself shining the redder of
the two, and the more bright.

The chariot glided toward the hill, toward a rounded aperture in the hill. Destination was no longer a mystery.

The hill towered up, loomed, burgeoned, blotting out the
brown sky, the horizon of green holocausts. Fear the friend
made much of the size of the hill, its yearning door.

Then came a sound out of the eerie soundlessness and the
rusty fluttering of the rain, a sound indescribable. The
damned screaming in hell?

An idea came to Vel Thaidis, led by the hand of fear the
friend. Am I dead already? Have I died, unnoticed; am I a
spirit, rightly borne into the realm of spirits?

Involuntarily, she brushed her face with her fingers; her
lips, her hair and eyes. She was as before, and yet, perhaps
all ghosts had so convinced themselves.

The cry of the damned blurred to nothing as the doorway
of the hill swallowed her up.

The dome, extending deep underground and rising
spaciously above it, bore its own unique set of directions,
known to all its machinery and accordingly accessible
thereby.

The side which faced toward the sun was Dayward, and
that which faced away from the sun, toward the black horizon, Nightward. The side of the dome that faced the direction in which the planet circled had been named
appropriately Travel. That which faced the area in space
from which the planet constantly revolved away, perhaps less
appropriately, had been called Return.

Situated on the twilight zone, between the day and night
sides of the planet, the exterior function of the dome (which
it performed in common with similar structures ringing the
whole world, just as the zone ringed it) was to retain intact
the air ceiling of the daytime side. The temples, which also
ringed the world along the boundaries of the sun-side estates,
shared in this function. Identical "temples," located on the
nightside, could additionally have participated in the activity,
had the oxygenated ceiling been extended across into the
dark, a scheme once considered, but put by.

Here, however, at the fading and blending of light and
gloom, of black and amber, atmopshere and void, the waste

products of the fabricated sky scaled constantly in an almost endless rain. Lightnings whipped their tails and occasional groanings were audible, both phenomena illustrating where blocks of air and non-air, failing warmth and frigid cold, perpetually collided. Only the incredible powers integral in the twilight domes held catastrophe at bay. Yet held at bay it was, and effortlessly, and doubtless forever.

The edifice which suggested a hill from the surface, a hole from below the ground, was the great master dome of the twilight ring, and had been designated Kae-nentem-Kae, or five hundred and five, but reduced thereafter to Kaneka.

Within, Kaneka was luxurious and beautiful; in the land of hell, a paradise, and invoking much of its two opposed neighbors.

Day and night came and went in Kaneka, both artificial, and yet both of a loveliness surpassing reality. Day began with an ambivalent sunrise. For no disc arose (as later, no disc fell), rather untrameled light itself welled up from every direction, burning through the darkness, through carmine and apricot and illimitable saffrons, into a clear day, water-green, powdered with small clouds and the luminous flying forms of birds and reptiles. The height of this day sky was five hundred feet, and looked a mile at the least. The shapes which ornamented it were fakes of the most elaborate and perfect kind. The coming of day required an hour, and its going another hour, during which the glory of colors sponged downward in reverse, and first a dusk and then an evening filled the apex of false, undeniably believable ether, rather as a drop of wine might soak through a fine green canopy, a central blush and a sultry and diffusing stain. In an hour jade had become jet, a vault of jet ghosted by the fragrant blue nimbus of clouds, and radiant patterned stars and sweet night winds. Day and night, needing an hour each to replace the other, lasted each a period of five hours only.

The floor of Kaneka was a garden. By day and by night, equally lush, secretive and sublime. Pinnacles and cliffs went up, and fountains of green aqua and white jets of pure air fringed their ledges. Forests proliferated, cacti with pods like rose velvet and trees with stems like fluted luminex, and funguses the shades of antique untreated bronze. Buildings grew out of the soil, out of the forests, and balconied from the recesses of cliffs. Silver buildings and gold, seeming less actual than the unactualities of the region. As if honesty alone were to be doubted.

241

Between the gold and silver buildings, the gold and silver mechanisms liquidly moved. Robots something like men and women, something like plants or insects, or simply like mechanical facets: wheels and pillars and spheres. They serviced Kaneka and the generating force of Kaneka, its energies and perfumes, its megatonal valves, its delicate arteries.

In a plastum marble hall, fenced by an avenue of brazen pillars, two screens stared at each other, quite blank, two sockets of emptiness, waiting to be filled by eyes.

They did not show, one: the young woman, the caressive day-breeze stroking her hair, the broad leaves of the trees framing her speechlessness her torn feet on smooth moss. Or one: the man, the platinum reed of a robot already before him, the last filament of a sunless sunrise like a pink wrapper left blowing on the lawn.

"We are here to serve you," said the robots. "Tell us how we may do so."

From habit, the prince and the princess, the aristocrats, gave their instructions, even in lassitude and disorientation. Neither beheld the other. The entire fabulousness of Kaneka was between them.

The day winds blew daintily. Waterfalls of flowers opened, trees showered their pastel parasols. Tricked too often, the man and the woman accepted, but did not honor, the dream, and reality lay down, quiescent, in reserve.


# Part Two


The sloping lawn hung like an island in the huge violet dusk, which, translucent and lambent, would fill the sky, the garden, for one-third of an hour. Stars solidified in flower-like clusters, high and far away across the illusory mile that separated the upper dome from its floor. Robot insects, each a flitting pair of pale luminous wings, scattered like leaves through the air, the bushes, and across the strings of the golden chame.

The girl sat before the chame, not attempting to play it. Its gold, and her own, the natural metal of her skin and undyed silken hair, were darkened and curiously simultaneously drained by this mystic after-glow. Vel Thaidis was learning the lessons of dawn, twilight, night. Repetition alone could convince her of their validity. But she was not afraid, having traveled, it seemed to her, through fear and beyond.

The first period of sun had been easy. In a bewilderment of familiarity, she had ordered the robots which so familiarly came to her, to tend her. She bathed, her hair was washed, her ruined feet repaired. Food appeared, recognizable, on recognizably fine plates, and drink in cut-glass goblets. An ambience of Hirz surrounded her, and she did not protest. She lay down to sleep on a divan, in a room where blue shutters of stained crystal brought the shade of a Maram-chamber. When she woke, total night had come, reminder of death and of Thar. Double-edged, her insecure amazement, suddenly washed of apathy and exhaustion, demanded of her to discover where she had come, and why.

The robots stood ready, peerless attendants, as at Hirz, and every one of them equipped with Voice, moreover a voice which pretended to breath and expression. She questioned them, employing Courteous Address though defiant and withdrawn: Explain to me this spot, its motive, what it will do. But the explanations which were rendered her, redolent of vast data, limitless and somehow therefore unsatisfying, drove her at length to the basis of her apprehension. "Am I dead?" she asked them.

"No, Vel Thaidis."

She relaxed weakly and they brought her wine and fruit. The machine which used Voice most often, a slender silver pin mounted on a noiseless runner, yet with a humanoid face and humanoid eyes and lips, murmured to her of night and of day, and of the zone between, and of Kae-nentem-Kae. She used the Distant Address thereafter, turning her head from the robots.

Later, she walked in the night. As the building of rooms she had been taken to was equipped with civilized appurtenances—chambers of sleep, bathing chambers, cabinets of books, stores of food and drink, of machinery and entertainments, so the nearer garden was formal. It had fountains and terraces. And on the sloping lawn which leaned against the hollow sky, a golden chame daubed with the glints of stars.

She sat by the chame, and did not play it. Presently, she

243

went away. A profound and weakening sadness overwhelmed her.

Reality which had been abrasive and destructive had become suddenly too beautiful. She did not know what she must do. She needed, though she did not recognize her need, fresh agony, fresh conflict to reassure herself she lived. Her sounding heart, the rise and fall of her lungs, her body's hunger, thirst, slumber, these were not enough. Where was the world? Not in this country of dreams. Where were the characters of her story? Where tragedy, terror and vengeance?

The Law no longer hunted her. Nothing did. She was alone in Paradise, and moment by moment, she softly, kindly died.

She pondered the tiny five-hour days and nights. The second day she walked a little farther in the garden. Distant buildings dazzled across lakes of moss, grasses, flowers. Should she go to them?

She perceived the tireless movement of ubiquitous machines. She did not ask her attendants any more about the states of being or not being. It was useless. They told her everything, but everything made no sense to her. There was, actually, nothing to be achieved in going forward toward the other buildings. Five hours and the day was gone.

A night, a day, a night, a day, she lay on the divan, sleeping, and on waking, suggesting herself again into sleep. I am weary, she repeated to herself. It was not weariness. Peace murdered her slowly.

But at the end of the fourth day, she could not drug herself any more. Her healthy, resilient flesh shouted for mobility and purpose. She called the silver robot.

"Am I to go back to the Yunea?" Like a petulant child, hearing the unfitness of the words, she stressed them more vigorously.

"No, Vel Thaidis," the robot said.

"You told me I lived."

"You live, Vel Thaidis."

"Then why shouldn't I return? Would the Law of the Yunea lie in wait for me—is that the prohibition? I should be seized and executed at the Zenith?"

"No, Vel Thaidis."

"No? Then I've passed beyond the Law. If I've passed beyond the Law, I'm dead."

"Legally."

"Then I can return?"

"There is no transport by which you might return."

244

This mundane equivocation startled her.

"The chariot I stole from Chure—"

"The chariot will not take you back."

"You mean I would be prevented from leaving here?"

"Yes."

"That's blatant," she said. For a moment, she was scandalized. "Can you, a robot, defy me? I see you can. How?"

"Kaneka," said the robot, "is Kaneka."

"How," she said, "if I tried to find the door from—Kaneka? How if I found it?"

"There is no need to leave Kaneka."

"I have a need," she said.

"Your needs will be served."

"Then let me go," she said, passionate for the wastes, the Slum, even perhaps for boiling death in preference to this temperate death drawing over her now.

The robot did not respond, and, in abrupt despair, her energy went from her. She sank down on the divan. Then in the dusk, she climbed the slope and sought the chame.

The coming and going of the robot insects fascinated her eyes. There was an illumination in the garden, even when full night entered it, more than that of the sprinkled constructed stars. Vel Thaidis turned her mind to Velday, and to Ceedres. She tried to experience anger, anguish, the wrath of the living. When she could not, she came to her feet and called out worldlessly across the quietly murmurous distances contained within the hill of heaven.

And then, seating herself again, she began to strike notes, chords, tearing seamless garments of melody from the instrument before her.

Almost immediately, an awareness of relief swept through her, as if she had unleashed, despite the inanimate calm of Kaneka, some power of living virulence.

So she played on, neither well nor attractively as, when a princess of Hirz, she had been tutored to do. But loudly, tumultuously, thrusting out as if with spears into the shadows, alert for reality to spring forth, from ground or air. Earth tremor, a great wind, a star crashing on the slope—anything to shatter the casement of indifference, the bars of the cage.

She played until her wrists and her arms, the joints of fingers and shoulders, her spine, her brain itself pleaded with her for rest, like sick children. Only when their pain translated into numbness did she let her hands drop from the keys and strings of the chame.

245

Nothing had altered, and the last solace of her frustration was to shed tears, or perhaps instead a tearless howling, such as the women of the Slum might give vent to in grief.

But before the paroxysm could be summoned, the darkness was split. Not by lightning or catastrophe. By a single motion, a glimpse of something that did not fit the tapestry of the garden—extraneous as herself.

She raised her head a fraction at a time. Her heart, unbeating, a rock, her ears two bowls of listening, her eyes enlarged to swallow the world.

About fifteen feet away, standing between the night-folded fans of trees, stood Ceedres Yune Thar.

For a second, she could not stir, finger or foot or limb. Then she rose, and she took a step.

She had no weapon, it was gone with the chariot, subtracted from her at the gate of paradise when she had barely noticed. She did not consider gun or knife, however, even a blow struck with the fist. The improbability of her enemy's arrival here had already occurred to her. She felt weightless.

"You are an illusion," she said. She held out her hand, half expecting a weapon after all to materialize in her grasp. "But your death may still comfort me."

The man came alive. He walked toward her, and the shadows dropped from his shoulders but strangely coalesced about his head. The night garden painted him with its glow. His skin was pale. Too pale for the skin of Ceedres, like ivory in the shade. She glanced at her arms where the loose drapery of Kaneka left them free. His skin and hers, the same in the world, dissimilar now as day and night.

"I am not," said the man, two yards from her, "who you think me to be."

He stopped. She stared at him. His gilt hair had soaked up the night and was black. His eyes were like two jewels, like the cold jewels in the sky.

"Your disguise is inadequate," she said.

"I am not Ceedres Yune Thar."

"His ghost then. His reflection."

He began again to approach, and her fear returned to her. Like many a longed-for gift, it was, in possession, unwelcome.

"No farther," she cried.

Once more he halted.

"My name is Casrus."

"Ceedres. Or his twin," she said mockingly. Her body

246

jerked on its bones, as if with illness. The illness which was a warranty of life.

"The genetic matrixes, white-black," Ceedres said to her, "have been induced to create near doubles, your side of this planet and mine. Corresponding. Even the names alike. But let me come nearer. There are sufficient differences."

He had not once copied her expressions. Suddenly she missed that everlasting gambit. Suddenly, she knew him to be another, not Ceedres, and absolutely here with her. She stood shivering, and said. "I see the proof of what you say."

"Good. I can come closer?"

"Yes."

He came to within three feet of her. He seemed to shut out the sky, the slope. She was alone with him in a space no larger than the space between them.

"It may interest you to hear," he said, "you also bear a resemblance to another. Some resemblance. The more I look at you, the less I see it. I believe that if you'll bring yourself to look at me, you'll find the same."

"You could not be Ceedres."

"No."

She gazed at his eyes, which seemed the color of the deepening sky. She was not really seeing him, but portions of him, now the black hair, now the outline of the cheekbone, the cleft in the chin, now the chiseled fold of cloak from the shoulder, the sculpture of forearm and hand. So much that was as she knew it, and so much that was not as she knew.

"The machines," she said abruptly, "never informed me I would have company. Are there others?"

"I think not. Just you and I. And the robots."

"You understand this place, and what has happened," she said.

"I have one fixed, perhaps erroneous, idea. But then, I was granted evidence you were not."

"I," she said, "I was granted nothing. Not even my enemy to slaughter."

"Maybe," he began, but hesitated, watching her. She could no longer bring herself to regard him. He offered her his hand then, with an unspeaking restraint, the ritual greeting of both their worlds, an unsuitable yet essential gesture. For a moment, she avoided contact, then shyly, like a well-trained adolescent girl, she put her palm to his. It cost her something. He was the image of so much that had shaken her, body,

247

heart and mind. But his hand was mortal, as was hers, and the hand of a stranger.

"So," he said, "I'll leave you now, if you wish."

Her hand separated from his.

"If you stay, I will be afraid of you," she said. "But I'm afraid of your going."

"Yes. Then I will go, but not very far."

"Where will you be?"

"Look up, and I'll show you."

She raised her eyes. He pointed into the dark below, toward vague trees, sewn by pearlized needles of water.

"Something like two staeds away," he said. "A building where the robots housed me."

"Will you explain to me what's happened?"

"What I understand of it, if I can."

"Not now," she said swiftly. "Next Jate—"

"You're more comfortable in the light," he said, "as I prefer the darkness. You see, my world is the dark side."

"Hell," she said.

"Literally, in part. As is your own. And this is paradise, Kaneka."

"Please go," she said. Her voice was low and hoarse. As he turned, he caught the glimmer of her hands involuntarily lifted, as if to clasp him, guessed at her lips opening to call him back. As he went down the slope, he heard her say aloud a name, but it was the name of the other. He walked on into the thickening of the night.

Since he had come from the recreation area at Kaa, the Fabulism on his mind, Casrus had dimly sensed the inexorable forward propulsion which had swiftly torn him, like a page, from his world. He had inadequately surmised it would be meaningless death he went to, the hot-side desert, which, though supporting a form of life, would not allow his metabolism to survive. But arriving in the mild warmth of the artificial country, seeing its dawn like that of one of those other worlds memorized by Klave computers, his primitive resignation to futility had cleared. The fact of a twilight zone he comprehended, as any educated member of the Residencia would have done. But the exquisite garden, prototype of the myth of heaven, intimated structures of thought and preparation. Though he had been brought here like a beast led by rope, yet some sort of program, and surely not a random program, had ordered events. The whiff of logic revived his logical intelligence. Soon, it seemed to him that within a framework of coherence his self-reliance and aptitude might be retrieved.

If he accepted that the Yunea was extant off a screen, its complementary values proposed a hideous parallel with the Klave. Both societies were absurd, with their core of godlike parasites and their hosts of condemned. Both, too, were patently doomed to collapse, each feeding on itself as it was, its technology running down or awry from unawareness and ignorance. Between these two habitats was Kaneka, also mechanical and also under the organization of machines. Kaneka, to which he, who had been the double face of his own society, had been brought. The key was apparently in his way, but he did not yet presume to name it.

(Nor, with the return of ego, the straightening of mental shoulders, did the wings of the dreamer carry him; he gained no sense of personal destiny. To Casrus, ego was an inner proposition, rather than a flare to be broadcast over outer regions. If he saw himself as in any way distinct, it was merely as an element of things as they were.)

Thus, unhurriedly, he let the robots of the garden attend him, beginning with them to erect a groundwork of clues. His questions, unlike the questions of the young woman two staeds away, were exact.

The ambient information which was dispensed to him, he assimilated; Kaneka's functions, external: the establishment of atmosphere and weather, and internal: the manufacture of a benign environment.

"For whom?" Casrus asked the robots.

The silver reed with the humanized face, which consistently replied, said to him: "For any that might come here."

"And who has come here?"

"Yourself, Casrus Klarn."

"Only myself?" The robot did not speak. Casrus said to it, "Tell me who else is here."

"A woman."

He went on questioning until it had given him her name and her biography, which ended in her flight to the twilight. Naturally, he had realized instantly who she was.

"And why are we here?" he said at length to the machine.

"You will live here."

Its obtuseness seemed of design. He said, "And why will we live here, she and I?"

"You cannot return to your own prior situations."

249

"Cannot?"

"Cannot."

"What will we do here?" he said.

"As you please," said the robot. In his physical weariness, Casrus had smiled at this curious joke.

Later, after he had slept, he walked out into a marvelous indigo darkness, and back over its blue lawns and black cliffs and silver floral staircases to the empty point through which he had come. He could not locate that entrance, nor had he thought to; it was merely his thoroughness.

He retraced his steps to his new apartments and began again a relentless interrogation of all the robots that would obey his injunction to come to him. Sometimes one would go away and another replace it. Sometimes several replied at once. They always would reply, but not always unambiguously. The more succinct the query, frequently the more nebulous its vocal reward. But gradually they gave up to him hints of vaults, libraries, banks of intellectual and practical acumen. It seemed he must seek these unaided.

"I'm to be tested, am I?" He thought of princes in Fabulism, and theatricals, infantile dramatized trials of valor and wit, unsuited to this dome.

"You must do as you desire."

"I desire to be shown the cache of books and records, printed or visual, which I believe you've alluded to."

"They are all about you."

"In this chamber?"

"In Kaneka."

Thereafter, for three periods of blue-winged darkness, unlike the iron cowl of space, three periods of fiery light, unlike any light he had ever known, he investigated the potential of the gold and silver buildings under the roof of heaven.

And found the records easy of access.

That he was practiced in such delving from his earlier investigations in the Klave assisted him. But the memorized visuals and the great books of the Klave were a synopsis and a prelude to what lay in the cortex of Kaneka. He recalled an ancient legend of Heaven's five hundred and five gates. Had it referred, not to numerical title, but facetiously to gates of stored intelligence? The history and science of a million planets and a million times-interrelated to his own, he cloudily saw, yet only by inference. In a few day periods and periods of night, some twenty-five hours, interrupted by one further indiscriminate Maram of two hours sleep, he could amass very little. What he absorbed served mostly to reveal the trek before him, all uphill.

At the fourth hour of the third five-hour day, he walked on to an avenue of brazen pillars and reached a marble hall.

As the doors of rose-stained glass drew aside for him to enter, a gust seemed to blow out over him from the chamber within. Only then did unnerving sensation decipher itself for him, showing as it did so, that it had been faintly with him all along. Pragmatic, Casrus did not deal much in impressions, those vapors of sensitivity that offered themselves as omens, inexplicable insights. Even in the otherworld of Kaneka, he had seen through the veil of legend. While Vel Thaidis had descried the dome's mystery, he had only descried its human application. Both had fathomed something the other had not. But now, the hall before him fashioning a slow tender light, no more harsh than the day, but seeming more false, Casrus checked, examining the bizarre idea which all at once riveted him. Which was that not a machine, but a living creature, had been here, on this area of ground, in this hall, not long before him.

He thought at once of the girl, but somehow acknowledged the girl, alien to him though she was, would not have left behind such a marker of strangeness and of presence.

He had had murmurs of this feeling previously, and dismissed them unexplored. The constant coming and going of the robots might have been responsible for them, in any case. But no longer, for the murmur had become a shout.

The hall had been occupied, and though seeming empty now, the occupation had splashed an opaque intellectual tinting over what remained.

Unarmed, and in the casually rich, nondefensive garments of Kaneka, Casrus crossed the room's threshold.

The tiles were a mirror of somber marble veined with cracks of jewel-work. A mail of bronze and silver and white platinum, brushed aside, displayed two vast screens confronting each other over five yards of shining floor. The screens reflected in the floor, one a dark thick gold, the other a burnished black, equally blind.

Dwarfed by them, disturbingly congruous, two elegant cushioned chairs placed back to back dominated the center of the dual reflection.

Casrus walked foward and set his hand on the central communal spine of the chairs. Each faced toward a screen.

The Fabulasts of the Residencia, Vitra and the rest, were a

tradition. The hot-side Yunea, rather more primitive than the cold-side Klave, had somehow loaned itself to be spied upon. Directed, presumably mechanically, through Vitra's feckless brain, the world of the sun had become a live and recorded diversion. Already he had placed this extraordinary happening inside the new framework Kaneka apparently offered. Guided by the computerized mechanisms of Kaneka, the mechanisms of the Klave had primed Vitra to become a transmitter. Another world of aristocratic pleasure and slavish toil had been caused insidiously to intrude, undermining the foundations of Klave society from its subconscious upward.

That the organizing machinery of either side, linked through Kaneka, should gear such a scheme into motion implied both enterprise and virtue. This was the logic Casrus had put together. But now the logic faltered.

The Klave observed the Yunea.

Some other thing had observed both Yunea and Klave, (gold and black, the sigils of the two screens were obvious.)

A computer, surely, did not require such screens to detect those it sought to influence. Certainly, it did not require *two chairs*.

Casrus turned. He went back through the mail curtain, and through the reopening roseate doors.

As ever, the scape of the garden, near and far, was glinting and fluid with the progress of robots. Along the avenue an opaline wheel approached, but such mechanisms paid the human voice no heed. Casrus raised his arm, hailing instead one of the slender silver kind. It seemed to blow to him on its runner, the mask of its face parting to take a needless, humanly reassuring breath before it uttered.

"How can I serve you, Casrus Klarn?"

Casrus beckoned it into the hall, and indicated the blind screens, the blinder empty chairs.

"Who sits in these?"

The robot breathed once more.

"How can I serve you?" it said.

"You can serve me by answering my question."

"Please repeat your question."

"My question was, who occupied this room formerly, and used the two screens?"

The sweetly armored face parted for its breath.

"How can I serve you?"

Casrus mused, watching it. This was the first time a forthright and complete refusal had met his request for enlightenment.

"You have been programmed not to discuss the matter."

"How can I serve you?"

"Instruct me on how to operate the two screens."

There was then the briefest pause.

The robot said, "The method is by thought, and will. There is no other method."

It must be so. Casrus had noted the absence of paneled keys, the absence of everything save the apparatuses themselves.

He let the robot go and stood some while before moving to the golden screen. He had faith in the quality of his concentration and the capability of his mind, but the prospect of so using them was unwelcome to him. That he preferred to attempt an evocation of Yunea rather than Klave was both challenge and evasion.

But the screen did not react. Unlike the key-motivated disc of the Fabulast, it demanded more than a wish to wake it.

An hour he kept himself there.

The hour gone, he seated himself reluctantly in the chair which faced the screen. Leaning back, the tension poured from him, his eyes blurred, and a picture came, great and glowing, filling the gold. Only for a second. He saw the girl, Vel Thaidis Yune Hirz, treading a road of metal and dust. Her hair, seared with the dye of Seta, as he had last seen it in Vitra's Fabulism, was folded within a dark veil. Her feet were folded in blood. This was a replaying of a portion of the biography the robots had told him of.

Only a second, yet the rays of the screen ran over him, informing him of her agony, her determination, the deeds she intended to accomplish—the acquisition of the gas-gun, the murder of Ceedres, her suicide.

He was jolted, jarred, both by what he received and by the way in which it came to him. As the screen wavered into returning blankness, he found himself stupidly obsessed by her two feet, slippered in blood. Vel Thaidis took on the character of the actress in Eres sector, she who by her bloody foot, her pain, and her desperation to prevail in the good will of the princes, had planted the towering tree of his guilt and his endeavor.

The screen had recalcitrantly shown him the past, in more ways than one.

When the sunless sunset began and he went from the hall,

253

all across the park, its uplands and rifts and blossoming laby-rinths, he heard the clamoring of the desolate crying chame.

He was drawn to her suddenly, she, his female counterpart in the wake of the appalling discovery. Drawn to her resolution, the pathos of her hurt and fear, her loveliness, like Vitra's, and not like at all.

He surprised himself, more than a little. After the hall and its aura, the search for human companionship, never indulged before, seemed ridiculous. Why, at such an hour, did a woman, whatever her worth or her symbol, compel him? Yet she was vulnerable, more vulnerable than he, understanding nothing of what had come about. There was some reason to go to her.

As he went, Temal was not quite forgotten.

Meeting Vel Thaidis, he did forget. Troubled by her trouble, he did not tell her much, or even warn her.


The second meeting, for her sake, was by day. Casrus had begun to reason that apartments and articles of clothing adjusted to increase or subdue for both of them the warmth or coolness of the garden, just as they were soothed by its robots and aesthetics. Whatever motivated the provision, he could do no less than a machine in considering her.

She waited for him on the sloping lawn, under a fountaining tree with delicate pale green ribbons. Three golden robots attended her. He was struck by a recollection of her stance beside the lake of Hirz. She would hardly have asked these robots: "You are sure it is Casrus who approaches?" Though if she had found the two chairs in the marble hall, she might have had some cause to ask.

She greeted him. Her etiquette was touching and admirable together, her means of holding fear aside.

He had been careful to give her advantages; the light, the chosen spot, the outdoors itself, native to her and foreign to him. She resembled Vitra only slightly, but by her eyes he knew he had stayed for her as Ceedres. He supposed the locked gates of Kaneka would supply them with the time to fade such comparisons. Already, the dynastic implications of a male and female brought here together and shut in had suggested itself to him, and probably also by now to her.

They strolled to a decline where green aqua flowed through a channel of stone. Robot fish darted in the currents and plumes of moss brimmed over from the bank.

Vel Thaidis and Casrus had adopted a veneer of propriety

254

and leisure, as if they conversed in some salon. Yet when she spoke, she asked at once: "We are prisoners?"

"It seems so."

"The two of us, served by these hundreds of robots." She smiled at the water, her slim golden hands folded tight upon each other. "It represents a worse extravagance than those of the Yunea."

"Or of the Klave. I'm afraid you have yet to learn of the dark-side counterpart to your world. I think there's a way here to show it to you. A screen that reveals my world, another that reveals yours. The past. Or, I imagine, the present."

"Casrus," she said firmly, confronting his name, but her eyes lowered on the acquatic fish. "I never knew of your world, except as a myth. Yet I can absorb the expression of it—almost too readily. It occurs to me there's some spell in this garden."

"Magic," he said gently. He remembered, her civilization was more primitive than that of the Klave.

"Not magic. Hypnotism, possibly. Or some chemical in the air, the scent of these flowers. How can I believe so much which, to me, should be unbelievable?"

Her oblique keenness intrigued him. She postulated a factor he had overlooked. If it was so, his earlier philosophies emerged in a different garb. Though there was no remedy, it was as well to know.

"This dome holds a hoard of instructions, applicable to both our worlds, and many others. It may contain explanations of itself."

"You said, when we met before, that you would tell me of the impulses of Kaneka. As you saw them to be."

"Perhaps I spoke rashly. I may be mistaken."

"I'd like to hear."

He glanced at her frightened hands and averted eyes. His inclination was to protect her and smooth her way with lies. Then he noted his error, for she would have to be told—the screens, the Fabulism, all of it. He reflected on the decision half a moment, debating as to whether he himself, or the force of the garden, prompted his judgment to speak.

Then he told her everything, sparsely, almost conventionally.

"And the machines of Kaneka order these things," she said when he had finished.

"The machines, at the direction of what governs them." He

255

had told her everything but the ultimate conclusion. She seemed on the verge of saying it herself, her face transparent with loathing.

"Vel Thaidis," he said, "we have to accept the notion that two persons have been watching every moment of our lives and the lives of those about us."

"But it's more than that," she said. "Isn't it?"

"They seem to have brought us here," he said. "Whoever they were, or they are, they could do that. Why not more?"

"Why not. Thar, which fell over some hundreds of years. That would be straightforward to negotiate, given such control of surroundings and machines."

*Or Klovez,* he thought, *a quicker fall, engineered for maximum effect.*

She spoke suddenly and rapidly, not to him. It was a prayer.

"But I suppose I shouldn't pray," she said. "I might be praying to *them.* Whoever they are. Gods. Cruel gods. *Playing* with us."

"Probably. I think not only machines were included in their scope. Our emotion, thought even, may have been capable of distortion via the screens. Without doubt, thought and feeling are relayed to whoever watches."

Even now their emotion and thought were perhaps transmuted, shaped, as the girl had deduced. He had uncovered the secret of the screens with small hesitation, and told it to her. And all the while they made no outcry. Horror, yes, but no rush to escape or to resist. . . . Kaneka was molding them. Not alone to the moods of night and day, but to an enormous insupportable complacence. And there was no help for it.

"Whatever it was, or whoever," he said, "has gone, but left its will behind it. I have the theory that we're to take its place."

The screens were ready, they had only to be mastered, and once they had been. Thought and will. Power beyond power. Until through the screens, as a Fabulast would form and disintegrate the lives of his or her inventions, so the denizens of Kaneka could make and break two worlds. As two other denizens had been making and breaking them for centuries.

A balance out of true.

Why not, when it was a story created purely to entertain? Where was the entertainment when no one rose, or stumbled, when none suffered or bled or died? If all were equal, all

256

princes, all happy, where was the narrative, and where the splendor?

He and she had been characters in a book of Jates and Marams. And now they could become, had indeed been chosen to become, its authors, the *heirs* to this wickedness. A wickedness beside which the foibles of Ceedres, of Vyen, of Vitra, were innocent and naïve. Blameless even, if their inclination, mind and soul, had been manipulated.

And Kaneka silently sang to its captives, mesmeric, caressive, when they slept or when they woke, convincing them that all was as it should be. That to rule as gods was fair and just.

The two who had gone away had left them that as their legacy, before they sealed them in Heaven.

"We could die," Vel Thaidis said quietly. "Would it be better to take our lives?"

"Perhaps."

For a long while they said nothing, and then he beheld how her hands had loosened and her eyes lifted to his face. They were beautiful, her eyes, within the charcoaled lines of their inner lids.

"I recall my brother, Velday," she said, "and Ceedres. And the vengeance I never came to."

*And what do I recall?* he thought.

The wretched warren of the Subterior, and the aristocrats who lived on it, beasts tearing at a screaming bone.

With the power of Kaneka, if such a power were truly within reach, maybe a game could be devised that set the imbalance to rights. You played god before, his heart said to him. And his brain: why not once more? And better.

"It's too grave an office to refuse," he said. The sentence echoed in his skull, the phrase of some other man who had spoken with his mouth.

They had been matrixed to be compatible with this, and with each other. The likenesses which had salted the performance were also a lure. It came to him to wonder if they bore a resemblance to those who had been here before them, those who had invented them.

"Why," she said, "did they leave their kingdom to us?"

"As well ask why they brought our ancestors to this star. Oh, yes, I think our races were taken from some other planet entirely, to be their toy. If we guess them to be gods, why stint them? Their avarice and callousness would be gargantuan. We can hardly fail to see that. Besides, the myths of

257

Klave and Yunea, the stories of wars, the traces of religions, even traces of Kaneka itself mixed in the law and semantics of our people. Yes, they brought us to this world and scientifically aided us in evolving to fit its scheme, eternal night, endless day. They generously gave us our stilted social hierarchies, dreamed up for us our slums and our palaces. The slums got worse and wider by their own graces, the technocrats more esoteric and dependent—something they must have predicted and counted on. For further amusement. But now, these gods—either they died, and choke some urn together, or else—"

An emerald fish leaped in the channel.

"Or else," she said, "they found some other exercise, and grew tired of this one."

She looked down, able now to turn from him without avoidance. She saw his image in the aqua when the fish had passed, and was soothed by it. She had loved Ceedres and denied herself in anguish. But here was a Ceedres from whom she need not withdraw in shame or self-denial. The beloved in the person of this good and honorable man. Her prosaic evaluation of romance also was comforting. That the processes of Kaneka had surely mated them was no more than a pale shadow in the recesses of her awareness.

Only awareness of vengeance, of worlds to be shaken and shattered, brought, for an instant, a far-off roar of fear that deafened her.

Only for an instant.

Robots were advancing through the tall mosses, bringing caffea. The silver stream drifted from the vessels of gold. She had lost all this, she had lived in despair and anticipated death.

His face was preoccupied. She studied it with a still and tentative joy. *We have been hero and heroine. And now how long before we learn the mechanisms, before we are god and goddess?*

Again, the vague note of fear, dying in the sound of leaves.

# CHAPTER EIGHT

## Part One

Velday, the last heir of Hirz, struggled to his feet. His attackers slipped from him, but in that moment, he realized they were no more than the silks of the divan. The lake of smoke and blood, in which he had seemed to be drowning, only the shade of the Maram chamber.

He stood, marooned, in the midst of the floor, and could not recollect coming here. Rarely did he keep Maram. The dream-wash was sufficient, and the intoxicated naps he slid in and out of during J'ara. The only picture that would come to his mind was of a dinner at Mansion Nu in the Slum. . . . Ceedres had presided. A woman with crimped creamy hair, had pressed a wreath of striped foliage onto Velday's brow, and held a wineglass to his lips. And then. . . . A door drifting aside, one of Ceedres' trained hierarchs bowing before him. Ceedres laughing. Ceedres was drunk too, but Ceedres drunk was a drunken god, no less. Women seemed to hang from him like flowers from a tree. A mouthpiece of onyx was between Velday's lips. He did not remember taking it up, but still he sucked in the fine granules of drugged dust. Ceedres' hierarch groveled to Velday now. Velday could scarcely see him.

"My lord the prince," said the hierarch, "says I should tell you."

"Tell me what?" Velday heard his own voice. far off, along an avenue of pavra, white caffea, wine and beauty.

"Your sister has escaped the Law."

"My sister?" His brain, which the pavra had expanded to a huge thrumming vault, focused on her more accurately than his eyes would focus on the sycophant. But what had Vaidi to do with the Law? Was she not at home, in Hirz—or no, not at home, and yet—

"Vel Thaidis has borrowed the chariot of the Yune Chures. She fled outwards to the Fading Lands. The Law lost her, gave her up."

"She has genius." The clear bronze of the voice, Ceedres' voice, filled Velday with pride, and with dismay. He tried to straighten himself, compose his face in lines of intelligence. To be worthy of Ceedres, to become Ceedres. Ceedres' golden cup was lifted. "To Vel Thaidis, last princess of Hirz!" It was a toast. Velday fumbled his glass and drank. Something worried at his thoughts, too feebly to bother him.

"How generous you are, Prince," one of the women was saying to Ceedres. "This is the second time she would have killed you. She's mad, for sure, that one."

"Gently," said Ceedres. "Not in the presence of her brother. I don't want to distress him." The laugh was low this time. The woman laughed with him. Velday, foolishly, laughed also, he did not know at what.

Now he knew. He had laughed at Vel Thaidis, his sister, who had grown insane. And Ceedres' laughter—that he had imagined or mistaken. Ceedres' heart was scourged by Vel Thaidis' plight, this much Velday understood. It was Velday's own guilt, his inadequacy and lack of strength that made him misinterpret the actions of others.

The dinner at Nu had run over into two or three J'aras, the Jates between spent in sport of hunting. Another incoherent memory: a robot approaching them as they paused in the bird chariot, offering a ridiculous admonition that the country beyond Hirz was being despoiled, over-hunted. What a ludicrous fancy. (A sudden image of Omevia Yune Ond clad in Ceedres' gift, a flowing garment fashioned from the bleached skins of immature antelines, mechanically sewn together with green jewels of Hirz.)

Velday felt a dislocation of awareness, between doubt and rejection of doubt. He went from the Maram-chamber, called a robot and asked for white caffea. Ceedres had left a flagon ready-chilling in a fountain that adjoined the upper salon of Hirz. At the sight of it, the touch of the enamel in his hand, Velday experienced an abrupt and undeniable sickness. Seeking to dispel it, he drank, but was only the more sickened. He sat down trembling on a cushioned bench, until gradually the motion and the murmur of the fountain refreshed him.

"Where is Ceedres?" Velday inquired of the robot.

"Ceedres Yune Thar-Hirz left word for you in the panel of your apartments."

"Oh." Velday considered returning to see, but his head rang. "I am unwell," he said to the robot. "Bring me something to ease me."

The robot went away, but a succession of figures seemed to come swirling out of the fountain to fill its place on the marble. When it reappeared, and bent to him with a thimble of medicine in its blond hands, he said uneasily, "When did I come back from the Slumopolis?"

"Three Jates, two Marams ago, Velday."

"What?" The medicine almost dropped out of his grasp. He swallowed it hastily, and holding gagging muscles in check, demanded: "You mean I slept so long?"

"Ceedres would have woken you."

"But I was too—too sluggish with wine to be roused?"

"Yes, Velday."

*And with berry juice and pavra. And with the women of Nu and their profligate flesh.* The medicine soothed him, body and soul, almost immediately. A sense of calm came over him then, spiced with an uneasy self-reproach. Sodden with poisons, he had slept three Jates away. Reviving, he had reached out to take fresh poison, as the matrixed child reached for the mechanical tube of sustenance.

Velday shut his eyes. On the lids, he saw Ceedres' kneeling hierarch.

"Tell me about my sister," Velday said to the voice robot.

"Vel Thaidis," said the robot, "is dead."

Velday seemed himself to die, and start alive again, in two atrocious spasms.

"What did you say?"

"Vel Thaidis is dead."

Velday saw everything, in instant retrospect—his sister's attempt upon the life of his friend and sworn brother, her exile to the Slum; his acceptance, his troubled dislike of her which muffled his troubled guilt. It seemed as if it were a year since she had gone away, or only yesterjate.

"How—what killed her? Did she take her own life?"

There was another picture now, a girl at Seta, one of Ceedres' women, Velday had assumed, a girl who resembled

261

Vel Thaidis. Or was it a dream? It must have been, for Ceedres had dominated it unpleasingly. He had spoken in a manner Velday could not recapture, but a manner vile and impossible; decidedly the stuff of bad dreams, like that of the smoldering lake.

"Vel Thaidis, formerly Yune Hirz, is dead in the legal form. That is, she has passed beyond the reach of Yunean justice."

Velday could not follow this.

"What do you mean?"

The robot spoke, in its high aesthetic tone, of the Fading Lands. Still, Velday did not comprehend. Vel Thaidis was dead, and yet he felt her life, as if she stood at his side. He remembered her eyes when she was an adolescent girl and he a boy, her eyes of love and admiration and jealous, controlled disquiet. He had been secure in her eyes, and had been annoyed by them, wanting her fascination with him, and not wanting it.

Velday rose and walked back to his apartment, to the message panel.

Ceedres' communication was brief. He had gone hunting with a chariot and three machines of Hirz.

If Ceedres was prodigal, did he not have every excuse? He had existed such a while with nothing. And he took now, as ever, with such charm, it was a pleasure to render him everything. Even the land and name of Hirz.

"I blame him," Vel Thaidis had said, "for his smiling schemes to *use* us."

The message panel mentioned nothing of Vel Thaidis. There were only these half mnemonic fragments, the kneeling hierarch with his words of escape, and Ceedres: *Gently, not in the presence of her brother. . . .*

All at once, Velday, with no opinions of his own to aid him, found himself beset by apprehensions of every kind. They seemed to have stolen up on him in his drug-clotted slumber, as if machines had mumbled in his ears all Maram, insinuating things. Now, awake, disarmed, wrestling with fear, there was no answer, no powerful arm against which to lean. He wished Ceedres had been there, to embolden him. Ceedres would have put all to rights. Velday was sure of this. So sure, he must repeat the surety aloud, over and over. Eventually it occurred to Velday, born of the repetition, that Ceedres had gone hunting. Velday would go after him.

At the thought, a warm flow of vitality replaced Velday's

sluggish depression. Out on the hunting lands, he and Ceedres would meet. They would discuss the kill and sip the minerally cold, fulvous last-chosen wine. Casually, Velday would require an explanation of the confused account the robot had given him. Perhaps the germ of it was that Vel Thaidis, rather than die, had been rescued in some way, which Ceedres had withheld from him till he should be sober. A part of Velday touched him with cold; deep within himself, he could now outguess his own hopes. However, the overhang of optimism persisted, the idea of Ceedres as a magician-hero who could cement everything together and make all bearable.

But despite this, and despite the scientifically magical restorative he had drunk, Velday noticed, in a glimpse of unexpected nervousness, how his own body had begun to undermine him. His youth and stamina seemed to have failed in several tiny, easily ignored, frightful ways. He ached. His spirit flagged and rose up inebriatedly, and flagged again. As the bird chariot pranced on its long legs across the staeds of Hirz, a wind of terror blew by him and was gone, leaving only the acrid dust of its passage.

He did not react to the temple until the chariot was almost level with it.

It was the Hirz boundary temple, alike, of course, all the others, the gleaming domes, the pillared walks, the lush lawns and trees. The Hirz temple, yet Velday Yune Hirz was hardly intimate with it. He had not ridden this route for years, had not specifically visited since boyhood. Not since the Jate he had sought the place with Ceedres, to swear kinship with him. Ceedres had been fourteen, and he himself nine or ten. Ceedres had humored him in this sentimental whim that had somehow forged a link of steel and gold between them.

Velday stopped the bird chariot almost inadvertently. The lower outer sun limned the ground with spurs and runnels of bright copper, and a green-gray cliff went up in the distance, over the border of the estate, out on the hunting lands. Direly, Velday's reverie had turned itself back toward the J'ara hunt, to Ceedres and Vel Thaidis in the Thar temple, his modesty, her rage, the knife, the cataclysm which profaned equanimity.

Before he quite knew what he did, Velday had left the chariot on the lawn. He was striding, hurrying, through the unintelligible, tinsely god-sound, toward the door of the Hirz temple, which opened for him as he advanced. When he

263

reached it, he was almost running. Bursting into the soft-lit columned space beyond, seeing the figure of the priest emerge before him, Velday admitted his desperate need. Uncertain of his ground, the child in him was looking over its shoulder to the omnipotent gods.

"Welcome," the priest said, spreading its hands in greeting.

"Priest, I am Yune Hirz." Velday's voice was still slurred. He swallowed and sighed. The title had been his sister's, before.

"Do you seek the Room of Prayer, Yune Hirz?"

"Yes," Velday said, He felt an urge to sob, and turned from the priest, as if it were human, as the floor began to rise.

He had not completely forgotten. The room was the same, the occult symbols on the walls, the myriad yellow globes, burning on their marble stands.

Velday crossed to a globe at random. He rested his palms over it, and lowered his forehead to rest against its light. His eyes were wet when he closed them. A tired child, he laid himself down before heaven for guidance, for some god to lift the burden from his shoulders.

Leaning mentally toward the supernatural, he was not surprised to have it almost at once within view. Like others, he had seen the vision long ago, the closed-lid imprint of the beautiful garden, some distortion of glare and shade focusing back into the pupils of the eyes—so, in adult parlance, he had learned to dismiss it. For, though sometimes worshipping gods, the Yunea did not permit itself to stray too far onto the abstract path of sheer faith. An ambience of security was all the aristocrats required, a guarantee that fate loved them. Of which guarantee Velday had been orphaned.

Seeing heaven, wanting to credit it, his eyelids clenched. Even so, the vision did not desert him.

There, a waterfall, there some creature in flight across a dome of sky. . . . Had Vel Thaidis seen such a mirage, before succumbing to murderous insanity by the Thar temple? No, she had seen a vision of hell, of black sky, white venoms, a sight she claimed Ceedres had forced on her.

Velday's eyes snapped open, and paradise was obliterated.

"Priest," Velday said. His mouth stayed wide, ready to blurt everything.

"Yes, Prince."

"Tell me about the upper room of this temple."

"The upper room of the temple contains its energies."

264

"What else?"

"Nothing else," said the auto-priest.

"Show me," said Velday, "the upper room."

What prompted him was a muddled vehement process of thought. All temples were alike, all robots basically similar, even the revered priests. It seemed the phantom of the upper room of darkness had haunted him all these Jates, Marams, J'aras, and now he must lay it by forever.

"No one goes there," said the auto-priest.

"Why not?"

"No one asks to go there."

"I ask," said Velday, with a resolution unusual and strained. "I am asking. Do you deny it?"

"No, Yune Hirz."

"Then, upward."

Immediately, the floor began again to rise; overhead, the ceiling to draw apart.

Velday gave a shout. It was a shout of alarm, but also of disbelief. And with the alarm and disbelief, a weird admixture of dull, acquiescing shame.

The floor was ascending into a great gape of blackness.

"No," cried Velday. "No farther."

The floor halted. Above, the black, and on the black a scatter of white gems, flaring into piercing brilliance.

"You informed me," Velday said, "the room contained the temple's energies."

"It does so."

"And the blackness, the lights—a facsimile of hell in the myth."

The priest's hairless cranium glowed in the cold sheen of white and dark. Its mortal plastum face looked blandly at him, as the bland face of Ceedres' priest must have looked at the princely council which interrogated it, the men and women who condemned Vel Thaidis. None saw these rooms because none asked to see them. Their function was unguessable, but their actuality was not. Ceedres had somehow come to knowledge of them, and now the phantom had grown to substance. For if Vel Thaidis had not fantasized about the room, what else had she been truthful in?

Some part of Velday shied from the simplicity of the revelation. Some part protested that Ceedres' deception could not have built itself so adamantly on such a flimsy base as mere ignorance. But another part of Velday, scalded by an intense mistrust of himself and all he had done, pushed deduction away. Was it not as he had always half suspected? He could not hide any more from his own baseness. His character and his honor had melted very thin. Only Ceedres now could save him, Ceedres his brother. Because Ceedres must, and would, have a solution even for this. (Ceedres' auto-priest, which had lied to the council and to the Law— was there a solution for that, also?)

And yet, no answer could be come at directly. It would be a time of testing; he, Velday, making test of Ceedres. This was unthinkable and nearly insupportable to him, but he felt a frantic motivation to attempt it. It would be straightforward, of course. Ceedres had always mastered Velday, been the stronger and the wiser of the two. Velday had only to let Ceedres go on in that assumption.

Velday turned to a golden globe and buried his face against it. Certainly, he had want of his gods now. Otherwise, he was quite alone.

It was the sixteenth hour of Jate. Hirz had entered the station of Aita in hespa. The painted Zenith window wall of the salon draped the chamber in its perpetual luminous gauze, lavender, cool yellow, and deep red.

Velday lay, like a stranded robot fish in the shallows of this lake of color and light. Ceedres' flagon of white caffea, two-thirds empty, and a crystal flask of wine one-third full displayed themselves as the remains of his breakfast. Velday looked sick in the cheerfulness, sick but merry,

When Ceedres entered, he came like the sung stroke of a clock, Golden and exact, freshly bathed and dressed after his hunting. He smiled at Velday, a smile of interest and liking.

"I tried to wake you," Ceedres said, "but you were past waking."

"Now I've breakfasted, I'm better." Velday's words were particularly malformed. He grinned ingratiatingly. "But tell me, do you think I take too much of this liquor?"

"Not too much. There are times when solace is necessary. I'll join you."

Ceedres took up the wine flagon and poured himself a measure.

"Solace," said Velday. "Yes. I have been thinking of—my sister, Cee. I dreamed of her."

"I should never have let you hear the news."

"The news?"

"Her escape into the Fading Lands." Ceedres' face was in-

266

tent and melancholy. He drank the wine. He said, "She was noble. She fought against iron justice until the end."

"The end—she's not dead, Cee?"

"No, my brother. Not dead. But lost. Beyond the Law. Beyond all of us. And she may die there."

Velday hiccuped.

"Could we not," he said, "go after her?"

"How would we find her?"

"Don't," said Velday pathetically, "don't treat me as an infant. Don't suppose I don't guess—you've kept things from me."

"Only to protect you, Vay."

"I know. But now I propose to search for her."

"The Law is absolute. I've tried to thrust it aside, to come at her and help her. But she's flung herself away from everything. It would be better to count her dead. I apologize for saying it, Vay. It pains me to say it. She was like my sister, too." The well-made steady hand trickled white caffea into the jade thimble and offered it to Velday. The other hand rested a moment on Velday's hand, the way a man would reassure a fretting beast.

Velday recognized the nature of the touch. The paranoia of suspicion had flooded him in the temple; he remained awash. The empty flagons, his appalling diction, were pretense. Acting the state with the facility of much genuine practice, he was conscious of anesthetized pangs of horror. He craved the alcohol before him now, and was glad when his performance permitted him to sample it.

"The Law," Velday muttered.

*The Law*, he thought, *How can the Law of the Yunea have borne the lie that no mythically black room existed?* He drank, and in a sort of fear felt the buoyancy the spirit instantly lent him, sickness only a faint blurring at its edges. *So, the Law is inadequate, had a blind spot. I must work on him without the Law.* Work on him—on Ceedres.

"The Law," Velday said again.

"Just, but harsh. My brother, let's forget this thing. We can do nothing. It's beyond us. You know I'd have done all I could."

They drank, and Velday shut his eyes. A whirling memory came to him at once, as if it had only been poised for the opportunity.

"Seta," Velday said. "We could keep J'ara there. There was a girl, wasn't there?"

267

"You mean my bitch Tilaia?" Ceedres smiled, lazy and generous, indicating to Velday that men might laugh secretly at women, from their deeper fellowship. "She's beautiful but, if you want her, yours."

"Not Tilaia. She was a—servant at the table."

The dream sequence was returning to him. Consider, and he could recapture it.

"Not Tilaia? Surely you don't mean some pot girl, Vay? Though I suppose if that's what you want."

Not a flicker in Ceedres' eyes, nor over the unique face. Nothing to convict. Yet the girl had been Vel Thaidis. Only Velday's stupor had kept him from knowing it before.

Cee had found Vel Thaidis. He had brought them together, brother and sister and friend. In the wake of so many falsehoods, equivocations.

There they all were. Velday could see them, even himself, minute figures, yet unmistakable. The girl wore the clothes of Seta, and the dyed brash hair, the rosy sunflower face. "Why are you doing this thing?" she said to Ceedres.

"If you mean your hapless brother . . . he has been drinking, inhaling pavra dusts. By Jate he'll remember next to nothing."

"No," the girl—Vel Thaidis—reasonably. "I meant to ask you why you've become a torturer. Your strategy, I follow, to obtain Hirz. But there can be no need for this."

"Recollect a black room. I went to the room to conquer my fear and know my conquest. I am enthralled with what I am. I intend to discover every facet, brain and spirit."

"And Velday is merely part of your experiment?"

Velday started at the sounds of his own name inside his skull. He listened determinedly, hotly, as if to voices overheard in a neighboring chamber.

"Oh," Ceedres said, "Velday. You and your brother, two spoiled brats."

"You never cared for Velday?"

"Do you imagine that in reality I ever could?"

"Velday," Ceedres said. Then, more loudly, "*Velday.*"

"What?" Velday started again, this time as if from a trance. He noticed that he had spilled the renewed drink of white caffea. That his eyes were also spilling burning tears. He shed them freely, unable to prevent himself, past embarrassment. He knew then that he had shed tears before, and during the same words.

*You and your brother, two spoiled brats.*

268

*You never cared for Velday?*
*Do you imagine I ever could?*

Ceedres stood over him now, the firm hand upon his shoulder imparting its quite spurious comradeship and compassion.

"Weep if it helps you, my brother. There's no loss of honor in that. I'll admit to you, I wept for Vaidi myself, once. I never told you. You take my humiliation from me, Velday."

Velday lay across the little table, not attempting to restrain his tears, or his mind, which moved on, clear and terrible, within his grief and above it. Now he understood. All she had warned him of was true. *His brother*—Velday was less to Ceedres than his whores, less than the napkin he used to wipe his lips after wine. Ceedres had played for Hirz, and got it. He got it across the theme of Vel Thaidis' tragedy and now across the theme of her death in some supernatural shadow beyond the world—if the story were even true. *He can somehow suborn the Law. Maybe he had her killed because she wouldn't crawl to him. For she'd never do that. As I have. Honor! He has none, and mine he's filthied. Vaidi—Vaidi— he has betrayed us both.*

Velday did not inquire why he should remember now. The trauma was too vast, it buried him in itself, refusing to be questioned or set aside. Velday, the optimist. The harshest lesson of all was that which ran contrary to the teaching of his own personality. There seemed in that moment no gladness and no future left for him. Then, he perceived where a warped gladness and a warped future lay in store. And as he cried, Ceedres' hands upon his shoulders, he made out, as if on a faraway slope veiled in mists, a knife with its blade in Ceedres' breast. Repetition of a previous scene, yet changed. Everything was changed at last. And suddenly, Velday desperately savored the encouraging firm hands of the traitor's unreal friendship, just as Vel Thaidis had savored the final unreal lover's kiss of his mouth. Knowing it was final. That the next words, even if unspoken, were to be: No and no. Forever and always, no to you.

The topaz beacon was alight and pulsing on the roof of Mansion Thirty-Seven. It was the nineteenth hour, and J'ara was well-established at Seta, the Black and Gold.

"Princess" Tilaia paced the mosaic salon, among the waiting flowers and flagons. She had no call on her to attend any person but Ceedres Yune Thar-Hirz. But Ceedres had not visited Seta since the J'ara when, at the door, he had heard

269

of the escape of Vel Thaidis. All hest-Uma sector had clamored with the tale, and the J'ara mansions were not excluded. The female aristo was now presumed dead, but an undercurrent of dissatisfaction persisted. No one had seen the woman die, and to witness at least a capture by the Lawguards was always expected in the event of a crime. The Slumopolis had been cheated and resented it. Tilaia, too, felt somewhat cheated.

Ceedres had sent her word he and the female aristo's brother were to use Seta this J'ara. But six J'aras had already passed since the J'ara of Vel Thaidis' vanishing. Also, Ceedres had relayed the message that Tilaia must eschew the rich aristo garments he had given her, the garments of Vel Thaidis, at least while Velday Yune Hirz was in the house. Tilaia had cunningly had made for herself instead a feminine version of Ceedres' attire of the J'ara when he had met Vel Thaidis in the supper room. Tilaia had had obscure notions of reminding him of her diligence on his behalf, in bringing the woman to Mansion Thirty-Seven. Now, clad in the white dress with its figurings of gold, its two chains of bronze crossed between her breasts, her inch-long nails, each with a black dagger embossed on them, Tilaia felt a momentary apprehension. He had been recently most often at Mansion Nu. He had visited the notorious Ler. And now, now he was late in arriving here.

One of Tilaia's robots vocalized at her.

"Tilaia, Ceedres Yune Thar-Hirz is entering Seta."

Tilaia jerked up her head as if astonished. She had been dilatory and could not alter her appearance now.

As she sent the robot out, she began to desire that Ceedres would not notice her sartorial jest. But, of course, he would notice everything.

Ceedres was ushered into the mosaic salon by the Princes' Friend. Velday came in behind him. The younger man was, as usual, sodden and virtually incoherent, supported by one of Ceedres' familiars. The familiar lowered Velday to a couch, and, in company with the Princes' Friend, went away at once. Tilaia slunk to Ceedres and carried out her normal obeisance. If he noted her garb, he did not say, but his face was in that dangerous immobile stillness it sometimes adopted. She had come to know that face, and fear it worse than the others, the mask of imitation.

He said little as the dinner was brought in. Three serving girls sufficed on this occasion, Tilaia officiating as his steward.

270

He had ordered no diversion, not even music. Coupled to his unspeakingness, the quiet made Tilaia ill at ease. Sometimes, when they were alone, Ceedres would permit her to eat with him; now she cringed a little when, handing him a goblet, a drop of green drink spotted the cloth. But no recrimination followed.

She comprehended she had failed him in the matter of Vel Thaidis. He had looked for a prolonged amusement there. The victim's disappearance had obviously been scored against Tilaia.

Tilaia, who had reached so high in her fortunes simply because an aristo had considered her a jot more toothsome than the rest, knew an always-ready leaden anguish. Was she, like many prior suns of the Slum, about to be put out?

The drunken, drug-incapacitated brother sprawled over the divan. This J'ara he seemed to have upset more than he imbibed, but despite this, the effects were disastrous. Tilaia had reckoned on Ceedres' plan long ago. The sister had ruined herself, the brother, Ceedres was ruining.

Much more than worship, Tilaia was afraid of her master. Velday was a frightful augur.

In that moment, Velday pronounced: "Taia is very lovely, Cee."

It was the clearest thing he had said thus far.

"Yes, Taia is lovely. Aren't you, Taia?" She kneeled at once and brushed the hem of Ceedres' draped tunic with her lips. "And such an elegant dress," said Ceedres.

She was too well versed in him to comment on the observation. She was saved from the silence again by Velday.

"You said to me," Velday mouthed, stressing the phrases with a sublime exactitude, "you said I might borrow Tilaia Yune Seta."

"Did I?" Ceedres studied Tilaia's bowed head. "It seems I've promised to loan you to my friend, Taia. What do you say?"

Tilaia drew her breath in a sharp small gasp. Under her powder, her golden skin had drained to yellow. She did not look lovely in that instant, as she raised her face. Ceedres, in all the while he had staked a claim to her, had expected that her favors be exclusively his. He had never ordered her to the side of others, save in her capacity as his dinner hostess.

"She's unwilling," said Velday. He laughed and upset the vase of wine he had been balancing.

"Oh no, Vay, you mistake her. Tilaia is always malleable, gracious. Aren't you, Taia?"

Tilaia quickly lowered her eyes.

"Yes, my prince."

"No, no," spluttered Velday. "She may think you'll be prepared to loan her to anyone hereafter. No, no, Cee."

"If it came to that, she would still do it, to please me. Would you not, Taia? To make my friends happy?"

"Yes, Prince."

"Then show my brother Velday that you're willing to console him."

Tilaia got up, her eyes apparently nailed by their lashes to her cheeks. She went to Velday, and positioned herself where the wine ran over onto the floor. She watched it run, and said, "Whatever my lord's friend wishes."

Velday floundered up. He caught hold of her, staggering, and Tilaia took his arm with a mannered precision.

"A thousand inspirations, Vay," Ceedres said. "Sweet J'ara."

The door opened. Velday clung to the girl for support. The wine cup he had brought with him; he slopped its contents on the ground and soon would slop on her white dress. Another girl had come to assist Velday. The three proceeded into an elevator, metal lattices swung over, and Ceedres' composed features were hidden. The elevator quivered, rose and settled.

Along a short passage hung with silks was the door to Tilaia's private apartment.

Velday handed his wine cup to the second girl.

"Leave—us." With an uncertain glance at Tilaia, the girl obeyed. "Is this," Velday inquired of Tilaia as they went the length of the passage, "where you bring Ceedres?"

"Yes, Prince."

Again, a door opening. They moved into the apartment.

The main chamber was much as it had been when Vel Thaidis saw it, smoking incense, sparkling gems and faceted crystal. The vanes of the amber ceiling were shut, and dull green apples of scented wax gave a somber light. Beyond a hand-woven, semi-transparent tapestry, a fountain danced in a basin of jet before a wide divan of golden satin.

Tilaia stepped to the tapestry, lifting it with her hand.

"This room will do," Velday said, "for conversation."

Tilaia spun about. More than the metamorphosis of his speech, now distinct and hard, her Slum woman's instinct registered some great metamorphosis that took in his whole self,

272

both bodily and in the metaphysical. A change that extended indeed over the entire room, blowing against her, seeming to stir her hair and gown.

"What is it, Prince?" she said, though it was an infrequent thing for her to talk first to a superior without some lead from him.

"What is it?" Velday repeated. "I'm not drunk, as you supposed me. That, I surmise, is what it is."

"Then you deceived—" she began, and stopped herself.

"I'm not the only deceiver. Tell me," Velday said in his pristine new voice. "How do you judge your master now?" She gazed and kept dumb. "Oh come," said Velday, "I saw your look when he gave you to me like a ring he was tired of."

"Forgive me," said Tilaia. "I was surprised. It will be my delight to serve you."

"And after me, who else will you delight in serving? Because it won't end with me. He likes the novelty. Didn't you see how he liked it? After me, all the princes who keep J'ara with him. You'll be recommended to each. Then later, his pet hierarchs. How will you relish that? You'll have guessed, no doubt. There's a girl at Nu. But it's unfortunate. I see you have robots. You'll lose them when the tech credits cease to come to you. When Ceedres stays away."

Tilaia's lips moved. At first no sound issued from them. Then she said, "Pardon me, but you're incorrect. Prince Ceedres Yune Thar has always been my protector."

"And mine, Taia. Look where it's brought me. Mindless with pavra and wine, my sister dead, my estate slipping from my fingers—into Ceedres' grip. But you knew as much, didn't you?"

"I know nothing," she said swiftly.

"Come," he said, "everybody knows. Not that he told you, but my decline is very evident. He's weaned me to toxics as if to meat."

Tilaia slid a narrow glance at him. Perhaps she saw his hands tremble.

"I have many assorted liquors here," she said. "What can I offer you?"

Velday smiled. Curiously, it was Ceedres' smile; yet maybe not so curious. "Offer me nothing. I crave those things, but there are medicines to assist me in putting that craving off. As I must. But I wonder how you'll fare, craving for tech credits and receiving none."

273

Tilaia flared abruptly, her instinct for disaster overwhelming her.

"You lie!"

"Now, Taia. You know that no prince lies to a Slum zenen or zenena. Ever."

Tilaia was quick to erase her fault. She bent her head again.

"Excuse me, but you make me feel afraid, prince Hirz. Why do you say these things of my master?"

"I'm trying to caution you. He's expansive with me, since he reckons me an addled sot. He boasts of what he will do. You're to be cast off."

"Why caution me then, lord prince," she whispered, with a trace of Slum guile. "What am I to you?"

"Nothing. But we share a bizarre affinity. He is an enemy to each of us."

"I don't accept my lord is my enemy. Nor that he is yours."

"He dismissed my sister with a crime of which she was innocent, and gambled she'd die of it, which she has, I think. He duped me."

Tilaia's eyes had brightened with a bewildered slyness. Too great a number of facts and implications were coming to her, she could not sort them, but she gulped them avidly against an hour when she might. She said impetuously: "If you have a grievance against him, go to the Conclave of the Law."

"Somehow," Velday said, giving the sentence the huge and terrible weight it deserved, "Ceedres has gained a way to pervert the Law. He can make machines tell lies to it, and they are credited. No, the Law as a weapon of vengeance is useless against him."

"What weapon will you choose, then?"

The vicious fearful side of Tilaia, the side which believed Velday's story, had uttered. The question unnerved her, and also Velday. Till that minute, he had not really thought in terms of murder. Now he did.

Ceedres the traitor, the besmircher of honor and trust, should be slain. But how, under the glare of the Law, which, unlike Ceedres himself, surely Velday could not blind?

He had talked to this woman from oblique motives, trying to discern her complicity, which was limited as he had supposed, trying to sour her against her lover, which it appeared he had done. For now, it was sufficient, and exhausted,

Velday turned from her, placing on a table as he did so the tech credits he had deliberately brought with him.

Tilaia was a statuette, but still with daggers on her nails.

"You're very generous, Prince, especially as I gave you nothing."

"It offends me," Velday said, "that he should keep you so long and then throw you over in this fashion. I understand something of your feelings. Hence, the credits."

He was at her outer door, when he heard the breathless cry: "Wait!" She must optically have counted the riches he had left. She ran to him and flung herself at his feet. For the first, he saw that she was beautiful, in the Zenith mode. Before, he had only seen that she was Ceedres' property. And now she bowed herself to the tiles, and kissed Velday's sandal. It was the gesture she offered Ceedres, her signal of total slavery, and a violent thrill shot through Velday, making him dizzy. Tilaia had, by transfer of the gesture to Velday, re-created Velday as Ceedres. And for a second, as Velday stood there, the pool of the girl's hair lapping his feet, her crayoned mouth on his skin, he *was* Ceedres. He felt Ceedres' body clothing his soul, Ceedres' face upon his own. He wore Ceedres' expression. When the girl lifted herself once more, and looked at him beseechingly, Velday intuitively mimicked her look. The effect on her was immediate. She too, obviously, beheld Ceedres standing in that second where Velday stood.

"Prince," she faltered, "I am your servant at all times."

When Velday reached the salon below, Ceedres had departed for another mansion.

Velday succumbed to the pull of home, and rode back to Hirz, sweating again with his need, and as he recollected how Vel Thaidis would have raced in this direction in the stolen vehicle of Chure. And sweating too as he thought of the weapon he must discover, by which to terminate the life of his friend.

The craving for pavra and for the white berry, the frenzy for wine of every type: the composite need Ceedres had brought him to, became Velday's close companion. It roused with him and walked with him and sat down with him. If he kept Maram, it lay at his side and whined in his dreams. He fought the craving now with all the ability that was in him, aided by the robots of his house and their scientific panaceas. Sometimes he succumbed, most often during J'ara, when he must pretend to sottishness. Even drunken, however, he did not now forget who had conducted him to this pass. And when he grew sick, when he writhed with anguish and physical hurt, he never now forgot whom he should blame. The weakness which Ceedres had nurtured in Velday to make him his puppet, now became, extraordinarily, the very thing which caused Velday to toughen and grow unsuggestible. And certainly, he hated Ceedres at last. That Ceedres did not see through the show, and guess it, was presumably only because of his vainglory and his sweeping confidence. These Jates and J'aras another Velday rode with him and drank with him. A Velday who acted and a Velday who hated and a Velday who brooded, awake and asleep, on a means to Ceedres' end.

Velday had vociferously thanked Ceedres for the visit to Tilaia. Velday had expressed worry that the girl had appeared distraught and peevish, apparently concerned that she was to become the plaything of Ceedres' favorites. Her invented oratory was duly punished, as Velday had foreseen. Ceedres presently sent Darvu and Kewel Yune Chure to her, with an instruction that she cater to them nobly. The Chures had been anxiously attentive to Hirz and to Thar since their unprecedented encounter with Vel Thaidis. They had protested to Velday that they had not known her in the J'ara slut, and that, on learning her identity, they had retracted all demands for restitution from the Law for her theft of their vehicle. At Ceedres' invitation, they went gladly to Mansion Seta, as if to prove their fellowship with Hirz.

It had seemed reasonable to Velday that his amorphous plans could afford to move slowly. He was not impatient that they should do otherwise, being unsure of his method, unsure basically of his goal, for Ceedres' death, though contemplated, had remained theoretical for him. (The alterations in Velday's character were still congealing, and yet to harden into rock.) He was only aware of driving Tilaia toward some brink or other, and that this might be of value.

And then, in the tenth hour of Jate, Velday entered the lower salon of Hirz, that room in which his sister had heard eight houses speak against her, and Ceedres, turning from a robot, said to him: "Now we know why the region's anteline herds are failing. We're not hunting them out, it seems. Three or four prides of lionag are at the work."

Velday, sallow from a wretched slumber, angry, and sullen that he had seemed forced to drink wine, blaming Ceedres, as always now, for his dependence and illness, put a hand to a bench to steady himself.

"Come," Ceedres laughed, and led him to a seat. "The notion of culling lionag never used to set you fainting."

"A lionag hunt," said Velday thickly, staring at the floor, Tilaia's wise habit. "I remember Ermarth Yune Zem was killed on the most recent one. I remember the dare-hunt when you were fourteen, the beast which leaped at you—"

"And which I shot with no trouble. Please don't quake for me, Velday."

Velday was seeing the old hunts dart before his vision. Lionag spelled danger and were revered for it. Ermarth was not the only young prince to give up his surety of three hundred years because of them. At nine years, Velday had crouched in terror, the sepia cat seeming to hang in the green air over Ceedres' shoulders. They had been lucky, that Jate. Or Ceedres had been lucky. If Ceedres had had less luck, the fortune of others might have persisted.

Even in his novel persona, this idea disturbed Velday, suggesting as it did the concrete facts of death.

"If I'm to hunt, I shall have to curtail my draughts of wine," he said aloud.

"Well, I never saw a drink spoil your aim, Vay."

Velday's blood seemed to rise up and choke him. In a split second, he reasoned everything and held the ultimate veracity in his hands. For he realized that Ceedres, whose plans till now had also been leisurely, saw in this unsafe hunt a way to be rid of him.

*He thinks me far gone on my road indeed, to reckon I'd not fathom the scheme.*

But Velday, frankly, (the former Velday), would not have fathomed it. As for the other princely houses, they had watched his decline with pity, brief sympathy, disgust. Yune Hirz mourned for his sister, and took to debauchery to alleviate distress. That they forgave. But when the debauch had not satiated itself, but progressed into vaster and more uncaring depravity, they had averted their faces and their thoughts from him. If he went drunken to a hunt and died due to the foolishness, they would lament the destruction of his title and his house, and know an unadmitted relief that the thorn had been cut from their flesh. He disgraced them, their finesse and their code. He would be better dead, with his deranged sister. Let the name of Hirz drift away with the dust, or let Ceedres, popular and superb, bear that name alone, with the wrecked name of Thar.

For all his knowledge, Velday felt a bitter fury. Hunting death, it would be easy to dispose of an intoxicated fool, so easy to let him in the way of slaughter, and no hint of guilt for anyone. Again, the Law blinkered.

And then, the unformulated floating threads of Velday's own plan wrapped together into a knot of steel. It was virtually as if another had sown the plot for him, cultivated and now presented it, seasoned, ripe, requiring only a touch to bring it from the tree.

Velday drank the wine Ceedres handed him.

"Years," he mumbled, "since we hunted Lionag. I will be thankful for the sport, Cee."

Ceedres immediately rewarded him, telling him some apocryphal tale of hunting. It was witty and made Velday laugh, through the white blade in his heart.


At the twentieth hour, the fourth of Maram, Velday entered Mansion Seta and was conducted to Tilaia's apartment.

Ceedres had gone to a supper at the Onds; Velday, politely invited, was too stupefied to accept, an event amazing to no one. When Ceedres had departed, most of the stupefaction was put away with the wasted flagons. In addition, Velday, who once in the vicinity of Ceedres had been his mirror, now assumed certain of the qualities of Ceedres during his absence. By the time Velday had come to Seta, these qualities had extended themselves. Until, when he stepped into the chamber and Tilaia was before him, the transfiguration seemed to Velday nearly complete. Last vestige of hero worship, it stimulated and uplifted him. On the girl, who seemed to note it well, it had another effect.

She kneeled to him, and cried: "Be kind—be lenient."

"What else?" said Velday.

Across her cheek was a murky welt, the same upon her shoulder. The Chures had not, apparently, included good manners in their attentions to her. But she had not approached the Law—what zenena would accuse an aristocrat? The injury nauseated Velday, but he simply remarked, "I trust you were recompensed."

Tilaia got up and met his gaze. Suddenly she appeared to accept this ally, or else she was as desperate as Velday had hazarded.

"They gave me nothing," she said. "They came as the guests of Ceedres." She let her eyes moisten with actual tears.

"That's too bad. I can't let you be treated in this way."

He gave her the credits he had brought for her. Her face became greedy and frantic, and she concealed it by kissing his wrists.

"He shows me no generosity. But you—"

"I'd be your protector," Velday said quietly, "to save you from his cruelty. But he would destroy both of us. Already I know he expects to kill me."

"Impossible—".

"No. Too possible. He'll evade the Law, as he did when he incriminated my sister to get a foothold in Hirz. He's clever, and there are means at hand—a lionag hunt. He won't find it unduly taxing to his ingenuity. When I'm dead, all Hirz will be his. I'm sorry, Tilaia. I don't envy you. If you run from him, I suppose he will merely provide a worse punishment."

Tilaia stole closer. Her proximity excited him, not to lust, but to strength, the strong identity of Ceedres.

"Prince," she said. There was a long interval. Eventually, the words projected themselves, inevitably. "You spoke of vengeance—is there no way?"

"Yes. One way. But it would involve your help."

At the outright confrontation, she recoiled. Then her hand wafted up to her bruised and lacerated cheek. Two practiced, mostly constrained, drops overflowed her eyes.

"You're an aristocrat. You say the Lawguards can be lied to. You might involve me, then sacrifice me to the Law in your place."

"You might do the same."

"I?"

He perceived she understood, even as she interrogated him.

"You'll be privy to my design, as I will be to your efforts to assist me. Equally guilty, how can one denounce the other? Yunean justice is flawed, I have seen that clearly enough, but it's to our advantage. I surmise Ceedres can die without suspicion touching either of us. As he intends to kill me without suspicion touching him."

"And you'd protect me? You would be my master?"

"Even if I wanted otherwise, I could hardly refuse. But in any case, I see your worth, if he ignores it."

"But you don't know my worth."

"Oh, he speaks of you, sometimes."

She was flattered rather than insulted, pure Slum-girl to her

279

roots, he thought. Dimly, unacknowledged, the Ceedres he had almost become glanced staeds ahead, and beheld Tilaia also removed, a blighted plant, from his garden.

She did not scan so far, or, if she did, she did not dwell on the sight. The present was her country.

"What must I do?"

"Get me some quick, debilitating, tactile poison of the Slumopolis."

"A poison?"

"The Slum's famous for such items."

"There are residues of the manufacts, drugs—some have been known to apply them—but they leave their mark, even in a reducéd dosage that does no more than cripple for a space. Anyone would detect murder."

"It doesn't have to dispatch him," Velday said flatly. "Just make an imbecile of him. What he would make of me. The lionag will do the rest."

An answering hate was in her look, and a nuance of insecurity, too, a shadow of loss, for worship had mingled with fear, as fear with worship. Ceedres was her god also, and to slay the gods took a weird courage, a temerity beyond all others.

Velday lightly raised her hand to his lips. There were flowers on her nails this time.

"Now you know it all," he said, and very softly, in the winning, mesmerizing tone of Ceedres, "will you resign me to the Law?"

Her lids fluttered down, her hands in his fluttered. Her emotion seemed spontaneous. She had given him power over her. She had given him power.


The smoke marker blotted the air, thirty feet over the plain. It was black, the danger color of the Yunea, for it indicated a major nest of lionag, a pride seven or eight strong, in a crevice of the rocks above.

The hesten border of the Hirz estate lay only seventy-one staeds away, but this was a tract of dry brown veldt. Treeless, it leased itself instead to stands of slender cacti that gradually mounted up on large shelves and staircases of auburn stone, dashed with that lower redder sun of the outer hunting lands. Far out and to hespa, an opaque scale of greenness revealed water. Here, the world baked in its clay. Amid the rocks, unaware the robot machines of men had spotted them, labelled them with a banner of black smoke, the lionag kept

280

Maram in Jate, poured over the ledges, or into the shelter of their rickety nest of reeds, cacti quills and the bones of creatures they had devoured long ago.

A quarter of a staed off, the lines of faceless hunt robots had halted, forming a ring. The spy kites, filaments extruded, had lifted above the steps of the rock, seeking noiselessly toward the nest.

The mortal hunters lounged in their bird chariots, around seven feet from the ground, and moderately quaffed their wine. Their pose was more affected than usual. The guns made a shining palisade between themselves and what might run down the natural stairway to greet them.

"This is too tame, Cee," Velday said. "Do you remember when we were boys, when we hunted without robots? That was something. But this—this—"

"Vay wants to tear lionag apart with his bare hands," said Omevia Yune Ond. Women did not generally pursue lionag, but she leaned on the rail of Ceedres' chariot, her hair tinted the color of its bronze, her black hide gloves dappled with orange gems, an enticement to blood.

"Why not?" said Velday. "I have white caffea here. After a sip of that, a man can do—anything."

"You should drink less with lionag in the offing," said Naine Yune Ond, Velday's neighbor on the other side.

"I have drunk very little," said Velday. He straightened himself. It was true, he did not seem as dehumanized as on other occasions.

"I also think," Ceedres added, "we might get in somewhat nearer. There are six of us and twelve robots. For myself, I propose taking a gun up to that ridge there. If the cats break away to hespa, we'll lose them."

There was a murmuring. Omevia said silkenly, "Six guns? You don't include me in the tally, Cee."

"Only as my inspiration."

One of the Yune Domms called over: "Ceedres is right. These things have been pilfering our hunting preserves, too. Sometimes whole carcasses are left to rot. They'll kill for sport and not eat, this nest."

Uched Yune Ket was swinging from a kneeling chariot, pointing a Ket voice robot to select a gun for him.

"I'm for Ceedres' plan. And I'll carry the gun myself. The robot can walk behind."

"And I," said Omevia, "I'm to languish here."

"Never languish," Ceedres said to her. He kissed her fin-

281

gers as Velday had kissed the fingers of Tilaia. "We'll leave six robots and the voice robots to guard you. And our friend, younger Domm, must stay and guard you as well. And Velday."

The younger Domm protested. Naine also protested at the foolhardiness of going up the rock on foot, yet he too swung down, his public bravery in the balance. Velday jumped from the upright bird and landed neatly.

"You see," he said loudly, "I'm fit as any of you."

"No, Velday," Ceedres said.

"Yes, Velday," said Velday. He flourished a bow to Omevia. "Gorgeous Mevi, tell my brother I'm capable of tearing lionag in two with my bare hands. Didn't you say I would? See, I'm fastidiously gloved as you are."

Omevia laughed desultorily and turned from him.

"Let him come with us," said the elder Domm. "He's just sober enough, and we have our half of the robots."

Omevia was already purring from Ceedres' chariot, striving to fascinate the younger Domm, her gold-leaf lids lax with incipient boredom. She had come to see a kill and to ride with Ceedres. She stared across the plain and up the sun-washed staircase. Soon, the five princes made their show for her by climbing it in limber, meticulous strides, the guns glinting in their arms or the digits of their hunt robots. All but Velday. Velday straggled, pace fluctuating. She had a startling premonition, and half raised her hand, ready to cry out to them. Then her hand fell. The younger Domm had begun moodily to talk of intellectual, mechanically composed poetry, to intrigue her. Omevia, reclining on the hot balm of the endless day, grew listless with suspense, not attending.

Near the top of the staircase, higher than the black marker, the climbers checked.

"The nest is through that crevice, there," said Uched.

"They'll have heard us. They'll be stirring," said Domm.

Ceedres gave an order to two of the six robots to proceed up and around the rock case, to come at the nest from the rear.

"This is too close for selective aim," said Naine. He shifted morosely. "I could go down a step or so."

"Yes, that's a good thought," said Ceedres. "We'll need at least one man to back us up on this side." Relieved, relaxing a fraction, Naine removed himself about ten feet down and poised, considering a further retreat. "What about you, Uched?" added Ceedres. "You've a keen eye."

"I'm comfortable here."

"Then, from here, I'll go up alone."

"Ceedres, we're on top of them now," Yune Domm said. A phlegmatic man, sense not nerves had prompted him.

"On top of them, and they haven't come to meet us. They're full of game, and sluggish. I think I can start the entire pride up and into our guns, if our placings are sound."

"There are eight cats to our five men."

"And the six machines. Some of the nest will be puny, young."

"Ceedres," said Velday, "is hunt master. Ceedres' decree is our law. I remember—"

Ceedres stood by Velday and slipped one arm casually about his neck.

"We must not brag, Vay, of our babyhood ventures. Go to the hest and set your gun. Or, better, the robot will do it."

*All my life, striving to emulate my hero. He knows what he does now I must follow. The more he puts me away, the more I rush onward. He knows.*

"Cee, I'll go with you."

Aloft, out of sight, a peculiar mewling snort.

Each man recognized the sound, and fell silent.

A spy kite sprang up into the sky and away, and filling the top of the rock after it was a lionag, burst from the nest below. Only one. Like a carving of the brown stone, it craned its serpentine head, polarized eyes gleaming like two black jewels. The collar of ruff was electric. It was impetuous, an adolescent of its kind. Reckless with bloodthirst, it launched itself straight off from the rock—and into the explosion of Naine's gun and Domm's. Uched's order to his robot to shoot was superfluously carried out as the animal spun, shattered and bleeding, from view, back into the crevice.

Shuddering with reaction, Naine cried, "That will give them something to ponder."

As if on his cue, a guttural snarling reverberated from the throat of the crevice. But no more cats came out.

Ceedres began, almost negligently, gun on arm, to ascend. He stepped through into the crack of rock just below the point where the first lionag had emerged. Domm cursed mildly. Recharging the stem of his gun with a deft sliding stroke, he went after Ceedres. Velday, gun in hand, thrust in front of him. Domm did not remonstrate. Naine with two robots on his lower stair, Uched crouched with a Ket hunt robot to hespa, were well stationed to pick off what might come erupting forth. The sixth robot trod after Domm, its feature-less mask tilted slightly to absorb the sounds from the rock, the decrees of the men.

The crack widened, and the nest appeared, untidily ag-glomerated between the cacti and the stones. The single re-maining young male of the pride prowled on the sloping ledge that ran up to the summit. About three yards below, the dead one lay. In the nest itself, the rounder heads of fe-males, two of them, poked up and snaked down again, and there was the glottal chatter of two or three cubs. All was in-decision now. Lionag could read death and its significance, and the spitting of guns. Then, with no proper warning, the king cat shouldered from the nest.

He was a colossus, some inches taller than a man from ear to pad, longer in his length than the brazen mechanical beasts which drew the princely chariots. Even polarized, his eyes gave off a redness, as of fire within. His thick tail lashed against muscled flanks fluid as oil. The younger male, impe-tus regained in the giant's presence, jumped to his side.

Velday thought, *So even they have their heroes.*

He swayed on his feet, slipping his hand from his belt to clutch at Ceedres' wrist and steady himself.

Tilaia's gift, a scrap of colorless cloth, no bigger than her flamboyant thumbnail, was held for a moment between Velday's gloved hand and Ceedres' ungloved wrist before skimming, unnoticed, to the earth. A moment was adequate for its purpose. It was impregnated by a dermal halluci-nogenic, distilled from the dregs of the Slum's manufact gut-ters, a slime gathered at Maram by several who indulged in or sold such commodities. The pores of the skin were recep-tive to it, but the veins of neck and wrist extremely so.

Alerted, not yet aware, Ceedres looked about at Velday. What Ceedres had determined to do, Velday was not positive, perhaps simply rely on Velday's imagined condition to fling him into misadventure. Behind them, in the crevice, Domm barked an alarm. Flank to flank, the two cats, the huge king, the lesser princeling, were flying forward off their ledge. Abruptly, one of the females cast herself after them.

Velday thrust to his gun. His marksmanship was excellent, and he was not drunk. Sighting between the foremost two lionag, he released the bolt, slowing and deflecting both of them, disabling neither. They crashed down, rolled and folded up with unsewn jaws of froth and flame. They ran im-mediately toward the guns, and the men who held the guns.

Velday seemed to be confusedly, sluggishly, recharging his weapon, dropping back. Domm tilted his gun stem and shot for the king, but the young one came between and spun over in a tangle of smashed bone, torn pelt.

Ceedres—

"Cee!" Velday shrieked, his voice high and thin as a girl's.

Ceedres had the gun angled incongruously toward the rock. He could not seem to maneuver it or keep it level. His face had grown mad, as if with an unlikely panic, and he mouthed something, but nothing intelligible reached his companions. Then the awkward gun volleyed, catching his shoulder, whirling him around and over, and under the body of the leaping king cat as it came down.

Separated and amplified as notes of music, Velday heard the monstrous horn claws stab in through Ceedres' chest and raked the length of his torso, through flesh, muscle, sinew, through the sculpted cavities of lungs and belly.

Ceedres began to scream. The screams sounded disbelieving, but they ended in a tumult of blood.

The she-cat hurled herself at Velday, and he shot her head from her neck. Her forepaws slapped harmless on the rocks in front of him. Domm was shouting and the robot fired. The king lionag bounced, wallowing, and sank back slowly, dragging Ceedres' cloak and entrails with it, smiling through its red teeth, dying.

Velday stumbled forward.

He stared down. He had known this instant before, this instant as he stared above the corpse of his friend, his brother. Velday, a terrified small boy, and to his everlasting shame, the tears, so familiar to him now, rained in Ceedres' wreckage. Until Velday saw that absurdly, unbreathing, speechless and disemboweled, Ceedres still lived.

The polarized lids had flickered up, the orbs of the eyes turned now hest, now hespa, either in shock or the continuing aberration of the drug. Ceedres grinned. It might have been the rigor of the final agony, a muscular contraction unmotivated by reason. It did not look to be. It looked to be a grin. And then the eyes fixed and muddied. Grinning like the lionag, Ceedres died.

Naine, Uched and their robots were approaching. The dense green sunlight magnified their clamor, let it go, and a burning quiet began.

Domm's heavy hand clasped Velday's arm. The clasp told

that here, if necessary, was a witness to innocence and accident beyond any breath of crime.

Somewhere Uched yelled, and a robot gun discharged, quenching the second female as she appeared on the ledge. Somewhere velvet heat, in motion as a breeze, sang along the plain.

Then the great quiet returned and multiplied.

# Part Two

A weapon of vengeance. . . .

But no one would seek vengeance upon her, upon beautiful Vitra Klovez. Besides, who was there remaining within the borders of her world to effect that vengeance? Ceedres had perished by the machinations of Vel Thaidis' brother. But Casrus Klarn had left no relative behind. Not even Temal, the suicide. And yet, foreboding clung to Vitra. The Fabulism she had thought to have invented now progressed dynamically without her aid. Klovez had collapsed. Casrus, who should have offered her his love, had declined to care for her, had passed to living death, and then mysteriously from life altogether. Everything had gone wrong. She was in the chains of a malign and baffling fate. She saw herself, lovely and doomed, catastrophe gushing upon her, no one to snatch her from its jaw. Except, perhaps, Vyen, whom she dreaded to speak to on the matter, who, when she did speak, swore at her, mocked her, ran away to Olvia Klastu.

Vitra turned off the "sun" in the Klarn salon. She could not bear it any more. Casrus, obdurate, unloving Casrus, was dead. He had been lost on the surface, in the scintillant black beneath the stars. Probably someone had killed him, some worthless Subterine outwitting the Law as she and Vyen had done. Oh, she was glad he had suffered and died. It was a suitable punishment. Yet, how his death hurt inside her. Now, certainly, she would never see him again.

And Vel Thaidis? What had become of her? Vitra had seen the last of her in the screen when Vyen depressed the keys.

Racing in the Chure chariot toward the shadows of the un-known twilight zone—obviously she had been lost there be-yond the sunlight, where nothing grew and the air ended. For, returning unwillingly to the screen, Vitra had seen no more of her. Instead, Velday's life had taken up the self-per-petuating drama. But none of them counted. Not Vel Thaidis, not Ceedres, nor even Velday, his handsome face oddly alter-ing to become a reflection of Ceedres' face, his tears watering the bloody murder he had engineered. All the princes strove to comfort him, Domm, Ket, Ond. He was more important to them than Omevia, screeching mindlessly, tearing her hair.

The Fabulism was magic. It might never cease.

Vyen sneered when Vitra postulated this. He persisted in holding her responsible. Some schizophrenic frailty of hers forced the Fabulism on. Useless to explain that even when she kept from Rise Iu, the story-making continued. Return-ing, she could replay long scenes which she knew she could not have created, and not been there to create. Of course, she dealt with Vyen wrongly. She did not attack him, she pleaded. She could not help it. She wanted him to save her.

Under the new, non-solar light of the salon, the amber fun-gyras had turned the color of sapphires and frost in their urns. Transformation dormantly lurked in all things.

Vitra rose and went from the salon, wan and pensive in her glitter.

Vyen was already waiting for her outside the house. They were to go to a J'ara gathering at Nle Stadium, a prospect that only added, to Vitra's fear and sorrow, the condition of boredom. Possibly, if she delayed, Vyen might grow con-cerned about her and come to fetch her. . . .

Vitra perversely turned to the stairway and walked to it, away from the house exit point. It was not until she found herself by the door that she realized she had retraced her steps to dead Temal's apartment.

A pang of horror went through Vitra. What was she doing here? An unfortunate idea came to her that if she caused the door to open, she would find the Subterine girl on the other side. Vitra's answering impulse would generally have been to back away, and it was with extreme agitation that she discov-ered herself going forward instead. As she did so, it seemed to her she felt eyes upon her, watching her, intensely, cruelly, and with fascination. The eyes of some fabulast who had created Vitra Klovez to play with.

The door folded aside.

Vitra let her breath out in a sigh.

The room was empty of a presence.

And yet, not empty, for the essence of that other woman remained strongly in evidence, had even intensified.

How curious, too, the heap of rent scarves and shawls had been left lying on the floor, the two leaves of the love declaration scattered with them, just as Vitra had left them.

The compulsion was inevitable: to read that declaration once more. Vitra glided into the room, her hands pressed to her mouth. She leaned over the heap of shawls, the pieces of paper, peering down, making out the words. *Love. Knives. Fires. Blood.*

Suddenly Vitra felt outrage. She, too, would have offered herself to a blade, a fire, would have spilled her blood for Casrus' love, of course she would, if he had ever asked her.

With a bitter, self-deceiving pride she turned, literally, upon her heel, toward the door—and stopped. For in the doorway stood Temal.

Temal, amid her dark ash of hair streaked with pale vermilion. Temal bloodless, yet streaked with pale vermilion blood, no bolster now to sop up that wound. Her eyes were closed, yet her mouth was open. She seemed to be laughing.

Vitra shrieked. In all her terrors, she had never known a terror like this.

"Vitra Klovez," said Temal, "your brother is waiting."

A film seemed to disperse from Vitra's eyes, while abruptly, and with a corresponding shock, she saw that it was not Temal in the door at all, but one of the Klarn robots. An extraordinary trick of the lamps, the unfamiliar shadows of the room, had played upon the dark and white metal of it, and upon the torn vermilion scarf which, in the way of such servants, it had retrieved from the floor at its entry. Not a ghost, after all.

And yet—

In a vile horror which, now, had no grounds for itself, Vitra fled from the room, running toward Vyen with a hopeless knowledge that he could no longer save her from anything that might be in pursuit, of flesh, or spirit, or her own mind.

It was a short journey to Nle Stadium, precluding much talk. However, after two or three minutes, Vyen spoke.

"Have you been to Iu this Jate?"

"No," said Vitra.

Silence.

"Oh come," said Vyen, "why try to camouflage your idiosyncrasies?"

"If you suffered as I suffer," Vitra exclaimed, "you would anticipate commiseration." This retort was habit. She was now beyond such retorts.

"I should get it, too. But then, you don't deserve commiseration. Probably you keep too many J'aras. That might account for your mental incompetence, the Fabulism you won't stop—"

Vitra's nerves snapped.

"I've told you—" She began to scream of bewitchments, phantoms, even of Fate.

"Use the dream-wash," cut in Vyen icily. "It will clear your head."

He smirked with half-closed eyes. He had grown less fearful over past Jates, as neither machine nor man linked Vitra's drama with their plot against Casrus. As for Casrus' death, it had consolidated Klovez' luck. That Vitra lamented for Casrus revolted Vyen, and with sulky humorousness he dripped acid in her wounds to pay her out. He had come to assume that the unwise lingering of the Fabulism was part of her lament. He did not believe, or would not let himself, that it had a soul of its own. After all, she had lied about it before, saying she had concluded it when she had not.

Before Vitra could reply, if she intended to, the Stadium of Nle spread its arbor of starry neons, and the chariot-car dashed in.

Just through the gate, a ramp ascended onto a balcony of rime-white tiers and arches that overhung a brazen racing track beneath. Here Shedri Klur was to drive one of the exercise chariots behind a team of four dogga. It was a fresh occupation for him, reminiscent of Casrus' feats. As the Klovez car pulled up, Shedri faced about and lifted his cup to Vitra in an archaic champion's salute.

In the middle of the rectangular track, a pylon of white silver threw fierce erratic blasts of blue light at the high ornamental roof. Nearby, unseen, the noise of gunshot and the hiss and scrape of fire-swords, cries of irritation and laughter. Vitra searched in vain for somewhere that her eyes and her ears might rest.

"Look," said Shedri, guiding her up the tiers, and pointing to three chariots currently clattering over the metal track. "It's not without risk, but I find it excites me." Vitra watched the expected slap of boredom stunning even her apprehension. "Ensid is racing against my cousin and one of the Klinns. Naturally, Casrus used to race. I never saw him, but I gather he was a fine rider."

"I'm sure you are the finer," said Vitra automatically.

"At least I haven't dishonored my name. Forgive me, Vitra, I shouldn't remind you of those unhappy events."

At the corner of the rectangle, Ensid's chariot, the usual steel plank slung between great wheels, careered out of continuity with the big dogga who hauled it. In a moment, Ensid was flung on the track, the chariot collided with the barrier, the dogga, harnessed two by two, reeled around on each other and began to fight.

Shedri grimaced contemptuously, a connoisseur.

Vitra stared with glazed eyes, seeing instead Casrus, racing very fast and with consummate skill, seventeen years old, about the Uta track.

"It's my race now. Ensid's is finished. You must time my speed by your chronometer."

Shedri went away down the tiers and stepped onto the track as Klastu robots persuaded the large snarling dogga from each other's throats. Ensid limped, pointing again and again to a metal-scorched calf. Vitra giggled and lowered her dark head to her goblet. Her oppression was almost overwhelming.

Olvia, in viridian furs, was offering candies to Vyen, who brushed them aside. Vyen would not look at Vitra.

On the track, Shedri was climbing onto his plank, securing the reins of the four pale beige animals, waving at her to notice him.

Vitra waved dutifully in return. The jewels on her wrist blazed in the blue pylon light.

While somewhere, far overhead, Casrus' bones were charring into the wastes of endless night.


Thinking of Casrus' death, Hejerdi spat, and his spit froze where it landed. It was one of the coldest Marams he had ever known. Ice had formed on his beard even within the facial shield. He kept J'ara perforce. Though his burns had healed, they had left him stiff, and Dorte had spurned him when he approached, begging his former employment as surface ganger. His share of Casrus' wage was gone with Casrus. What followed was predictable and inexorable. Credits unpaid, he was ousted from the hovel in Aita Slink. Now he sat out the freezing misery of the hours in one of the Subterior's shack-like taverns, drinking alchafax much diluted by the free ice that hung from the internal rafters. At the other side of a tiny basin of coals squatted Zuse. Being himself in work, he had bought the coals, and the drink. He had also, in a stuttering growl, related his enforced part in Casrus' slaughter. Reiterating frequently, "Dorte, that piece of dirt, he forced me to it—I couldn't do anything but what he said," Zuse had confessed taking Casrus to the curious building on the planet's surface, strangely like a temple associated with the sun-side Fabulism. Over and over, Zuse retold the climax of the venture, as if Hejerdi must get it by ear to recite. "The floor went down and shut him in. I'd vowed to release him next Jate, and sew up some tale for Dorte about an escape. But when I did come back, the floor opened—and Casrus was gone. He's an aristo, I said, he'll have tinkered with the machinery, got free on his own. So I searched about a bit, but never found him. And he never came down here again. There was no route out of that under-room that I could see. But the other thing, did I say?" "Say it again," said Hejerdi. And Zuse would comply. "The first time, when we shut him in, after the floor closed over, I seemed to see a glow—a glare—come up through it. We took ourselves off—the other was with me—I was frightened. Then, when I came back for Casrus, I'd reasoned myself from that, and there wasn't any light. But I wonder—some burst of energy from the planet's vitals, could it be? Enough to—" Zuse dropped his voice on each occasion when he said, "to incinerate a man, skin, skeleton, clothing, as if for an urn?" "Maybe," said Hejerdi. And on the fifth retelling, he spat.

He was uncertain precisely what he felt. Anger at Zuse, of course, snarling impotent range at Dorte. But for Casrus, what? Eventually, he was able to assure himself that the grief in his stomach was simply, and quite properly, at the forfeit of the shelter and credits Casrus had shared with him.

Presently Zuse drank himself into a maniacal bravura, and rolled woodenly from side to side, threatening Dorte and scheming his demise. Hejerdi stayed quiet, and his mind ranged on its own black wanderings.

Since Casrus Klarn and fortune had deserted Hejerdi, a select memory had involved him. The memory was of the aristo woman, the blue and silver princess, who had come to the door-mesh and shaken it, and to whom Casrus had said, *You intended that I be sent here.* Her name was Vitra— Hejerdi had heard that too, before Casrus had requested pri-

vacy with her. But naturally, though Hejerdi had willingly
given them privacy, he had not moved too far away. He had
supposed they might warm to each other when alone, and
had been intrigued by the idea of Klarn displaying passion.
But the passion had been all on the woman's side, and, since
she had often utilized her vibrant little lungs to the full,
Hejerdi had acquired more knowledge than he subsequently
admitted to.

At the hour, Hejerdi had been vastly interested, but had no
dream of acting on the interest. It appeared the princess had
falsely incriminated Casrus, insuring his banishment to the
Subterior. That was Klarn's problem, not Hejerdi's. Hejerdi
had neither the inclination nor the incentive to pursue this
phantom.

Now, however, Casrus absent and doubtless slain, it had
come to Hejerdi that if the princess Vitra and her brother
could outwit the Law one way, they could do so another.
Dorte had appeared to give the order for Casrus' sub-surface
immuration, and give it as a torture rather than a death sentence. But maybe it had been a definite sentence all along,
put into practice by Dorte—but at the explicit, if concealed,
order of Vitra.

Alone and desperate, Hejerdi contemplated a crazy whim.
Vitra and her brother were dangerous, but she had impressed
him mostly as a silly hysterical hussy. And there was a limit
to the crimes they could essay without detection. They had
everything to clutch onto, and he nothing. Walking out from
the Fabulism that was her art form, Casrus had said to
Hejerdi, *I recall sufficient to damn my enemies.* A few Jates
after Casrus' disappearance, Hejerdi had visited the recreation
area at Kaa Center and looked for himself. The hypnotism
had made a haze of much of it, but having determined to, he
salvaged enough to recognize a plot built on falsehood, culmi-
nating in a fall to a Slum. There was, too, something uncanny about this hot-side Fabulism. The Subterior, never
quite recollecting it succinctly, yet seemed to throb and hum
with unconsciously retained images and concepts. There were
drawn suns on several walls, weird beasts and vehicles; some
of the women had taken to dyeing their hair yellow and
brass, there was a coarse tavern rhyme that mentioned a
bright green sky. There was, too, an undercurrent of newborn
antipathy for the aristocrats. This very Jate, someone had
been vividly describing how an aristo had died, torn to
shreds. Fantasy, Fabulism, whatever it was, the mood in hell

292

was not quite as it had been. Like a turgid brew with a chemical agent in it, remodeling everything. Hejerdi had analyzed what the remodeling entailed. Before, they had foregone hope, lain down in brutalized quiescence. Now, they cursed fate and themselves. Now they kicked against the load, the whip, the very cold foul air. Now they were waking up from the frozen centuries.

Perhaps the presence of one aristo, reduced to their depth and cast among them—Casrus—had also helped to activate the key.

Where the program ended, Hejerdi had no proper concern. He must, as must they all, look out for himself. And it seemed to him, as he sat over the shallow basin of coals, that Vitra, the Fabulast aristo, might be the answer to his personal dilemma.

Presently Zuse rolled over on the ground and snored. Sometime in the last phase of Maram, the alchafax would disturb his glorious drunkenness, causing him to vomit, to groan, to pray to nonexistent, no-longer-titled gods. This alchafax, if absorbed in quantity, generally did, but men went on drinking it, nevertheless. A couple of hours of warmth and undespair seemed worth the price of an eighth of a Jate of misery. If the guts were rotted, no matter. Death was everywhere here. Why not anticipate?

Hejerdi, though, a mere quarter cup inside him, had only its sour taste to contend with. Leaving Zuse with a grunt of off-hand pity, Hejerdi adjusted his facial shields and went out of the tavern, along three or four alleys, across two or three spaces, under and through the barren forests of icicles and stalactites, stepping over the islands of sleepers, and by the chill-stinking holes of Subterine mansions.

He reached the center at Kaa and went in. A ramp lifted him. He was shown in passing places of expensive joy, of food and soft slumber, the area of the Fabulism, the medical section, cold as ice, cruelly able to make men well that they might go out and grow sick once more, and sicker; that they could die. Finally, a cubicle, a voice which asked Hejerdi's name and quest.

"It's this way," said Hejerdi sulkily, staring at the plastomil flooring. "An aristo visited me in Aita Slink. Her name was Vitra, a princess who was a Fabulast. . . . She took a liking to me. She wanted to make me an Upperling, have me with her in her palace in the Residencia City, the way they sometimes do with us, the aristos. But I was an idiot. I got angry.

293

I said she might go—I said she might go away. She said if I thought better of it, come to a center and ask for her to be told. I had to give my message a certain way so she'd know it was me. You see? I've changed my mind."

"You wish a message to be relayed to Vitra Klovez?"

"Klovez. . . Yes, Vitra Klovez."

"She may decline to receive you now."

"Not if you give the message as I was to phrase it."

"You are sure you are unmistaken."

"No mistake. Contact her. You'll see."

Herjerdi did not like conferring with a machine. As with most Subterines, robots and mechanisms were to him alien, untrusted things. But useful, no doubt, most useful. Now, at least.

"What is the message you require given to Vitra Klovez?"

"Oh," said Hejerdi. He had planned out the words so carefully that in this vital instant they almost failed him. Then he visualized Casrus Klarn, incinerated in a burst of sub-planetary volcanic radiation, erupting as Vitra Klovez must have known it would. Jealous, greedy little cat. Spoiled, vicious, meddling little cat. Well, others could meddle. "The message was," said Hejerdi. He felt an upsurge of courage and determination. "Princess, I heard and remember everything you said when you came to the Subterior, to the hovel in Aita Slink. I remember, too, your clever Fabulism. I remember the wisdom of its plot. Let me come into the Residencia to you, and prove my admiration and loyalty."

The machine merged its panels in colored lights.

"Your message to Vitra Klovez has been recorded and will be delivered. It is doubtful you will be called to the Residencia. Leave the center now."

Hejerdi slunk from the chamber, and the ramp sung him back into the dreary cold of Maram. Best run to cover, now, in some chink he had grown fit enough to fight for. The Klovez might send Dorte or another after him, though he doubted it. Too many inexplicable corpses, however tenuously linked, would besmirch their reputation.

And Vitra was not very intelligent.

Her response to his message would be swift panic, and the effeminate brother's the same. They would send for Hejerdi. He would be carried into the princes' city, and then—his brain suddenly balked, unable to proceed. Tripped up by his own deeds, the circumstances he had set in motion, Hejerdi lunged off into the warren of the Subterior.

294

Shedri Klur had completed his chariot exhibition. He had engaged the course with a rigid nervous gusto. There had been no accident or dislodgment of vehicle or driver, and now and then he had demonstrated tricks, such as shifting the right foot over onto the back of the nearer right-hand dogga, or, enwrapped with reins, presenting his back a moment to the team. But these fireworks of skill were performed with an asymmetrical adherence to detail, for Shedri was afraid to move intuitively. All had been conned, as it were, by rote. A single departure from the lesson would have inaugurated disaster.

But he was proud of himself. He came to Vitra with a swagger, offering her the magnificence which was himself. She reacted with the proper display, but her eyes were dull, vacant. He tried not to register her eyes. Then, when he could no longer overlook them, across the glasses of thin turquoise wine, he said to her: "You seem oppressed by something."

"No. Not at all," said Vitra quickly. The dull eyes screened themselves behind black lashes and silver paint.

"Yes. Come, Vitra, confide in me. Is it Casrus' reputed death which troubles you?"

"Oh," said Vitra. Now she lowered her head and hid her whole face in a brief, forward-falling wing of black hair.

"He was your enemy, but his death is a profound shock to each of his peers. My sisters talk of nothing else."

"Don't speak of him," said Vitra.

Surprised, embarrassed, Shedri stared. He had thought himself gaining on her, as had happened once or twice before, always, admittedly, with the same result, that he was shown he had not gained. Not quite aware of what he did, he cast a sideways frown at Vyen. Shedri had come to see that Vyen was his rival, Vyen, whom he usually liked and was happy enough to be in company with, Vyen's razor edges deflected by Shedri's easy-going nature, or admired by Shedri's princely arrogance—or else merely missed by Shedri's slowness. But Vyen, as Vitra's possessive brother, was another being, and Shedri had come to censor him for Vitra's indifference. Though during this J'ara, Vyen appeared to have left Vitra wholly alone. The thought inspired Shedri. Unkindly, lovingly, he said to her: "You've quarrelled with your brother, and it's upset you." She said nothing, still hiding in her hair. Confident of having pierced the target at last, Shedri

295

went on: "Dear Vyen has too much mastery of you just lately. He's a year your junior, and should be more respectful. I'll be your brother instead, your elder brother. How would that be?" He waited tensely, playfully, for her answer.

He never got it.

A platinum sphere, which, unseen during their interchange, had been wafting gently through the stadium, now settled in the air before Vitra.

"Vitra Klovez," said the sphere, "I have a message for you."

The novelty stirred the nearer groups on the tiers of Nle. Most of the Klovez' acquaintances were there; thus who should send messages? Olvia laughed, and made some facetious remark about an unknown worshipper. Vyen, his plastivory face abruptly taut as the carving it resembled, turned to his sister for the first time that J'ara. He seemed to sense, as the others did not, the terrible crystallization of foreboding which Vitra was experiencing.

Vitra said nothing. The sphere rested before her, featureless and perfect in the blue gleams of the pylon.

"Vitra, do ask for the message," said Olvia. "We're in such suspense."

"The message isn't for you, but for my sister," Vyen said harshly.

"Oh, very well, let's go up to the next tier," Olvia snapped.

"You go," said Vyen.

"And I?" said Shedri.

Vitra said nothing.

Vyen stalked along the tier, and the others swaved aside, drew back, began to move away to a discreet distance. murmuring, gesticulating damningly at his uncharacteristic uncouthness.

"Vitra," Shedri said.

"Please—" said Vitra—he hung from the pause, waiting— "please go."

Scowling, pushed away into the crowd, Shedri went.

"What is it?" Vyen said to his sister, gripping her arm.

"I don't know, how can I know—"

"Ask it then."

Both trembled, both were white. Both felt. it seemed. the cloud of imminence, in a world without clouds, which had gathered above their delicate skulls.

"Give me the message," Vitra said to the sphere.

An aperture unsealed, a bead dripped out. Vitra automatically extended her hand and the bead settled in her palm. The sphere drifted away across Nle stadium. She stood there, and she recalled the bead of message she had sent to Casrus, the invitation into the snare, his initial step toward the door of death.

"Activate it."

"Vyen—"

"*Activate it.*"

He had been so blithe before, cuttingly, jeeringly blithe. He had reckoned on safety. Now his eyes swam in his white face as if he might faint.

Vitra's thumb activated the bead.

"This message is relayed from the Subterior, from one, a man. Name: Hejerdi. As follows."

Vitra and Vyen froze, holding their breath, or breathless.

"Princess," said the bead, with a new male voice. "I heard and remember everything you said when you came to the Subterior to the hovel in Aita Slink. I remember, too, your clever Fabulism. I remember the wisdom of its plot. Let me come into the Residencia with you, and prove my admiration and loyalty."

Vyen and Vitra watched the bead as if it might spring at them. But it was motionless, and said no more. It had said indeed everything that was necessary.

"Hejerdi," she faltered eventually. "He was with—he was with Casrus. I don't recollect him, he was like the rest of the worms, ugly, in rags, obnoxious—but I recollect the name. He *listened.*" Her face lightened momentarily with an unsuitable righteous indignation. "And now plainly he threatens me—he's guessed—Vyen, what shall I do?"

"Do?" A livid color rushed through the pallor into Vyen's cheeks, mostly into his eyes, inflaming them. "You should have done it long ago." She stared, her lips parted. "You would not stop it, would you? Your *Fabulism.*"

"I tried to," she croaked, no moisture in her mouth.

"No. On and on. You would *not.*"

"I would have—couldn't—"

"No. *Would not.* And now, as they had to, one of the rabble has sussed you out. You've ruined us." He raised, not his voice, but his hands into the air, flagrantly gorgeous with their rings. "Ruin. . . . Go and slice your wrists, you worthless, witless bitch!" The hands flashed. The two blows caught her across the face, one after the other, and she dropped on the floor of the tier.

She was inert, had entered a state where everything was of horror, flowing to all horizons, and beyond.

As she lay there in the gray nightmare, a paroxysm of movement and noise broke out before her and above. Then she heard Shedri Klur shouting.

"Whatever your disagreement, you don't strike an aristocratic woman when I am by."

Vyen sounded obscurely, terrifyingly nonchalant.

"Oh, but she's my kin, Shedri. That gives me the privilege of being able to strike her, don't you understand?"

"Vitra is under my protection now."

She raised her lids, and saw Shedri slash Vyen, in peculiar imitation of what had gone before, full across the mouth with his open hand. The blow was reasonably powerful, even Shedri was more of an athlete than Vyen. Vyen staggered, caught one of the arches, and saved himself. He bled, neatly, from both corners of his lips. His eyes gradually filmed over.

"What's this," he said, speaking awkwardly through the blood. "A challenge to a duel?"

There was a huge silence. Not only on the tier, but throughout the Nle stadium. On the track the teams had been reined in, the chariots were static, their drivers gazing up. From the chambers of swords and guns, princes and princesses had emerged. Always alert for theater, the Residencia had faultlessly relayed, in a few minutes, the impact of the scene which had built between Vitra, the message sphere and Vitra's brother. Somewhere, maybe an eighth of a staed away inside Nle, a gun sounded, some practicing marksman that the alerting current had not yet reached.

Shedri felt the moment fly to his shoulder like an arcane bird.

"Yes, I'll challenge you. For the sake of Vitra Klovez, her honor and her welfare. You accept?"

"Why not?" said Vyen. "I suppose you intend to the death."

Shedri rocked a little.

"The death?"

"Oh yes. That's legend, Klur. A means to legal murder." One of the Klinns started to call from the upper tier. Vyen cut him short. "I'm willing." He began to walk toward Vitra, Shedri hurrying after him, grabbing at him, Vyen thrusting him off. Vyen kneeled by Vitra. "I've bruised your face. It serves you right. If we fight with fire-swords, Shedri can kill me, and that will serve you right, too."

"Don't," she said. She sat up and flung her arms around him. "Don't fight him."

He held her tightly.

"We've lost everything," he said. "The idea of the Subterior frightens me. The cold and the vileness. I'd rather die here. And you'll watch me die. I'll do it prettily, Vitra. And wittily. I'm scared, but never mind that, I'll give you a last picture of me that you'll be proud to remember." He twisted her hair cruelly. "And you can say, 'I brought my brother to that.'"

They began to cry into each other's necks, while Shedri, feeling and appearing stupid, loomed in the background.

Soon, unable to bear his redundant position any longer, Shedri snarled the traditional question.

"Weapons!"

Vitra clawed at Vyen's sleeves, but he rose, pulling free. He wiped his eyes and the blood from his mouth with elegant studied gestures.

"Fire-swords, Shedri Klur."

"Very well."

Shedri was also becoming afraid, and he stammered slightly as he gave orders to the Klur robots. The duel would be legal, certainly, but the stigma might not. Though the Residencia loved drama, it did not love those who provided it. But, of course, despite the heated dialogue, they would not battle to the death.

One of Shedri's sisters and a woman of Klef were supporting Vitra. Klef and Klarn robots glided behind. The tier was emptying of aristocrats, as the concourse swarmed through into the lower rooms of Nle, toward the arenas of combat. Far off, the practice gun had ceased firing.

Vitra took each step very properly. She looked straight ahead but saw nothing, not even Vyen now. Vyen was chattering to Ensid, to Olvia who was entreating him, to the Klinns. Feverish, nonsensical chatter. She could hear him, not the words.

Now they went under an arch, idled on an escalator. On the walls glassy draperies sewn with drops of gold sheered up in the breeze of their passage. Vistas of ice caverns behind translucent plastic—more beautiful than the Subterior, but as cold.

Death was so close. The prolonged death of exile. The man called Hejerdi had sentenced the brother and sister. Or was it Casrus, reaching out to them from the black geography of

299

space in which his soul had been netted? Or was it Temal, the omen of Temal, clawing a way back from her ashes?

How lovely the ornamental balustrade, its flutings and curlicues of polished copper.

Perhaps it would be simple to die.

Perhaps it would not be necessary.

Perhaps she had imagined everything. Shedri and Vyen about to exercise together, an athletes' bout with fire-swords. And shortly they would drink wine and sample alcohol sticks, and dine in someone's palace. And Casrus would meet Vitra on a thoroughfare, handing her a jade rose copied by machines from the memory bank of a computer. Casrus would love her. She would not be guilty or liable to retribution.

A weapon of vengeance. . . .

The arena was one of the smaller chambers of its kind. A red light pervaded it, conducive to affray. Aristocrats congealed at the low marble rail. Without prologue, she found she would see everything.

Where had Vyen gone to, and Shedri? To be dressed, to select swords—

The two women were tired of supporting Vitra. Through fright, she had grown to be a dead weight in their arms. They gave her to her robots, or the robots of Klarn which now were hers. The arena whispered as friend elaborated to friend, princely house to house, on how Vyen Klovez and Shedri Klur had come to blows and now to a duel. The robots had taken their vow and willingness both to fight to the death. It was a legal formality, obviating blame. But neither would actually slay the other. Such a thing had not occurred for centuries. Young men yawned to detract from their avid eyes. Young women stared, eyes like jewels, fingernails like enameled claws. Vitra knew their beastliness. She had invented them. This was a Fabulism.

The fighters came out and were cheered, more loudly than at a practice bout.

They wore the thin protective and nonflammable garments of the combat, traditionally one black, one gray, which covered even hands and face. Contestants might be singed but not set on fire. Not, at least, from a superficial blow.

A weapon of vengeance.

A fire-sword.

The blade was two feet in length, about one inch in width, tapering to half an inch at the point, and was forged of calvium steel, absorbent of, but resistant to, heat. There was no cross-grip, the hilt was part welded into the gauntlet, both also of calvium seel. From hilt to point on each broadside of the blade ran a quarter of an inch channel, partially closed by narrow rings, fine as wires, and treated to extreme hardness. Small chips of fosscoal had been forced into these tubes, and trapped there by the rings. The sword had then only to be plunged in a scoop of burning oil to set it alight.

Once lit, the flames wreathed the entire weapon to the hilt. They were in shade a vaporous blue, with flushed tongues which would darken slowly into red the longer a fight continued. The calvium glove, padded on the inside with cooling, heat-impervious layers of phosphor and plastics, protected the swordsman from his own blade.

The fiery aspect of the sword was mostly for spectacle, yet coupled to the instinctive human fear of damaging fire, which even when restricted to a singeing was unpleasant, the weapon called up unique impulses of defense and attack in the combatants.

Complementary to the fire-sword was a plaque of fresh-cut ice clenched in a light steel vise and carried in the other hand. At the battle's commencement, when the ice was immature, it could be employed effectively to block an opponent's weapon. The oil on each blade prevented the flames from relapsing, but meetings of ice and fire were marked by explosions of steam. As the ice decayed, the more rapidly the more often it met the fire, its use as a ward became less. In the more stretched bouts of such fencing, ice gone, the steel vice was thrown aside.

Casrus Klarn, it was well known, had practiced the art with robots, who could be set at phenomenal speed and reflexive ability, and could fence indefinitely. Most princes preferred to pit their talents against other men, fallible as they themselves. But then, they fought to win, even at exercise. Casrus had fought to tone his muscles and to quiet his mind.

Neither Shedri in gray, nor black Vyen, though concealed from head to foot, evoked Casrus. They were altogether too light, too fragile. The arena sizzled with their combined ethos of apparent hate and frenzied indecision.

Shedri's voice cracked as he instructed a Klur robot to signal the start of the bout on a count of fifteen. The robot's voice came shrill and flawless after it.

The two princes seemed posed like runners, leaning on the atmosphere itself, dipping their swords at nente, the tenth nu-

301

meral, the blades hissing, throwing out large petals of flame, the ice handed to them by their machines through the smolder.

The fifteenth numeral was achieved.

"Begin," said the robot of Klur, and wheeled rapidly to the arena's edge.

Vyen's suicidal impulse had already dissipated. To be replaced by an immediate assurance that he would still die. Shedri the better fighter, would kill him. And ironically, through Vyen's spasms of dread and bewilderment, came the conclusion that even the threat of the Subterine Hejri or Hezeddi, or whatever foul name it was, might have been dealt with, fobbed off. For what had seemed, in that distraught second, an insurmountable destruction, had now shrunk to its proper size—too late.

Shedri's eyes were enclosed behind the tinted fireproofed lenses of his nonflammable mask. Shedri had disappeared altogether. He had put on the clothing of the killer, and become a killer. And yet (even in utmost fear, Vyen could see it) Shedri was such a clot, could he truly mean to kill? Had he the metal for it? As if along an echoing tunnel, Vyen heard in memory Shedri's stammer.

Shedri's blade, smoking, flaring, leapt across Vyen's breast. Vyen thrust the plaque of ice tardily between. White steam roared, and under its cover both combatants danced back. Vyen had been stung, a slight hurt, but a presage. His limbs turned to fluid and he almost fell. But how ineptly Shedri had moved—

Vyen had not fought with a fire-sword for six or seven years. Even in play, it had been literally that, a vessel for jokes, which his opponents had allowed him, amused by his antics, or wary of his more agile tongue. Suddenly, a compulsion overcame Vyen, caught between premonitions of death and contempt for Shedri Klur, to attempt a joke, a pitfall for all clots.

Klur was advancing once more. The flaming blade wove stripes of light and after-image on the air. Vyen sidled away, halted, wriggling his fingers loose in his gauntlet. He hefted the blade, freed his hand, and threw the whole assemblage at Shedri.

As the sword left him, Vyen cursed himself for an idiot. If Shedri intended business, Vyen had insured his own mortality. But Shedri's reply was exactly the reply of Shedri and his fellows six or seven years ago. Accompanied by gasps and cries from the princes at the low rail, Shedri ducked and gargantuanly sprang aside, lost his footing, stumbled, righted himself, ungainly, on one wobbling knee and hand. Vyen's sword, which had been given neither the force nor the direction to do more than touch smoke from Klur's protective garments in passing had he remained stationary, now plonked noisily on the arena, as if to underline the buffoonery.

The watchers were laughing now. Vyen failed to realize it was the laughter of disappointment. They had wanted, though not quite believed in, a kill. Elation washed through him, despite the quavering of his pulses. He strolled diagonally, well clear of Shedri, kneeled, slid his hand back in the gauntlet and stood up. Then beheld his irretrievable error.

Shedri had reckoned himself clottish enough. Now, writhing with humiliation, restraint and timidity had abandoned him, or he them.

He charged at Vyen, and his sword was a volcano spewing fire from his hand. Vyen's answering terror robbed him instantly of all equilibrium and all coherent thought. A few ill-recalled lessons slunk in to supply reflexes instead.

The volcanic blade smashed forward, and Vyen's ice-ward clipped up to stay it. Boiling steam jetted over them, but Shedri did not withdraw. He lashed out with his ice itself, catching Vyen across the neck, following through to clap him across thigh and ribs with flame. This time the singeing blow was excruciating. Nerves raw from trepidation, Vyen called out.

Shedri's sword cut for his head, and Vyen jerked away and ran two or three paces, his own blade flailing like a useless third member.

"Shedri," Vyen panted through the mask. "Shedri, you're being too serious. It was—a jest between us—wasn't it?"

"No jest," said Shedri. His tone was blurred, swallowed, as if he were drunk.

"Come, Shedri," said Vyen. He strangled on his own spit, coughed, and crowed: "I will apologize to you—whatever you like."

"I like *this*."

Vyen did not see the sword move. Pain came like a shriek inside his arm. He looked, and beheld the torn smoking fabric, the blue-crimson ignition of his own blood.

Vyen screamed, clapping the ice (another old lesson, instantly regained) to the wound, the running flame. One pain went out, a worse replaced it. The arena swung, and Vyen's senses began to go from him.

The laughter had long since perished on the crowd's princely lips, letting in again the feral savagery of the death-wish. Every figure strained across the rail—no higher than mid-calf to the women—the rail which fenced them from yet barely kept them out of the arena. They knew that minute how it must be. The duel was absolute, and real. They saw Shedri's passion, his clumsy deadly smitings. They saw Vyen drooping, about to go down. The melting ice of his ward slopped on the ground. The tip of his sword was down already and drinking at it thirstily. Shedri's blade swirled. It seemed to take a very long time. Perhaps etiquette was reasserting itself, sobering Shedri, hanging on his arm to prevent him.

And the crowd broke into uproar, thinking they bellowed at him to stop, in fact, wordlessly bellowing for a crescendo, for slaughter.

Vitra had perceived the sequence, too. She beheld the absurd joke and Shedri's rage at it, she beheld Vyen's punishment, Casrus' vengeance claiming him. But she did not see with clarity. It seemed a Fabulism, acts controlled by external projection. And then clarity stabbed through her anesthesia.

Clarity told her that Vyen was within an inch of death, but that death hesitated. Shedri's sword seemed to float, a rift of soft red flame, gentle, checkable.

She had been a mistress of events, a maker of stories, she knew what she must do, and how she must do it.

She moved from the support of her robot attendants, stepped easily across the rail. Then she sped toward the fighters, and as she did so, she cried Vyen's name once or twice.

At her cry, everything was altered. Like a wondrous catalyst, she acted upon it all, without herself swerving one iota from her goal.

She was two yards from them, when Shedri, surfacing from his excitement to see himself blatantly culpable, turned his head, lowered his sword as if it were too heavy. His eyes, focusing on Vitra, pale and frantic and running to beg his mercy, sent the signal to his intellect: *If I spare him, she will have to thank me for it the rest of her life.*

As she reached him, he dropped the sword, and let her white hands extend to fasten on him and her white face offer itself to him in supplication. And as this happened, Vyen, hardly conscious, hearing his sister's crying of his name, was yet galvanized by it, and accordingly, in sightless delirium, tore up and forward with his burning blade, delivering a towering blow against Shedri. Or intended against Shedri. Something had come between, an obstacle; an obstacle which gave a high pure singing note, and blazed up, a slender torch of vari-colored flame. Vitra.

Vyen's sword had entered her side, almost ripping her in two from the determination of the stroke. It ended her life before she really felt the fires which scaled her flimsy garments, her skin, her hair, imparting an agony of cold rather than heat.

Her scream was not rational, it owed nothing to her reason. She had the space only for a fraction of horror, amazement, despair, beyond all horrors, amazements, despairs. And then the world poured from her, poured away as if into a bottomless urn. And the pale mouth of nothing at all closed upon her.

The silence roused Vyen. He wondered what he had done, or what Shedri had done, to cause such soundlessness.

He stared some while until his faintness drew away, and his eyes, his nostrils and his spirit informed him.

Hejerdi, his stomach gnawing on its hunger, his back braced against the ice-thick wall of Center Kaa, rubbed his forehead in hurtful monotony against his cloth-wrapped, frost-darkened knuckles. He did not know what to do. In a few more Jates, lack of work and therefore of food and shelter would have decided for him.

He had come to Kaa Center, then his nerve had absconded. He had sat down to wait.

It was two Jates, and a Maram between, since he had sent his message to Vitra Klovez. That she had not responded alarmed him. Could she be brave enough, silly enough, to risk his revelation of her calumny to the computers of the Subterior? Or did she imagine he would not be credited if she spoke in denial? Was she correct?

Now another enforced J'ara was beginning for Hejerdi. He had chipped icicles earlier and sucked them for moisture. Over by the lop-sided tavern that perched above Kaa Slink, a ghastly thing had happened. Hejerdi had managed to steal a chunk of concentrated food from a sleeping man. Out of sight of the Stare-Eyes of the Law, such an event was sometimes possible. But having stolen, having chewed off a corner of the edible, Hejerdi had withered in sudden conjunction. As

305

once before, with Casrus, he found himself putting back in the owner's pocket what he had taken. This awful failure of the survival trait in himself disgusted and frightened Hejerdi. He returned to Kaa and desperately resumed his vigil. Which was not, however, nor showed evidence of, being rewarded.

Presently the mid-Maram bell clanked Hejerdi from a nauseous doze.

Something made him get up and blunder into the building, toward the ghostly prospect of his last hope. Although, once again confronting the faceless machine, Hejerdi peered at the floor.

"Did the princess Vitra Klovez reply to my message?"

A hesitation of mechanisms.

"There was an accident in the Residencia, at Nle Stadium. Vitra Klovez is dead."

Hejerdi's life-systems seemed to fragment, and he tottered. As if he had loved her. He had: she had been his road to security. At least, perhaps, a road away from his own annihilation.

"How," he said brokenly, "did she die?"

"This does not seem," said the machine, "to concern you."

Hejerdi laughed and wept.

"Not concern me? Not concern me?" A sick anger roiled in him. He found himself imploring, not comprehending yet why he did: "Was my message delivered to her before she died—was killed?"

"Yes."

"Her brother," said Hejerdi. That was all. The logic had revealed itself.

Her brother, the brother she had betrayed to Casrus, the brother she had called—what was it? Ven? Vyer?—her brother had learned she was discovered, that therefore both were implicated, she, and he himself. And he, this Vyre, had somehow arranged a most fortuitous accident—before she could betray him further.

"Her brother killed Vitra," said Hejerdi.

"That is so," said the machine. "An accident during a practice bout with fire-swords. A duel."

To kill his own sister. . . . To a Subterine, normally denied, by the planning of the matrixes, any known kin, mother, father, brother or sister, the Residencia's family status had a certain luminous quality. Now defiled.

And if Ven-Vyer-Vyre had slain his own known flesh and

306

blood, he would not avoid slaying Hejerdi. It was, in fact, a miracle Hejerdi had escaped till now.

Till now, when his only recourse was to tell everything, all he had overheard, all he suspected, the Klovez plot, Casrus' murder by order, Vitra's murder by hand. That Hejerdi himself had tried to profit by the knowledge, might cause him to be chastised, but that was better than death.

And while he was assisting the Law of the Klave, the Law would feed him, would it not?

His anger and frustration crunched together hotly in him, like settling coals.

"I have something to confess," he said.


Vyen Klovez sat in his black chair, shivering, always shivering, his eyes enslaved by the pointless motions of the ice-green robot dancer on its pedestal. The blue-green light had also been innovated at Klarn, and the bird-shaped window gouged in the wall. But the newest innovation of all was that Vyen was, involuntarily, alone.

Olvia Klastu had been with him constantly, not that he had wanted her. Nor Shedri's cousin, nor the women of Klinn or Klef.

He was afraid. So afraid. He could not explain to himself his fear, or dispel it, or conceal himself from it. The ministering of his admirers had seemed to make it worse, but now they had gone away he knew it had not, for isolation was the worst of all.

He was alone because the computers of the Law had summoned him. Because they had sent machines to him which postulated how his sister Vitra had boasted a stratagem of false witness to Casrus Klarn in the Subterior, and been overheard. The whole plot had been put together. The motive had been assessed (correctly). Lastly, the murder of Casrus was hinted at, and then they had suggested that Vyen had killed his sister, judging her emotions, her movements, scheming her destruction as he had schemed the rest.

He had sat in his chair, shiver-shivering, the fiddle-toys whirling or snapping or flopping from his fingers. They had asked what he would say. He said:

"You t-t-take the word of a Sub-ter-ter-erine ag-against m-my own-own?"

"Are you guilty?" the machines had asked.

"N-no. I-I am n-not."

"The Fabulism, to which the man Hejerdi directed us, has

307

been observed. There are criminal similarities, beyond doubt. Do you still maintain you are guiltless in your dealings with Prince Klarn?"

"I-I d-do. I am-I am-I am not guilty—"

"And your sister?"

"An acci-accident."

But he was the machine, not they, spouting mechanical sentences. They had reevaluated. They had delved and probed and collated. They knew. They knew it all. They had established truths that were not even true. The immaculacy of the Law had been caught out. The computers would not forgive him that.

And he. He sensed some part of him was wrenched away. The sword wound was healed, another, more obscure, gaped wider. He said things without conviction because that missing portion was not there to add its feather weight, its brilliance like a diamond or a star. It was all Vitra's fault. Her stupidity, that which he had mocked, had wrecked them. Poor Vitra, in her lonely silver urn. She should have paid for this, not he. Not Vyen, poor Vyen.

The machines had gone away. When they returned, they had gifted him with their summons. He must present himself at the designated computer complex. Others had also been questioned. A verdict had been arrived at, and awaited him. Shortly, the robots of the computer complex entered Klarn.

"Wh—wh," said Vyen. He giggled, remembering Vitra's giggle. "What if I w-won't g-go?"

"You will be required to go."

"You m-mean I-I shall be forced-forced to?"

Vyen rose. He leaned on the arm of his chair. A Klarn robot came to support him.

When he was five years old, he had been acrobatically tilting himself over the rail of a chariot-car, and tipped on the ground. He had sat on an avenue, retching and terrified, with a discolored thumb which pointed the wrong way. Vitra, who was six, had held his head, and when the hurt and the disfigurement had been corrected, Vitra fed him candies. They had sat together and watched the erratic light of Rise Uta skim the ceiling of the room. They had told each other macabre stories in the unlit everlasting dusk.

He wanted Vitra to be with him now. But he had killed her. She was a silver urn.

The way down into the planet was cumbersome and sym-

308

bolically desolate amid its cold metals, cold tiles, cold grumblings of machinery.

There was an Upperling in the Subterior. His name was Dorte. He had been apprehended. At first he had refuted the charge of murder, but when it was proven, he had agreed vehemently that two aristos had certainly coerced him, bullied him, into illegal homicide.

They were building lies against Vyen, as he had once built lies.

(Had any of Vitra's little-girl stories ever mentioned the planet's hot-side, a golden veldt, jade-green sky, tindery hills?)

He was in the chamber where he had rendered the fabrication against Casrus Klarn.

He sat on the cushioned couch, smiling and shivering. He tried to pour and drink the liquor that stood at hand, but the liquor spilled, just like his life, through his fingers.

The platinum ovoid spoke to him. It told him all that had been discovered and the tests applied to the discoveries, and the results. Then it told him he was condemned.

Vyen went on smiling, shivering, spilling the liquor, not glancing up, or anywhere.

"Vyen Klovez," said the machine, "in accordance with that which has gone before, your murder of Prince Klarn and of your sister Vitra, there can be no clemency, no appeal. The sentence is final, and it is death."

Vyen cried, and the tears married with the wine. His long lashes, sticky black with wetness, stuck to his cheeks.

"But," said the machine, "we do not allocate the harsh dishonorable death of exposure at the surface, the death of oxygen deprivation in the vacuum. You are granted, if you will, a more tender execution, here in the Residencia."

Vyen went on crying, a child that was not to be placated with a shadow play.

The robots of the Law carried him to the little cell and laid him on the divan. Here he curled himself tightly together, screwing up his face, winding his arms about it. In this position, he cried aloud for Vitra until the room was flooded with an invisible, odorless, painless poisoned gas.

In the screens of the Fabulism, the sun-side drama went on. It was unquestioned, by human or by machine. Only Hejerdi was perplexed, only he was properly aware it had been Vitra's. Could it be some other aristo Fabulast had

309

adopted it, or had some mechanism of the Fabulast chambers run amok? There had been a jeweled insectile aircraft darting through the feathery cirrus of the green sky. Velday Yune Hirz had reclined within the craft, and Tilaia, the J'ara girl, had kneeled to him with a dish of cakes. He had taken her to live in Hirz. He had acquired a taste for her, or for her homage. But in the Slumopolis, their taste was for revenge, furiously submerged. An aristo had avoided justice as no Slum-dweller ever had. Vel Thaidis Yune Hirz had fled into the dusk beyond the sun, but who believed she had died there? She was a princess, and the Law had allowed her the privilege of life no zenen or zenena could have bought, once saddled with crimes of Vel Thaidis' magnitude. Seeds of revolt had been tossed upon the dusty and infertile land. The sun might shrivel them, or it might not—

But how could such seeds, scattered across the Subterior's frigid rock, find any spot to root in?

Conscious of strange undercurrents murmuring all about him, Hejerdi marveled, flinched, meditated. Other strange things had happened, the strangest only half a Jate ago. The computers, which had reached into the princely city to penalize, had reached out again to Hejerdi, and grasping him firmly in the toils of the Law, assured him he was not to be disciplined in any form for retaining his evidence, nor for seeking to profit by it. His adverse circumstances had been accepted as excuse sufficient. But Dorte had been deprived of his status as Upperling; he had been tattooed on the forehead with the mark of a pardoned assassin. He had no work, and might well starve. The man who had helped Zuse imprison Klarn in the "temple" building had been beaten with steel, but not Zuse himself—

Hejerdi mused over the wholesome wine the Center had provided him. He had been told to recruit men for surface work. If he were canny, he might aspire to be an Upperling himself. The jump in his fortunes was fantastic. He had begun almost to suspect some destiny. . . .

Yet not a destiny as another Dorte. There were enough of those. Casrus Klarn had taught him something. He must search within himself for what it was. His extraordinary cascade of luck influenced him. When a woman came and plucked his sleeve, he lifted his hand to cuff her, then stayed his hand.

"You were with Klarn," she said. "I know it. Will you do as he did? Spare me a credit chip."

310

Her face was hollows and stark bones.

"Casrus was mad," Hejerdi said. He pried a chip, his advance wage, from its ring, and gave it to her. Her face became smooth and beautiful. And he—he became Casrus Klarn.

An intolerable humbleness and joy went through and through him. Probably the wine made him susceptible, but already he had inaugurated the avalanche. There was no path back.

Later, he gave away another chip. Later still, he took on three men for a surface gang, and asked no tip from them for his goodness in putting the work their way.

He had been awarded Casrus' hovel in Aita-Slink. He went there, and looked at the drawn cat pouncing in the firelight on the wall, and felt the seeds of metamorphosis putting their roots into the bare stones all about.

Next Jate, a man rushed Hejerdi. Hejerdi broke his nose, then sent him to a center for healing and left him credit.

Two men who had never met Klarn face-to-face, sought Hejerdi out and inquired what Klarn had been like.

Herjerdi had become an interpreter, a prophet, more or less through wild quirks of fate. The hour for a leader, a messiah, had not yet arrived, for the seeds were barely rooted. In the dark or in the sun, they would need a margin to grow.

# CHAPTER NINE

"So even Casrus was not immune to the wish for vengeance. That surprises me, in particular as regards the girl. He had impressed me as chivalrous to the point of banality."

"You mistake him. I studied him more closely than you. I think his plan was otherwise, but the reality of what he could achieve with the screen disturbed him. He relinquished control of his characters some moments too long."

"Explain."

"Oh, it's simple. Casrus worked on Hejerdi's limited mentality, persuading him to send the message to the Klovez. Vitra was intended to allow Hejerdi into the Klovez-Klarn palace, where he would flounder in luxury, granted whatever he wished in return for his silence. Vyen would hold himself aloof, and Vitra would try to pretend Hejerdi wasn't battening on them. Then Casrus would introduce compunction into Hejerdi's brain. He would feel bound to do as Casrus did, take over Klarn machines to aid the Subterior. In that way, Hejerdi would be in the supreme position, a foot in both camps, to offer himself as spy or messiah, when the full germ of rebellion takes hold—perhaps two or three years from now. An interesting gambit."

"I see. Yes, that's more like Casrus. What happened?"

"I surmise he controlled the emotions of the brother and sister inadequately. They became hysterical and brought death on themselves. Hejerdi's betrayal of Vitra's boasts to Casrus, which made sure of Vyen's execution—I think that, too, was Hejerdi's own fright rather than manipulation. In a short time, Casrus will probably have the computers of the Residencia gift Hejerdi with certain robots of Klarn—a reward, say, for his brave confession, that brought wrongdoers to justice. Then the plan will go on as before."

"Vel Thaidis, on the other hand, took her revenge with enchanting ruthlessness."

"Yes. Did you relish it, brother?"

"It was—educational. More so than your own cowardly and uninventive method, darling sister."

"I disdain to comment on the word 'cowardly.' It was a logical act and appealed to my masochistic persona at the time. As to invention, I think myself to have been more inventive than yourself. Consider the reprojection via my screen here at Deneder, and that eerie fulsome little message—How strange, too. I might almost have been prophesying that Vitra—"

"Oh, don't become a mystic, my dear. I really could not bear it."

"Very well. Our protégés shall be mystical for us both. They have resolved on a future uprising, possibly on a messiah. In the Slum and in the Subterior. Two guilty aristos paying out their peers, those peers who left them to the wolves."

"Ideal. Apt."

"Yes. I suggest we have been talented."

"Are we not always so?"

"Certainly we always assume we are."

The man laughed. The woman watched him, pleased by, but not joining him in his brief mirth.

They were, in either case, physically similar to the persons they had projected, actually impersonated, if physical was a condition that might be attributed to them, for their nature was not quite that. . . .

"You know," he said a length, "I think Deneder is more attractive than Kaneka, though Kaneka is the larger of the ruling domes. Kaneka's more gaudy. Better for the newcomers."

The woman turned her smile to the open doors. Beyond this chamber of screens, marbles and gems, spread a garden-park, unlike the garden of Kaneka in many ways. Here days and nights were prolonged, the stars moved over the dark, and a white globe occasionally arose, altering its contours phase by phase for the enjoyment of watchers. There was grass in Deneder, and curious trees. Few robots moved here; instead animals padded the walks, as flying things circled the sky, which, by day, was not the color of the sky of the Yunea. Whether these creatures were mechanical or not was moot.

Dere-nentem-dere, three hundred and three, abbreviated to Deneder, was the somewhat smaller sister dome of the planet's twilight zone. Its function, in common with all the

313

rest, concerned the upkeep of atmosphere; its inner function, as with Kaneka, was to provide a haven, a paradise. But it was situated at a distant juncture of the world-ringing zone from Kaneka. It had not passed into the mythos either of light or dark side, since it had been in existence a mere thirty years.

The slightly aphysically natured brother and sister (the original "players" who had inhabited Kaneka and operated their game through its two screens and left their chairs behind there to perturb the two who came after) had caused Deneder to be constructed when they contemplated their game's newest innovations.

They had been playing a great while, first bringing their human toys to this world, causing them mostly to forget their origins, next experimenting with various forms of civilization for them, then choosing the hierarchies that presently obtained. But the dual societies, darkside and light, locked in their changeless environments, began to deteriorate. Their machinery ran down, their virtues diluted—initially this promised action, upheaval. When none came, the brother and the sister began to weary of their gaming boards, the stagnant dark, the fruitless light, which had even ceased to worship them properly as half-remembered gods.

When the first innovation occurred to these gods, and then the second, Deneder was made in readiness, and complex fore-programming took place in Kaneka itself.

Rather than observe and direct, the gods would put on mortal flesh. They would participate in the worlds they had fashioned.

By a form of emancipated psychic projection, they launched themselves from their protective domes and into the matrixed embryos they had put ready for themselves, (they had organized the matrixes for centuries, and the appearance of what came from them) one on the cold side, one on the hot. Their own supernal bodies were discarded, and mechanically borne to Deneder, to be resumed on their psychic return. The instant of which return each knew exactly, since each also knew, with a self-tolerant delight in wild adventure, that, as humans, they would die shocking deaths. They had actually chosen and designed these deaths, just as they had chosen and designed their temporary mortal forms, as infant, man and woman. Just as they had chosen and designed the pre-programmed impulses which would still be fed in at the

screens, in their absence, to turn the wheels of lives, to per-
petuate the story line through its desired stages.

With their astounding abilities of mechanized and tele-
pathic control, it had been inevitable they would seek for
something extra. To dwell as men, and act mankind's fear,
arrogance and foolishness, titillated them, but even that
would, of course, pall. To that end, the death of each had
been arranged to afford escape. And to that *second* end, the
second innovation had been programmed.

The second innovation being the propulsion into Kaneka of
Vel Thaidis Yune Hirz and Casrus Klarn.

The woman had glided from the marble chamber onto the
broad green lawn. She gazed toward the blue hills that rose,
apparently miles off, in the direction known as "Travel." She
and her brother were free to leave the screens whenever they
wished. Usually the programming their wills had previously
enforced would continue, whether they took note or not. But
at this time, neither exerted any influence at all on Yunea of
Klave. They left the game to Casrus and to Vel Thaidis.

For now.

Therein lay the second innovation, the reason for the making of Deneder, and for the birth, manipulation, summoning
and installation of a prince and princess in the master dome.
The game that had once been so engagingly played singly,
might resume its energy when played *against another*. One
against one for the existences and fates of the dark-side. One
against one for the existences and fates of the sun-side. Even
if Casrus did not know it, nor Vel Thaidis guess, as yet, that
they were not alone in their rule, that they had *opponents*.

"I do think," said the woman, gazing on the hills to Travel
of the marble chamber, "trees might improve the prospect of
that ridge."

"Have them planted from the seed bank," said the man.

The sun, which really dawned and set in Deneder, glinted
on his gilded hair. Her hair, black against the blue of the sky,
was more silken than it had been in her "life." But they were
much the same. Anyone would have known them, and if not
by their looks, by their names, which it had been their irony
to have themselves given again in the world.

"When shall we recommence with the screens, Ceedres?"
she asked him.

"Tomorrow? Or the next day, perhaps."

She smiled once more. He was to play against Vel Thaidis
as in the Yunea, though currently unknown to her. And she,

315

Temal, would play against Casrus, who, with his matrixed resemblance to her brother, intrigued her very much.

It had amused and tantalized her to love Casrus, to die for Casrus. The reprojection of her "ghost" to appall Vitra, the impassioned post mortem note—Temal had rejoiced in those, yet partly she wished now the story had gone on for her, in the life, as it were. Just a little longer. . . . But there might be a future occasion when she could indulge that fancy, even yet.

Ceedres, proud, stimulated by the rending of the claws of lionag, recalled the event with a dazzled, agonized sensation, very nearly nostalgia. To live. To die. Such depths and summits of expression.

They did not think beyond these things, only of next day, or next. Or backward, to the adventure they had lived, the pains and traumas and the strange human emotions. Naturally, in the end, either Casrus or Vel Thaidis, replaying former actions from the story on their screens, would come to see that, of all the characters, only Ceedres and Temal did not give off a true aura of emotion, that now and then, they, and they alone, were quite indecipherable and might only be presumed to have, or deduced to have, felt anything.

They were long lived in their own essence, that essence not quite physical. There were eons before them, and behind. They had to have such toys, Temal and Ceedres, the true tyrants of this overshadowed and malignly fortuned planet. Destruction they would wreak heedlessly, torture and despondency. For, beyond the opulence and the tyranny, was not their situation worse than any other's?

One day, or night, one Jate or Maram or J'ara, might come the end of all the roads, the going out of all the lamps. One day, every game might stale, every innovation pall.

One day, like human aristocrats three hundred years of age, they too might die of boredom.

**DAW** ⊕ **sf**
**BOOKS**

## Presenting MICHAEL MOORCOCK
## in DAW editions

### The Elric Novels

### The Runestaff Novels

### The Oswald Bastable Novels

### The Michael Kane Novels

### Other Titles

---

If you wish to order these titles,

please use the coupon in

the back of this book.

# DAW BOOKS

## Outstanding science fiction and fantasy

To order these titles,

see coupon on the

last page of this book.